THE WORLD OF DRAGUNS

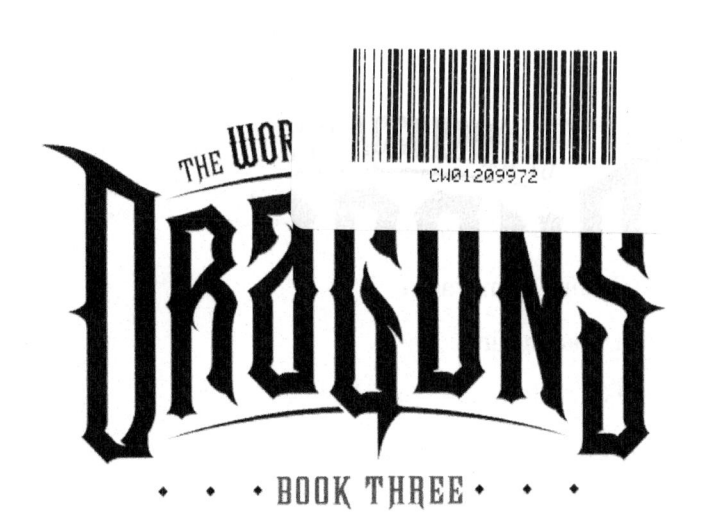

· · · **BOOK THREE** · · ·

HARMON COOPER

Copyright © 2023 by Harmon Cooper

Copyright © 2023 Boycott Books

Edited by Celestian Rince

Proofed by Andi Marlowe

Art by Daniel Kamarudin

Font by Shawn King

Arcane Card design by Yulia Volska

Arcane Card art by Sor Cooper

Map design by Chaims Cartography

Audiobook produced by Tantor Media and narrated by Wayne Mitchell

All rights reserved. This is a work of fiction. Names, characters, places, and incidents either are products of the author's imagination or are used fictitiously.

Map of the
Four Kingdoms of the Sagaland

Map of the Kingdom of Icenor

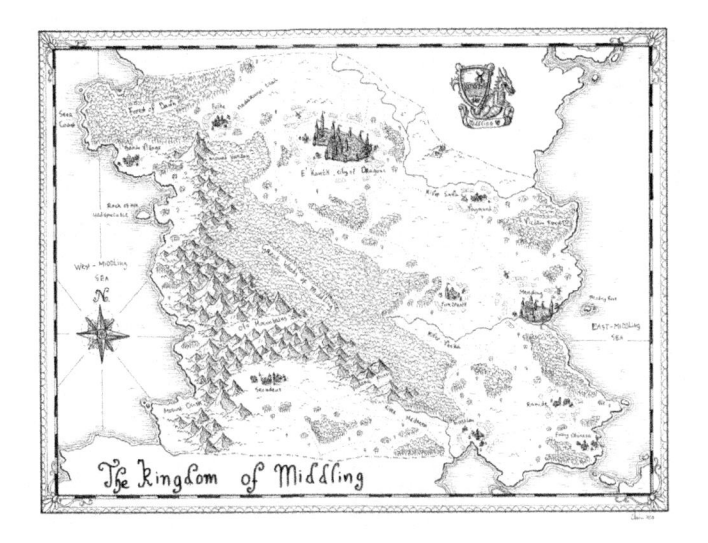

Map of the Kingdom of Middling

Map of the Kingdom of Southfall

The World According to Dragons (recap)

Contains spoilers!

Book One

Jhaeros Shotaro Vos, or Twillo, as he was called by his mother, starts the yearly Artifance by getting a neck tattoo. Later that night, as he roams the streets of the city of E'Kanth with his cart full of mapstones and other rare items, he has a chance encounter with Princess Embla. The princess recognizes him from their shared youth, which could be problematic because of his past.

Twillo uses a hallucinatory dust to escape the princess, and is chased by one of her guards, an elven orc named Rowian. Twillo manages to escape Rowian by using one of his relics known as the Enkiro Ring of Animation. From there, he hides out in a stave church that is run by a pair of monks named Olaf and Vradon. It becomes clear Twillo needs to get out of the city due to his alleged assault on Princess Embla. Before Twillo leaves, he meets the tattooist from the previous night and gets information about a relic outside of Padrian Sands, one known as the Quill of Katzimo.

Twillo meets a mysterious elven man on his carriage ride to the northern city of Padrian Sands. The elven man turns out to be a kitsune in the form of a human, and the two become fast friends. Katashi invites Twillo to look him up if he's ever in Icenor's capital of Vendir.

In Padrian Sands, Twillo finds the fixer who has the mapstone for the Quill of Katzimo. Anneli Vrignava is an elven orc who works at a tavern known as Storgata. After he gives her a prized relic known as the Tongue of Ravenna Megren as collateral, she gives him the mapstone. Twillo visits his safehouse in Padrian Sands, one that is in an abandoned stave church, and heads to the desert.

Upon locating the cave where the relic is rumored to be held, Twillo notices all the signs of a terrible yokai known as a wolvencree. He waits to enter the cave until he's certain the beast is sleeping. As if by fate, another yokai known as a rake appears and releases a terrible sound, which wakes the wolvencree. Twillo is attacked and torn into two pieces.

A voice comes to him at that moment, asking him if he wants to soulbind. Without any other options, and bleeding profusely, Twillo agrees. The dragon known as Adventus takes shape and saves him. Twillo's legs are also restored.

What Twillo doesn't realize yet is that all of this has been orchestrated by Livia, the Goddess of Luck. He also doesn't know that the Goddess has been working behind the scenes to set him up for decades, starting with his father, Shotaro Vos, who became obsessed with a relic he thought would bring Twillo's dead mother back to life. The relic happens to be the wristlet that Twillo now wears, which was how he sparked the dragon in the first place.

The only problem now is that the wristlet isn't powerful enough to fuel Adventus for very long. To get stronger, and to summon the other two dragon forms Adventus can take, Twillo must visit vortexes and ziggurats. The vortexes are located across the Four Kingdoms. They were places where dragons could recharge. The ziggurats are hidden and Twillo will have to hunt for them. Not only that, Twillo will need to learn to cycle and use dragonessence. Adventus can teach him several things, but he's limited in what he can tell him because the Goddess that helped free the dragon—Livia—has wiped part of his memory.

Twillo returns to Padrian Sands and finds that Anneli the barkeep has left town with his relic. During this discovery, he also gets a first glimpse of what summoning power will be like by absorbing energy in the stave church. He meets with Vradon the monk, who is now in Padrian Sands studying. The monk tells him that the church back in E'Kanth has some text he can't translate in the crypt. Seeing it as a lead, especially because Adventus will be able to read the Sagic script, Twillo returns to E'Kanth.

Once in E'kanth, Twillo and Adventus view the text, which tells them of two ziggurat locations. The first location is near the Oraibi Monument in the kingdom of Southfall. The second is in the north, beyond the fjords of the City of the Dead. After getting dragonessence from the vortex in E'Kanth, and getting scolded by Olaf the monk for falling asleep outside and drawing too much attention to himself, Twillo heads to the desert kingdom of Southfall.

On his way to the Oraibi Monument, Twillo encounters a Stylite nun named Sister Tonandi. Once she hears of what he plans to do, she grants him the power to access his dragonessence core. She also introduces him to his dragonaura. In doing so, she forfeits this power herself. Twillo continues on, and eventually finds the ziggurat. The guardian of the ziggurat presents a challenge to him, one in which he is transported to a pocket realm and forced to fight alongside his father during the night that Shotaro Vos was killed. Before he's transported back to his world, Twillo also meets his former combat teacher, a woman named Renda, who reminds him how to cycle dragonessence through combat.

Upon completing the challenge, Twillo is granted the power of the ziggurat. This allows him to summon Adventus in his wyrm form, known as his vordic form. They are soon attacked by a dragon rider, one of the Senja. Twillo manages to defeat the Senja warrior while Adventus battles the dragon in the sky above. They travel back toward E'Kanth, and stop in Firebreath to recharge, where he encounters an old acquaintance in the form of a shieldmaiden named Rose. Twillo experiments with turning off his dragonessence entirely in Firebreath, which is something he'll have to do in the future to avoid detection.

Upon arriving in E'Kanth, he finds that Olaf has been killed inside the stave church. Twillo is ambushed by Rowian, knocked out, and taken prisoner. He wakes inside a carriage heading toward Vendir alongside another prisoner. Twillo frees himself from his cuffs and fights back against Rowian, leaving the elven orc to die in the desert. The second prisoner turns out to be Anneli. She no longer has his relic tongue, having traded it to a fixer in E'Kanth for a bracelet similar to the one Twillo has. Together, they go to the cave that contains the Quill of Katzimo and retrieve it, where they are attacked by a seemingly possessed wolvencree.

After being saved by Adventus, the two return to Padrian Sands to drop Anneli off. Twillo plans to speak to Vradon about the death of his life partner, but puts this on hold for the time being so he can reach the second ziggurat. He flies to Vendir, where he reunites with Katashi the kitsune. While having his old family sword worked on, Twillo trains with Katashi, who has spent time studying combat with the Brethren of the Tribute Islands. He also upgrades the sword his father gave him. The blade is now able to shoot a bolt of dragonessence.

Together, the two head to the City of the Dead. They encounter another Senja warrior, a female who nearly bests them. She escapes with her life after Twillo and Katashi are aided by Ash and other ashinagatenaga, the name for a yokai with extremely long arms and legs. After a meal and some recovery, Twillo ventures toward the sea with Adventus. They fend off a yokai known as an ohatsu and reach the ziggurat beneath the water.

Forced to go forward on his own, Twillo squares off against a large stone statue of an infamous kitsune named Corobashi. He uses his newfound skills to defeat the statue, and is given the power of the ziggurat as the walls around him come crashing down. Twillo is saved by Adventus, who is now in his dragon warrior form. They escape the ziggurat, to find a new dragon flying about in the air. This is Seondzus, a red female dragon now in need of a rider.

As Twillo returns to Katashi and the ashinagatenaga, Livia watches on. She does so in a melancholic way, aware now that Jecha has taken Rowian's body, who Twillo left to die in the Icenordian desert.

Jecha, the God of Carnage, now has a host.

Book Two

The second installment of *The World According to Dragons* begins with Twillo in the Stormking Mountains of Icenor, where he hopes to find a relic known as the Yamauba Paintbrush. After defeating a ghost-like yokai known as a goryo, he is rewarded with the paintbrush and a pair of gauntlets that glow with dragonessence.

Twillo heads to Padrian Sands next, where he plans to regroup, connect Anneli with Seondzus, his new dragon, and meet with Vradon to tell him of his Olaf's death. Twillo is forced into a bar fight after trying to get information on Anneli's whereabouts, but eventually learns she is in E'Kanth.

Things heat up the next morning when he goes to the Monk's College to find Vradon, Twillo encountering Rowian instead. The elven orc is supposed to be dead. Before Twillo can confirm anything, Adventus takes his third form and tells Twillo to run. As he flees, Twillo spots Vradon in one of the windows of the college. He flies up to the tower using dragonessence and joins the monk, promising to explain everything later.

They are able to escape, and in doing so Twillo learns from Adventus that Jecha, the God of Carnage, is now in Rowian's body. While this news is bad, the news Twillo must break to Vradon about the death of his partner is equally bad. After some time to process, Vradon tells Twillo that he has found several of the ziggurats and vortexes. He also mentions a passage about something known as Arcane Cards, which Twillo hasn't heard much about.

They take several days to reach the eastern Middling city of Mending, where Twillo meets a relic hunter named Garnax at a tavern. Garnax tells him he knows someone Twillo should meet to ask about Arcane Cards. The next day, Twillo goes to the home of Ashimori, who teaches him about Arcane Cards after Twillo beats Ashimori's pupil, Geneva, in a battle. Twillo is given a single card known as Ripple Tide and told to meet with a Magi named Marianne in E'Kanth.

To recharge his power, Twillo and Vradon go to a vortex on Mending Rock. From there, they seek out a ziggurat in Victrin Forest, where they are attacked by a Senja Warrior. They defeat the warrior. Twillo is given three additional Arcane Cards after figuring out he can absorb another person's dragonessence core. He also takes the warrior's wristlet, which contains a black dragon named Ramide. Twillo puts the wristlet on, doubling his power. In E'Kanth, he has more of the dragonessence system unlocked by Marianne. Twillo is classed as C-Rank in

Martial Arts Mastery, which he hopes to improve. While he works to upgrade his Core Eruption power using matches, Vradon locates Anneli, who has since retrieved the Tongue of Ravenna Megren. Katashi the kitsune also joins them and the three leave for Folke that night after agreeing to meet with Vradon in Seondzus.

They camp out using one of Katashi's relics, which allows them to rest in a portal dimension. They train the next day and Twillo transfers Ramide to Anneli's wristlet. They journey to Folke, where Twillo hopes to gather some supplies before they head to the Forest of Dawn in search of a relic and the next ziggurat. Twillo is surprised when the relic merchant turns out to be Vitharr, the God of Fate. Vitharr has a message directly from Livia. He tells Twillo to take out the Magi named Korin who is working for Jecha who is responsible for finding dragons in the Realm of the Formless.

After recharging at the vortex, Twillo, his dragons, and his companions head deep into the forest. They encounter a bear named Walth, who is the leader of numerous yokai. He offers to give Twillo the Brooch of a Demon Bear if Twillo can defeat him. Upon doing so, Twillo receives the brooch, which spawns a bear named Yasuna, who just so happens to be Walth's sister.

Anneli completes the next ziggurat, and once she has done so, their group heads toward the mountains in the southwest in search of the final ziggurat that Vradon has discovered. They find a dead Senja Warrior at the entrance to the next ziggurat. Twillo takes her cards and core. He severs the wristlet on her wrist, which contains the dragon named Nalig. Katashi takes this one, and together, they complete the ziggurat's challenge.

Their next stop is Seondzus, where they expect to meet back with Vradon. Twillo also hopes to confront Romulus, his father's old friend. He suspects that the man knows more about his father's death than Romulus has let on in the past.

Instead of finding Romulus, he encounters Princess Embla, the Crown Ravenna of Icenor. She has been led to Twillo by a tip from Vitharr the God of Fate. Now, Twillo knows without a doubt that Livia, Vitharr's daughter, is blessing their journey. Embla tells him that Romulus is in E'Kanth, which happens to be where he needs to go to take out the mage helping Jecha find dragons.

Embla and Twillo separate from Vradon and Anneli, with plans to meet them in a week in the Southfallian city of Nalig. Once Twillo and Embla arrive in E'Kanth, they take refuge at a home owned by a woman who was once injured by Embla's father. Before they go for Korin the mage, Twillo deals with Romulus alone.

What is supposed to be a conversation about the past and perhaps Arcane Cards becomes a fight once Romulus reveals the truth, that he was the one who sold Twillo's father out so many years ago. He tries to attack Twillo and Twillo ultimately kills him, but not before Romulus tells him he has a few choice Arcane Cards at his home in Seondzus, which happens to be on the way to Nalig.

Before they leave, Embla and Twillo sneak into a keep and kill the mage that is freeing enemy dragons. They are chased by Renda, Twillo's former sword instructor, and by Jecha, Twillo finally coming face to face with the God of Carnage. Jecha nearly defeats them, Renda seems like she may be dead after being consumed by fire, and Twillo and Embla are able to escape through their combined powers and the two dragons.

Twillo now understands what he is up against, and since he doesn't have a lot of time to grow stronger, he will need all the help he can get from his friends, the power from more ziggurats, and Arcane Cards.

Chapter One

One Last Trap

SEONDZUS, THE MIDDLING CITY known as a winter and summer escape for the Four Kingdoms' richest, was quiet. Too quiet.

It was late in the night now, the streets well-lit with the soft, distant glow of lanterns expertly made by the dwarves of the Tribute Islands. Even with the light, there were still plenty of shadows perfect for thieves and cutthroats, perhaps even Senja Warriors, to call home.

But Twillo wasn't expecting Jecha's worst at the moment, not after what had happened a few hours ago on the outskirts of E'Kanth.

And what a battle it had been, Twillo forced into a fight with Jecha, who had taken the body of an elven orc named Rowian and now carried a pulsing red and black sword. Had it not been for Adventus and Seondzus, the two dragons he was able to summon, Twillo would have likely died, or worse, Jecha would have enslaved him somehow.

Yet he had made it. He had survived.

Princess Embla, who was with him now, had also played her part. And she had played it well. The Crown Ravenna of Icenor had proven to Twillo just how surprising her power was, and how much she had learned in the years of his absence. She could fight, she could use Arcane Cards, and she knew a thing or two about dragonessence.

Twillo only hoped it wasn't a pyrrhic victory.

Being defeated by a mortal had likely stirred a fire in Jecha, one that could only be quenched by the carnage he was famous for. He might not have had the ability to easily resurrect more dragons now that Twillo had killed the Magi that was pulling them from the Realm of the Forgotten, but Jecha was still alive. He was still active, and the only way for Twillo to beat him would be to band with those brave enough to stare down the God of Carnage himself, and to get stronger.

Not an easy task for the shunned saracent from an Icenordian city known as Sparrow's Rise, a relic hunter who had taken on this task after soulbinding with a dragon on his deathbed. But Twillo was up for the challenge. Now, he was able to use dragonessence, he had access to a dragonessence system. The more ways he could utilize the system, his relics, his Arcane Cards, and his combat knowledge, the better his chances.

But how many more would he have to lose along the way? There had been Olaf, Vradon's partner. And to find out that Renda, the elven orc who had raised him to fight, had joined Jecha, was certainly a knife in the back.

But hopefully, she was dead now.

Twillo had seen her burn himself. And if he could get out of this war with the God of Carnage with just two deaths, Twillo would be incredibly lucky.

The companions that he planned to meet in a few days were on the forefront of his mind now. Vradon the monk, Anneli the elven orc, and Katashi the kitsune—they were the people that mattered. Alongside Princess Embla, Twillo wanted to make sure they survived all of this when the day came.

Not only did he have to do this for the Four Kingdoms, the people who would either prosper or suffer during the coming Rebirth of Dragons, he had to do it for them. He also had to do it for his own legacy, even if it was something that he would never want to gain notoriety from.

Regardless of who he was, Twillo's father had betrayed the Ravenna of Icenor, who just so happened to be Princess Embla's father. This was a form of redemption for him, a way to make things right. He was at the point now that he lived for his destiny. He just needed to reach the end. And then, if everything worked out in his favor, Twillo could disappear again.

Back to the life of a relic hunter.

"Are you sure about this?" Princess Embla asked.

The princess braided her long white hair with its unique blond streaks at the back of her head, revealing more of her face, her long neck and elegant features. She was a far cry from Twillo with his tattoos and piercings, yet they did have one thing in common in the way that their eyes gleamed. Icenordians could see in the dark, but their eyes, like an animal, often gave them away.

"Well, Jhaeros?" Embla asked him, her eyes flashing yellow. "Are you sure about this, or do you think we should wait?"

Twillo let out a short breath. "I think we will be fine. There's no way he could have gotten word to the city this quickly."

"We don't know that, and it isn't Jecha that I'm worried about."

"If not Jecha, who could she possibly be worried about?" Seondzus asked, the red dragon's voice now in Twillo's head. Adventus was there too, yet he was quiet at the moment.

"She wants to know what you're worried about," Twillo told the princess.

"Romulus. He may have had something set up to happen if he died. It was a couple days ago. Word could have reached here by then, especially if someone used the Emperor's messengers."

"You mean Romulus could be leading me to a trap?"

"Your final confrontation with him wasn't exactly pleasant, was it?"

Twillo remembered Romulus' confession, how he had been the one who had ratted out his father. The giant of a man had tried to kill Twillo in their last encounter and Twillo had acted. On his deathbed, Romulus had told Twillo of a stash of Arcane Cards at his home.

That was the plan at the moment. Get the Arcane Cards, and then continue south, where they were supposed to meet the others in the western desert city of Nalig.

"We will be careful," he assured her. "Extra careful."

They had just left the stave church, where they were able to recharge their powers via its vortex. And not a moment too soon. By the time they arrived, Twillo was quite low on reserves.

He took a moment to look at his status as he considered their options for reentering Romulus' oldest estate.

Name: Jhaeros Shotaro Vos
Tier: Apprentice
Rank: S

Class: Martial Arts Mastery

Rank: C

Secondary Class: None

Tertiary Class: None

Dragonessence: 325/325

[Arcane Cards]

Arms of Vikan Wood, Level 1

Core Eruption, Level 2

Eternal Cycle, Level 2

Firebreath, Level 1

Flash of Fata Morgana, Level 2

Nadakunai's Might, Level 1

Ripple Tide, Level 2

Vard's Blessing, Level 1

Twillo was only able to have three cards on deck at any given moment, which meant that it would take a moment to rearrange. He did so, now with Firebreath, Core Eruption, and Flash of Fata Morgana at his disposal, *on deck* as it was known. His current line-up gave him a way to fight someone, a way to charge an object if need be, and a way to confuse opponents, if it came to that. The rest of the cards went back into the box that he kept them in.

"I'm ready," he told Princess Embla. "Let's keep to the shadows."

They reached the back of Romulus' grand estate to find that the lights were on.

"It seems like someone is home," Seondzus said as Twillo pondered how this could be.

"It could just be a precaution," Adventus told her.

"Perhaps. Or this could be a trap of sorts. How about summoning us, relic hunter, and we can simply burn the entire place down? That is an option here, is it not?"

"He needs the cards. We aren't here to torch every place we visit. Stop acting like such a dragon."

"I don't even know how to respond to that," Seondzus told Adventus.

"What are they saying?" the princess asked Twillo. She had been around long enough now to recognize when the dragons were communicating in his head, which could be quite the distraction.

"They think it's a trap. Or one of them does. She is suggesting we burn it down. I don't think that's a great idea, either."

"You three really don't appreciate the power of a good fire," the red dragon said.

"Let's go to the same door that I went in when I surprised you there," Embla said. "It's this way."

Twillo remembered how she had seemingly appeared in Romulus' home, how surprised he had been. Princess Embla had been guided by Livia, same as Twillo. In this way, their destinies were intertwined. "That could work."

"You were surprised when I appeared, were you not?" she asked playfully.

"Not in the least bit, Your Regalness. Let's do this."

Twillo and the princess circled around to the side of the enormous estate, where they reached an ivy-covered wall made of stone. The pair floated up over the wall and landed on the other side. They crouched near neatly arranged box hedges. Once they were sure no one was watching, they followed a gravel path through a garden, one with vibrant flowerbeds, and the melodious sound of water trickling out of a fountain made of marble.

Princess Embla stopped and inhaled the fragrance wafting off a rose garden. She locked eyes with Twillo, shrugged, and continued on. The two reached a lily pond that had a wooden footbridge crossing its still waters.

Twillo shook his head, which Seondzus noticed through her next comment: "All this opulence, and for what? I suppose one could say it is in honor to me, considering the name of the city. Perhaps I should look at it like that."

Twillo gestured to a gargoyle-like dragon statue that was short and stout. "Dedicated to you, I'm guessing?"

"You're lucky I don't torch you for that. That is *not* supposed to be me," Seondzus told him. "Absolutely not. You've seen my face. Do I look like a bloated dragon who has spent the majority of her life barbecuing wolvencree pups?"

Twillo didn't answer.

They reached the side door where Embla quickly picked the lock, as if she had spent years of her life as a thief. When she got it open, she drew her dragonessence-powered dagger and stepped in. Twillo followed close behind her, his hand on the hilt of his father's blade.

They paused at the end of a narrow hallway, the lanterns ahead all glowing. Embla shook her head, her ears flitting back slightly. "Something seems off."

"It shouldn't," Twillo said. "It really shouldn't."

"Summon one of us, and we can go ahead," Seondzus told Twillo. "It is safer that way."

"She wants to come here."

"Would your dragons even fit in this hallway?" Embla asked as she gauged the distance between the floor and the ceiling. She shook her head. "It's best if we just do this quickly. And then we can find a place to rest. I don't know about you, but I could use some."

"There will be plenty of places for us to relax for a spell, I assure you. We just need to get these cards first."

"They will probably be in the study."

"It's a good place to start. Lead the way," Twillo told Icenor's Crown Ravenna. Over the last several days, he had grown used to her being around, yet it still struck them as fortuitous that they had grown up together, and had somehow united. And it was always fun to tease her a bit about her status.

She moved ahead quickly, Embla light on her feet. Twillo floated after her and caught up to her once they reached a tapestry depicting the River Vaska, which flowed from the Great Woods of Middling out to the East-Middling Sea. It was a fine piece, one that showcased the river's white shores reminiscent of the snow of Twillo's home kingdom.

"Admiring the art, are we?" Seondzus asked.

"Always pleasant to fly over that river," Adventus said.

"I wonder what will happen to all this stuff," Twillo told the princess. "Some of these tapestries are priceless. Which tells me he might have stolen them."

"I really do not know. Come on."

Twillo kept to the side of the hallway. They came around the corner, the relic hunter now recognizing the area. He had come from the opposite direction last time, Twillo certain of it. They reached the study and stepped down into the lower space.

Fwitt!

Fwitt!

A pair of throwing knives zipped through the air. One of the knives grazed right past Twillo's shoulder. Had he been just an inch or so to his left, it would have done some serious damage.

"Careful, Left-Handed One!" Adventus said.

Twillo drew his sword and moved straight into action against a pair of warriors dressed in all black, their faces concealed. He knew what they were. And he knew how much they would have trained to be where they were.

A guild of assassins out of the Tribute Islands, the Brethren were considered some of the fiercest warriors across the Four Kingdoms. Twillo didn't know why they were in Romulus' estate, but he knew now wasn't the time to ask questions.

He swung his sword. One of the Brethren assassins met him using a gauntleted blade. Twillo's sword clinked off the strange weapon.

He activated his Flash of Fata Morgana power, which had his opponent turned around in a matter of seconds. The assassin was still fighting ferociously, yet he couldn't find Twillo as he cut through the air with his two bladed gauntlets to stave off the sudden hallucination.

Meanwhile, Princess Embla had already dragged her opponent to the ground, her legs wrapped around his body as she jabbed him in the chest with her dagger.

Seeing this took Twillo off guard. He had no idea how she had gotten the man into that position so quickly.

It was certainly a testament to her skill.

With his opponent still dazed, Twillo quickly slashed him down with his sword. He stepped over him and delivered the deathstrike.

Princess Embla's eyes shone hard. "When there's two—"

Several more Brethren assassins stepped into the room, these ones armed with swords with angled protrusions jutting off their blades.

"Let me handle it," Seondzus said.

"Sure." Twillo gladly summoned the red dragon. She appeared in the room in her magnificent red-scale armor, her hands on the hilt of a giant sword. Rivets of gold accented the deep red of her hardened exterior, culminating in a helmet that completely covered her face and revealed a pair of glowing blue eyes.

Much to their credit, the Brethren didn't flee. They hardly flinched. The assassins came at Seondzus, leaping over furniture and spinning into action. Yet her speed, fierceness, and the sheer size of her sword gave her an instant advantage.

The first assassin to reach her lost his head. The second woman got close enough to Seondzus' armor to get a strike in, yet was quickly cut down. Seondzus ducked under the next attempt, swiveled, and hacked the man down. She finally drove her sword through the last assassin's chest just as he was lunging for her.

By the time she was done the room was filled with dead or dying Brethren. Twillo could almost taste the blood in the air, and he didn't like it.

"This one is still alive." Seondzus nudged the man she had stabbed in the torso with her foot. She brought her sword under his chin and lifted it. "Who sent you?"

The man, who was coughing up blood until she placed a sword under his throat, glared at her. He gritted his teeth, the enamel covered in red.

"They won't speak to you," Twillo said. "Most take vows of silence."

"Then he is no use to me." Seondzus kicked him away.

"Shall we get what we came for?" Adventus asked Twillo, the white dragon's voice surprisingly calm in such a visual of suffering.

"I was thinking the same thing." He turned to Princess Embla. "Where do you think they are?"

"If we split up and search, we will be able to find them. We're looking for cards; they will probably be in something similar to what you carry yours in," she said, referring to the box that the Magi in E'Kanth had given Twillo.

"I'll search as well," Seondzus said as she walked over to one of the shelves. She began knocking some of the books out of it. She then tilted it over entirely, the shelf crashing to the ground.

"With finesse," Embla told her with all the command of a Crown Ravenna.

Twillo was surprised to hear her take that tone with Seondzus, yet the red dragon warrior heeded her warning. While she searched in the study with Princess Embla, Twillo explored the rest of the mansion.

He reached Romulus' room on the second floor, where he found a large, circular bed that was made in a way that it appeared as if it were floating off the ground. The walls were covered in elaborate sexual paintings of fleshy women spooling over one another, buried in bosoms and flowers and lustier than some of the work

Twillo had seen in pleasure houses. "You were a fool, Romulus," Twillo said as his eyes dropped to a protrusion on one of the pieces, something just slightly out of place.

The casual observer might not have seen it. But to Twillo, a relic hunter, a man who had spent the majority of his life looking for treasure, it was obvious. He approached the painting and placed his hand on the protrusion, discovering that it was a small handle. Twisting the handle allowed Twillo to open a portion of the painting to reveal a safe.

Now, the only thing standing between him and the Arcane Cards was the lock.

Twillo tapped his Enkiro Ring of Animation against the lock, which caused the lock to come alive. The piece clicked to the right and fell to the ground, where it writhed for a moment before settling.

Twillo opened the safe to find a purse full of platinum coins, as well as promissory notes. At the back, stored in a small card box, were a trio of Arcane Cards. The first one was exactly what Twillo had been looking for, a way to store all the cards without having to manually place them in his chest. He would have to get some guidance on how to actually use it, but he had a feeling Princess Embla would know more.

Codex Vault

Legendary Heart Card

Level One

Codex Vault is a passive card that allows you to store an unlimited number of Arcane Cards.

CODEX VAULT - LEVEL 1 - LEGENDARY

Codex Vault is a passive card that allows you to store an unlimited number of Arcane Cards.

The card featured a woman wearing bright purple robes as she spun a handful of Arcane Cards in front of her body.

The next card seemed equally helpful.

Warding Glyph

Ultra-Rare Sword Card

Level One

Using this card, you can inscribe a glyph on any surface. Anything passing by it will trigger an explosion of dragonessence.

WARDING GLYPH - LEVEL 1 - ULTRA RARE

Using this card, you can inscribe a glyph on any surface. Anything passing by it will trigger an explosion of dragonessence.

The Warding Glyph card had a hand on it, similar to his Core Eruption card. Rather than depict an image of the hand charging a stone, Warding Glyph showed a hand charging a brick wall.

He could imagine a number of ways to use the third card as well, which featured the image of three mages pointing at one another as if they couldn't figure out which one was the doppelganger.

Enchanting Deception
Legendary Shield Card
Level One
If legend is to be believed, the Enchanting Deception card was first created during the War of Ambrose to create a mirage of an entire army. Use it to enchant your efforts to confuse your foes.

ENCHANTING DECEPTION - LEVEL 1 - LEGENDARY

If legend is to be believed, the enchanting deception card was first created during the War of Ambrose to create a mirage of an entire army. Use it to enchant your efforts to confuse your foes.

Twillo took the cards and the platinum coins, but left the promissory notes.

He met Embla and Seondzus downstairs. "Well?" the princess asked.

"A good haul. One card in particular, I want to get your opinion on it." He showed her the Codex Vault card.

"This is the one I was telling you about, another way to store Arcane Cards rather than keep them in a physical container. Put it in your chest. It will stay there and act passively." She smiled at the relic hunter. "You really are lucky, you know that."

"So I've been told," Twillo said as he placed the Codex Vault card in his chest. He then sent all of his other cards in, doing so with no issue. "And then I just invoke which one I want to use?"

"That's right. One of the Brethren I studied under back in Icenor had one of these cards."

"I didn't think that they used these kinds of powers."

"They do. They are from the Tribute Islands, which are known for artificers. And while magi are the ones who have been generating these cards since the time of Yanzon the Undisputable, they were known to craft them as well. After all, an Arcane Card is simply a piece of parchment that has had a dragonessence code inscribed into it. Think of them as instant spells, and the number you can use as spell slots."

"Should we check them for cards?" Twillo asked the princess as he turned to the dead Brethren.

"I already did. Nothing."

Seondzus faked a yawn. "Are we going to sit around here and hear a full explanation? Or are we leaving? It's a rather grim scene, even if the assassins had it coming."

"Agreed. Let's go to the Oto mountains," Twillo told her. "It's time to recoup before we find the others down south. And who knows," he said as he extended his grin from Seondzus to Princess Embla, "maybe we'll find a relic or three along the way."

Chapter Two

Discovery

TWILLO AND PRINCESS EMBLA touched down in the Oto Mountains just as the sun was starting to come up. Adventus had found a clearing, one large enough for the dragons to perch. It just so happened to have an old hermitage near it as well.

"By Livia, I'd say this is almost as good as a summer home in Sorzol," Twillo told the princess, his hands on his hips as he admired the hermitage. Meanwhile,

Seondzus playfully bickered with the white dragon behind him, the two snapping at each other.

"You're serious?" Princess Embla asked, her face a mask of skepticism.

The hermitage was built into the side of the rock, the wood packed tight with a mortar that looked almost fibrous. It was an unusual way to create a building like this, but Twillo had seen these constructions before, especially closer to the border of Southfall.

"It will do for the day," he told the princess as she joined him. "Unless you want to head back to town." Twillo jiggled the coin purse he had taken from Romulus' mansion. "We could stay in a pretty nice place with this amount, Your Grace. For a long time, even. We could probably even buy a place."

"Looking to settle down, Jhaeros?"

"Things will catch up with me at some point if I don't." Twillo pried the hermitage door open. He looked inside to find that the space was completely protected from the elements. The hint of ancient sage that lingered actually made the place smell pretty good. "Look at that. Perfect for someone of your status," he said as he motioned Embla inside. "Perfect."

"Funny."

She sat, and Twillo took a place next to her. He felt a pulse of dragonessence as the dragons returned to him. "And... they're back."

"I could go hunting for you all," Seondzus offered Twillo as he got comfortable.

Twillo pulled his bag around and went through some of the things. "We have some food," he said, referring to some of the stuff they had taken from the stave church in Seondzus, which consisted of day-old bread and a kind of yak butter they made in the western cities of Southfall.

Twillo got the bread out and used a small knife he carried to butter it. He took his first bite, and swallowed it down. The bread wasn't great, but it would do.

"None for me?" Princess Embla asked.

"I assumed you wouldn't want any. It isn't exactly fine dining."

"Fine dining? You assumed wrong."

Twillo buttered some bread and gave it to her with just a little flair. She laughed, they ate a bit more, and prepared to sleep, the two Icenordians sleeping back to back for additional warmth. There wasn't much time for Twillo to think about all the things that happened in the last twenty-four hours. He was out in a flash, exhaustion pulling him to sleep quickly.

He awoke hours later, his mouth dry.

A spur of panic came to him as he sat up. For a moment, Twillo didn't know where he was. But then he remembered that they had found an old hermitage in the Oto Mountains, that as far as he knew, the two were safe for now, and everything was going to plan. They just needed to reach the southern city of Nalig and wait to meet the others.

Twillo stepped out into the clearing and took a deep breath in, observing the mountains beyond. Their location was certainly high up, to the point that he couldn't see the ground, only a thick gray mist. The setting sun cast blue and purple slivers across the mist, the visual one that Twillo wouldn't soon forget.

"Finally, you awaken," Seondzus said in his head, which halfway brought Twillo out of his peaceful morning reverie.

He yawned. "Care to take a look around?"

"I thought you would never ask." Seondzus took shape, the red dragon smoothing her wings back as she settled before him. She tilted her head up and let out a small puff of fire, one that formed a perfect orb before disintegrating. "Let's fly."

Twillo mounted up, and soon, the two were gliding around the mountain, and over the crest of another. Seondzus came in close enough to bring her wing through the snow. She spun a few times, Twillo hunkering down as the cool wind blasted against his face. They were just finishing a full circle when he noticed something on one of the peaks.

"Closer to that," he said as he pointed to what looked like the spires of some ancient building. It was hard to tell this high up in the mountains, but there were similarities. He was fairly certain the structure was man-made.

"What do you think it is, Left-Handed One?" Adventus asked, his voice still audible even though Twillo was currently whisking through the air on the back of the red dragon.

Seondzus veered right, used the tip of her wing to take out some icicles, and returned to the structure.

"If it is what I think it is, then we are in luck," Twillo told Adventus as they grew closer.

There wasn't much space for Seondzus to land, so Twillo hopped off her instead and floated down in the snow. He bent forward, his body pressed against the rock as she disappeared. The wind roared past, twisting around the peak of the mountain, banshee-like. It brought with it snow flurries, Twillo forced to clench his eyes shut for a moment as the wind finally settled.

At a distance, the two objects he was looking at resembled crumbled bits of stone. Yet it soon became clear that they were statues, remnants of the guardians that once protected the sanctum beyond. Twillo's eyes traced over a door carved into a rock. The coloration of the stone was a deep, somber gray, with subtle veins of red running through it. But these weren't visible from a distance, only once Twillo approached.

Twillo placed his hand on one of the statues. It was textured, rough and weathered, a testament to the elements that had battered the peaks of the Oto Mountains since long before the Age of Giants. He wondered who had built this so high up in the mountains, and why they had gone through what he knew was certainly a lot of trouble.

Twillo dusted some of the snow away, hoping to find some Sagic writing, but didn't come across anything. "That would have been at least somewhat helpful," he said to himself.

"What kind of place do you think this is?" Adventus asked.

"Only a fool or a hermit would live this high up in the mountains," Seondzus said. "Perhaps both."

"Neither. It was likely a place of sacrifice," Twillo surmised once he saw another rock formation that resembled an altar. It was hewn from the very same stone as the door, veins of red twisting throughout, likely hematite.

Twillo used his sleeve to dust the altar off. He imagined that it was once stained with blood and he found the channel from which the blood would have flowed. Twillo followed this channel across the ground, into a place where one could set a stone bowl. He saw the remnants of these bowls around as well. There were so many shards.

"Definitely used for sacrifice. Although I don't know what they were sacrificing up here, an animal, or maybe something else."

"That door seems pretty solid," Adventus told Twillo.

He approached the stone door and looked up to the top. "It does." Twillo had opened doors like this before using some of the supplies he carried with him. There was always a chance to blow the stone away using guardian shards and basanic fire. But a place like this had a sanctuary aspect to it, and he was superstitious enough not to want to enter it this way.

"Well?" Adventus asked.

"We do have a few more days before we are supposed to meet the others. Although, I don't know how much the Crown Ravenna will enjoy exploring whatever lies beyond."

"You are hoping that your relic hunting is contagious," Seondzus said.

"I am. There could be something useful."

"There could be something useful anywhere."

"There could," he told Seondzus.

"But there often isn't."

"You could send Yasuna in as well," Adventus said, referring to the demon bear brooch that Twillo wore. "Or one of us. That is, if you can get the door open."

The wind picked up again, howling and hissing. Twillo ducked his head for a moment, and waited for it to pass. When it did so, he spoke again: "I will see what she thinks. Maybe Her Highness will have a solution for opening this door as well."

"Yes, night will come soon. Perhaps you should attempt to enter the sanctum in the morning," Adventus suggested.

"In the meantime, I can get you some food. I love hunting," Seondzus said.

"Yes, that would be nice," he told the red dragon.

Once again, she formed into existence, batted her wings and took off, Seondzus never touching down or saying anything before her departure.

This left Twillo alone with Adventus near the entrance to the recently discovered sanctum. "Good. In that case, I suppose we should go." Twillo glanced at a ledge ahead, one arched in a way that would allow him to dive off the side of the mountain. "That will work."

He floated over to the top of the stone, prepared himself, and jumped.

Adventus appeared beneath him.

Twillo latched on to the white dragon and bent his head forward, the wind rushing past him as they swooped upward. They eventually came around to the other side of the hermitage, where they found Princess Embla waiting, a slightly annoyed look on her face.

"For a moment, I thought you were going to leave me here," she said after Twillo had landed.

"I would do no such thing, Your Ladyship." Twillo playfully got on his knee and bowed to her. "I am at your mercy. Do with me what you will."

She laughed. "Oh, stop it. Where were you?"

"I might or might not have found a good place to look for relics." He motioned for her to follow as he pointed out a nearby peak. "In that direction. Treasure."

"But you didn't actually find something?"

"Not exactly, no. I haven't even gotten inside the front door yet," he said as he adjusted his long white hair. "It's going to take some work to get through the entrance. But there is probably something there. I get hunches, you know."

"About relics?"

"And other powerful items, yes. And I have one here. There is something in there that we could use. That is what I am feeling at the moment."

Embla looked at him skeptically. "Are you sure you aren't simply telling yourself that?"

Twillo shrugged. "Maybe I am, maybe I'm not, but we do have time before we have to meet the others, and it is probably good if we stay out of sight for another day or so. So what do you say? Do you feel like relic hunting with me?"

She crossed her arms over her chest. The princess let out a yelp as Seondzus dropped a charred goat onto the ground and landed beside her. "Dinner is served."

His belly full, Twillo slept peacefully that night in the shelter next to the Crown Ravenna of Icenor. He felt as if he were so far away from the turmoil in the land below, Jecha's encroachment, the Senja Warriors looking for him. These were the kind of nights he loved as a relic hunter, nights spent out in the wilderness, under a blanket of distant stars, on the eve of some grand, new adventure.

Whatever the sanctum he had discovered possessed, Twillo would find and take it. It wasn't often that he came across these hidden nooks entirely on his own, the tangible evidence of a past that still existed even if it was buried in the sand. Or in this case, cut into the side of a mountain that had been glazed with decades of snow.

This was truly what Twillo lived for, and even if the journey to get him here had been one rooted in betrayals and painful secrets, it was worth it.

Upon waking the following morning, Twillo left Embla to begin his morning practice.

He was still at the Apprentice Tier, and hoped to rank up, which would give him an additional Arcane Card. After dusting fresh snow off the ground, he took a seat and reviewed the Tiers that were possible if he was able to level up.

Tier 3: Adept

Warrior monks and arcane cultivators are strengthening the foundations of their journey

at this tier. They can use level two and three Arcane Cards, and they can have up to four cards on deck.

Cultivators at this Tier can choose a new class to start minoring in, which will become their Secondary Class.

Tier 4: Guardian

Warrior monks and arcane cultivators are further enhancing their journey at this tier. They are considered experts in their field. They can use level three and four Arcane Cards, and can have up to six cards on deck.

Certain cultivators can begin their study of Warding Magics.

Tier 5: Magus

Once they reach this tier, warrior monks and arcane cultivators are amongst the top practitioners in their field. They can use level four and five Arcane Cards, and they can have up to eight cards on deck.

Cultivators at this Tier should be nearing an S Rank in their first class. They can begin their study of their final branch, their Tertiary Class.

Tier 6: Protector
Only highly skilled warrior monks and arcane cultivators are able to reach this tier, where they can begin their study of Blood Magic. They have mastered a wide range of techniques and disciplines. They are highly respected for their knowledge and expertise.
They can use level five and six Arcane Cards, and they can have up to ten cards on deck.

Tier 7: Master
Warrior monks and arcane cultivators at this tier have surpassed the highly skilled and experienced practitioners in their art. They have mastered at least one class. They can use level six and seven Arcane Cards, and can have up to twelve cards on deck.

Tier 8: Mythic

Warrior monks and arcane cultivators at this tier have mastered all known techniques and disciplines. They are both revered by their peers and feared by their enemies.

They can use level eight Arcane Cards, and they can have up to fourteen cards on deck.

Cultivators at this Tier should be S Ranked in one class, and nearing S Rank in the other two. They can begin their study of Realm Travel at this stage.

Tier 9: Legendary

Warrior monks and arcane cultivators at this tier are legends. They are considered god-tier, amongst the greatest of all time, and sometimes, this title is granted posthumously.

They are able to freely travel realms. They can use level nine and ten Arcane Cards, and can have up to sixteen cards on deck.

Those at the Legendary Tier should be S Ranked in all 3 classes.

"Just one more and I'll be happy. For now." Once he was ready, Twillo stood and accessed his dragonessence core. He sent it hovering in front of him. As he swung his sword at the glowing orb, Twillo maintained an expert grip on his father's blade. He wished he knew more about the weapon, how it came to be in his father's possession, and how it acted as a conduit for dragonessence.

But that was likely something he would never learn.

"Are you ready?" he asked Adventus, who had control of his core.

"I am."

With a flick of his wrist, Twillo sent a bolt of dragonessence flying out of the tip of the sword, one that struck a rock and caused a bit of snow to fall. He brought the weapon back to the ready and chased after his target, his core always a step ahead.

After warming up, Twillo put his blade away and brought his fists up.

He proceeded to practice a series of punches and kicks, which warmed him even further. Toward the end of his session, he peppered in elbows, recalling the techniques that Renda had taught him so long ago.

After a quick break to catch his breath, Twillo checked his status and took a quick mental scroll through his Arcane Cards.

[Arcane Cards]
Arms of Vikan Wood, Level 1
Codex Vault, Level 1 [Passive]
Core Eruption, Level 2
Enchanting Deception, Level 1
Eternal Cycle, Level 2
Firebreath, Level 1
Flash of Fata Morgana, Level 2
Nadakunai's Might, Level 1
Ripple Tide, Level 2
Vard's Blessing, Level 1
Warding Glyph, Level 1

Now that he was able to store his cards in his chest, Twillo wanted to practice cycling through them. The first one he accessed was his Arms of Vikan Wood card. He cracked his forearms together, noticing how much stronger they felt. He picked up a stone and used Core

Eruption to charge it, Twillo tossing it away as it exploded.

As his dragonessence core cycled around him, Twillo used his Firebreath power, producing a gush of silvery-green flames. He focused on a stack of stones not far from him and toppled it using Ripple Tide, the free-flowing energy strong enough to cause a small avalanche that brought snow and other stones crumbling down the side of the mountain.

"You are a terror," Seondzus said, her first words of the morning. "Perhaps I should check and see if someone is down there. They will need rescuing after the avalanches you have caused."

"That sounds like an excuse to spread your wings," her counterpart said.

"And if it is? It gets so stuffy in here."

Twillo shook his head. "No one is down there. Well, there may be some yokai or a few animals. But no one that we need to worry about."

"It could be a good breakfast...?"

Twillo continued on, now with Nadakunai's Might as he once again swung his sword back and forth through the air. He used Flash of Fata Morgana next, which backfired to some degree and caused everything to turn upside down for a moment. To settle, Twillo dropped to his knees and bowed his head, waiting for the effects to end.

He was getting the hang of it. Transitioning between the cards wasn't as hard as he would have anticipated. He could only have three on deck at a time, but Twillo was mentally able to cycle them out, which almost eliminated the need to have more on deck at any given time.

Yet there was a delay. That was something that he definitely noticed. And in an actual fight, it might be much harder to swap out his powers, especially under duress or with adrenaline pumping through him.

Twillo was now ready to try out his new cards.

He started with Enchanting Deception, which created a replica of Twillo that stood directly before him.

It was uncanny.

Twillo didn't normally see himself this way, his long white hair swept behind his ears, the tattoos covering his arms and neck, his numerous earrings, his piercing eyes—it led Twillo to stagger backward. Yet his replica remained standing, as if it were awaiting orders.

"I can barely handle one of you, now two?"

Twillo ignored Seondzus as he stepped over to his clone. He reached his hand out and pressed his finger right through its body, a ripple of energy spreading outward as he sunk his arm fully into the front of the replica's chest.

"Run that way," Twillo said, an idea coming to him. He pointed toward the end of the ledge that he was training on, some thirty feet away.

His replicant took off, leaving no footprints behind as it reached the ledge and continued into the sky until it fizzled out.

"So use it as a deception, got it." Twillo could think of a number of ways this would help him in the heat of things, or simply as a means to escape. He accessed the card again and his replicant took shape. "Draw your sword."

His replicant did as instructed.

"Attack me."

It charged at Twillo and swung its sword, the blade passing right through him.

"This is most excellent," Adventus said. While his voice was somewhere in the back of Twillo's head, he still controlled Twillo's dragonessence core, which hovered nearby, almost as if it were a casual observer.

"One last thing to check before we wake Her Highness up." Twillo adjusted his cards and accessed the new one known as Warding Glyph. From his reading of the description, it sounded like it would be an explosive that was triggered by movement.

With this card, you can inscribe a glyph on any surface. Anything passing by it will trigger an explosion of dragonessence.

Twillo touched the side of a stone, its surface bitingly cold. A portion of the stone grew warm as he channeled dragonessence into it. It glowed, but as he moved his hand away, the glow dissipated.

Twillo stepped back.

"What now?" Seondzus asked.

He took an even bigger step back and picked up a small rock. Twillo tossed the rock at the piece he had just charged. It exploded upon impact, kicking up a small cloud of debris.

"You could use that for a trap," Adventus said.

Once it had cleared, Twillo tested the power again. But this time, he tossed a stone in front of the piece he had charged, rather than touching it. This also produced an explosion, one triggered by movement.

"It would certainly be a good way to escape something," Twillo surmised. "And by the looks of the explosion, it's bigger than what I can do with Core Eruption." He shrugged, satisfied with himself. "I guess Romulus came through after all, even if he tried one last time to kill me."

Twillo turned back in the direction of their camp.

It was a perfect morning for relic hunting.

Chapter Three

Unhanded

TWILLO REACHED THE HERMITAGE to find Embla ready to go. Once they mounted their dragons—the princess riding Seondzus, Twillo riding Adventus—they took off toward the ruins he had spotted the previous day.

Wind and bits of snow whisked past Twillo as Adventus hugged the side of the mountain, the white dragon less reckless than his counterpart. Seondzus flew overhead, a bit wilder than her counterpart as she guided her wing through clumps of snow, occasionally dislodging icicles while Princess Embla hung on for dear life.

It soon became apparent that there wasn't much space to land. After conferring with one another, the two dragons hovered nearby while both Icenordians dismounted and floated down to the natural ledge created by a rock formation that seemed to have been cleaved in two. After the dragons returned to Twillo's wristlets, they approached the two statues. Embla stopped in front of the altar that had been used for sacrifice. She wiped some of the fresh snow away, and found the grooves where blood had once flowed freely. "Animal, or human sacrifices?"

"No way to tell."

"That's grim."

"Sacrifice often is." Twillo joined her at the altar. After examining it for another moment, he approached the entrance and looked up at the giant stone doors.

"And how do you plan to get in there?" Embla asked.

"I have an idea." Twillo motioned to one of the statues. "I can create an explosion that will be large enough to bring one of the doors down. Stay back here, though. I don't need Her Highness ending up as collateral."

"You're already in enough trouble kidnapping me."

"Exactly."

Embla stepped away to allow Twillo to observe the door once again. He grazed his fingers over the cold stone and knocked on it, gauging just how thick it was. Once he was ready, Twillo used his Warding Glyph card to charge up a portion of the stone. He moved far enough away from the door that he could trigger it without being caught up in the blast.

"Cover your head," he told the princess. Twillo used a spare rock to activate the explosion, which blasted bits of stone into the air.

"That would explain the noises I heard earlier," she said as she waved away the dust. "I thought you had picked up mining."

"Maybe in another lifetime." He was just about to approach the door again when he stopped. Twillo looked up at the top and noticed it was swaying to some degree. He jumped back, his dragonaura amplifying his movement.

Wham!

A single side of the stone door fell forward, and with it came a noise like a deep hiss, which emanated from the inside of the ancient sanctum as if it were having a bout of geological indigestion.

"What was that?" Embla asked.

"If I knew, I'd tell you. Let's take a closer look."

Twillo stepped onto the door, portions of which had crumbled. He passed into the opening, the hallway beyond dark at the other end. Twillo approached the torch and pointed to the Sagic script written next to it. "What's it say?" he asked the dragons.

Adventus replied: "It says you can use this torch to light all the other torches in the sanctum."

"Using dragonessence, I'm assuming." Twillo waved his hand in front of the torch. It burned alive with the silvery green glow. This produced a cascading effect as all the other lights in the hallway came on as well, which gave the chamber that followed an eerie, spectral feel.

Twillo exchanged glances with the princess. "Shall we, Your Eminence?"

"I'm not going to respond to that."

"It is sort of fitting, no?"

"No. And really, Jhaeros, aside from thinking up ways to tease me, is this really what you've been doing over the last twenty years?" she asked as they continued on, her soft voice echoing down the chamber.

"What do you mean exactly?"

"Exploring random locations that you happen to blow out of the side of a mountain—you know, things like that."

"In a way, yes."

She considered this with a huff. "It suits you, you know. Being a relic hunter. Don't you remember?"

"Remember what exactly?" Twillo asked as they reached a set of stairs carved into the stone of the mountain. He looked around for any writing, any warnings, but didn't find anything aside from a few tools that had been used to do the carvings. He then checked around for traps. Twillo did so with his eyes open and his eyes closed, just to be sure there wasn't something that had a dragonessence glow and was waiting to ambush them.

"That summer. Maybe a year or two before you disappeared."

"I didn't disappear. Not by choice, anyway. I guess to you it must have seemed that way. But if you had just headed a bit south to Vendir, you would have found me at an orphanage, where I didn't last very long. Then you would have found me as a street urchin, pickpocketing to stay alive. Then you would have found me in Middling near the coast, doing anything I could to survive." Twillo let out a troubled breath. "Sorry. I learned a lot during those years, mostly about the way that we exist as a people and the depths we go to survive. Lessons like that. It makes doing things like this look easy," he said as he swept his hand forward.

"Don't say that just yet, relic hunter," Seondzus told Twillo. "We don't know what we will face once we move deeper into the chamber."

"You really don't remember that summer?" Embla asked, who wasn't privy to what the dragons told him when they weren't physically around.

"I don't, sorry."

"Think back, Jhaeros. I found that hidden passageway in my room. It was behind a painting. But I was too scared to go in there by myself. You weren't. As soon as I showed it to you, you opened the hidden door and stepped inside. I wasn't going to follow you, but you called out and told me that it was safe."

"Hidden passage?" Twillo asked. Try as he might, he couldn't recall finding a hidden passage behind a painting in her summer home.

"It was a secret escape route, one that fed out into a tunnel beneath our summer home. Don't you remember? We walked in that tunnel for several hours before we came to the forest outside of Sparrow's Rise."

"The forest outside Sparrow's Rise?"

The memory returned. Twillo recalled what it had been like to step out of the cave, the cold air rushing by them, the chattering of birds beyond as they moved through the foliage. He remembered just how deep the underground tunnel was, and how he felt like they'd never reach its end. While he hadn't shown it at the time, he was certainly scared.

But he was also curious.

"I remember it now. The passage."

Princess Embla grew visibly excited. "We talked about sneaking away and going south to Middling, to E'Kanth, then taking a caravan to the coast and heading to the Tribute Islands from there. I can't remember what we said we would become."

"I remember! I wanted to be a firewater brewer," Twillo said with a sad laugh. "Imagine me as a brewer."

"Because your dad liked kvoss."

"Yes, and I wanted to make a special batch for him. We were going to go to Firebreath, you and I, so I could study making kvoss. Yes! I remember it now, we really were going to sneak away, weren't we? How youthfully stupid of us."

"I remember that part, but not the part about what I was going to be. Surely it wasn't a firewater brewer. The ingredients reek and it's hard to get the smell off your clothing. I know firsthand. I took a tour of one of the breweries several years back as part of a mission for my father's court. I had to get rid of the dress afterward."

"You don't remember?" Twillo stopped and turned her. "You said you wanted to be a barmaid. That you liked talking to people and making them happy. I would make the kvoss, you would serve it. I told you at the time that you had never met a barmaid."

"I hadn't," she said with a sheepish grin. "But I still think I would have made a good one."

"Are you certain, Your Grace?"

"Yes, how hard can it be? Take orders and serve them."

"That and deal with all sorts of things, from throwing out drunken men for slapping your rear as you pass by to cleaning up loads of vomit."

"The first person to slap my rear would lose the usage of their hand," she said pointedly. "And I wouldn't let them get close to vomiting. I'd monitor their intake."

"How queenly of you."

"It is noble, yes."

"So you'd take their hand, is it? Cut it right off? If that's the case, then you would likely get sent to jail or worse depending on who you de-handed," Twillo told her.

"Unhanded?"

He laughed. "Defisted?"

"Unfisted?"

"Unwristed?"

"Dewristed?"

They both laughed. Twillo continued: "You know what I mean. Honestly, I can't believe I forgot about that.

That passage was everything to me that summer. Our little secret."

"That's what I'm referring to. And it's likely why we are here now, why you became a relic hunter. You were so keen to explore at that time, Jhaeros. You would have certainly explored that tunnel for the rest of the summer had it not been for the staff finding out that I had located the escape route."

"They found out? I don't remember that."

"I never told you. But after you left that day, I received a tongue lashing from the head of staff of our summer home, poor Anita! They were already bending the rules a bit by letting me hang out with you, especially as I had reached the age. You know what I mean. There was chatter."

"I don't recall anything," Twillo said, even if he faintly remembered her filling out her robes just a bit more that summer than she had in the past.

"But they knew that we had grown up together, so they overlooked this small transgression. They sealed up the secret passage after that. Or at least that's what I was told. I didn't dare try it again."

"They act like something happened between us in there," Twillo said as he nudged a stone over with his foot. "Nothing ever happened between us. Never."

"It didn't, but it could have."

"You think?" Once again, Twillo stopped and turned to her. "You really think?" He raised an eyebrow at the princess. "Between us?"

"You were a saracent. Who else was I supposed to marry? If anything, it would be someone like you. That is generally how it goes. In a way, that is why you all exist, all saracents."

"I'm no longer a saracent."

"You keep saying that, Jhaeros, but I'm not convinced. We Icenordians like to keep our blood pure, but we aren't inbreds like some of the other rulers of the Four Kingdoms. A large pool of viable saracents accomplishes this task."

He scrutinized her for a moment. "You really think we would have gotten married?"

"I could have ordered you to marry me."

"That would have been ripe. You should have done it down in the tunnel."

She rolled her eyes and they continued on. It was a moment before the princess spoke again: "I'm not married now, so clearly I didn't approve of any of my suitors. And my father knows better than to arrange a marriage for me. I would have his throat."

"That's a bold statement. Usually, if someone threatens harm against Vraizard the Blade, I'm supposed to report them to the Honor Guard. I guess you get a pass."

"Thanks," she said as she stuck her tongue out at him. "But he is starting to put pressure on me now that he's getting older. Soon, I will take the throne, and he is interested in a successful succession."

"Successful succession, huh?"

"So my marriage status is a conversation that continues to come up, and frankly, I'm sick of it."

"You think you will marry now?" Twillo asked.

"I think I might have to. What do you say?"

"About what?"

"Getting married, Jhaeros. Married to me."

Twillo suddenly felt light-headed. "I..."

She burst out laughing. "The look on your face. I wish you could see yourself right now!"

"She's toying with you," Seondzus told Twillo. "Tease her back!"

Princess Embla shrugged playfully. "I'm kidding but..."

"But?"

"But you are a saracent."

"Formerly so. No longer, Your Liegewoman. You, of all people, are aware of this."

"My father could restore that title in a heartbeat. If he didn't, I could. I have enough favor in the court to see anything like that through if it's something that I really want. I don't like using my influence that way, but it is a possibility."

"Last I checked, your father's men are still after me."

"He's not the one that ordered them to find you. I sent them after you because I wanted to talk to you about this, and now..." Her demeanor changed. "Now, Olaf is dead, and that is the result of that order."

"What Rowian did isn't your fault and you know that, Emmy," he said, using a nickname that he hadn't used in twenty years.

She blinked twice and continued on. "But if you must know, that is why I summoned you. That, and I wanted to tell you about the dreams that I've been having."

"I don't know what to say," Twillo told her after a long pause. "No one has ever proposed marriage to me before."

"I'm not exactly proposing, Jhaeros! You make it sound like we don't know each other. Like we couldn't have a spark or never had one before."

"Marriage to you or anyone is the last thing that is on my mind, or has crossed my mind since, well, since ever." Twillo shook his head. "I don't know how to respond. I'm flattered? Wait, are you actually asking me?"

"Ugh!" She stormed ahead. "We have more important things to do right now, you know, like saving the world from impending doom. Those kind of things. But it is something that you should think about. And it is something that needs to happen. I guess in that regard, you'd be doing me a favor. My other options aren't that great."

"You could always marry some wayward nutter saracent from Sorzol and adopt."

"As progressive as my father is, and as the court has become since the death of Yanzon the Undisputable, I don't think that that is an option on the table. We are traditional in that sense, at least. Anyway," she said as she slowed to some degree, "something to think about. We have much more pressing matters now, and I'm going to have a lot of explaining to do once I show up again considering I'm technically missing."

"That may prove challenging in the future, perhaps less so in Southfall. The desert holds many secrets, as they say."

"So I've heard," she told him.

"We might not encounter many people out there aside from water harvesters and Stylite monks and nuns who wouldn't care or know anything about who you were."

"Although they may be curious as to why a group of Icenordians are traveling alone, along with whatever form Katashi decides to take."

"Likely so," Twillo surmised.

A loud hiss indicated that they were closer to whatever lay at the depths of the sanctum.

"Your marriage talk can wait," Seondzus told Twillo. "We're close. Be ready to summon us."

***

The two continued to talk as they explored the sanctum, Princess Embla just switching to the topic of warrior monks and nuns when they reached a hallway that looked to be filled with statues. Twillo knew otherwise. These were ash warriors. "Prepare yourself," Twillo told the princess as he drew his sword.

He cut down the first ash warrior just as it was coming alive, just as the sandstone guard lunged at him with a pike.

Twillo looked ahead to the other side of the chamber, hoping it had a door that would seal in some way. If not, they would have to figure out a different way to stop the ash warriors because of their supernatural traits. As soon as their bodies crumbled, ash warriors took shape again. They could even merge together, making them almost impossible to stop.

But maybe there was another way.

Twillo slashed another one of the ash warriors aside.

Currently, he had Core Eruption, Warding Glyph, and Firebreath on deck. He decided to go for it. Twillo produced a plume of dragonessence fire from the palm of his hand, a test to see what it would do.

The flames covered the ash warrior, silver-green dragonessence flickering all over its body as it writhed in pain.

Twillo's experiment had worked.

"Hit it with whatever dragonessence you have," Twillo told Embla, who was already in the process of cutting away ash warriors with her dagger. She was fast on her feet, able to dodge their polearms with ease. Within moments, Embla produced a sphere of dragonessence, one that twisted forward and exploded.

This gave Twillo an idea. "Come on!"

He raced ahead, Embla soon catching him as they reached the other side of the chamber.

Using Warding Glyph, Twillo set a charge along the side walls while Embla flicked her dagger at some of the ash warriors, producing a bolt of dragonessence.

Twillo stepped back, Embla doing the same. He assumed that the ash warriors that were left would charge them and he was right. They attempted to reach the pair of Icenordians, only to be blown back by a blast of dragonessence. Flashes of green and silver fizzled across the room as the ash warriors all stopped moving, their bodies crumbling.

Dragonessence was the key to defeating ash warriors.

"For a moment there, I thought you were going to have to call me," Seondzus said.

"What were you saying earlier?" Twillo asked Princess Embla as he caught his breath.

"I was asking what you knew about warrior monks and the skills that they use against one another."

"I've seen them fight; I learned to access my dragonessence core from a Stylite nun."

"So you know about their mudras?"

"Mudras?" Twillo asked.

"Mudras are the hand gestures that they used to orchestrate dragonessence commands. It's quite fascinating, you know. For example, this one activates your dragonaura."

She reached her hands out and tapped the back of her knuckles together. "Of course, you already can access this in other ways."

"I can simply summon mine," Twillo said as he tapped the backs of his knuckles together anyway. Nothing happened.

"There's a reason behind that, you know," she told him as they continued on. "And it is the story of the Kingdom of Southfall itself. Arcane cultivators, water harvesters, warrior monks and nuns—these were the first to access and use the dragonessence system. They still are able to use the system in its original form. It is not like what you see, your status screen. It is arranged differently, and they can multiclass in ways that we cannot. The Emperor's Magi, archmages from our kingdom, and arcane artificers from the Tribute Islands—these are newer interpretations. Southfallians are the original users of the system."

"I honestly did not know that. And Arcane Cards?"

"They can use those too."

"But did they invent them?"

She shrugged. "That, I don't know. But back to the point I was trying to make. Mudras are what warrior monks and nuns use. They are hand gestures that can produce effects. Aura Blast is one of those techniques. I actually know how to do that one."

Embla turned away. She quickly sent her left hand out and punched her right hand forward, opening it as she did so. This produced a rippling bolt of dragonessence that speared off toward the chamber they just came from.

"Pretty awesome, right?"

"So they are hand gestures and movements that produce dragonessence?"

"They are."

Twillo sighed, but it wasn't a sigh of exasperation. It was a sigh of appreciation. There were so many ways to use dragonessence. The topic fascinated him to no end. There was the way that he had originally learned by simply feeling it out; there were Arcane Cards; there was the ability to encode magical powers in objects; and now, he was learning there were also mudras.

"And this is what the water harvesters use, right?"

"Actually, no," she said, referring to the Southfallians responsible for freeing water veins and bringing them to the outer cities. Their efforts, and especially their voluntary service, were legendary across the Four Kingdoms. "They don't use mudras. Well, some do if they were raised by warrior monks or nuns. When they're eighteen, they take part in what is known as the Trine Ceremony. This is entirely by choice. They don't have to take this path."

"I believe I've heard something about that."

"They have the system activated within them, and a water harvester's class is chosen. There are three classes. From that point forward, they dedicate seven years of their lives to searching for these hidden water veins across the desert kingdom. To make things easier for them, their memories are wiped."

"That part I didn't know," Twillo said as they came to a chamber with a high ceiling.

The hallway was nearly three times his height, yet he could reach both arms out and touch the walls.

She continued her explanation: "Not all of their memories. But memories of their parents, loved ones. These are returned to the water harvesters once they have completed their seven years, and what is known as the Rite of Fulfillment. Something like half of them die out there in the desert."

"Surely, there is a reward."

"There is. They are given notoriety, and prestige. But even with the money, even with the fame and the fact that they can pretty much do anything they want after they finish their service, many of them continue to work either as regional harvesters, or they go on to study to be warrior monks and nuns. There's also the role of desert mage. And some of them, like the Stylite nun you met, some of them do things like that. Many simply have children that they then raise to take the role, even if they know that their children will forget their faces and could die during their service."

"Crazy." Twillo laughed. "How did we get on this subject?"

"Mudras, I believe. You asked if water harvesters use them. I went off on a tangent about water harvesters and their practices."

"She is good at these tangents," Seondzus said. "I suppose this comes with the territory considering her upbringing and how everyone is required to listen to her when she speaks."

"But even I am learning things," Adventus said.

"You are too encouraging to humans," the red dragon told her counterpart. "Sometimes, I feel that they have this inner urge to talk incessantly just to fill the air."

"Like you don't always talk."

Seondzus laughed. "I can be chatty, but the things I say are generally of importance."

"We are about to be in Southfall; this talk seems important."

"Jhaeros." Princess Embla poked Twillo. "Are you listening to me?"

"Sorry. The dragons were talking in my head. What's up?"

"Do you feel that?"

Twillo stopped walking. He noticed that there was something different about the air. It was stuffier, heavier in a strange way. He also heard more of the hissing sound that he had noticed earlier. The noise was louder now, and there was a metallic clank that joined it.

"Strange."

"Whatever is guarding, or perhaps cursing this place, is up ahead," she said. "How do you want to do this?"

"Please send me, please send me," Seondzus told Twillo.

"Before we call out the big swords, let's see what it is ourselves."

Chapter Four

Sanctum Sentinel

WHAT FOLLOWED REMINDED TWILLO of the ancient innards of an Icenordian stave church. That was the only way he could frame how the opening of the next room was shaped, the ceiling high enough that he couldn't see the top, yet the space itself surprisingly small. In the center of the chamber stood a suit of armor, one without a head. There were chains attached to its arms and legs that dangled to the ground and pooled in front of its body.

"You think that's what was making the noise?" Princess Embla now had her dagger at her side, prepared for whatever lay ahead. She stood next to Twillo, who had since drawn his sword.

The headless guard shifted toward them, its chains scraping against the ground.

"I would say that this is certainly a possibility."

"Summon us," Seondzus told Twillo. "Best we handle this one now."

Twillo nodded in agreement. Seondzus appeared in her dragon warrior form alongside Adventus. As he had seen before, Adventus carried a large glaive, while Seondzus had an enormous sword, both of which matched their armor to the point that their weapons seemed like an extension of their beings. The two contrasted heavily against one another, Adventus in a silvery white armor, chunky and oversized; Seondzus in gold and red armor that fit her slender form. They did have one thing in common through their eyes, which glowed a bright blue.

Seondzus pointed her sword at their staggeringly large opponent. "Wherever your head is, prepare to join it."

"Is she always like this?" Princess Embla asked Twillo.

"Generally, yes."

While the headless guard didn't have a face, Twillo got the sense that it was laughing at the way that Seondzus had challenged it. The armored monster lifted one of its chains, and whipped it against the ground, cracking the stone. This produced a ripple effect, one that extended all the way around the room, and up to the top of the ceiling.

It did it again, the second ripple morphing into pure dragonessence that formed into an animal made of energy, its body like that of an enormous bull, with the head of a horned lion. The armored sentinel sent one of its chains at the lion-bull, which wrapped around its neck. It pulled the bull's body toward it with a quick tug, mounted up, and took off toward Twillo and the others.

Seondzus shot right, Adventus left.

The white dragon warrior brought his polearm to the side, prepared to cut the lion-bull's feet out from beneath it. As he did, his weapon pressed right through the spectral bull, allowing the headless soldier to strike Adventus in the chest with his chain. This sent the dragon warrior sprawling, the sound loud and percussive.

The headless guard reared up just as Seondzus moved forward to cut it down. The guard whipped its chains at the red dragon warrior and pulled her legs out from beneath her, sending her straight onto her back.

"By Livia!" Twillo said as he jumped out of the way, his dragonaura pushing him forward just in time to avoid one of the magical chains. He ran to the side and Adventus moved in again.

"Stay away from it!" Adventus called out as he prepared to strike the headless guard. He managed to clip their armored opponent in the leg, but ultimately was tossed away as the headless guard brought its chains down against the back of Adventus' shoulders.

Now on the sidelines, Twillo cycled through his dragonessence cards. He chose Arms of Vikan Wood, Enchanting Deception, and kept Warding Glyph on deck. Twillo used Enchanting Deception to create a clone of himself, one that he pointed toward the opposite side of the room.

"That way!"

It took off toward the other side of the chamber, the headless guard turning to the replicant just as it was about to approach Princess Embla.

Seizing upon his opportunity, Twillo dropped down to the ground and charged up some of the tiles using Warding Glyph. "Try to bring it this way," he called to Adventus and Seondzus, who had moved back into action.

The two dragon warriors took turns feigning strikes, both jumping out of the way to avoid the headless guard's endless barrage of chains as it ran at them, the lion-bull also prepared to strike with its horns. Adventus jumped into the air, and landed just in front of the Warding Glyphs that Twillo had charged.

The headless guard bolted toward him, but Adventus zipped out of the way at the last moment. The bull dashed his hooves against the Warding Glyphs, which caused an explosion that shot it backward, causing the lion-bull to completely disintegrate.

"That's it!" Princess Embla said as she prepared a charge of magic. "We're going to have to take it out with dragonessence." She fired a twist of mana that broke into three pieces. The dragonessence oscillated around the room, amplifying as Seondzus distracted the headless guard. Princess Embla's strike came down all at once, shattering some of their opponent's armor.

The headless guard spun both chains in a frenzy as it cut deeper into the ground. By this point, Twillo had cycled out his Warding Glyph power for Ripple Tide. He used his next opening to unleash a wave of dragonessence.

More cracks in the armor appeared as their opponent got to its feet. The headless guard seemed to grow in size, its armor expanding as veins of glowing power connected.

Adventus ran the end of his glaive through the headless guard's back. The tip didn't press out the front, but he did manage to force it to stumble forward, where Seondzus struck the armored protector with her enormous sword, the dragon warrior wielding the weapon as if it were a bat.

Twillo saw a hunk of tile on the ground, one that had been dislodged in the explosions caused by his Warding Glyphs. He grabbed it, and mentally sent his Arms of Vikan Wood card away, calling upon Core Eruption. Once it was ready, and as Adventus and Seondzus continued to hack away at the headless guard, Twillo charged up the piece.

He moved close enough that he could fling it at their opponent. Twillo let it go and jumped out of the way.

The explosion caused their opponent to fly forward, where it hit the ground, cracking more of its armor. The headless soldier was struck by a spear of dragonessence, one conjured by Princess Embla. This shattered more of its armor, which fell off into huge chunks revealing a body made completely out of glimmering energy.

It was all dragonessence.

While it was the same color as the dragonessence Twillo was used to seeing, it was clear that they were dealing with some sort of titan made of pure mana. But what was it doing here? How did it get here in the first place? And what was it protecting?

Ripple Tide back on deck, Twillo struck the headless guard with another wave of dragonessence.

Their opponent was starting to lose steam. While it continued to whip its chains at Adventus and Seondzus, both of them beat it down, their strikes causing it to eventually fall to its knees.

It was Embla who delivered the death strike, the final blow that stopped their opponent.

Her blast of power shattered what was left of its armor, leaving smokey entrails of dragonessence twisting up to the ceiling. For a moment, Twillo thought they were set to fight something else, but then he looked up at the way that the ceiling glowed, a platform lowering to them.

Whatever it was on the platform, he was certain it contained a relic.

The platform settled on the ground, the sound of shifting jewels and gems filling the strange space.

"By Livia," Twillo said as his eyes traced over what was clearly a treasure. He didn't run into things like this as often as he would have liked but knew, without a shadow of a doubt, that this was something that had been hoarded.

He glanced over to Princess Embla, who didn't seem as impressed. "You were expecting a relic, right? It looks like you're getting jewels instead." She approached the platform. "All that work for jewels and coins. We could have just raided the royal treasury."

"You have access?"

"I'm kidding, Jhaeros."

"Most would be happy with jewels and coins, Your Gracefulness. Myself included."

"While you two divvy up the spoils and discuss the finer things in mortal life, I'll check for an exit." Seondzus flashed away and reappeared in her vordic form. She whipped her tail behind her as she spiraled toward the top of the chamber, where there was no light.

Adventus joined Twillo. "It is quite the haul."

"That it is. Let's take a look, shall we?"

Twillo started searching through the loot. He found ornate necklaces, ones with intricate metalwork that were covered in gleaming gemstones, everything from amethysts to garnets. There were smaller gemstone scepters, elegantly carved, their orbs inlaid with diamonds. He found jade statuettes and a variety of brooches and scattered rings. There were also coins, platinum and gold.

Twillo examined one of these coins. "These alone would make someone a rich man ten times over. I'm no expert, but I would estimate that these ones are easily two or three hundred years old. Yanzon's face is on them," he said as he pointed out the elven ears of the individual on one side of the coin. "Otonashi had everything re-minted once he took the Four Kingdoms."

"Then what good is it to us?"

"It's worth even more with Yanzon on there. You can sell these to the royal mint for a premium but I'd just as easily take it to a fence, who will then take it to E'Kanth and sell it to the mint."

"There are definitely some pretty things here. But what use is this to us, Jhaeros?"

"Unfortunately, we need money," he said. "Especially if we are going to operate in a way that you have never experienced before."

"I know what it means to move in a clandestine way."

"We may find ourselves in positions where we need to pay people off. Wherever we stay, we will have to pay more than we normally would, especially if someone recognizes you," he reminded her.

"They won't recognize me."

"Even if they don't see your face, you have a way that you move that signals that you are royalty. You may not believe it, Emmy, but it is true."

Embla took a step back. She stepped around the platform, as if she were trying to examine the way that she walked. "Are you saying I move like royalty?"

"You do, Your Ladyship, regal and purposeful," Adventus told her. "You have the grace of someone who understands the finer things, yet your gait has a humbleness to it as well, like you don't want people to think that your blood is stronger than theirs."

"There's no difference between my blood and theirs."

"Grab as much as you can," Twillo told her. "Small things that we can trade. The rings, the coins, necklaces. Leave the chalices and the scepters, unless you want a scepter. Wait. Let me check them first because there has to be a relic here. I can feel it."

Twillo focused on the pile of jewels, looking for any signs of dragonessence. He moved some of the items away from the center, and sifted through more gemstones and diamonds, everything that his world labeled as valuable. He found a small box, one that could have been overlooked had it not had sharpened corners.

The box glowed with dragonessence.

Twillo opened it and found a compass crafted out of gold, the face adorned with celestial symbols and Sagic characters. A massive gemstone served as a needle, one that glistened with various hues depending on how Twillo shifted the compass.

One thing he noticed, however, was that the needle didn't move.

"Strange," he said as he located a piece of parchment, one with handwritten directions in the old Sagic language. "What does this say?" Twillo asked Adventus as he handed him the small slip of parchment.

The dragon warrior examined it. As he did so, they heard Seondzus cheering from above. It sounded like she was making her way back toward them.

Adventus translated the text: "It says that it is the Pathweaver's Compass. That is what the artificer named it. It will guide the owner to whatever destination they desire."

"Whatever destination I desire?" Twillo nodded, impressed. "This could be helpful. This could be really helpful."

Seondzus appeared overhead and dipped down toward them, her fanged face stopping just a few feet away from Adventus. "Ready to go on a ride?" she asked her counterpart. "You will need to take your vordic form, old chap. There's a way out, but it's going to be a tight trip. You'll fit, but it'll still be tight." She turned her head to Twillo. "Did we get everything we need?"

"Almost. Let me fill my bags as well."

Twillo joined Princess Embla, who continued to scrutinize the jewels. "What did I miss?" she asked. It was clear by the look on Embla's face that she had changed her tune regarding the jewels. Twillo didn't blame her; there were some amazing pieces here, the craftsmanship unlike any he'd seen before.

"I found what is known as the Pathweaver's Compass," he told Seondzus as he scooped up more of the gold and platinum coins. Twillo was aware that this was enough wealth to disappear forever. He could buy a villa in the Tribute Islands, never to be heard from again. But that would be boring.

Once he had gathered as much as he felt comfortable carrying, Twillo placed his hand on Embla's shoulder, who was scrutinizing a necklace.

"We need to move. We will reach the city of Nalig by nightfall if we leave now."

"And we're just going to leave all this behind?"

"For the next relic hunter," he said with a wink. "We got the best stuff, but the journey will still be worth their time."

"Do you all usually do that?"

"Leave something behind? When it's necessary. I very much practice a 'take what I need' philosophy of relic hunting."

Twillo looked up at Seondzus, who continued to hover above them, her form slightly coiled. "Finally," she said with an exaggerated breath out. "We will go first, you and I, and Adventus and her Royal Highness can follow. Ready?"

"Let's do it then," Twillo said.

It was more difficult to hold on to her vordic form, yet he soon found a way after he floated up to the dragon, prepared to leave the sanctum. As soon as he was secure, Seondzus shot toward the top of the opening, moving fast enough that Twillo had to buckle down, his head forward, white hair whipping at his face.

They twisted into a dark, cavernous hole, the wind whistling past them, the light nonexistent. Twillo knew to trust her. Yet the points when portions of her body struck solid stone formations, causing stones to crumble, had him on edge.

"Incoming!" she called back to Adventus.

They took a sudden turn and then another, Twillo clenching his teeth now, his eyes shut, everything moving too quickly for him to make sense of where they were. All he knew was that they were deep inside a mountain, a cave system long forgotten.

After another fast turn, one that caused Twillo's sense of gravity to shift, light filled the tunnel. They exploded out of an opening, bursting through the snow.

Seondzus came to a sudden stop. She twisted around, awaiting her counterpart.

"Fun, right?" she asked.

Twillo let out a deep breath, the world settling around him. "I don't know if I would call it that."

The relic hunter would never know that he was being watched at that moment. He would never see Livia's robes, the way they draped all the way down the slopes of the mountains as the Goddess of Luck watched him settle on the back of the red dragon.

Soon, Twillo would be joined by Princess Embla, and they would leave for Nalig together.

This was both good and bad. It was in Nalig that Twillo was about to receive quite a shock, one that she had no way to warn him about.

Livia hoped that he would survive the encounter.

If not...

She shook her head. Perhaps there was a way.

Chapter Five

Skeletal Giant

SEONDZUS TOUCHED DOWN BRIEFLY. "Get off," she said in a playful tone.

Once Twillo dismounted, the red dragon smoothed her wings behind her and threw her head back as the pair waited for Adventus and Princess Embla to join them.

"Ugh. He was much faster back then, you know."

"Adventus is plenty fast," Twillo told her as he checked his dragonessence levels.

Dragonessence: 269/325

He still had plenty of power, yet Twillo knew that it would be necessary for him to recharge before they reached the southern city of Nalig, a place that just so happened to be named after the dragon that was currently summonable by Katashi the kitsune.

Katashi had soulbinded with Nalig, a green dragon, and the two were with Vradon the monk and Anneli the elven orc. Anneli had a dragon of her own, Ramide, the largest dragon of the bunch, with black scales, a tank of a body, and an enormous horn on the end of his snout. Ramide remained the most intimidating dragon that Twillo had yet to see by sheer size alone. He even made Adventus look small.

While Twillo was aware that he had a few more days before he needed to meet with them, he hoped to reach the city of Nalig early. That would give him time to unload some of the loot at a fence and get the lay of the land. Years had passed since he had last visited Nalig, which was known for its labyrinthine streets and wild night markets, and he was looking forward to it. Yet they also needed to make sure that the Senja weren't going to be in the city, where they could potentially ambush them.

Jecha had seen Twillo and Princess Embla fly south. There was a high likelihood that he would be scouting some of the southern cities, and it made sense to start near the border between Southfall and Middling.

They would need to be alert at all times.

While he waited, Twillo retrieved the Pathweaver's Compass and examined the relic again.

Seondzus turned her head to him. "Ooo, shiny."

"We should try it out. Got any place you'd like to see?"

"I have plenty of places I would like to see, starting with Sorzol in western Icenor, but only because I knew Sorzol the dragon and she hated the cold. But unfortunately, your princess is almost here," Seondzus told Twillo as she peered up at the sky. "Such a slow dragon. He's not that much larger than me, yet it takes him twice as long to get here." She produced a small puff of fire. "We might need to put him down at some point."

"Put him down? I don't even know how to respond to that." Twillo ran his thumb across the top of the compass. He focused on the needle and decided to try a phrase: "I need you to take us to the nearest vortex."

Twillo continued to rub the face of the compass. Soon, the piece began to vibrate. He watched as its needle spun counterclockwise and continued doing so as Adventus landed.

"I thought you'd never get here," Seondzus told her counterpart.

"I fly gracefully, not recklessly."

Princess Embla floated down to the ground, her hood over her head as she approached. "What is it?" she asked once she saw how fixated Twillo was on the compass. "Did you figure out how to use it?"

"I believe so. I'm having it route us to a vortex. We might as well recharge, spend the night, and take our time getting used to the city." The needle stopped spinning on a point toward the southwest. It twitched, and settled.

"Which way?" she asked.

Twillo thought of the map of Middling and its place in the Four Kingdoms. "The vortex is near Mount Dusk?" he asked the compass, even though it wouldn't reply. "Mount Dusk. That's southwest of here."

"It is. And luckily for us, we were heading in that direction anyway," Seondzus said, a bit of fire leaving her mouth as she spoke. "How will we know when we are near?"

"I have no idea," Twillo told her. "That wasn't part of the instructions it came with. I suppose we should just travel in the direction it is pointing, and if we are lucky, it will let us know when we need to change our trajectory."

"In that case, let's go." Seondzus threw her wings back and let out a haughty puff. She moved into the air, her powerful shoulders propelling her forward. She steadied out, thrust downward, and then used the wind to move even faster as she made two complete flips and stopped directly in front of Twillo.

"Are you done playing around?" Adventus asked her.

"I've only just begun, old man."

Adventus let out a huff of steam.

"Hold still for a moment," Twillo told Seondzus. Soon, he was mounted up, the two zipping toward the southwest with Adventus and Princess Embla on their tail. The ground grew further away, a vast panorama of mountains nestled in the thick forest.

Even though he was ducking now, his hood over his head, Twillo kept an eye on the compass. Whenever it shifted, he guided Seondzus by placing a hand on the side of her neck, and lightly putting pressure on it. This annoyed her at first, but she didn't say anything as the dragon continued directly toward the setting sun.

The world beneath them seemed to crumble away and reform as the foothills of Mount Dusk rose from the ground, the famous mountain itself with its sharp peak. It wasn't as large as some of the other mountains, and paled in comparison to its southern counterpart, Mount Dawn, known for the three enormous swords that jutted out of its exterior. But it certainly took up a large portion of the skyline, its flanks a patchwork of craggy stones carved by years of erosion.

Much to Twillo's surprise, the compass seemed to shift in a direction just past the famed mountain.

"Want me to find a place to land?" Seondzus asked.

"No, keep going. Keep going toward the sea," Twillo said as he glancd at the compass.

"I'm not your trusty mount, you know." The red dragon shifted right, the wind passing beneath her belly and flowing over her scaled form. She leveled off, and slowed until Adventus and the princess joined them.

"Where are we going exactly?" Princess Embla asked.

"It is still pointing us to the west," Twillo called over to her. He looked down at it again, its face illuminated by an increasing number of stars and a bit of moonlight. "Continue west."

The Pathweaver's Compass began to vibrate as they grew closer to the coast. Twillo gazed out at the ocean beyond. If he wasn't mistaken, the compass was leading them directly toward the water.

This sparked a memory. He remembered what it had been like to dive beneath the surface with Adventus, to clear the ziggurat that freed Seondzus.

Twillo hoped this wasn't the case this time around. He really didn't feel like getting wet.

The wind changed as they reached the sea, becoming colder, and with a briny scent to it that made him want to pinch his nose. The waves crashed below and produced magnificent white crests riddled with bits of red seaweed. Twillo was well aware that the western sea was much more violent than the east, but to view it like this was a new experience entirely. He could see the waves as they lapped against the shoreline. He knew how strong they were.

The compass vibrated even harder as they reached a series of stone rock formations that had somehow managed to survive the tumultuous sea. The tower-like rocks jutted out of the water, their surfaces long and flat.

"It's one of those," Twillo said as Seondzus shifted to the side, allowing him a more panoramic view.

"Are you certain?"

"That's what the compass is telling me," he told the red dragon.

"Hang on tight." Seondzus moved forward, a gull rushing past them as she reared up and finally landed on the first sea stack. The next sea stack was near, only about ten feet away. Each was wide enough to hold a good number of people.

Twillo floated down from Seondzus. He stepped to the edge of the surface and looked out at another one of the buttes, to a large pile of crumbled stones. He paused for a moment as the water lashed at the rocks below.

Seagulls soon appeared to investigate their sudden presence before moving on quickly due to the dragons.

Seondzus, always one to put on a show, blew a puff of fire at one of the seagulls and caught its tail on fire. The seagull spiraled down to the water below but ultimately took flight again.

"That was unnecessary," Princess Embla said as she approached.

"Perhaps. But we don't want seagulls around, Your Royalness, trust me."

She gave Seondzus a skeptical look and turned her focus to Twillo. "What do you think?"

"It's around. I can sense it." Twillo closed his eyes. He noticed the glow from the large pile of stones on the sea stack across from them. "There. That's it."

Twillo used dragonessence to float to the next stack. He was joined by Embla, Adventus and Seondzus staying behind.

"This?" the princess started to ask.

As if it were answering her question, the crumble of rocks came alive, silver-green mana tracing around its form. It wasn't a golem, as Twillo initially thought upon seeing its movements. As its form clicked into shape, he realized it was the skeleton of a giant. But how? How had the skeleton of a giant gotten out of this sea stack of the western coast of Middling? And what was it doing on top of a vortex?

Adventus landed behind Twillo, instantly taking his dragon warrior form.

"Behind me, Left-Handed One, Your Ladyship," he said as he produced his massive glaive, which was now rimmed with power.

Adventus took to the air just as the skeletal rock monster swatted its fist at him. He drove the glaive into one of the ribs of the giant skeleton, only to be batted to the side.

Seondzus flew in and slammed directly into the skeletal giant, causing it to stagger backward. The skeleton almost grabbed her feet, yet she managed to flap her wings and lift away just in time.

Back on the attack, Adventus took another swing at the skeletal giant but did little to no damage.

Twillo was still entirely startled by the sheer size of their opponent, who must have been a hundred feet tall. Taking it on was a daunting task, the skeletal giant terrifying in size and the way its bulging boulder-like bones mocked the human form. It moved with an uncanny agility, able to swing at Adventus and easily knock him to the side.

Twillo had to do something.

Once he had run through the cards he had on deck, Twillo hit the skeletal giant with a blast from his sword, one amplified by dragonessence. This did little damage, but it did allow Seondzus to swoop in again, the red dragon throwing her body into the skeleton's shoulder yet again.

It became clear what she was trying to do once she struck it again. Seondzus was trying to shove it into the ocean, where it would present much less of an issue for them. They could recharge and leave. The water below would also crush it.

They just had to push the skeletal giant over the edge of the sea stack.

Twillo stepped back as Princess Embla fired a blast of dragonessence at the skeletal monstrosity. He locked eyes with her. "Over the edge," he said as he summoned up the courage to do what needed to happen next.

Twillo raced forward. He skidded to the side to avoid being struck by a giant skeletal fist. He reached its foot and leaped onto one of its boney toes just as the giant tried to stomp him. Adventus appeared again, this time taking to the air so he could distract their opponent.

As the giant slammed its foot down, Twillo held on tight and charged its toe using his Warding Glyph power.

Twillo took to the air, and was seconds away from being swatted down by the giant when Seondzus flew in and grabbed him with her talons.

She deposited the relic hunter over by Princess Embla and turned back to the fight, snarling as she let out a puff of fire. Seondzus ripped forward, the red dragon slamming into the skeleton just as Twillo's explosion blew bits of bone into the air.

The sudden explosion caused the skeletal giant to lose its balance. As it began to stumble backward, both Adventus and Seondzus collided with it. They continued striking the giant relentlessly, and forced it to the edge of the rock formation, where it wobbled for a moment before ultimately falling to the crashing waves below.

Twillo raced over to the other side to see what had become of the creature. He watched as it clawed at the base of the stone in a final, desperate attempt to pull itself back up. Even though it was a skeleton, there was something akin to terror in its eyes as enormous waves came crashing in, foaming white.

It managed to grip the stone base of the sea stack and pull itself up, only to be struck by another wave, one that pulled its arm out of its socket. The arm was flung to the side, and the next wave that came in hit it hard enough to separate its cranium from the rest of its body.

The skeletal giant stopped fighting at that point, and was quickly engulfed by the sea.

"By Livia," Twillo said as he ran his hand through his white hair. Even though it was cold, there was nervous sweat on his brow. "How did that thing get here?"

Adventus approached. "That was a gashadokuro."

"So that's what it's called," Princess Embla said. "I've read about those things before. The skeletal remains of a giant that have been animated by dragonessence." She raised her hand out at the vortex and started to recharge. "There is a lot here."

Twillo continued to watch the water below. Even if the giant was gone now, he still wondered how it had reached a platform in the first place, how the bone had been deposited here. Had the gashadokuro died here long ago? Was it ever even alive?

"Do you want to jump in after it?" Seondzus asked after she'd morphed into her dragon warrior form. She approached Twillo. He could sense her presence behind him, her sheer size and the prideful energy she gave off.

He turned and looked up at her. "I was just wondering about it."

"The relic hunter wonders about many things," she told Adventus, who nodded in agreement. Seondzus patted him on the head. "Many things."

"That is because he is intelligent."

"Why would it be here anyway?" Twillo asked after he'd slapped Seondzus' hand away.

"Only the gods know," Adventus said. "Only the gods."

Twillo approached the vortex and watched as the ground came alive with dragonessence, the power exploding into myriad strings. He felt the mana enter his system, warming him as it coursed through his veins, recharging his levels. Twillo looked out over the ocean and huffed as a light breeze traced over the tops of the buttes.

For some reason, he felt better.

"It would make a strange camp, but it could be beautiful as well," he finally said.

"Let's do it then," Embla told him. "Seondzus can deal with any wayward seagulls."

She snapped her teeth. "Gladly."

"Once we meet up with Katashi, we will be able to use his pocket shelter. You'll like that one." Twillo started to explain how it worked but the princess stopped him.

"I know what that is, remember?"

"Well, that would be handy right about now." Twillo sat near the vortex. It felt warm like a glowing hearth, warm enough to make him want to sleep. "I love sleeping outside," he said.

"You really haven't changed, you know," the princess told him as she took a seat near him. "You were the same as a child too. How many times did you sleep outside the window of my summer home? Do you remember?"

"You mean in the Everberry tree?" Twillo smiled. "I remember. I'll tell you one thing. I'll never forget the ants that love those sweet berries. I woke up several times covered in ant bites."

"They have ants in Icenor?" Seondzus asked. "I assumed it would be too cold for something like that."

"They do, but only for a limited time in the summer." Twillo lay down on his back and placed his hands behind his head. He yawned.

"Look at you," Seondzus said. "Acting like you just slayed a giant skeleton."

Adventus laughed. "Are you standing guard? If so, I will conserve power."

"I'll be around," Seondzus said. "It is a nice night, and it's been a while since I've seen the western sea. Plus, someone has to deal with these seagulls. If anyone would like one for a snack, let me know."

"I'm good," Princess Embla said.

"Are you certain?"

"I'm with Her Grace. We're not eating seagulls tonight," Twillo told the red dragon.

Chapter Six

A Day of Leveling

As always, Twillo was up well before Princess Embla the next morning. After gazing out at the sea for a moment, and enjoying the calm breeze with a noticeable absence of seagulls, he began his practice. He started with cycling dragonessence, Adventus controlling his core while Twillo swung at it with his father's sword.

Twillo was still at the Apprentice Tier, S-Ranked, which meant that he would move up to the Adept Tier soon. He had to keep working at it, training and growing his power. Once he reached that Tier, he would be able to have an additional Arcane Card on deck at all times. Even with the Codex Vault card allowing him to store everything in his chest, changing cards still required a process, where having them on deck would allow instant access.

Pausing, Twillo took a look at the upcoming Tiers by accessing his status. He read the text, yet it also spoke in his head in a strange way. Twillo still didn't quite understand how the system presented itself, but it made sense, and he could access it, and that was what mattered.

Tier 3: Adept
Warrior monks and arcane cultivators are strengthening the foundations of their journey at this tier. They can use level two and three Arcane Cards, and they can have up to four cards on deck.
Cultivators at this Tier can choose a new class to start minoring in, which will become their Secondary Class.

Tier 4: Guardian

Warrior monks and arcane cultivators are further enhancing their journey at this tier. They are considered experts in their field. They can use level three and four Arcane Cards, and can have up to six cards on deck.

Certain cultivators can begin their study of Warding Magics.

Tier 5: Magus

Once they reach this tier, warrior monks and arcane cultivators are amongst the top practitioners in their field. They can use level four and five Arcane Cards, and they can have up to eight cards on deck.

Cultivators at this Tier should be nearing an S Rank in their first class. They can begin their study of their final branch, their Tertiary Class.

Tier 6: Protector

Only highly skilled warrior monks and arcane cultivators are able to reach this tier, where they can begin their study of Blood Magic. They have mastered a wide range of techniques and disciplines. They are highly respected for their knowledge and expertise.

They can use level five and six Arcane Cards, and they can have up to ten cards on deck.

Tier 7: Master

Warrior monks and arcane cultivators at this tier have surpassed the highly skilled and experienced practitioners in their art. They have mastered at least one class. They can use level six and seven Arcane Cards, and can have up to twelve cards on deck.

Tier 8: Mythic

Warrior monks and arcane cultivators at this tier have mastered all known techniques and disciplines. They are both revered by their peers and feared by their enemies.

They can use level eight Arcane Cards, and they can have up to fourteen cards on deck.

Cultivators at this Tier should be S Ranked in one class, and nearing S Rank in the other two. They can begin their study of Realm Travel at this stage.

Tier 9: Legendary

Warrior monks and arcane cultivators at this tier are legends. They are considered god-tier, amongst the greatest of all time, and sometimes, this title is granted posthumously.

They are able to freely travel realms. They can use level nine and ten Arcane Cards, and can have up to sixteen cards on deck.

Those at the Legendary Tier should be S Ranked in all 3 classes.

There was another thing that he confirmed regarding the Adept Tier. According to the system, he would be able to learn another class. What did that mean for someone like him? He hadn't been trained in the way of a warrior monk or arcane cultivator, nor did he have any of the skills of a southern water harvester, who used a similar system to manage wind, water, and terrain powers.

What Twillo really needed was someone to work with him, someone who had a better understanding of the system. Unfortunately, he only knew a few people that had knowledge of the various dragonessence systems. There was the Stylite nun somewhere between here and Shetro Ketl, but it would be very difficult to reach her, especially from his current location. He also knew of a Magi in Mending, the one whose student he had bested in a sparring match. But again, that was on the other side of the continent. And there was no promise that he'd actually get any help from these people.

Perhaps Embla knew someone...

Twillo looked over to the sleeping Crown Ravenna, who rested on her side. She looked beautiful in her slumber, her cheeks slightly flushed. He got the sense that she wasn't actually sleeping, yet she never opened her eyes and looked at him.

Maybe she knew someone.

Twillo returned to his practice. He slipped into an almost meditative state as he continually swung his sword and reversed the energy at the very last moment.

He didn't need to do this. The vortex near them still had power. What he was doing was mostly for practice, to better his skills and hopefully trigger a level-up.

After a few more practice runs, Twillo decided to work with his various Arcane Cards. He wanted to level all of them up if possible, and he had an idea of how he could do this. He was well aware of the fact that he wouldn't be able to bring them to Level Three until he reached the Adept Tier, but he could at least try to get them to Level Two.

He took a quick look at his list of cards.

[Arcane Cards]
Arms of Vikan Wood, Level 1
Codex Vault, Level 1 [Passive]
Core Eruption, Level 2
Enchanting Deception, Level 1
Eternal Cycle, Level 2
Firebreath, Level 1
Flash of Fata Morgana, Level 2
Nadakunai's Might, Level 1
Ripple Tide, Level 2
Vard's Blessing, Level 1

Warding Glyph, Level 1

Twillo put Vard's Blessing on deck, which allowed him to heal himself alongside Arms of Vikan Wood, which improved his natural defenses, and Nadakunai's Might, which improved his strength. Twillo would work on these first, and then he would try to do the same with Warding Glyph, Firebreath, and Enchanting Deception.

"This is going to hurt," he said under his breath as he turned to Seondzus.

"What's that look?" she asked.

"I need to level up six of my Arcane Cards."

The red dragon, who now sat on the ground with her legs crossed beneath her, looked up at him. "And you want what from me exactly?"

"I want you to hit me," Twillo said, knowing that he was going to regret saying that.

"Ooo, I like the sound of this." Seondzus got to her feet and drew her sword. "I'll try not to kill you."

"She won't kill you," Adventus said, his voice at the back of Twillo's head.

"Aware. I need to have injuries to heal from. But first, let me put on my gauntlets." Twillo returned his dragonessence core to his chest and he put on the gauntlets he had picked up in the Victrin Forest. "I currently have three cards on deck, one that heals me, one that strengthens me, and one that gives me power."

"And you want me to cut you down?"

"Not with your sword. Put that thing away. I need you to injure me to some degree, a slight degree. Nothing serious." Twillo clipped his gauntlets on and lifted his fists. "I am aware that this is going to hurt."

While the red dragon's armor had a mask that covered most of her face, it did reveal her mouth, Twillo watching as a big smile took shape. "This will be fun."

Seondzus came at Twillo hard and fast, with a fury of fists that seemed amplified by dragonessence. He blocked what he could, and certainly took some damage. His moans and grunts eventually woke Princess Embla, who fixed her long white hair as she approached the two of them.

"Enough," she said, glaring at the two of them. "What in the name of Yodane is going on here?"

Twillo spat some blood on the ground and grinned at her. "I'm trying to improve my Arcane Cards, Your Ladyship."

"I can see that."

"We can't leave until night anyway. Not with the dragons."

The princess took a look around. "So we are here all day then, is it? Stuck on this rock in the middle of the ocean?"

"It's not just any rock, it's a sea stack."

"The technical term, yes?"

"Yes. After we finish up here, we will go to Nalig. And tonight?" Twillo sat on the ground. He showed his palm to Seondzus, an indication that he needed a break. "Tonight I will unload some of this jewelry and see if I can't learn anything from the relic hunters in the city." He looked back up at the red dragon, who seemed to loom over him. "Give me a moment. I'm going to heal. We are going to do this a lot."

She playfully cracked her knuckles. "I can't wait."

"Take care of yourself, Left-Handed One," Adventus said. "If she hits you too hard, let me know. We have yet to spar."

"I'll keep that in mind." For the next hour, Twillo went through the stages of getting injured and then healing himself. He added his own attacks to the mix with Seondzus' permission, Twillo wanting to amplify his Nadakunai's Might card.

He checked his status throughout, and was pleasantly surprised that he had done exactly what he intended to do.

[Arcane Cards]
Level up!
Arms of Vikan Wood, Level 2
Codex Vault, Level 1 [Passive]
Core Eruption, Level 2
Enchanting Deception, Level 1
Eternal Cycle, Level 2
Firebreath, Level 1
Flash of Fata Morgana, Level 2
Level up!
Nadakunai's Might, Level 2
Ripple Tide, Level 2
Level up!
Vard's Blessing, Level 2
Warding Glyph, Level 1

"Good," he said with a long breath out. "Good."

"Did it work?" Embla asked.

"It did, all three. Now, it's time to do the same with Enchanting Deception, Firebreath, and Warding Glyph." Twillo put these cards on deck, and prepared. "Do you mind if I attack?" he asked Seondzus.

"You can try."

Adventus flashed into existence, which caused Seondzus to take a step back once she saw him in his warrior form. "I believe I will find something for you all to eat," he said. "I'm growing bored and disturbed watching you take damage."

"Poor relic hunter," Seondzus said.

"I will go with you," Princess Embla told the white dragon.

"As you wish." Adventus stepped away and morphed into a dragon. He got down low so the princess could mount up. Once she was ready, he took to the air, and twisted toward the beach beyond.

"Good, just you and me." Seondzus brought her fists up. "Wait. Am I attacking you, or are you attacking me?"

"It's my turn this go-round. Sorry in advance." Twillo activated Firebreath and blasted her with a plume of pure dragonessence. He used Enchanting Deception to send a clone of himself running forward. He charged bits of stone with Warding Glyph, and had Seondzus trigger them. Her armor fully protected her from the explosions. He wasn't strong enough to actually do much damage, and even if he could, she could simply recharge through the vortex.

"At least make it fun for me," she said at one point as Twillo came forward and released another plume of fiery dragonessence. Seondzus pretended to cower. "It hurts," she said as she dramatically fell to her knees. Even on her knees, she was still about Twillo's height.

"Come on," he told her. "Stop playing around."

He used Enchanting Deception to create another version of himself, one that was gesturing toward her to stand. Twillo noticed more and more that usage of this card, and the replicas he created, were tied to his very last action and how it was coupled with his very last thought.

He assumed that once he got used to using the card he would be able to do grander things with it. But for now, it worked as a distractionary measure.

They continued to train until Adventus and Princess Embla returned. The dragon had caught a large fish with gleaming green scales, which he currently carried in his mouth.

"You know what to do with that thing?" Seondzus asked Princess Embla.

"Gut a fish? Yes. I do."

Seondzus laughed. "How? Aren't you used to having food prepared for you, Your Highness?"

"We would go fishing in the summers," Twillo told the red dragon.

"I stand corrected."

As Twillo and Seondzus continued to train, Adventus aided Embla in her effort to make a meal. Just about the time she finished, Twillo checked his status to find the good news.

[Arcane Cards]
Arms of Vikan Wood, Level 2
Codex Vault, Level 1 [Passive]
Core Eruption, Level 2
Level up!
Enchanting Deception, Level 2
Eternal Cycle, Level 2
Level up!

Firebreath, Level 2
Flash of Fata Morgana, Level 2
Nadakunai's Might, Level 2
Ripple Tide, Level 2
Vard's Blessing, Level 2
Level up!
Warding Glyph, Level 2

Everything was looking up. Twillo was certain he would rank soon, which would allow him to start pushing his Arcane Cards' powers to Level 3. He figured it would take more grinding to get them there, but he was fine with that.

As fun as the last couple of days had been, from spending more time with an old friend to exploring a long-lost sanctum, Twillo knew that Jecha awaited them. The God of Carnage, whatever dragons and warriors he had, Renda, Twillo's former teacher—Twillo sensed it would all come to a head soon.

And while he didn't know where this was going to happen, he had a feeling it would take place in Southfall. As far as he knew, the ziggurats in Icenor and Middling had all been tapped. Perhaps there were some in the

Tribute Islands, but Southfall, the southern desert and its vast mysteries, likely held the bulk of what was left.

Twillo was certain of it.

This fish was good, even without any seasoning. Twillo ate, and then he rested into the night, until it was the perfect time to take their dragons to Nalig.

The gateway to the desert, and their uncertain future, awaited them.

Chapter Seven

The Gateway to the Desert

THE CITY OF NALIG was protected from the nefarious desert yokai by towering sandstone ramparts carved with depictions of Southfallian triumphs featuring the battles they had won, the water harvesters they championed, and the legendary giants who had once ruled over the southern desert lands. In front of them were watchtowers with vertical flags hanging from them, the towers managed by desert mages. Twillo knew these to be former water harvesters, the mages capable of wondrous things.

He had only seen them in action once, years ago near the walls of the lower eastern city of Endrus. Dune howlers, a huge group of the wolves that could walk on two legs, had attacked the city in a large pack. The desert mages outside were able to fend them off using wind, water, and a unique ability that let them shape the desert ground as if it were clay.

Twillo had nothing but respect for those desert mages, and he wasn't surprised to see a pair of them approach once they spotted the two Icenordians.

"A long way from home," said the male on the right, the one with a white marking painted across his forehead. The water harvesters of Southfall wore these markings to identify their various sects. Twillo didn't know which one it was, but he did see that the man's marking was different from the other desert mage, a female with darkened skin, her sect marking featuring three dots over each eyebrow. Other than their markings, they simply wore long robes, nothing really distinguishing them from one another.

"It has been quite the journey," Twillo told the man. "Quite the journey."

"You didn't come in on camelback? How peculiar."

Twillo pretended to squint out at the desert. "We were in the city earlier during the day, got some great stuff from one of the markets and decided to head out for a desert picnic. What can I say? We got a bit lost. I'm not ashamed to admit that."

The desert mage exchanged glances with his counterpart. He then gave Twillo a curious look. "Two Icenordians picnicking in the desert? I suppose it is spring and still cool enough to do something like that. Still. It is a bit strange. Unless you were linking up with one of the caravans."

"We did, in fact. Not far from here." Twillo pointed toward a series of ridges rimmed by the remnants of a setting sun. "That direction."

"Ah, I know the one," the other desert mage said, her voice soft and feminine. "They usually camp for several days and host a fire festival."

"Yes, the fire. Even in the daytime it is a sight to behold, and the feast that followed. Let's just say we made a mistake bringing our own food," Twillo told the mage. "And I'm quite full from it. A little drunk too, if we're being honest." He drummed his hands across his stomach. "Been a good day."

"Your Ladyship, Your Lordship," Princess Embla said, her voice carrying the unmistakable tone of decorum and respect that one would associate with a background growing up in the royal courts of Icenor. "We do have plans with a few friends tonight, and apparently, stories to tell of our fiery exploits. If we might be on our way…"

"By all means," the first mage said. "Please, Your Ladyship, go with Vard's intent." He swept his maroon robes away and stepped aside, allowing them to pass.

Twillo and Embla entered the city of Nalig, where Twillo immediately grabbed her hand and pulled her into an alley.

"I cannot believe that worked," she hissed. "Who would believe we'd been out picnicking? How did you know? Really, we should have just snuck in. That could have ended poorly."

"Yet it didn't. People picnic down here during the spring," Twillo assured her. "It's a thing, believe me."

"But two Icenordians? And without guards or an entourage?"

"The world has changed, Your Highness, bit by bit, but changed nonetheless. Besides, it's not easy to sneak into Nalig. It's impossible, really." Twillo grinned at her. "Well, maybe there are ways, but you saw the caravan as well as I did when we were flying overhead. This worked, did it not?"

"You surprise me daily, Jhaeros."

"I surprise myself sometimes."

The two came to a set of steps. They reached the bottom and came to a large street, one with stone buildings that had crenelated battlements. Unlike the alley they had just come through, which was covered by canopies in an effort to blot out the sun, the road that ran through Nalig was wide open, with shops and bars on either side. Beyond were the nicer homes of the city, many two and three stories with tiled roofs.

They were miles away from the ocean, yet there were plenty of items brought up from the sea. Numerous caravans moved between Nalig and Karakorum in the south, which was the biggest city on the western side of the continent and right next to the sea. Twillo could see the remnants of these caravans, many of their carts put away for the night, allowing those who planned to travel back, or perhaps further east, the freedom to move about.

And move about they did.

The people in Nalig were known for their conical hats, which differed from other parts of Southfall, most notably the east, where Twillo once trained with Tonandi the Stylite nun. Because of the mountain range that cut through the kingdom of Southfall, it wasn't easy moving from east to west. Unless one went through the high desert, a notorious stretch of land between a chain of mountains known as No Man's Crossing, the only way to reach the opposite side of the kingdom was to travel north through Middling and loop back around, or sail around the peninsula. This created a civilization that had ties with one another, but also their own unique customs and practices.

Like the conical hats.

Twillo knew these hats were useful in the sun, but he didn't like the fact that they obscured everyone's faces, making it hard to find people yet equally hard to catch the eyes of someone tracking him.

There was a reason the two had come at night. It was much easier to travel during that time, and the two Icenordians certainly stood out in their current garb. They would need to change that.

There were night markets in Nalig, and the one that Twillo and Embla eventually came to was bustling, full of sights, sounds, and numerous strange smells. The locals called these famous night markets the Bazaar of Stars, and they were known for the sizzling meats that they sold out of old stalls, meats garnished with various exotic fruits and served on freshly baked bread loaded with yak butter. The spices were otherworldly, and they were never what one expected.

One expected something from the desert to be bland. It was not. One expected something from the desert to be spicy. It was anything but.

Much of the food of Southfall was savory and sweet, sprinkled with a type of sugar made from powdered dates. That, or it was aromatic to the point that you could taste the food without actually tasting it. The cuisine was so different from the things they ate in Icenor, the root vegetables and the imported fruits from Middling.

"This is something else," Embla said as they came to a stall selling conical hats. Twillo quickly bought a pair and placed one on her head.

"And just like that, you're from the south."

"I am, am I?"

"You look like a camel herder, Your Liegeness." Twillo tucked his ponytail up and placed his hat on his head. Upon seeing how he hid his white hair, Embla removed the hat and did the same.

"Next time warn me before you put something on me," she told him, her playful smile now obscured by the shadow cast by her hat.

"Are you hungry?"

"I am."

"Then try this." Twillo found a booth that sold skewered meat. It was drizzled with a spiced honey, the heat lingering long after they'd both finished their skewers.

"I've been to Southfall and I've never tasted something like that," she said.

"Stick with me and there will be plenty more good food."

The princess laughed.

Lit by the faint glow of lanterns, their light flickering over the stone walls and cobblesand streets, there were as many thoroughfares in the market as there were dead ends. It was certainly an easy place to lose oneself. Because Twillo knew she didn't have experience with something like this, he once again took the princess' hand and led her toward the back of the market, where he would be able to offload some of the jewelry to a fence.

There was also a pretty good relic hunter tavern in the area. The last time he had been in Nalig was several years back, on a journey through the Desert of Heroes to Leenaka's Gift, a fishing village where there was said to be good relics. Twillo couldn't exactly remember what he had picked up at that time. He had them written down somewhere, but he had long since traded the item.

The pair of Icenordians continued until they reached an open area, where Embla whipped her hand away. "You act like I've never been out on my own."

"It can be dangerous at night in the desert."

"We are in the city," she said.

"A city in the desert."

"If anything happens, we will able to do something about it," Seondzus chimed in, which was the first time either dragon had spoken since they landed far outside of Nalig.

"It's best to stay close," Twillo told Embla. "We'll deal with the jewelry, perhaps grab a drink, and get on with it."

"Do you have a good idea where we can stay tonight?" Princess Embla asked. From the way that she lifted her chin, Twillo got the sense that she didn't want to admit that sleeping outside for the last two nights wasn't exactly her cup of tea.

"I don't have a room in the stave church here, where we'll eventually meet the others. So we'll have to find lodging."

"You're about to have more money than you know what to do with," she told him as a couple merchants passed by, ones looking to offload more wares. They carried sacks over their shoulders, the duo ready to sell all night if that was what it took.

"Are you suggesting I buy the stave church?" Twillo brought his hand to his chin. "I hadn't considered that."

She rolled her eyes. "Of course I'm not suggesting that. But it would be nice to find a comfortable place, especially with all the traveling that we have been doing."

"Anything for the Crown Ravenna. This way, Your Serenest Serenity," Twillo said under his breath as he gestured her into what looked like an alley. There was a shop at the back, the light on inside.

"This is it?"

Rather than answer, Twillo stepped up to a wooden door and knocked. He waited. A slit opened to the side. "What is it?"

"Got something here."

"Yeah?" the voice on the other side asked, a male. "And what's that, Icer?"

"If I told you it was treasure, the likes of which you've never seen before, would you believe me?"

Twillo heard laughter, followed by the door unlocking. It creaked open and Twillo removed the conical hat from his head, letting it slide down his back and stay affixed via a string around his neck.

"Two icers, eh?" the fence said in lieu of a greeting. "Must be a reason you've made it to Nalig." He was an older man, one who stooped over, the ends of his leather vest hanging like wings. His thin gray hair was parted over to one side and he wore a pair of square spectacles, the lenses scratched up. The fence took a seat behind the table and increased the intensity of a lamp. "Well?"

Twillo placed the jewels on the table one by one. He did this for anticipation's sake, the fence certainly interested by the time he had placed the third or fourth piece down. "Where did you two get these?"

"I'm a relic hunter," Twillo said matter-of-factly.

"And her?"

"She's my younger sister."

"She hunts relics too?"

"Sort of. She's more of my assistant," Twillo said, which caused Princess Embla to scoff.

"And you don't have any relics for sale?"

"Not at the moment, no. If I did, I would go to a fixer. No offense, fence."

"The fence takes no offense." The bespectacled man continued to watch Twillo place jewels on the table. He gestured his chin toward a back room. "Do you mind? This is going to be quite the haul."

"By all means."

The fence pressed away from the table and stepped out of the room, leaving Twillo alone with Princess Embla.

"Where is he going?" she asked. "And your sister? Really, Jhaeros?"

"Younger sister."

"You're older than me by just a few days."

"I know, hence the term younger sister."

She puffed her cheeks out.

"To answer your other question. With a transaction like this, well, you'll see." Without skipping a beat, Twillo continued to put the jewels on the table. The fence returned from the other room, and was joined by a younger man lingering in his shadow.

He was clad in worn leather armor, which hung loosely from his slender frame, the pieces mismatched. The belt at his waist was fastened to the last hole and covered in nicks and scrapes, enough that Twillo wondered if the belt had been passed down through several generations. Despite his shoddy armor, there was a spark in his hazel eyes that held a bit of cunning. Twillo could see in an instant how he'd fill the armor out in a year's time and provide a much more intimidating guard.

"He'll be monitoring," the fence said.

Twillo shrugged. "Fine by me."

"Tell him you have two dragons with you," Seondzus told Twillo.

He ignored the red dragon's voice and continued until all the items he had lifted from the sanctum were on the table.

"By Livia," the fence said as he began examining the pieces. "These are hundreds of years old. Relics themselves!"

"And worth something, I assume."

"As long as they're not fake," the fence said. Both Twillo and the man laughed. "I know they're not fake. But when it comes to dealing with something like this, I like to have an extra person in the room. Hope you don't mind."

Twillo glanced from the fence to his added security. The young man swallowed hard.

"Like I said, it's fine by me," Twillo said.

The fence offered his counterpart a short nod. The man produced a pouch. "I'm going to lowball you here," the fence told Twillo. "Not because these aren't worth something, they clearly are. I just know how much trouble it'll be to actually sell them, especially in Southfall. If you were in E'Kanth, that would be a different story. But to unload these, I'll have to travel there, and that's not the best of journeys with a load of jewels and old coins. I hope you understand."

Twillo was about to say something along the lines of, *there's plenty more where that came from*, regarding the jewels. After all, he had left quite a bit back at the sanctum. He could always fly back and get more. There would likely be complications with taking that journey, but it wasn't completely out of the question.

Instead, he merely nodded. "I'm willing to negotiate."

And negotiate he did.

In the end, Twillo ended up taking several platinum coins and a handful of gold for all of the loot. It was considerably more than he had ever gotten before by selling off treasure, yet he knew it was worth more, that the fence was right in saying he should have taken the stuff to E'Kanth.

Twillo was fine with that. He needed the money now, especially if he was to entertain a princess.

Twillo left after a bit of small talk and a cup of lukewarm tea. Rather than lead Princess Embla to the place that he had planned for them to stay—the upstairs of a quaint tavern near the night market—he took her to one of the nicer hotels on the western side of Nalig. If someone came checking for them, he figured they would start at the kind of place where royalty or saracents would stay. The hotel he had chosen was a step below that, yet it was still grand.

"Not too bad," he said as he took in the place.

The building had a sandstone façade with lanterns suspended from intricately wrought iron baskets. This created a welcoming glow along the path that led to the entrance doors, which were carved from Sunblaze Cyprus and tall enough to fit a giant.

"After you, Your Radiance." Twillo respectfully stepped aside and offered the princess a short bow.

"You're too much," Princess Embla told him as the two entered the hotel.

A grand chandelier held court over the foyer, the flickering candles along its rims causing the light in the spacious room to dance. Twillo paid for a nice, second-floor room, and he paid a little extra for discretion.

Still maintaining the conical hats over their heads, Twillo and Embla were led to a suite with a pair of comfortable beds covered by fine silken sheets.

Ornamental screens over the windows added a touch of privacy, yet there was also an open balcony that overlooked the hotel's lush courtyard, one with fountains and blooming flowers.

"See?" Twillo said once the hotel staff left. "This is how you live like a Ravenna and do so discreetly." He swept his hand at the room's furniture, which was expertly carved and had mother-of-pearl inlays, the seats with plush velvet covers.

"What is so discreet about this? You literally paid the people at the front not to mention any Icenordians were staying here."

"I suppose you're right." Twillo lowered onto one of the beds and kicked his feet up.

"Boots off. You act like you weren't raised in Sparrow's Rise."

"Was I?" Twillo asked as he sat back up and popped his shoes off.

Princess Embla approached one of the tables. She examined the basket of fruit and ultimately chose a date. She ate it and leaned against the table as she looked Twillo over. "You really need to think about what happens after all of this."

"You act like this will be a quick victory against Jecha, Your Loveliness. I would wager that it isn't."

"I meant what I said before, that you would be deemed a true champion and worthy of your name being restored. You already should be considering what you've already done. It's remarkable, Jhaeros. You need your title back."

"I do, do I? And what do you need again?"

"I need someone to help me rule Icenor."

"Is this her way of proposing to you?" Seondzus asked.

"It seems like she's the type that just wants to be ready for what is to come," Adventus told the red dragon. "There is nothing wrong with that."

"Correct me if I'm wrong, but it is out of the bounds of Icenordian customs for a woman to ask a man to marry her," Seondzus said as Twillo continued to stare over at the princess.

"They grew up together," Adventus reminded the red dragon. "It makes sense. I wouldn't call it out of bounds."

"You just want to be part of his wedding. Imagine flying in on dragonback, how grand that would be. They could hang tinsel from your tail. Maybe they could even paint you an interesting color, something much better than white. Might I suggest red?"

"Red!? I would never allow anyone to paint me red, and you know that."

"Enough," Twillo told the dragons in his head. "And let's just get to that point first before we start making plans, Your Illustriousness, the point where we've defeated Jecha and we're looking for our second act. Third act? Fourth act? Speaking of acting, you act like this is going to be easy."

Princess Embla ate another date. "I don't think it's going to be easy. It's just something that's on my mind. I have a life to go back to after all of this, you know."

"As do I."

"Who's to say that you couldn't continue to do what you'd like, Jhaeros?"

"If I were to marry you? How would there be time? Who's going to take care of all of our wonderful children?"

Embla blushed. "Now who's the one getting ahead?"

"Well, that is your proposal. And I would assume we would have a whole clan of boys and girls. We could summer in Sparrow's Rise and winter in the Tribute Islands, or perhaps Nalig if you like a little desert flair."

"Stop it." Princess Embla approached the balcony door. She opened it and stepped out. Twillo felt the breeze shift into the room. Even though everything was clean, he could see the dust that the desert was capable of bringing. He imagined the upkeep it would take to operate a place like this and shuddered. That wasn't a life for him.

Twillo left Embla alone to her thoughts as he relaxed onto the bed and stared up at the ceiling. It had been painted with murals of Southfall, famous landmarks such as the Three Pillars of Mount Dawn. He continued to gaze at the mural, focusing on a section that depicted humans in a battle against what he assumed were the gods.

"What is it?" he finally asked, his question meant for Adventus. "The mural."

"I believe it is a mural for the Tournament of the Gods. Are you familiar with it?"

"No, I'm not."

"Gods get restless. They choose people from across the Four Kingdoms of the Sagaland to compete against their own skills, against others, and finally against the gods themselves. At least that was what it was like in the past. I couldn't tell you if it is still something that happens, but the people here remember it."

"The gods have a tournament?"

"They do, or perhaps they did."

"And whom do they choose to compete?"

"Water harvesters, warrior monks, the Emperor's Magi, Icenordian archmages, the Brethren—people who have power and access to the dragonessence system," Adventus told him. "Whoever those people may be. It could have changed now."

"I knew someone that competed and won," said Seondzus. "But she had her memory stripped afterward, so she never quite knew of her accomplishment."

"So it's real?" Twillo asked as he placed his hands behind his head. His eyes traced over the mural again. It was strange to think that the gods would organize something like this, but he believed it. He would believe anything that had to do with the gods now, especially after what he had seen from Jecha.

He didn't know why they liked to meddle in human affairs, or why his realm, the Realm of the Formed, was so important in the grand scheme of things. But Twillo planned to do his part. In the morning, or in the afternoon depending on how late he slept, he would visit the stave church of Nalig and leave a message with the monk there.

At some point in the next three days, Vradon would arrive in the city with Katashi and Anneli. The monk would get the message Twillo left, and then he would be able to meet them at the hotel. From there, Southfall and all of its mysteries would be at their disposal.

In that regard, the city of Nalig truly was the gateway to the desert.

Twillo was up before Princess Embla the next morning. There wasn't space in his room to cycle dragonessence, but it would be possible in the large living area of the hotel room if he moved things around. As quietly as ever, Twillo shifted the furniture until he had a suitable place to move around.

"Are you ready, Left-Handed One?" Adventus asked.

Twillo looked up at the high ceiling, and then to the furniture that he had shifted aside. "Let's do this."

He removed his dragonessence core from his chest and sent it forward, where Adventus took over.

"What about a sparring buddy?" Seondzus asked in a way that indicated she already knew the answer to her question.

"There's not enough room for you in here," Twillo told her. "Apologies."

"You will be fine," Adventus said as an afterthought.

"Let me control his core. You always get to control it."

"Absolutely not."

"You act like this is hard—!"

Twillo watched his core twist off to the right. It flipped back in front of him, and then zipped to the left. He tried to grab it and ended up running his knee into the corner of a desk he'd moved. The core blasted around him again and Twillo swatted at it.

"Hey," he said after his core did a complete circle around the room. "Let's be a little careful with that."

"Fine, I'll let him do it," Seondzus said. "But you owe me one."

For the next hour, Twillo worked on cycling dragonessence. Because of the confined space, he decided not to access his Arcane Cards and test them all again, but at least he had brought each of the cards to Level Two.

Twillo was slowly starting to accept that he wouldn't be able to reach the higher levels that he wanted through the dragonessence system, not in the time given. While he didn't know when things would come to a head with Jecha, to really rank up, to move to the higher Tiers such as Magus, Protector, or even Master, would take him years. Even with the way he had learned to somewhat game the dragonessence system through ziggurats, instantly increasing his reserves, the actual leveling wasn't something that he could do as quickly. There was no quick way to the top.

Yet he was fine with this. Since the incident years ago, his father killed, Twillo left to be raised by the streets, he had always been scrappy. Maybe that was why Livia had chosen him.

In thinking this, Twillo gripped his sword tighter and put more of his power into swinging his weapon. He caught a glimpse of some of the tapestries on the walls, all depicting the Tournament of the Gods. Twillo knew that the trajectory of these legendary warriors was different from his, yet in a certain light, they were the same. With what he had been tasked with doing he was Livia's champion, the person that she had put her full faith behind.

And as much as what had been asked of him was sheer pressure, it was also inspiring. The thought of this weighed him down at the same time that it lifted him up.

Princess Embla joined Twillo at about the time he was finishing his practice.

"I hope you rested well, Your Regality," he told her as he returned his father's sword to its scabbard. He stood with his hands behind his back, at mock attention.

"At ease, Jhaeros," Princess Embla told him with a yawn.

"She always rests so well," Seondzus said. "Did you notice how much the princess likes to sleep? That would be something to consider if you were to marry her. Do you want a sleepy bride? Some people would like a sleepy bride, especially if they were a morning person."

Twillo gritted his teeth. He hadn't yet thought about the whole marriage thing that morning and didn't want to think about it now.

"What is it?" Embla asked as she made sure that she was covered up. She had totally misinterpreted the look on his face.

"Just some voices in my head," Twillo told her. He reached his hand out to his dragonessence core and pushed it back into his chest, a warmth instantly moving through him. "I need to leave a message at the church."

"I can go with you."

"We really should be careful," Twillo told her. "It is clear that we are Icenordians."

"I thought that's why we got the hats." She motioned to the conical hats that Twillo had purchased last night. They were both hanging from a rack near the door.

"That is one reason, but—"

"You worry too much." Princess Embla stepped over to her bag and retrieved a scarf. She wrapped it around her neck and pulled it up so it covered the bridge of her nose. "Hats and something like this? We'll be fine."

"Maybe you're right, but it's best that we go while it is still early."

After writing a message for Vradon on a bit of parchment, Twillo fashioned a face cover for himself using a cloth that he traveled with. Usually, this was for polishing various relics, but it would do. The pair left the hotel with hats on their heads and their faces covered, Twillo guiding the Crown Ravenna toward the Icenordian district.

Most of the cities in Southfall had an Icenordian district, some larger than others. This was because of the trade between Southfall and the Tribute Islands years ago, during the time of Yanzon the Undisputable, the Icenordian ruler that had banned dragonessence. These districts were fairly easy to find if one could see above the sprawl and catch the tip of the stave church.

Twillo did just that as he headed toward the west, yet again navigating the mazelike streets of Nalig as if he had been born there. He spotted the spire of the stave church, the apex featuring a dragon carved out of Vikan wood. The wood had been beaten soft by the constant winds and sand, yet the dragon stood strong, the church expertly maintained over the years.

As Twillo and the princess approached the church, he noticed that it had recently been repainted black, which was something he never quite understood because this color always faded in the desert sun. Two statues of Livia with her flowing robes cast thick shadows into an X-like pattern along a cobblesand walkway that led up to the entrance. There was a well on the side, and beyond that a courtyard where Twillo sensed the presence of a vortex.

"Grand as always," Adventus said, the white dragon taking a deep inhale even if he wasn't currently in his physical form.

"This is certainly one of the nicer ones," Twillo said, a statement for both Adventus and Embla. He turned to the princess. "Perhaps I should leave the message. The monk here may recognize you."

"In that case, I will sit here in the courtyard." Embla turned to a wrought iron bench. She took a seat, her conical hat and scarf obscuring her face.

Twillo stepped into the stave church, the smell of hundreds of years of incense instantly reaching his nostrils. He looked up to the rafters, at the various dragon carvings, many in their vordic forms. He navigated the pews and came to a door on the side that opened to an interior hallway.

Twillo stepped onto a red carpet that had bits of sand on it. He followed the carpet to the end of the hallway and found a group of monks seated on the ground amidst several scrolls and books that had been placed on velvet pillows. They had little side desks near them, other books open. It looked like they were forming part of a ritual.

"Your Lordships," Twillo said to the monks, all of whom had their long white hair braided and wrapped around their necks. *"Vekh Vekhran."*

They all looked up at Twillo, yet only one spoke. "*Vekh Vekhran*. May I help you?" the leader of the group asked, the man an older monk with a crooked posture.

"I am expecting friends, a monk named Vradon and a few others. He will come here looking for me. I would like you to let him know that I am at this hotel." Twillo produced a piece of parchment. The monk nearest to him took it, folded it open, and examined the information.

"For your troubles," Twillo said as he produced a few coins. He placed them one at a time in an offering bowl near the entrance and bowed his head slightly. "Your Lordships."

"What is your name?" the monk who had spoken earlier asked.

"Twillo."

"Twillo. Such a curious name. Of where?"

"Hoersung," he lied. "And yes, Twillo was a nickname. My real name is Maron Brunvigna. I have papers if you'd like to see them."

"No, that is fine, Twillo. Such a curious nickname. I can't say I've heard it before."

"Many haven't," he said. "I trust that you will deliver the message when the time comes. It is of the utmost importance."

The lead monk grunted a positive response. "We certainly will. Your patronage is always appreciated."

"I understand." Twillo put a few more coins into the offering bowl, each one plinking as it reached the others that he already donated. "For your troubles."

"It is no trouble."

"For your discretion."

Twillo left, and soon joined Princess Embla in the courtyard.

"How did it go in there?"

"It went well enough."

"So everything is set?" she asked.

"It is."

Twillo and the princess left the church. Once again, they navigated the maze-like sprawl of the city of Nalig, where it became dense to a point that he couldn't see more than a few feet in front of them. The crowd seemed to have swelled during the day, herders in town to gather supplies for the long summer to come. There were also water harvesters by the looks of it, Twillo noting a particular group of young men all in maroon robes, with white markings on their foreheads.

The pair reached one of the city's numerous squares, where they came across a squad of elven orcs that had just marched out and were beginning their patrol. Twillo touched Princess Embla's arm and moved her in a different direction. "What is it?"

"Your father's Honor Guard is here."

"In Nalig? I've never heard of them coming this far south."

"Rowian must have sent them," Twillo said. "Or should I say Jecha."

She glanced around nervously. "You think there are others here?"

"I couldn't tell you. But we shouldn't stick around to find out."

"Be on guard," Adventus warned him, even though he didn't need to. Twillo was already moving as far away from Rowian's men as he could.

"They might be looking for me," the princess said. "I wouldn't put it past my father to send small squads to all the main cities. He is certainly worried about my absence."

"Do you think he would have sent them to any city south of Seondzus, where you were last seen?" Twillo asked as they slipped around a man leading a donkey cart.

"That would make the most sense. Actually, it would make sense for him to send them here considering our proximity to Seondzus."

The two dipped into an alley, one shielded from the sun by multihued canopies. Twillo paused for a moment. He didn't know how they were going to be able to get to the other side of the city without crossing that particular square. He had an understanding of Nalig, but the city was dense and the layout seemed to have changed since the last time he'd visited years ago. Perhaps they could figure a way to leave Nalig itself and loop around.

"Sometimes, I wish we could simply use the dragons," he said.

"Wouldn't that be easy?" Seondzus asked Twillo. "We could pick you up and drop you off at the hotel."

Twillo turned to the wall behind him. It seemed to separate the alley from someone's small yard, where there was laundry hung from clotheslines. "Let's make this quick," he told Embla as he offered her his hand. "I have an idea."

She took it and the two floated over the wall. He landed in the yard, where they found a young Southfallian girl playing with a wooden doll in the shade. The girl looked up at them, instant fear in her eyes. Twillo imagined how intimidating they must have looked, their faces concealed, conical hats casting shadows over their eyes.

"Just passing through, youngling," he told her.

The girl's lips quivered.

"Please don't scream," Embla said as she crouched before the child. She removed her face covering and offered the girl a kind smile. The princess pressed her hat back, allowing her white and yellow hair to spill out.

Twillo would never have admitted it, but she looked like an angel in that moment, especially with the dusty city of Nalig as her backdrop.

"What are you doing here?" the girl asked.

"We're just looking for a way to reach the outskirts of the city. Do you know which way that would be?" she asked in a sweet voice.

The girl, who was now wide-eyed having seen the princess' long hair and pointy ears, gestured toward an open gate. "That way."

"Thank you," Twillo said as he slipped through the gate. From there it was a winding trip down a set of steps that had recently been washed to cut back on the dust. They came to a smaller neighborhood market, which wasn't as dense as the night market they had navigated the previous evening. It was clear that the people in attendance were mostly locals, Twillo and Embla safe for now.

They continued in the same direction as the girl had pointed them, which sent them directly beside a stable full of camels and other desert beasts. The smell was strong and pungent, and Princess Embla pinched her nose at one point, but they were finally able to reach the outskirts of Nalig, where they once again came to the wall that protected the city from the elements.

There were desert mages at the top, a small cluster of them seated as they stared out at the rolling sand beyond.

As Twillo looked up at them, a bead of sweat rolled down the side of his temple. He wiped this away, let out a quick breath, and began scanning the wall and the buildings around it for a way to continue toward their hotel.

The density of Nalig left some of the homes themselves pressed up against the wall. Twillo got the sense that the one nearest to them had a yard, which he was able to see through a crack between two of the mudbrick buildings. From there, it was more open. But to get to the yard, he would need to pass through the building.

"Hopefully this helps," he said as he produced his coin purse.

Twillo approached a low door and swept the curtain covering it to the side. "Your Lordship? Your Ladyship?" he inquired.

A woman responded. She quickly approached, the woman with a mixing bowl in her hands and flour splattered across her apron. She eyed the two Icenordians suspiciously. "What are you doing here?"

"Just passing through," Twillo said as he placed a silver coin on the table. "We thought we might use your yard."

The woman looked from the silver coin to the back door, and finally returned her gaze to Twillo. "And if someone asks if I've seen two curious Icenordians?"

"Then you tell them you haven't seen anyone that fits that description." Twillo placed another silver coin on the table.

"And indeed I haven't." The woman motioned her mixing bowl to the back door.

Soon, Twillo and Embla were in the yard, where they were able to exit out onto another side street. They had to wait for a moment behind a pair of men carrying buckets of water on their heads, but they were eventually able to squeeze around them and continue on.

The two came to another yard, this one full of sheep. Careful of the sheep droppings, and careful of the one with horns that seemed very protective of his flock, Twillo and Embla reached the end of the next yard, and were finally able to take the stone steps that led into the nicer district, where their hotel was located.

"We made it," the princess said with a deep, satisfied sigh.

Rather than respond, Twillo led her inside the hotel. "New robes," Twillo told the clerk as he produced his coin purse again. "Actually, a tailor is in order, and make sure it is something that is more appropriate for the desert."

"Yes, Your Lordship," the man at the front told Twillo. "We have one on call who can be here in about an hour. Does that suit you?"

"It does."

"In the meantime, we will provide mint water and lunch."

"Even better," Princess Embla said. "Please have food delivered to our room."

Chapter Eight

Ariosto

LIVIA WAS THE ONLY ONE who knew how close Embla and the relic hunter had come to being discovered.

The Goddess of Luck was also well aware that one of the toughest encounters of his life to this date was right around the corner. While the honor guard was indeed in the city of Nalig, someone else had just arrived, a person with a past that directly intersected with the reason

Twillo had survived the storming of his father's home so many years ago.

Yet she wanted him dead.

Renda was the swordmaiden who had trained Twillo, an elven orc whom Twillo's father had secretly loved. Twillo and Renda had even met years later, after he had journeyed to the eastern coast of Middling. Yet everything that had happened to Renda after that point was the reason she had finally given in to the influence of the darker aspects of dragonessence.

There had been redemption, there had been a struggle, but for her to survive, for her to continue onward, she had found herself in a position directly under Rowian. Naturally, once Jecha took Rowian's body, Renda came under his influence. The God of Carnage knew how to tap into the evil inherent in everyone's soul. Everyone. It was one of the reasons he could grow so powerful in such a limited amount of time.

Livia looked out across the city, the thousands of inhabitants both young and old. Every single one of them had this evil within them. Every one of them could be persuaded by Jecha. It was one of the reasons why she needed to stop him. Once he gained some control, his influence would proliferate with startling speed.

The gods needed to know, and much to her chagrin, Livia's father *did* know. Yet there'd been no action. Were they so foolish? Did they fully trust a mortal like Twillo? What were the gods aware of that she herself didn't know? Since her request for her father to get involved, Vitharr had retreated to his strange home, the one with Livia's favorite koi fish in the pond out front.

She had tried paying him a visit, yet he had simply kept his door shut. Something was afoot.

Livia didn't know what it was, and she knew that interfering in the lives of mortals was something that was frowned upon. But she also knew that the gods operated in ways that made little sense. As an example: they had their tournament, the one in which they pitted the strongest of the four kingdoms against one another. Was that not interfering? Was that not directly intervening in the lives of mortals?

She had brought this up numerous times, yet the argument had never landed. This was one reason Livia didn't like to associate with the other gods. They didn't practice what they preached, and many were pompous and out of touch. Without any competition, they had grown used to their lifestyles, with no concern for those that suffered in the Realm of the Formed. They simply didn't care, and this angered her to no end.

Even with all those concerns, what Livia really wanted to do was warn Twillo.

Yet she didn't have that kind of power. She could, however, influence what was set to happen in a way that would give him a leg up. It was time to try one more thing, something Livia had been planning for just the right moment.

As easily as she was hovering over the Southfallian city of Nalig, she was now directly above a courtyard in the Southfallian city of Karakorum. Karakorum had its similarities to Nalig, yet it was pressed up against the sea, with a lively port, the rest of the city surrounded by slums.

It was in the monastery quarter, in a hidden courtyard, that Livia watched a warrior monk finish training a group of water harvesters. There were five in total, one of whom had classed as an arcane cultivator. This young man, this arcane cultivator, wasn't destined to meet Twillo, yet he had an interesting destiny of his own in the days ahead.

The warrior monk teaching them, however, could be of service.

The man, who wore a conical hat, beneath which were a pair of green eyes, had been alive for centuries. His graying, orange hair peeked out over his ears. There were vertical writings tattooed down the sides of his temples, Sagic words that he didn't understand, which made him similar to the relic hunter.

While he had taken the form of a man, he was actually a bakeneko, a type of yokai that could morph similar to Katashi, Twillo's close companion. This warrior monk, who went by the name Ariosto, was perhaps one of the strongest mortals currently alive when it came to utilizing dragonessence in ways that had been forgotten for centuries.

Now, as Livia floated over the courtyard, she saw one of these ways that he had come to understand the power. The sand that Ariosto and the five water harvesters currently stood on glowed with dragonessence. He had made this vortex himself, one that continually replenished power. As Ariosto instructed the five harvesters, Livia settled nearby.

She smiled as Ariosto shifted his gaze in her direction, his eyes gleaming with recognition. He stepped aside and one of the harvesters produced a blast of dragonessence by using a mudra known as Aetheric Crescendo.

Livia was early, yet she knew that Ariosto had seen her.

She waited, her robes moving on their own accord as time for Ariosto and his five trainees sped up. Time remained the same for Livia, and soon, Ariosto had returned to the courtyard alone.

It was now night.

"Ariosto."

"You have come about the boy?" he asked her, referring to the arcane cultivator, the most unique of the group of water harvesters who had just been training. Jaden was of age, but to someone like Ariosto, a bakeneko who had lived for quite some time, he was still a child.

"I have not," Livia said, her voice only audible because of the white sand that Ariosto now stood on. The warrior monk sat, his legs crossed beneath his body. He maintained his human form, yet he now had a cat's tail, one that curled in the air as he continued to look up at her.

"He is on his way to the Three Pillars of Mount Dawn with the others. Please guide your robes over his journey."

"Their journey is not what interests me, but I do wish him and the others well. There is another, and your guidance would be helpful."

"Another?" Ariosto asked. "Is this about the Tournament of the Gods?"

"It is not. That is my father's hobby, not mine."

"Ah, Vitharr."

"Yes, my father. This is about your world, your realm, and everything that could happen if someone doesn't intervene. Jecha has returned, and he has taken the body of an elven orc."

This statement brought a look of concern to his face.

Livia continued: "The pieces are in motion now for confrontation between Jecha and an Icenordian relic hunter who goes by the name Twillo. It is set to happen soon, in the coming week."

"I see," Ariosto said with a slight purr to his voice.

"You may be one of the only mortals I can communicate with. If I could, I would raise an entire army to bury him, but Jecha already has access to something like that and that could easily backfire. So maybe it is best we do it this way."

"And the other gods?" Ariosto asked.

"I do not believe that they will intervene. The tournament. They are more interested in that."

"A pity that they would sit by as the rug is pulled out from beneath them."

"Truly."

"And where do you see me in all of this?" Ariosto asked.

"Twillo the relic hunter is going to need your help soon. He is north, in the city of Nalig. He is staying at the Desert Breeze hotel with the Crown Ravenna of Icenor."

"The Crown Ravenna?" He considered this with a huff. "What is her name?"

"Her name is Embla. And it is a complicated story, but here's the overview: Twillo was once the son of the Saracent of Sparrow's Rise, where he grew close to the princess during the short summers up north. Through a series of events, no fault of his own, he was put onto the path of poverty, became an orphan, and later an accomplished relic hunter. I mean it when I say that he is cunning and good at what he does. He now has access to the dragonessence system, but it is not the same that you utilize down here. It is a broken version, one created by the Emperor's Magi."

"You would like me to go there, Your Ladyship?"

"I would, and I don't believe I will be able to communicate with you about it further. Unless you can bring the sand with you."

"I don't think that's a possibility," Ariosto told her. "I put everything I have into the sand. It is the source of my power. While I can bring a vial of it, I don't think that would be enough to communicate with you. What about a Dragon Meridian? What if I took them there? Would you be able to speak to Twillo and the Crown Ravenna there?"

"A Dragon Meridian?" Livia considered this.

Warrior monks were able to use what were known as Dragon Meridians. These were the names for the five meridians on a person's body that produce dragonessence. There was one below the navel, one in the chest, two at the shoulder, and one at the forehead. Normal dragonessence users, from relic hunters to water harvesters, rarely knew about these points, even if they were the source of their powers. But warrior monks and nuns could access them by portaling to these meridians and clearing out blockages.

"I believe that would be a possibility," she finally told Ariosto.

"Then I will make that happen. I will leave for Nalig in the morning, and I should reach there by the evening. But first," he said as he got back to his feet, "I have a few more things I need to take care of in town."

"Do hurry. This will all come to a head soon."

"You can count on me," he told her with a slight bow.

"I knew I could."

Chapter Nine

The Flower Festival

THEIR NEW CLOTHING WAS DELIVERED the following afternoon, the dark blue robes made of a light cotton material like Twillo had seen other Southfallians wear. He could move more freely in them, and the tailor had even designed the clothing to have the high collars that Icenordians were fond of wearing, even though they had told her that this wouldn't be necessary.

"What do you really think of this stuff?" Princess Embla asked after the tailor and her two assistants had left. She spun once, her gesture bringing a smile to Twillo's face as she finished her movement with a graceful curtsy.

The more time he spent with her, the more Twillo remembered how much he liked being around Embla. It was something he had certainly felt years ago, but he had been so far removed from their youthful summers together in Sparrow's Rise that he had forgotten this about himself.

Another thing he had thought of over the last day was her proposal of marriage. She hadn't proposed to him in his traditional Icenordian way, reading her yoika poem and having a monk or nun oversee it, but he knew that she would gladly go through these rituals if this was what it came to.

Was this what it was supposed to come to? Were all his years of struggle simply a long and winding road back to the top, to a seat at a table that he'd long since abandoned? It was hard to consider, especially with the threat of Jecha and the rebirth of the Age of Dragons. Yet he couldn't stop thinking about it.

Being adjacent to the ruler of a kingdom was simply a role that Twillo couldn't imagine himself in. All the circumstance and pomp of living in Icenor's capital of Vendir would be compounded by the fact that he'd be dealing with the Ravenna's Court, the titles, traditions, the rituals, and everything else that would come with being married to Princess Embla.

And it wasn't like he would be king, a true ravenna himself. Twillo would always be considered a Prince Ravenna. But if they had children, one of his children would grow up to lead Icenor, and with Twillo's knowledge of the world, perhaps he could do some good here. Perhaps he could raise someone that would lead Icenor into a renaissance never thought possible in the northern kingdom. Maybe that was a better way to think of all this. The sacrifice of the rest of his life for the betterment of the future through his offspring.

He knew things weren't that simple. There would be a lot of work that would need to be done before he would be allowed to take that role, enemies that would need to be silenced or quashed, like Ananda Min, the woman who had come for his father. How would she react to something like this? Furthermore, how would Embla's father, Vraizard the Blade, take his daughter's proposal?

Twillo was actually glad that they had a current mission in clearing the rest of the ziggurats in Southfall and stopping the God of Carnage. In certain ways, it was easier than staring down his future and making decisions that very well could affect the entirety of the Sagaland. It was an important and necessary distraction.

As he often did when staying in the same place for too long, Twillo grew restless toward the early evening. Perhaps this was another reason that he wouldn't do well in Icenor's capital of Vendir, where he would be well-fed behind the walls of the Embla's sprawling castle grounds.

He tried cycling dragonessence to kill time. When he wasn't doing this, Twillo busied himself by pacing, thinking, and organizing his things. There'd been the conversations with Embla, and of course a little playful banter with Seondzus while Adventus occasionally commented, but Twillo had reached a breaking point. He needed to stretch his legs.

"What do you say?" he asked after he knocked on Princess Embla's door that evening. "Night is upon us,

Your Highness. Shall we enjoy the city in a clandestine manner? Who knows what we'll discover."

"Do what now?" she asked from the other side. "Please, come in."

Twillo opened the door to find Embla seated at a desk with a bit of parchment in front of her. From the looks of it, she'd been drawing the flowers that bloomed every summer in Sparrow's Rise.

"Think of it, Your Grace. Is there a better time for us to explore all that Karakorum has to offer? Surely there isn't. I'm about as bored as someone living in Legends Fall during the long winter," Twillo told her, a saying that poked fun at one of the northernmost cities of Icenor where they only got eight months of sun a year.

"Aren't you the one that thought it was best if we stayed inside?" she asked.

"I think many things, but that doesn't make them right."

"Such a restless relic hunter," Seondzus tsk-tsked.

"I suppose it couldn't hurt." Princess Embla pressed away from the desk. Yet again, his eyes dropped to the flowers she'd been drawing.

"I didn't fancy Your Ladyship as an artist."

"I get bored easily as well," she said, her voice without the same command that it normally had. "It's something I learned to do back in Vendir during winter breaks. Of course, with my position, I had actual artists train me."

"I can tell," Twillo said. "This could be in a gallery in E'Kanth, you know."

"Stop it." She approached Twillo and placed her hand on his arm. "If we're going to leave, let's do it."

"I'm serious. It could be in a gallery. I have a paintbrush you could use," he said, which was a joke that only Seondzus seemed to pick up on.

"You'd need blood for that paintbrush, relic hunter," the red dragon said.

Not privy to the dragon's voice, Princess Embla looked at her drawing and shrugged. "People would assume that someone else painted it, or that I paid to be in the gallery. You know that."

"Then you'd make it a live demonstration. You could do the art right there in front of them. Just think of all the spectators, how much clout you would have once people find out that you are not only a princess, but a talented artist as well. The entire Sagaland would be envious—"

"Stop," she said as she moved past Twillo and reached the door. "Do we have to wear our hats?"

"It's probably for the best, especially with our new robes." Twillo placed his conical hat on his head. He approached the princess and fashioned her hat into position as well. He even strapped it beneath her chin, his hand touching her face for a split second longer than it should have.

She certainly noticed, but she didn't say anything, only offering Twillo a smile as they left the hotel.

It was time to see what they could get into.

Twillo and the princess reached the same public square where they had seen the honor guard a day earlier. There was no discernible presence there any longer, the square filled with various booths that were part of some flower festival. It was surprising to see how much merchants had brought into Nalig over the course of a few hours.

Vibrant red poppies interspersed with patches of lavender, and clusters of desert lilies all stood alongside one another. There were various bouquets that had been preassembled, woven garlands hanging from the booths and other flowers blooming in ceramic pots. Lanterns illuminated the festival, the gentle light reflecting off petals and adding to their vibrancy.

Even with the cold desert air, the scent of the flowers was overpowering, a sweet reminder of the day-long celebrations that looked to be continuing. A parade started up from the western side of the square, the people of Nalig in conical hats and with strings of flowers draped from their necks. Some of them wore colorful masks, and as the children chased each other through the festival grounds, their laughter filled the air.

Princess Embla brought her hands to her waist. "I was not expecting this."

"I've heard of it, but figured it would be another day or two," Twillo told her as they remained on the outer rim of the festival. "I'm surprised you didn't see the crates of flowers outside of the city. None of this is from here, you know."

"Some of it is," said a man in a conical hat, one that was suddenly standing at Twillo's side. The man wore light gray robes, the sleeves of which had been rolled up to reveal a pair of thin arms with veins running up them. There was something peculiar about his voice, a hum to it as he spoke again. Twillo caught a small glimpse of his face and noticed there were Sagic tattoos on his temples. "Water harvesters in the area help with the desert lilies. Those are from here. The sunflower blooms and the saffron orchids are also from this region, too," he said as he pointed to a series of orange flowers that rose along green stems like ladders.

"I did not know that," Twillo said.

The man merely nodded.

Twillo was just about to ask him more about the flowers when he noticed something on the other side of the festival. People were moving away, as if someone was pushing through the crowd. The festival-goers began to scramble and push one another to make room.

"I would suggest we move," Adventus said, his voice ever-present.

"Come on," Twillo told him as he took Embla's hand. Yet before he could step forward, the princess was already leading them in a different direction, one that would push the pair to exit on the north.

"This way is faster, Jhaeros. Less people."

"Works for me," Twillo told her as they neared an exit to the square.

He turned back to look toward the center of the festival just as a wave of dragonessence rippled through the crowd. It forced people to fly left and right, the blast followed by the screams of children and panicked citizens.

Two of the Senja warriors used dragonessence to leap to the top of the festival stalls. They carried blades rimmed in power, which cast sinister blips of light onto the fleeing festivalgoers beneath them.

"Summon us!" Seondzus said.

"Not here," Twillo told her. The dragons were a last resort. And he certainly didn't want to reveal them to the public in such a way. Even if they could take their dragon warrior forms, it was best to see how much they could handle on their own.

Because there was no point in fleeing.

It was clear that the group of Senja had spotted them. And they seemed to have little to no concerns that there was a crowd of spectators still fleeing the area. The Senja fired bolts of dragonessence indiscriminately as Twillo raced toward them, his father's blade at the ready. Embla wasn't far behind with one of her daggers, the princess boldly ready to assist in whatever way she could.

The first warrior lunged for Twillo, only to miss, and punch his sword directly through the replica Twillo had created using his Enchanting Deception card.

Twillo came up behind the man and swung his sword into his side. His blade, amplified by dragonessence, cut through the armor and brought the Senja warrior down. Twillo pulled his sword out and then drove it into the man's back.

He barely had his blade up in time to reach another assailant, this one of the elven orc variety. The man was much stronger, his strike powerful enough to cause Twillo's knees to buckle. The man was blown to the side by a spear of dragonessence courtesy of Princess Embla, who continued to dodge the strikes of the other Senja warrior.

Coming to her aid, Twillo attempted to strike him down. In doing so he was kicked directly in the chest, the Senja warrior much faster than Twillo expected. He flew through one of the flower booths, and landed in a mess of thorny stems. This also had a way of sending flower petals in the air, which Twillo ignored as he got back to his feet.

He glanced ahead to see Embla deliver the finishing blow. Somehow, the princess had slipped around the Senja warrior and had driven her dagger into an opening in the armor at the back of his neck.

"You're going to need us now," Adventus said.

At first, Twillo didn't understand what he was referring to, but then he saw that they were completely surrounded by Senja warriors and members of the Honor Guard. Renda was with them now, Twillo's former instructor approaching with two swords drawn, her face obscured by the demonic helm that the Senja warriors wore.

Renda became Twillo's only focus as he brought his blade to the ready, just as she had taught him so many years ago. The elven orc flourished both of her swords, and tilted her chin up, as if she were looking down at Twillo with disgust. "Jhaeros, we meet again."

"It doesn't have to be like this," he said, even though he knew this was the only way. That was how Renda had trained him, to fight with victory in mind, to never give in to an opponent no matter how stacked the odds were.

And they certainly were stacked.

"Left-Handed One, summon us!" Adventus said.

Twillo did as instructed, both Adventus and Seondzus appearing in their dragon warrior forms.

This would have given them leverage had it not been for another pair of combatants, the two standing behind Renda and wearing all black armor. These were dragon warriors as well, which meant that Jecha and his scouts had uncovered more ziggurats.

Like Seondzus and Adventus, the enemy dragon warriors wore heavily modified armor that seemed to be an extension of their scales.

"We should do this somewhere else," Twillo said. He wasn't often the voice of reason, but there were still people trying to flee the square. The fight that was to come could easily spread out to the city and cause havoc.

"I tend to agree," came a voice to his right. As if he had been there all along, the man in gray robes and with face tattoos that Twillo had met earlier stood with his fists at the ready.

"This isn't your fight," Twillo told the man.

The man tapped the back of his knuckles together, dragonessence sparking and quickly bathing over him to create a brilliant dragonaura that was stronger than any Twillo had ever seen before.

Renda didn't seem fazed by his display. "Then you will die with him. Kill both the men," she told her squad, "and spare the princess' life. Jecha will be pleased."

The mysterious man in gray moved like the wind. Suddenly he was beside some of Renda's forces, where he quickly disarmed a pair of elven orcs through amplified movements. Twillo knew now that the man was a warrior monk, but he didn't know the term for the movements he was performing. All started with a hand gesture that quickly shifted into various dragonessence-based attacks.

Renda came for Twillo, wielding both swords as Seondzus and Adventus moved to address the two dragon warriors. This left Princess Embla, who had already started to engage one of the elven orcs, the man keen not to hurt her.

Renda swung her swords in a way that seemed haphazard, yet Twillo knew just how in control she was. He had seen her fight for her life once before, just barely, a glimpse of her moving forward as he fled his childhood home.

Twillo blocked her next attack, which caused a spark of silvery mana that blew him backward. He would have landed on the tops of his shoulders had it not been for his dragonessence, which he was able to use to right himself at the very last moment. The kick she landed next hurt, one delivered right to Twillo's chin.

He arced to the side and broke through another flower stall, yet was able to somewhat roll to his feet. He was now covered in various flowery perfumes, the smell overwhelming. Twillo needed some space, which would give him the chance to battle Renda on his own terms.

He bolted toward the outskirts of the fight, and turned just as she approached. The swordmaiden sheathed both of her blades and raised her fists.

"Do you remember what I taught you?" she hissed.

"What—?"

Suddenly, Renda was directly in front of Twillo, delivering a punch that seemed like it had drilled a hole through his stomach. Winded, Twillo fell and rolled onto his back. Renda placed her foot on his throat like she was going to crush it, her eyes dull and lifeless as she looked down at her former pupil.

A burst of dragonessence quickly engulfed the swordmaiden, causing her to stumble to the side. Twillo had used Firebreath, yet it did little to damage her armor aside from bits of whatever she wore beneath, the fabric smoking as she reapproached.

"You use Arcane Cards and trickery," Renda said as she tried to stomp Twillo. "How pathetic."

Twillo pushed back to his feet, and caught a glimpse of his father's sword, which was just out of reach.

Even though he was winded, Twillo brought his fists up, and went for his demon bear brooch, which summoned Yasuna. It was a cheap trick, but he could barely breathe at the moment, and he was also concerned with the fight taking place closer to the center of the square. He had a feeling that the honor guard wouldn't harm the princess, but he had to be sure.

As Yasuna gave Renda utter hell, the big demon bear swatting at Renda and roaring in her face, Twillo grabbed his father's sword and limped back to the main battle. He sent a blast of dragonessence into the side of an orc trying to wrangle Princess Embla. She finished him off with a knee to the face as he fell, one that Twillo sensed may have killed him.

"Tsuh!" The man in gray robes produced a blade of dragonessence with the palm of his hand. He sent this forward into the body of one of the elven orcs, quickly killing the woman. He whipped her to the ground and delivered a high kick to an incoming combatant. The warrior monk came down hard with an elbow attack, one that sounded as if it had caved in the man's skull.

The clashing clink of the dragon warriors instantly drew close attention as Seondzus and Adventus battled their counterparts. This was much more destructive than any of the humans that were fighting. In the short time it took Twillo to sidebar with Renda, the dragons had cratered the courtyard and taken down some of the statues. Adventus grabbed one of the dragon warriors and flew him directly into the final remaining statue, which sent huge bits of stone crumbling to the ground.

Dust, debris, flowers, misted blood, and the cries of men and women in combat filled the air, Twillo certain that they would soon have more company. As he engaged another elven orc, one wielding a mace, great gusts of wind blew into the square, scattering everything they came into contact with. Whole carts were tossed to the side, rocks and plants tossed about.

A pair of desert mages landed, both with white markings on their foreheads that told Twillo that they had once been water harvesters.

Two of them had control over the wind, and the third instantly began taking control of the stone and creating a combatant out of it, one that was even larger than Adventus in his dragon warrior form. This one was a stoneshaper.

Three desert mages, two of which were galecallers and one of which was a stoneshaper.

"She is the Crown Ravenna of Icenor," Renda said as she reached the main theater of the fight.

Twillo glanced back to where he had last seen Yasuna. She was lying on the ground, and looked as if she were dead. As soon as he locked eyes with her, the demon bear returned to the brooch, which Twillo now held in his hand.

He would have to check on her later. Twillo thanked her under his breath as he looked ahead to see what the desert mages would say. They were all seasoned harvesters, each in their thirties. The one that spoke was female, her hair braided behind one ear. "Everyone here will be taken to the keep, Crown Ravenna or not."

"I don't believe that is necessary," the man in gray robes said. He stood close to Twillo, his face still obscured by his conical hat.

The desert mage seemed to recognize him instantly. "Ariosto? What is the meaning of this?"

"I'm not able to—"

Renda rushed forward with her swords drawn in an attempt to kill the desert mage. She was met by a fist of wind that sent her flying backward, over a hundred feet. The fight was back on, and after seeing what Renda had done to Yasuna, Twillo wanted to deal with her once and for all.

Twillo slipped away, and soon reached the other end of the square to find Renda lying in a pile of stone, her helmet now missing. Twillo pointed his sword at the woman who had trained him.

"You would kill me like a coward?" she asked, blood trickling down her lips.

"No, I will not. I don't know why you've done it, but the dark influences you are part of have warped your mind. You will destroy the Four Kingdoms if Jecha's wishes come to pass. You realize that, do you not?"

"Aside from my time in your father's house, the Four Kingdoms have done nothing for me." It was then that Twillo noticed that there was something sticking out of her stomach. Renda had been impaled on a rusted weapon once held by one of the statues in the square. The desert mage that had attacked her had been much more precise than Twillo would have imagined.

"You are dying," Twillo said.

"I am, Jhaeros," Renda told him. Even though she had tried to kill him, even though she had joined the side of the God of Carnage and had likely been directly responsible for countless deaths, Twillo couldn't help but feel sorry for her.

Renda had been the closest thing he'd had to a mother after his had died. Her strict lessons, the way she always kept him on his toes, how Renda had taught him so much more than swordsmanship—all of it had played an instrumental role in the man Twillo had become. Without her lessons, he wouldn't have survived on his own. Without all of the training that she put him through, Twillo would be dead by this point, unable to do his part in saving his world. If he had lived, he would be a much weaker man than the ones standing before her.

There was still some activity happening behind him, a fight that was dying down, yet Twillo paid little attention to it as he got down to one knee and looked at Renda. He reached his hand out and she took it, a tear rolling down the side of her face. It was only one tear, and it was a defiant one at that, but it was genuine.

"How do you want to do this?" he asked. Twillo continued to hold out his hand and look into the eyes of the woman who had raised him.

"I deserve to suffer."

"No, you do not. Wherever you go next, be it the Realm of the Forgotten or a worse hell, go knowing that without you, I wouldn't be here. I wouldn't be able to stop Jecha, and if we're being honest, I probably would have died at the manor. How do you want to do this?"

"If you leave me here, I will die eventually."

"I do not want you to suffer," Twillo said as he got back to his feet. He drew his sword from its scabbard. "Thank you for all you have shown me. I will do my best to honor your name, and go forth with everything you have taught me in mind. Livia knows I'm going to need it. Goodbye, Renda."

"Goodbye... Jhaeros."

Twillo swiftly ended her life and pulled his sword away. He looked down at her dead body, blood dripping from the tip of his blade. Twillo saw that there were flowers nearby. He stepped over to them, and turned back to the swordmaiden's body, where he placed several flowers at her feet.

Twillo did all this as if he were in a trance, completely blind to what was going on behind him. In finally turning around, he found that the Honor Guard and the Senja warriors were all dead. The two dragons were gone. Now that he thought about it, he had heard them take to the air at some point, which must have startled the three desert mages.

Twillo approached, his head hung heavy, strands of his white hair now in his face. He didn't know when he'd lost his conical hat, but hiding his identity was no longer necessary. "It needed to be done," he told Princess Embla. "It had to be done."

"You slayed her compassionately," Seondzus said, her voice now back in Twillo's head.

"We caught the end of it," Adventus told him. "It was indeed with dignity. Now we have other things that must be handled. This has been quite the calamity."

"And the other dragons?" Twillo whispered, just to be sure what he had heard.

"They left with a pair of riders heading north, toward E'Kanth."

Twillo steeled himself. "In that case, it's better that we leave."

"It is," Adventus said.

Twillo examined what was once the flower festival, which was now a square of smoldering craters, pulverized flower arrangements, and dead bodies. As gruesome of a scene as it was, he was reminded of something else: this was what he was working to protect the Four Kingdoms against.

With Jecha's growing influence, this was merely a preview of what was to come.

Chapter Ten

Dragon Meridian

Twillo joined the man in gray robes known as Ariosto, who was just finishing up a conversation with the three desert mages.

"We will leave the city now," Ariosto said, Twillo instantly noticing that there was something different about his voice. It seemed to echo in a way that had the three desert mages nodding along, as if they were enchanted by his words. "I'm sorry that things came to this. It is rather unfortunate, but I assure you I can explain. Right this way." He gestured toward a southern exit.

"We need to take our things from the hotel," Twillo told the warrior monk. "And leave a note for our companions."

"In that case, you lead the way. But we don't have much time."

"Come on." Princess Embla grabbed Twillo's wrist. She led him toward the exit nearest to their hotel, Ariosto following behind, the warrior monk light on his feet.

"Who are you?" Twillo asked once they were away from the water harvesters, who had already begun using their powers to start cleaning things up.

"It is best that we save an explanation for a bit later," Ariosto said, "once we are out of Nalig. I was sent by a friend, I can assure you that you are in good hands and that my intentions are true."

"He isn't human," Seondzus told Twillo. This caused the relic hunter to pause, which allowed Ariosto to step in front of him and continue along with the princess. The man looked human to Twillo, but he knew that yokai were capable of things like this. Was that what he was? Was it something else?

Twillo kept an eye on him, the way that he moved with the gait of a feline. The warrior monk could have been a hundred years old as easily as he could have been in his early thirties. From certain angles he seemed older, and the way he spoke was certainly something that came with age, his dialect just a bit different than what Twillo was used to hearing. Yet his features were of a man that was much younger, youthful even.

They reached the hotel and gathered the bags Twillo kept his relics in as well as a few of Princess Embla's items. "Where should I tell them to meet us?" he asked Ariosto as they headed down to the lobby of their hotel. "Our companions will be here any day now."

He gestured toward the chandelier. "And they were set to meet you here at this wonderful hotel?"

Twillo nodded. "Yes. We ran into a little money and I thought, why not spoil a princess?"

"Don't listen to him," Princess Embla said.

"Perhaps we can greet them in the desert. I think it is important we speak to someone before we do so."

"In the desert? But the desert is vast," Princess Embla told Ariosto.

"That it is. You may leave a note, but I don't believe that will be necessary."

Twillo left one anyway, telling Vradon and the others to meet at the stave church. It would send them from the church to the hotel and back, but he didn't know Ariosto well enough to fully trust him and figured they could return to the city if the desert didn't pan out.

They left Nalig quickly, Ariosto leading the way. He seemed to know the city like the back of his own hand, the warrior monk navigating the narrow streets as if there were a wide boulevard that he'd walked thousands of times. Once they reached the desert beyond, Ariosto turned toward an outcrop of stones that lay beyond the city, one with the signs of old quarries.

"An explanation," he said as they started around the hills of stone. "You are owed that. How much contact have you had with Livia?"

"She has used her father to speak to us," Princess Embla said.

"Ah, then you know why she has spoken to you, what is at stake."

"We do," Twillo said, relieved to hear that following the warrior monk had been the right idea after all.

Ariosto turned to Twillo and the princess. "She came to me yesterday while I was finishing up with some students."

Twillo felt a flutter in his heart. "She came to you? Livia?"

"I am what is known as a bakeneko," Ariosto said as his tail started to take shape. He removed his conical hat, which now hung by a leather string around his neck. While he had a human face, Twillo could see cat-like features through the way Ariosto's eyes and ears were shaped. It made complete sense. "I hope my transformation isn't too troubling."

"One of the companions we are waiting for is a kitsune," Twillo told him. "We are familiar with the possibilities of yokai transformations."

"Ah, then you are aware that we yokai can live longer than humans and elves. I have lived numerous lives. I have been a water harvester, I have traveled the Four Kingdoms, I've even had a family before. In the end, what interested me the most was the dragonessence system, the original one, the one provided to arcane cultivators, water harvesters, and warrior monks. You have a version of the system. Livia told me this."

Twillo nodded. "I didn't know the versions were so different."

"They are. The capabilities vary. One of the things I have improved in my own study of the powers is the ability to transcend realms to certain degrees. I have also reached a point where I can imbue objects with dragonessence, not unlike an arcane artificer. I have such an object at my home in Karakorum, sand that I have poured as much power into as possible. This was where she came to me. It was how she was able to come to me in the first place."

Twillo felt moved by the man's words. He knew that the Goddess of Luck was guiding her robes over his journey, yet he still couldn't imagine what it would be like to actually meet her. "What was she like?"

"Livia? She's not like the other gods, I can tell you that. Livia doesn't want to watch humans test themselves and battle for their pleasure. She doesn't want to watch our world turn to chaos. She believes in you, your power to stop the God of Carnage. This, I don't quite understand, but how could I? I've only just met you, I couldn't possibly know what she sees in you, or what she knows of the future, however murky it may be. But I can assist by allowing you to meet her."

"We would actually meet Livia?" Twillo asked.

"Yes, through one of my Dragon Meridians. Are you familiar with this practice?"

"It is where warrior monks and nuns draw their power," Princess Embla said. "A meridian is the name for one of the five points on the body that actually produce dragonessence. Other users don't have access to these points in the same way. I know a little bit about it, and was given an overview of it. But that's about it."

"Good, then you will understand what is about to happen. How about...?" Ariosto looked to some of the hills not far from them. "Up there. That will be a safe place to do this. I will let you ask her any further questions you may have. That is not my role in this."

The hill they found provided a good view of a desert valley beyond, yet the wind blew stronger here, spiraling at times and kicking up sand. This was made mesmerizing by the moonlight, which caused the sand to glitter in a way that made it almost resemble dragonessence.

Even if Twillo had spent a considerable amount of time in Southfall, there was something mysterious about the desert that always drew him in. It was a place that was both scorching hot and bitterly cold, a place of contrasts through its sheer expanse and comforts one received upon arriving at the various cities along its border. It reminded Twillo of Icenor without the frost and the hallucinatory Fata Morgana.

Twillo and Embla were now seated in front of Ariosto, who had his shoulders pressed back, his meditative posture showing signs of a man who had done this for much longer than Twillo had been alive. It was contagious in a way, Ariosto's calmness, the way he maintained his focus. Even Seondzus, who normally commented on everything around Twillo, had quieted down.

"While this is something that you will likely never be able to learn, I believe it is important for you to understand what we are about to do. You would need to be an arcane cultivator or warrior monk to be able to do this," Ariosto told Twillo and the princess. "Even if you have access to the dragonessence system, yours has been..." He paused for a moment as he searched for the right word to describe it. "Let's call it coded differently. Yours has been coded differently. And once you have access to the system, only a select few are able to modify, to fix the kinks in the system you are using, a semi-broken system that is the result of years of both experimentation and oppression."

"Oppression?" Princess Embla asked Ariosto.

"Yanzon the Undisputable. His actions of banning dragonessence so many years ago and putting severe restrictions on those who were allowed to practice it led to a clustering of skills." He touched the ground and used it as a map of the Sagaland. "Southfall, here, with its warrior monks, water harvesters, and arcane cultivators. The system originated here around the time of the Age of Giants. Dragons later utilized the power itself as a fuel source, but it is much older than them."

Twillo nodded. He knew where Ariosto was going before the warrior monk continued:

"In Middling, here, you have the Emperor's Magi, who are often recruited from Southfall. When this happens, the system is adjusted. Over time, the separation between the two and these adjustments led to two different systems. If you move all the way up the continent to the Kingdom of Icenor, here, you get the secret of archmages, which I'm assuming you know more about than you are letting on," he told Princess Embla.

"I've been quite clear of what I've learned from a variety of teachers," she said, mostly for Twillo.

"Again, a different interpretation of the system that originated here in the desert. Once we bring in the Tribute Islands, you have arcane artificers using yet another interpretation of this system to imbue objects. I know this is a long explanation, and I'll get to the point. This is why you won't be able to use Dragon Meridians. It is coded into the original dragonessence system. But there may be other things you can do."

"Like what?" Twillo asked.

"Mudras. But we can look into that in the morning." Ariosto tilted his chin back and peered up at the sky. "It is almost morning, isn't it?"

"It is," Princess Embla said.

"In that case, I will make this quick." He laughed as if this were an inside joke. "I'm sorry. When you go to a Dragon Meridian it is essentially portaling into yourself. Time doesn't move the same way as it does here. That was why that was funny to me."

Twillo's eyebrows twitched upward. "We are portaling into ourselves?"

"No, you are portaling into one of my meridians. I suppose I should explain that as well. There are five," he said as he placed his hands just beneath his navel. "The Core Nexus. The next is the Chest Meridian, known as the Heartflow Conduit. Followed by the Left Shoulder Meridian, the Lunar Channel; and the Right Shoulder Meridian, the Solar Channel. The final is the Forehead Meridian, the Mind's Eye Pathway."

"Five Dragon Meridians," Twillo said.

"Correct. Warrior monks are able to visit these meridians and clear out blockages within themselves. It isn't as complicated as it seems yet it is vastly hard to explain, but in clearing these blockages, they are able to learn new skills and enhance their dragonessence here in our realm. There are dangers associated with traveling to the meridians. The creatures that are able to attack them in these spaces can take their dragonessence cores, but we won't need to worry about something like that tonight. Are you ready?"

Twillo and Princess Embla exchanged glances. He spoke: "And this is how we will meet Livia?"

"It is," Ariosto assured them. "Now, close your eyes."

Twillo did as he was instructed. He let out a deep breath, and with his next inhale he was suddenly standing in a vast desert, not unlike the one that he had just been seated in. Yet there was something different about this desert.

The colors were all off, the sand black and the sky an ultraviolet purple. They were near an oasis, one surrounded by fluorescent fauna that glowed brightly with pink, turquoise, tangerine, and sunflower yellow. Ariosto stood before them; he didn't look the same way he had moments ago. His entire body was made of energy, his face obscured by a conical hat. There was a light at the tip of his tail that Twillo noticed, one that changed color as he motioned for them to sit.

"This is incredible," Princess Embla said.

Twillo looked to her to see the same thing, Embla's body made of light, her hair blindingly white. He glanced down at his own hands and saw that they were also made of energy.

"Adventus? Seondzus?"

"They won't be here," Ariosto told Twillo. "But they are safe with your body back in our realm. Do not be alarmed. They are still with you."

"And we're just sitting there in the desert?" Princess Embla asked.

"We are, but we are safe. You have dragons with you, do you not?" Ariosto looked to the oasis behind him, the water gleaming. "I suppose it is time."

As if he had conjured the Goddess of Luck himself, the water rose into a single column. It took on the form of a woman with simple, almost nondescript features. The oasis faded away, the water in the sand around it becoming the woman's long robes. The robes extended even further until they had entirely masked the blackened desert around them.

They stretched beneath Twillo, yet they didn't feel like robes when he placed his hands down by his sides. It still felt like the sand. All of it was beyond magical to the point that it was confusing to see.

Twillo let these thoughts drift away. His focus now was on the woman who stood before them, Twillo entirely speechless, the sense of awe he was experiencing profound.

"Jhaeros, Embla," she said, her voice soft and divine. It seemed to come from all directions, echoing in Twillo's head. "I'm glad you are here. And thank you, Ariosto."

Twillo didn't know when he had moved, but the warrior monk now sat next to him also looking up at the Goddess of Luck.

"It is an honor, Your Ladyship," the warrior monk said with a bow.

She looked back at Twillo and Princess Embla. "This is the only time that we will speak, so please listen carefully. If you had asked me when this all started, I didn't think we would ever communicate. I don't see the future in that way. To me, the future is murky at best, and it is visible to me in multiple ways. There are the positive outcomes, neutral outcomes, and the negative outcomes, the ones I hope to avoid. Jecha's resurgence is one of those outcomes. But there are others, including your death."

"My death?" Twillo asked. Princess Embla shot her hand out to him and gripped his wrist. She quickly let go.

"Yes, it is certainly a possibility, certainly something I have foreseen in the near future. You were in Southfall weeks ago, yet even then I didn't think to link you up with Ariosto, I didn't foresee this. So I have to be wary of the visions I have, and the strength I give them. If you didn't already know, Jecha is here in Southfall. He is on the eastern coast and rapidly moving toward the high desert, toward No Man's Crossing."

"I figured as much with Renda's appearance."

"Yes, I'm sorry you had to witness that."

"I'm just glad it's over," Twillo said honestly. "That she can finally rest."

"Yes, sometimes that is best." It was a moment again before she spoke. "There are two ziggurats left in Southfall. One is in the high desert, and the other is deep in the Harvest Mountains. If Jecha reaches either of these ziggurats, your chances of survival become incredibly slim. If you can reach them and unlock the power in time, as well as the dragons present, then you will be able to defeat him."

"How many dragons does he have?" Twillo asked.

"He has four. But in clearing these ziggurats, he will be able to access all of the dragons in the Realm of the Forgotten. That was the point of these installations in the first place, to hold the dragons back. By reaching them and unlocking their powers, you are breaking the spell cast long ago by Father Dawn. So either way, they will be part of the Sagaland yet again."

"So the fight now is about who frees the dragons, and where their loyalties may lie."

"To some extent, yes, Jhaeros. But there are more good dragons than there are bad. Jecha's power over them will be absolute if he is the one that can free them all. This would lead to all-out war across the Four Kingdoms. If this were to happen, I think the gods would intervene, but his power would be great enough that there wouldn't be many ways to stop him. The entire realm, the Realm of the Formed, could come under Jecha's control. It has happened before, you know."

"With Jecha?" Twillo asked.

"How do you think Father Dawn took the realm? It was a benevolent takeover, but it is possible. Because of my nature, I don't see things along the same timeline as you may. I see them over the course of decades, up to hundreds of years. There are so many options, so many opportunities, and so very many serendipitous occurrences possible that it is impossible to truly know how things will be. This is the issue with the power of luck. Before I leave, I want to impart this to you: if you fail, the Four Kingdoms will be in ruin by this time next year. It will affect everyone; any magic left will be used to conquer further."

"I understand," Twillo said, even if these words were hard to process. How could he understand something like that? The entirety of the Four Kingdoms ruined so quickly if he failed? He let out a deep breath, one that did little to relieve the weight on his shoulders.

"You must reach the high desert ziggurat before Jecha. But before you do so, you will join your companions later tomorrow. Ariosto will guide you there."

"I will?" the warrior monk asked.

"You will know the signs. After No Man's Crossing, you will head south to the Harvest Mountains where you will find the last ziggurat. At that point, I'm certain that Jecha will be on your heels. His forces will have moved into Southfall, taking the cities. There are too many scenarios that will play out by then, too many ways that this could go. You just need to reach that point." Livia raised her arms, and as she did her robes began to disappear and push back. "Know that I am with you every step of the way. Know that."

And with those words, Livia faded, the oasis reappearing as if she had never been there in the first place.

"I knew what I was getting into, but to hear it from her, to even imagine what could potentially happen"—Ariosto shook his head—"how terrible. And now I truly understand how important our roles are in righting things. This is for the future and the past."

"I don't even know what to say," Princess Embla whispered. "Never in my life would I have thought that I would actually meet the goddess."

The warrior monk tilted his head back and looked up at the starlit sky above. "Our world, or should I say our realm, is a wondrous thing. Shall we return?"

"We should," Twillo said. "It's best we update the dragons, and I need to check on Yasuna."

Ariosto brought his arms into an X and placed them over his chest. He bent his head forward, and within seconds, they were back in the desert, back in their world.

The interrogation started immediately, Seondzus leading the way. "Did you actually meet her?"

"I did," Twillo said as he got used to being in his body. It felt different, it felt heavier than his astral form, or whatever he had been in moments ago.

"And?" Adventus asked.

"We'll meet the others tomorrow and head to the high desert from there." A smirk took shape on Twillo's face. "What am I saying? The high desert? Only a fool travels on foot through No Man's Land. Isn't there an old song about that?"

"There is," Ariosto said, "but there is a hidden meaning to the words." The warrior monk cleared his throat and sung a song Twillo had never heard before.

"Only a fool goes foot by foot, 'neath the wrath of midday light. Rather float on air so cool, far from the land's fiery bite. With burning sand and a giant stride, the crossing doth implore, a journey made without a glide, shall be a journey nevermore."

"I don't get it," Twillo said.

"Do I need to sing it again?" Ariosto asked.

"I'm sorry," Twillo said as he sat back and let out a deep breath. "My mind is still processing what just happened. We just met Livia. Is that not profound? People will live their entire lives and pass on to the Realm of the Fortunate and still never have a chance to see her. I guess I'm still just thinking about it."

"It was rather more remarkable. As for the song, the answer is in the lyrics. One doesn't walk across the high desert, they float." Ariosto tapped his temple. "Simple as that. They float using dragonessence, which is something that any water harvester worth their weight in sunstones would know."

"Do you think we will encounter any?"

"We may. Harvesters are certainly about during this time of year. Although the groups that patrol the high desert don't normally move there until late spring. But you never know. If we're lucky, or should I say, if they're lucky, they won't encounter us. It is best that they know nothing of what we are doing. Best that the world doesn't know." Ariosto let out a deep breath. "I suppose we should call it a night. There's much to do in the morning."

"One more thing before we do. Also, do not be alarmed. Yasuna is harmless. Well, sort of." Twillo used his brooch to summon Yasuna. The demon bear approached, shame in her eyes.

"I'm sorry I failed. Walth will never let me live this down."

"Fail? You didn't fail," he said as he placed his hand on her armored forehead. "You helped us succeed."

It was a moment before the demon bear finally grunted a response. "I'll do better next time."

HARMON COOPER

Chapter Eleven

Mudras

IT WAS HARD TO SLEEP THAT NIGHT. Even though it had been a long day, it had also been a day in which Twillo had survived an attack by Jecha's forces, a day in which the woman who had trained him had died, and a day in which he had met the Goddess of Luck herself.

Twillo found it nearly impossible to sleep after something like that.

Too much had happened, and even though the desert was peaceful at night, the breeze nice and cool as it whispered across the sand, Twillo could never get comfortable.

He eventually gave up. Twillo sat for a while and watched as the sun warmed on the horizon, the desert filling with an orchestra of subtle sounds. Princess Embla rested near him as did Ariosto, the warrior monk in a deep sleep-like meditation a few feet away as well.

Twillo yawned.

The sun looked like a pink bubble at first, but it soon took its place in the sky, the desert before him transforming. Twillo had seen dawn break over the desert before. He knew how the sand, currently cold and uninviting, would shift to a warm golden palette that glowed in the morning light. Yet it was still remarkable.

The tranquil scene was interrupted by the shrill cry of distant birds that cut through the silence, the landscape continuing to reveal its harsh beauty as a gray cloud that had settled overnight pressed away, desert shadows growing long and jagged.

It was going to be a hot day.

Twillo could feel the heat from his new robes. But it wasn't too bad. The breeze seemed to pass through, cooling his skin. It was a strange sensation, the outer surface of his robes warm, Twillo remaining cool beneath the clothing. In continuing down the hill, he was able to find some shade, and was just about to sit when Ariosto appeared.

It was as if the warrior monk had been standing there the entire time.

Ariosto was still in his human form, and he now had a cat's tail that was hooked in the air. Even though Ariosto had slept in the desert, his gray robe seemed perfectly pressed. He also was alert, as if he had been up for several hours.

"Daybreak's grace," he said as he motioned for Twillo to follow him. "We don't have a lot of time, but I will show you a few mudras that may help you."

"Wait," Princess Embla said as she came down the hill to join them. She smoothed her hands over her tailored clothes and offered the warrior monk a curt, royal bow. "I'll join you all."

"Look who's up early," said Seondzus, which was the first time she'd spoken that morning. Twillo thought about summoning both the dragons, but decided it was best to conserve his power for now.

"Did I miss anything?" Embla asked.

"Just a morning greeting," Ariosto told her. The warrior monk took a look around. They were near a small clearing, a gully of sorts. There was a bit of dust on the hardtop, but it was a pretty solid place to train. "I thought about what I could teach you last night in the relatively short amount of time we have together, what would best aid you along your journey. First, both of you already have your own ways of activating your dragonaura. Yet I can show you another."

"I just summoned mine," Twillo said.

"Same," Princess Embla told Ariosto. "And I know the warrior monk way to activate it as well."

"Good, we do this." Aristo tapped the back of his knuckles together. His dragonaura flared out, brighter than any that Twillo had seen before. "Summoning it this way is stronger in most cases. You will understand with most mudras that there is something about the force that is put behind them which helps propel their power. I will show you a mudra now. I will do it slowly, and then I will pick up the speed."

Ariosto sent his palm forward and grabbed his wrist with the other hand, he quickly pulled away. In doing so he created a blade of dragonessence out of the palm of his hand. "This one is called Etherfang Blade. It is a common technique that warrior monks use. Now, I'll show it to you faster."

He performed the same gesture, but this time Twillo barely saw his hand grab his other wrist. The blade flared even stronger.

"Do you see what I mean by the force to put behind something? Keep that in mind as we go forward. But perhaps Etherfang Blade is a bit advanced. First, try activating your dragonessence in this way."

Both Icenordians tried this technique. Embla got it after the second attempt. Twillo kept at it, the relic hunter cracking his knuckles together until there was a spark of dragonessence that coated his entire body.

"Good," Ariosto said. "Did the voice come to you?"

"No voice for me," said Twillo as he looked to the princess.

"A voice let me know that I leveled up my Dragonaura mudra."

"Ah, the two of you have different systems, it seems. Different interpretations. That's fine. You can check your full status once we finish here," Ariosto told Twillo. "Now that you know how to activate your dragonaura the old-fashioned way, let's go through some warm-ups. Then I will teach you things that may help."

Over the next thirty minutes, Ariosto led them in a series of quick jabs and right and left hooks. It was a form of calisthenics to be sure, an intensity behind it that had Twillo gasping for air by the end.

"Tough, right?" Princess Embla asked. She threw her head back and took in a deep breath through her nostrils. She then tied her hair into a bun and brought her fist to the ready again.

"She certainly has spunk," Seondzus said. "And what about you, relic hunter? You're going to let a spoiled princess show you up?"

"The limitations of the human body can be tiring, you know that," Adventus told her.

"You always come to his defense."

"We are soulbound. He generally doesn't—"

Ariosto punched his fists together, which created a wave of dragonessence. "Ready? The next mudra I'm going to teach you is called Scaled Lash. It's funny, you know. I taught this very same maneuver to someone last year. It was helpful for him, and I'm sure it will be helpful for you. That is a story for another day."

"Scaled Lash?" Twillo asked. "Describe it."

"How about I show you how it works instead?" Ariosto took a quick look around. He saw a cluster of cacti, one of which stood taller than the others. "Watch carefully."

He stuck his left hand out and threw his right fist forward. Rather than deliver a punch, Ariosto opened his fist at the last moment and ran it across his hand, creating a clapping sound. What followed was a lasso of dragonessence, which he controlled with his right hand. He used it to cut the top of the cactus off, the piece falling to the ground, cauterized.

"That's not all I can do with it," Ariosto told them as he looked around again. He saw a rock and used the power once again. This time he hooked his dragonessence lasso around the rock, and was able to toss it to the side. "You can also use it to latch on to something. Doing that, you will scorch whatever it is you touch. Look at the rock."

Twillo and Embla approached the rock that Ariosto had just tossed to the side with dragonessence. There was a clear burn mark around its circumference.

They began practicing the movement. As she had before, Embla was the first to understand the maneuver. Her lasso dragonessence wasn't very strong, and she certainly couldn't wield it in the same way as Ariosto could. But she was able to cut through the cactus. Twillo only got it right in the end, but this didn't frustrate him. Embla had spent a lot more time training than he had. He would get it, he would work on it for however long it took.

"So now you know how to activate your dragonaura through using a mudra, and you know the mudra for Scaled Lash. Finally, I believe I should teach you a move known as Dragonflight. You can already float using dragonessence. But you may reach a point where you need to move even faster than that. This is where Dragonflight will come in handy. Observe."

Ariosto extended his arms back and shaped them like a dragon's wings. He shot them to the ground and burst into the air. He landed in a flash of silver-green mana. Twillo had moved fairly quickly simply using his floating capability, but this was something else entirely. This would allow him to reach a high ledge. It would also allow him to avoid an attack, to get a vantage point and then return to a fight. This particular mudra was certainly one that he needed to master.

Twillo was the first to get it this time. He brought his arms back like they were wings and cast them down to the ground, an explosion taking shape at his feet. He nearly came down like a book falling off a high shelf, yet was able to catch himself just in time.

Twillo rolled onto his back, placed his hands on his stomach, and laughed. "That was close."

Embla, who was still attempting the move, stepped over to Twillo and offered him her hand. "It would be the irony of ironies if you had killed yourself by playing around with dragonessence, especially just before stopping Jecha. It would be a tragedy, for sure, but it would certainly be ironic."

"I'm with the princess on this one," Seondzus said. "On your feet, relic hunter, and try not to die."

"I'm not going to die," Twillo told the dragon in his head.

Once he was ready, Twillo performed the move again. This time, he was able to control his ascent and his descent. There weren't any high ledges around them, but it was certainly something Twillo would practice when they encountered something like that. He could see in his mind's eye how helpful this technique would be.

There had been numerous scenarios in the past where being able to burst in the air would have made his life a lot easier.

"You can do it, Your Grace," he told Embla after watching her try a few more times. "Just pretend you're a dragon."

"Pretend I'm a dragon? How does one pretend they are a dragon?"

Twillo flapped his arms as if they were wings.

"Funny," Princess Embla said.

"I should eat you for that," Seondzus said, which brought a laugh from Adventus.

It took her a few more attempts, but eventually, Embla was able to perform the Dragonflight mudra.

"Good. That should at least give the two of you a taste of what is possible."

"There's one more thing I wanted to ask you about, now that I have an expert," Twillo told Ariosto.

"Oh?"

"I'm interested in learning about whatever it is that warrior monks use to, I don't know, negate power? That's not the right word. What I'm referring to is the tournaments I've seen where they are throwing punches at one another and it seems like they're absorbing them only to release the energy later on. I understand that this has something to do with a dragonaura. And I learned a little bit of this from the woman who taught me how to fight. At least the theory of it. But I want to know the mudra."

"There are two mudras that help monks and nuns perform these maneuvers, Voidshift and Voidrift. For you, Voidshift might be the most useful. You aren't really going to be doing too much hand-to-hand combat, not that sort that you've seen in the past from warrior monks. But you could use this mudra to absorb a strike and then release it. I'll show you how. Put your sword away."

Twillo did as instructed and stepped over to Princess Embla. The pair watched as Ariosto quickly brought his fists back and then pushed them forward, pressing them together. Doing so created a glowing circle of energy that quickly dissipated. Yet closing his eyes, he could see that it was still there through his access to dragonessence.

"Strike me," Ariosto said.

Twillo came forward with an attack. Ariosto moved like he was going to block it, yet Twillo never touched his forearm. Instead, he hit something spongy. It still felt like he had punched Ariosto, yet there had been no response.

"Again."

Twillo delivered another strike, Ariosto absorbing this one as well. As Twillo brought his fist back, the warrior monk released a burst of dragonessence, pure stored power. This forced Twillo backward, the relic hunter ultimately losing his footing.

"Like this?" Embla asked as she brought her fists back and sent them forward.

"Exactly. And the way that you would cycle dragonessence, pressing forward, but maintain your control over it. You should feel as if you are forming a circular shield."

Twillo tried a few times but was unable to get it. Embla seemed to get it, however, and once she was ready, she blocked two of Ariosto's strikes.

"Good. Now, release it. Release the power."

Embla did as she was told, the princess releasing a flare of energy that quickly dissipated. It reminded Twillo of his Ward Glyph card, the way the dragonessence almost exploded forward.

He kept at it, trying to learn the skill himself, but ultimately was unable to do so.

"You'll get it," Ariosto assured him. "It isn't often that someone learns several mudras in a day. The fact you can use them at all is a testament to your skill. You two are very powerful." He tilted his chin up as he looked them over. "Made for each other in a certain way."

"Thank you for your lesson," Embla told Ariosto, her eyes bulging at his last comment.

"Before we leave, check your status. What you find may surprise you."

Twillo did as instructed. Sure enough, mudras were now listed at the end.

Name: Jhaeros Shotaro Vos

Tier: Apprentice

Rank: S

Class: Martial Arts Mastery

Rank: C

Secondary Class: None

Tertiary Class: None

Dragonessence: 221/325

[Arcane Cards]

Arms of Vikan Wood, Level 2

Codex Vault, Level 1 [Passive]

Core Eruption, Level 2

Enchanting Deception, Level 2

Eternal Cycle, Level 2

Firebreath, Level 2

Flash of Fata Morgana, Level 2

Nadakunai's Might, Level 2

Ripple Tide, Level 2

Vard's Blessing, Level 2

Warding Glyph, Level 2

[Mudras]

Dragonaura, Level 1

Dragonflight, Level 1

Scaled Lash, Level 1

Twillo had learned three mudras, and now, he needed to level them up. Once he had time to train, he would work more on this Voidshift power and hopefully learn it. It seemed like it would be useful.

Chapter Twelve

Relic Hunter Extraordinaire

THEY HAD TO BE CAREFUL with the dragons. While it would have been easy to simply hop on their backs and fly, Ariosto still preferred that they travel toward the high desert in a more clandestine manner, one that matched the song he'd sung them.

The sensation of floating over the sand using dragonessence, especially when traces of wind picked up the grains and swept them aside, made Twillo feel much more powerful than he was. Occasionally, they would stop and take rests, Ariosto meditating while Twillo and Princess Embla enjoyed the stunning, if bleak, views of No Man's Crossing. At one point they came to some old ruins, the kind of lithic scatter that excited Twillo. There were relics out there, he could almost smell them. Finding these long-lost items, however, would be something else entirely.

As he had sensed earlier that morning, it was going to be a hot day, yet Twillo's new robes kept him cool. They were just light enough for the breeze to continue to strike his skin as they floated. Once they landed, the robes protected him from the intense rays of the sun. It was an eye-opener to some degree. Twillo knew how hot it could get in Southfall, but to see it like this during spring was something else entirely.

It made him wary of whatever summer would bring.

The desert that unfurled before Twillo was an endless tapestry of sun-bleached sands surrounded by staggering mountains. Some of the cactus they came across stood like sentinels, solitary, their forms casting long shadows. Occasionally, a capricious desert wind would pick up, swallowing the sand and spitting it back in mesmerizing patterns as it revealed hidden rocky outcrops, ones with reddish hues that broke the monotonous beige. It was around some of these outcrops that Ariosto picked a certain kind of root, one that tasted sweet after it had been washed.

This was another thing that Twillo had noticed about the warrior monk. Not only did he have a native's understanding of the desert, he seemed to have some control over the elements, able to pull water from the hardtop, and conjure bits of it in the air that allowed him to fill a large canteen that they were sharing and wash anything they came across like the roots.

"And you can do that because you are a water harvester?" Twillo asked him as he filled their canteen yet again.

"It's an advanced technique. Even those that are aquaseers have trouble doing this."

"Aquaseers?" Princess Embla asked. "That's right, they're one of the three harvester classes. Stoneshapers, aquaseers, and galecallers."

"Correct. Generally, water harvester sects have two galecallers, two stoneshapers, at least one aquaseer and the leader. Some have more. But that is how these sects are commonly maintained."

"Why only one?" Twillo asked.

"Because there isn't much water here. Of the three, the aquaseer is likely the strongest, but only if there is a large water source nearby. It is the other two classes that are generally more helpful in finding these hidden reserves, water veins as they are known. With galecallers, you can scout ahead and you can also deal with certain desert yokai. A stoneshaper allows you to do numerous things with the soil, and they are monstrously helpful in places like desert dungeons."

"Desert dungeons?" Twillo asked as they began floating again.

"The giants that once called Southfall home had great keeps that were built, and later covered by the sand. Humans built things on top of these keeps. Oftentimes, they are simply called desert dungeons because of the things that lurk inside them. Where we are heading, toward this ziggurat, could certainly be considered a desert dungeon."

"Dungeons, huh? That is sort of my specialty," Twillo said, a statement that caused Embla to laugh.

"You are an overly confident relic hunter," Seondzus told him. "And Her Royal Highness seems to agree."

"That is because he is a good one," Adventus said. "She knows."

"See? This is what I mean when I say you always take his side."

"We are—"

"Soulbound, I know," Seondzus told her counterpart.

Twillo ignored them as he tuned back in to what Ariosto was saying: "Water often gets trapped in these places, so galecallers and stoneshapers are instrumental in helping the aquaseer find the water. They have continued these traditions for quite some time now, and they will continue long after we are gone, that is, if the world is not destroyed."

This ominous statement had a way of quieting the group for a spell as they continued in a southerly direction. The sands shifted and Ariosto stopped. He removed his conical hat to reveal a feline face complete with whiskers and ears, yet he still maintained the body of a man. "My senses are sharper this way," he explained as his whiskers twitched. "Let's continue in this direction."

Twillo and Princess Embla exchanged glances, but neither said anything.

Ariosto floated forward. Later, they reached a rugged enclave of stone, which soon became an orchestra of rock formations and weathered boulders with sunbaked surfaces. Larger rocks towered above the smaller ones, the jagged contours forming an intimidating skyline that reminded Twillo of the capital of E'Kanth from a distance.

As they landed, he merely heard voices. Then they came around a particularly large rock, one with a heavily eroded surface, to find Vradon, Anneli, and Katashi seated in the shade.

"By Livia," Anneli said as she hopped to her feet. Her hand was on the hilt of her blade, but she quickly lowered it upon seeing who it was.

"By Livia, indeed," Twillo said as he came forward with a big grin on his face. "And I've got a story about her for later."

Vradon rushed over to them, the portly monk looking a little thinner than he had the last time Twillo had seen him. It was clear in his eyes and his weatherbeaten face that they had been through quite a bit during that time. He embraced Twillo and then turned to the princess, offering her a short bow.

Katashi approached, the kitsune in his half-fox, half-human form at the moment. "I see you've met a bakeneko," he said as he greeted Twillo.

"That's the reason we are here. Livia sent him to help us."

"Ah, even better. It's nice to meet you," the kitsune told Ariosto. The warrior monk's features were back to normal, his face obscured by his conical hat. The kitsune motioned toward the others. "This is Vradon, Anneli, and I'm Katashi."

"So we aren't going to Nalig now, it seems," Vradon said. There was a hint of disappointment in his voice, one that Twillo instantly picked up on.

"We brought the party to you instead." He grinned at his old friend. "Besides, the ziggurat we need is somewhere in the high desert, south of here. And Nalig is boring. Or, at least it's not a great place for us to visit at the moment, trust me. Again, I have a story for you. But first, the ziggurat."

"I know exactly where it is," Vradon said. "We were coming to tell you that we had already located it, but have yet to figure out how to get inside."

"What do you mean?" Ariosto asked as he took a seat. He looked up at Vradon as the monk spoke again:

"It has to be the ziggurat. Everything I have translated up until now points to this location, yet there is nothing there aside from a flat stone platform with three runes on it that I've never seen before. So that's what we were coming to tell you. We found it, but we don't know how to access it. We figured we would reach Nalig, regroup with you all, and then we'll fly together to the location."

"And I take it that Ramide and Nalig are well?" Twillo asked, referring to the dragons Anneli and Katashi had access to through their wristlets.

"They are more than well. They are great," Anneli said.

"Well, bring them out then," Seondzus told Twillo. "And bring us out too. There's no one around to be bothered by our dragonly presences."

"Is it okay if they come out?" Twillo asked Ariosto.

"Don't ask him. You don't need the cat-man's permission," Seondzus told him.

"I believe that will be fine. We shouldn't do any flying until later tonight, though."

Soon, Twillo and his group were surrounded by four dragons, one white, one red, one green and a black one that was larger than all the others, the big horn on Ramide's nose not unlike the jagged rock formations stacked around them.

"I wish we could stretch our wings," Nalig said as she looked up at the sky.

"I'm right there with you," Seondzus told her.

Ramide took a step closer to them and then dropped onto his belly, which caused the ground to shake and dust to fall from some of the surrounding rocks.

"Easy," Anneli told the dragon as she approached. She placed her hand on his horn and Ramide sighed deeply, the low sound emitted by his throat also causing dust to fall.

"He might be the sleepiest dragon that has ever existed." Seondzus threw her head back and let out a puff of fire.

"It's already hard enough," Adventus told her. "Why must you always push things?"

Ariosto watched them for a moment, the warrior monk clearly intrigued by the dragons. He'd only seen Adventus and Seondzus in their warrior forms. From the way he was looking at them, it was clear that this was his first time seeing actual dragons. He maintained his cool—the warrior monk always seemed to be in control of his emotions—but it was clear that he was impressed.

"Anyway, that's our update. There is another ziggurat in the Harvest Mountains, but we haven't made it that far south," Vradon said.

"But you have details about that one?" Twillo asked him.

"I do. Better details than the one here. This is the one that we were looking for and got a little bit lost. It is not easy to maintain directions in the high desert."

"Did you run into any water harvesters?" Embla asked as she too sat in the shade, the Crown Ravenna of Icenor unperturbed by the dragons' low chatter.

Vradon nodded. "There were some not so far from you. I wouldn't be surprised if they stop by later. They insisted on checking on us."

"We may be in for quite a day tomorrow, so it is best if we rest now and then deal with the harvesters as they come," Ariosto said. "We can leave in the early morning while it is still dark out. I don't mind if the harvesters see the dragons. Their memories will be wiped—"

"What now?" Twillo asked him.

"Water harvesters have their memories stripped away when they take this unique role. This is so they have less attachment to their family and friends back home."

"Ah, Her Grace mentioned this to me."

Ariosto continued: "Once they complete their seven-year service, and what is known as the Rite of Fulfillment, harvesters have these memories restored and some of their newer memories are stripped from them, unless they decide to move on and become regional harvesters or warrior monks and nuns. What I'm trying to say is something like seeing a dragon would be a memory that wouldn't exist for them forever."

"Maybe it's best if we normalize dragons," Twillo said. "The rebirth is upon us anyway."

"True. But if any harvesters do come, it will give anyone who wants a chance to do some sparring with powerful cultivators, ones who have only been focusing on a particular elemental skill. Would you be interested in something like that?"

"As long as I don't get swept away in the wind…"

Katashi laughed. "That is most certainly something that will happen. In the meantime, we can make this a proper rest. And we're going to need some food."

"I got it," Seondzus said as she pressed her red wings back. "What? You said it doesn't matter if they see us anyway. Let me do some hunting, please. I live for this sort of thing. My nickname used to be the Huntress."

Nalig the green dragon laughed. "No, it didn't."

"Shhh, they don't know that!"

The red dragon took off. Once she was gone, Twillo turned to the others.

"You aren't going to believe what has happened since we last saw each other. It all started in E'Kanth…" Twillo launched into the story, and watched as their eyes widened once he got to the meeting Livia part.

It was quite the tale.

Seondzus returned later with a goat, one with long wooly hair and horns that stuck straight up from the top of its forehead. She dropped it onto the ground and joined the other dragons. "Water harvesters are en route." She stretched her wings and fell onto the ground in the shade next to Ramide.

"I'm going to assume that you brought them," Adventus said.

She snapped her teeth at the white dragon. "I was discreet. Well, as discreet as a graceful dragon like myself can be in an endless desert. They were curious."

"I'm sure they spotted you from miles away," said Nalig. "Look, look at that giant red bird."

Seondzus made a cooing sound with her throat, which pleased the green dragon. "I should have done that. And then turned a bit of the sand near them into glass just to let them know I mean business."

"Anyway," Katashi said, who had just been detailing more of their journey. "All of Vradon's scrolls are in the pocket shelter if you'd like to see them."

"They are the old Sagic script, yes?" Ariosto asked him, the warrior monk still seated, his tail curled in the air.

"They are." Vradon stood with his hands behind his back, obedient as ever. Behind him, Anneli had already started to deal with the meat. Princess Embla had joined her, taking instruction from the elven orc.

This brought a smile to Twillo's face. It was a side of Embla that he had yet to see, but it made sense. She had always been curious. Embla had never been dainty, and she'd never minded getting her hands dirty. The fact that she was with him in the high desert now was true evidence of this.

"Unfortunately, I never learned to read the old script," Ariosto told Vradon and Katashi. "Now, that is something I regret."

"You can always start," Katashi said. "I started late and I'm certainly not as fluent as Vradon over here, but I can read some of it. The more common words."

"I could, and so could anyone. But I don't want to spend the next several years of my life trying to decipher the scrawlings of the past." Ariosto grinned at the kitsune. "Someone has to be tending to their garden."

Twillo got to his feet. "Let me know if you need anything," he told the two women as he approached.

"What we need is water. Look at this dirty thing," Embla said as she motioned to the beast. "Covered in dust and dragon spit."

"I can help with that," Ariosto called over to her. The warrior monk stepped away from the group. He returned a minute or so later, a hazy trail of dew following him. "One of you will need to hold it, or I suppose I can do that for you as well." He lifted his hand and the goat floated into the air.

Ariosto was able to clean the goat with a quick gesture, yet the muddy water never hit the ground. It remained in the air, where it formed into a bubble of watery filth that he eventually floated over to some shrubs that had taken refuge in the shade.

"I'll leave you all to it," the warrior monk said. "Unless you'd like me to keep the goat suspended."

"Now that it's clean..." Anneli looked over to Katashi. "I need to head down to the shelter for a moment."

"Certainly." Katashi produced the pocket shelter. He set it in the shade, the wooden frame growing until it was large enough for someone to climb through. Anneli took the stairs to the bottom and returned with a rug that looked like it was used for this kind of thing.

Princess Embla, who had yet to see the pocket shelter, was suddenly curious.

"Do you want to check it out?" Twillo asked her.

"Is it wrong if I do?"

"Not at all, Your Royalness, it's fascinating." He led her over to the opening. "Just one word of advice. Don't go over the edge down there. Stay on the platform."

Twillo turned back to Anneli, who had since placed the rug under the floating goat. Ariosto lowered it onto the fabric. "I suppose I should go ahead and meet the harvesters, to let them know what they are about to encounter. I will be bringing them shortly."

"I don't know if this is enough food for all of us," Anneli said.

"They will have something," Ariosto assured her. "They generally do."

The warrior monk turned in a direction that Seondzus had come from earlier and was soon gone.

While Princess Embla explored the pocket shelter, Twillo helped Anneli with the goat. She made the initial cut at the hind leg, carefully slicing it up the groin area, the elven orc instructing him where to hold and what to do even though he knew how to clean a goat.

They loosened the skin and peeled the hide away, which Twillo placed on a rock so it could dry. While they did this, Katashi and Vradon made a fire, the two moving larger rocks around it so they could keep the goat in place.

By the time Ariosto returned, the warrior monk now with a small group of women in maroon robes around him, the goat was slowly being roasted.

"These are the Tidecallers," Ariosto said as he gestured to the group of women, all of whom had deeply tanned skin and white diagonal lines running down their cheeks.

Aside from their leader, a woman who looked to be about fifty, the harvesters were all youthful. Several of them carried hardened looks on their faces, evidence of lives in the high desert that Twillo could hardly imagine.

The others seemed fresher, like they were new to the group.

The way they had approached prevented them from seeing the dragons that were resting off to their left. Once one of the harvesters caught sight of the dragons, their expressions instantly changed. Their mouths dropped open, the women all speaking quietly to one another as they seemed to back away as a group.

"Don't worry about us," Seondzus said as she looked over at them. She let out a tiny puff of fire as a peace offering. "If we wanted to do something to you, it would be done by now."

"Your Ladyships," Adventus said. "Welcome to our camp. Please, make yourselves at home."

"Hiya," Nalig said as she offered the harvesters a very toothy grin.

Ramide merely grunted, the big dragon barely opening his eyes to look at them.

Twillo approached the sect. "I won't bother telling you all of our names because—"

"Is he the Icenordian that is looking to spar?" one of the women asked. Her dark hair was braided into two large coils behind her ears.

"I was anticipating we would do something like that, yes," Twillo told her. "Only if it is something you would like to do."

"Good. Are we doing that now or later?"

Twillo gave the aggressive harvester a funny look. "Aren't you interested in relaxing for a while?"

Her eyes widened dramatically. "With Icenordians and dragons?"

Some of the girls laughed. Their leader said something sharp to the harvester under her breath.

"Sure," Twillo said. "We should let the goat cook for a while anyway. Plenty of time. Where would you like to do this?"

The water harvester with braids now stood across from Twillo, her hood pressed back, maroon robes beating in a slight breeze. It was with her next statement that he understood where the breeze came from. "I am

Sereyn, B-Rank, Guardian Galecaller of the Tidecallers Sect," she said, revealing her class. "State yourself."

"State myself?" he whispered. "Um, Twillo, er, Jhaeros Shotaro Vos, Twillo."

"Twillo," she said, pronouncing it in a way that told him she'd never heard this kind of name before.

It was a strange place to do battle, a stretch of hardtop just beyond the dragons, enormous boulders surrounding them and the sun setting on the horizon, the sky a mystical pink. But it was also the perfect place for something like this.

"Only in the desert," Twillo said as he used Codex Vault to rearrange his Arcane Cards. He kept Enchanting Deception, Flash of Fata Morgana, and Ripple Tide on deck.

They had already agreed that he wouldn't use a sword, just in case things got out of hand. It was clear with the ferocious way that the galecaller stared him down that this was a real possibility. She seemed ready to push things to the limit.

"Well?" Sereyn asked.

"Well?" Twillo replied.

"What is your rank? What are you?"

"Twillo, S-Rank Apprentice, Relic Hunter Extraordinaire."

The other water harvesters laughed. They had all gathered on the left with their leader, who had yet to say much. On his right were his companions, Anneli with her arms crossed over her chest, Princess Embla standing gallantly beside her, Katashi with a slightly annoyed look on his face, Ariosto with his features obscured by his conical hat, and Vradon with his brow furrowed in worry.

"Remember, we're not trying to kill each other," Ariosto said as he stepped between Twillo and Sereyn. The wind tracing through the ends of her robes died down. "But this is a good test for both of you. A bit of fun."

"We should be eating," Anneli called over to him. "Or heading to the ziggurat."

"We should, yes," Ariosto told her. "But it is tradition for the Tidecallers to challenge those they come across if feasible. We will honor those traditions. Now, are you ready?" Ariosto asked Twillo, a bit of force behind his voice now.

"I am."

"And you?"

"I am," Sereyn said.

"Let's begin." Ariosto conjured his sphere of dragonessence. He lifted it into the air with one hand and brought it down onto the ground. He jumped back, the fight kicking off.

The wind that struck Twillo was a force unlike anything he'd ever experienced before.

It whipped him backward, Twillo barely able to push himself forward using his dragonessence. He landed and activated his dragonaura through the mudra Ariosto had taught him, Twillo strengthening the shield of mana that he hoped would protect him.

He could feel the change around him, the way the air crackled with power. His dragonaura certainly helped once another gust of wind twisted in his direction and struck him head-on.

This time, he wasn't whipped away from the hardtop. As soon as there was a break in the galecaller's attack, Twillo used Ripple Tide, which produced a surge of power that rushed forward like a wave. It struck her before she got out of the way.

Sereyn hadn't anticipated he was about to do it, and had been midflight when it hit. This tossed Sereyn off to the side, where she landed on her knees. She flashed back to her feet, fury tracing across her eyes.

Twillo reached her, and was just about to deliver an amplified strike when she conjured a shield of wind. Punching it wasn't what he expected. Her wind shield wasn't springy like he would have expected it to be. It was as hard as stone, Twillo immediately feeling the results of the strike deep in his bones.

His dragonaura protected him, yet it still transferred pain forward, Twillo instinctively backing up.

He held his arm for a second, only to be blindsided by a strip of wind that launched him into the air yet again. He fell in a controlled way, and landed just before the galecaller.

She reared back like she was going to strike him. Twillo hit her instead with the Flash of Fata Morgana, the galecaller instantly backpedaling. Not only did Twillo's attack affect her, it affected anyone in the vicinity, which included a few of her fellow water harvesters.

The ground began to shift. Twillo assumed it was because of his card, which produced vivid hallucinations. It was only when he stumbled into a hole and noticed the surface move again then he realized this was the result of one of the Tidecaller's stoneshapers who had accidently been hit by his power.

Ground shifting, rock churning beneath them, the wind raging overhead, Twillo used Dragonflight to push him away from the main theater of the battle. He needed space, just a moment to gather his wits.

Upon landing, he realized that he had not been struck by the Flash of Fata Morgana, that he had actually used it in a controlled way. Yet the shifting ground made him assume this had been the case. Twillo had even kept his head low as if it were a real Fata Morgana situation, like the ones he experienced up north in Icenor.

Twillo quickly sucked in deep breaths. The rules of their fight weren't very difficult. First one down lost. But they hadn't quite defined what was considered down.

Rather than merely move back on the attack, Twillo dropped to the ground and sent a clone forward using Enchanting Deception. The timing was just right, and Sereyn moved to attack the clone as it neared her. Using this to his advantage, Twillo exploded back onto the scene with an amplified punch, this one actually landing.

He struck her windshield with his fist and forced her backward, Sereyn cutting a trail in the dust.

Seondzus produced a puff of flame, which made all of the water harvesters bristle.

"She won't attack," Adventus said as he glared at his counterpart.

"Who promised that?" she asked him playfully.

"Tsuh!" Sereyn landed a wind-powered kick just as Twillo was getting the upper hand. He wasn't blown backward, but he certainly felt it in his chin, and he was afraid for a moment that his jaw had been dislocated.

Twillo jumped away from her and spat blood. He looked back up at the galecaller, and changed his card arrangement once again using Codex Vault.

Even as the wind spiraled around him, Twillo took the time needed to make sure he had certain things on deck. For one there was his Firebreath power; he also went for Nadakunai's Might to amplify his attack power; finally, he went for Core Eruption.

Twillo bolted to the other side of the hardtop, and was quickly met by Sereyn, who appeared before him and attempted to deliver another wind-fueled kick. It hurt, but he was able to follow it up with a strike that actually shattered her shield. Or at least that was what it felt like as the wind exploded in tendrils all around him.

Twillo reached some of the stones on the outskirts of their fight, grabbed the largest one and began to charge it using Core Eruption.

Sereyn came forward in a fury of wind, a mini tornado amplifying her movement. Twillo hurled the charged stone down into the gust at the very last moment, exploding the rock. He fell back and brought his fists to the ready as he waited to see if his attack had landed.

Sereyn now lay in a small crater caused by the combination of her power and Twillo's attack. She slowly pressed herself up and glared at Twillo as he approached.

He offered her his hand.

The galecaller hesitated, but she ultimately took it.

"You are an incredible fighter," Twillo told her.

"Your mouth is covered in blood."

He grinned at her, his teeth red. "But all my teeth are still there, right?"

This seemed to soften Sereyn's mood to some degree. "They are still there, Icer."

Ariosto approached. "Tidecallers, the demonstration is over. Relax your guard. There will be no more for today. Let us have a feast, and then we will be on our way, and you can be on yours. It isn't often we run into each other in a place like this."

"It isn't often that you run into anyone in the high desert," Sereyn said, which came coupled with affirmative grunts from her sectmates.

"No, it is not. But Livia is guiding us these days," Ariosto said, "and for that we thank her."

The warrior monk couldn't see the Goddess of Luck at the moment, or how she sat on the edge of one of the larger boulders nearby, her robes dripping all the way to the ground. But she smiled at him like he could anyway.

His role with the relic hunter could come to an end soon. This was nothing to be concerned about. It was the way of things, but it did make her wish that there was more that could be done to keep him with the others.

Ariosto was a solid addition to their group, a voice of calculated reason, and a powerful arcane cultivator.

But she could be wrong. What happened next was murky, and there were numerous outcomes. Even as the sand settled, the horizon remained obscured. Jecha was on the move, and the relic hunter and his companions needed to hurry.

Chapter Thirteen

Sand Wraiths

AFTER THEIR FEAST with the Tidecallers Sect, one which turned out to be quite the affair as the sect produced various jerkies and dried desert fauna, the group of water harvesters demonstrated some of their unique class capabilities. It was fascinating to watch how fluidly they were able to use dragonessence as an elemental magic, shaping the sands and controlling the winds, carving stone as if it were pudding, their lone aquaseer demonstrating her unique power by shaping water into various forms, from dragons to weapons.

Each time, Twillo and his companions clapped and cheered the women on. Twillo knew it was an experience that most in the Four Kingdoms would never get to enjoy. A pity, too. These kinds of cultural exchanges would do a lot to bring the people together.

They bid farewell to the group later that night. Once they were gone, Twillo and the others packed up what little they had in preparation to find the ziggurat.

"We should reach there in a few hours," Vradon said. "But it might be best if you examine the runic markings in the morning. I'm assuming that we will want to get some rest."

"Yes, that's important," Ariosto told him. "And that will be fine. As long as we get there tonight. In the morning, you all can go ahead, and I will keep watch."

"One of us should keep watch with you," Katashi told Ariosto. He motioned between Twillo, Anneli, and himself. "Someone with access to a dragon."

"I would volunteer my services, but..." Vradon swallowed. "I'm afraid that they wouldn't be much help. I'm always here for moral support, however."

"What about the next dragon? You're getting it, right?" Twillo asked Princess Embla. "Once we reach the ziggurat and complete whatever challenge it holds, we will unlock the power of a dragon. At least I'm going to assume this is what will happen. I have been to one before where there wasn't a dragon given as a reward. But if there is a dragon, it's yours."

"Who doesn't already have a dragon?" Embla asked, even though she likely knew the answer to this question.

"I don't, and I do not think that's a good idea for me," Vradon said. He covered his wrists with his sleeves. "I am not the dragon tamer type."

"Dragon tamer type?" Seondzus asked.

"No offense!"

"I don't believe that is my role in all of this," Ariosto said.

"Face it, Your Ladyship," Anneli told her as she stepped beside Princess Embla. "You're getting a dragon. Just imagine what it will be like once you are the Ravenna. I don't know how many hundreds of years it has been since Icenor was ruled by someone who could summon a dragon, but I'm suspecting there will be quite the celebration."

The look of apprehension never left the princess' face as she offered Anneli a firm nod. "I see."

Anneli turned to her dragon. "Ramide."

The large black dragon got to his feet, the ground trembling around them. Ramide lowered his head so Anneli could climb up to her mount.

"I believe I will go with her," Vradon said.

"In that case, I will ride with you," Princess Embla told Twillo. "Ariosto can use one of the other dragons."

"We aren't mounts, you know," Seondzus said, which brought a huff of agreement from Nalig. "You treat us like a group of wayward sunstriders. But who am I kidding? We sort of are." The red dragon turned into Ariosto. "Are you ready, warrior monk?"

"Ready as I'll ever be. And speaking of sunstriders, have you ever actually seen one?"

"The winged camels of Southfall?" Seondzus did a dragon's version of a shrug. "I've hunted one before."

Soon, the four dragons were soaring through the sky above the high desert, Nalig in the lead, followed by Seondzus, Adventus, and Ramide.

It felt like it had been a while since Twillo had ridden Adventus. The white dragon was much calmer than

Seondzus. The way he flew was more balanced and steady, with fewer jerky movements or sudden stops.

Princess Embla held on tightly to Twillo, even though she didn't necessarily need to do this. This made Twillo think of her suggestion of marriage. He knew this was the last thing that he should be thinking about, but her familiarity, and her current closeness pushed this to the forefront of his mind. What would it actually be like? If he was able to pull all of this off, what would it be like to settle down, to gain a type of status that he had only gotten a taste of in his youth?

Perhaps he could talk to Vradon about it alone. Whenever Twillo had a private matter, and he happened to be in the capital city of Middling, he often conferred with Vradon or the late Olaf.

He valued their advice.

The desert winds grew colder as they cut through the night sky, Twillo noticing the sand shifting below. He saw great beasts he didn't know the names of prowling about the dunes, shadows that seemed ominous, rocks shaped like giant monsters. Southfall was a foreboding place, and if someone had asked him a year ago if he thought that he would ever be anywhere near No Man's Crossing, he would have laughed in their face.

Yet here he was.

Ramide shifted toward the ground and landed first. The other dragons circled around him and found good spaces. There were no rock formations here, the stretch of land defined by its towering sand dunes. As Twillo looked around, everything illuminated by the moon, he tried to make sense of where they were, and where this ziggurat was located.

He floated down to the sand and carefully trailed to the bottom of one of the dunes, where he joined Vradon and the others around a rectangle of stone. It was about ten feet long, and buried deep into the ground, a platform of sorts.

Ariosto took a quick look around, the sand dunes surrounding them large enough that they resembled hills. "We should be fine here for the night. And this is certainly it. I can sense the power."

Twillo closed his eyes. Sure enough, the platform glowed with dragonessence.

"We can use the pocket shelter," Katashi said.

"No, that won't work here," Ariosto told him. "One of these dunes could collapse and fill it with sand."

"You really think that would happen?"

"Why do you think there aren't many pocket shelters left in our world?" the warrior monk asked the kitsune. "They do have a tendency to get abandoned often due to the fault of their owners. Now, it's best if we sleep out here tonight and take turns standing guard. I don't mind going first."

"I can go first," Anneli said.

"No, let me. I have a mudra for this sort of work," Ariosto told her. "And if you are one of the ones who is going to explore this ziggurat tomorrow, you will want to rest. In fact, anyone exploring should rest."

"It's probably best if I stay here," Vradon said as he turned to Twillo. "I was thinking about it in the sky. I will only get in the way down there."

"No, you should come," Twillo told him. "You can read the old Sagic script."

"The dragons can too—"

"But they can't read it in the dark. Katashi or Anneli can stay here with Ariosto."

"I'll stay," Katashi said. "You all might want Ramide."

"They may want me," Nalig told him from the perch she'd managed to make on top of one of the dunes. Not only were the dunes casting shadows onto them, the dragons were doing so as well, blocking much of the stars and the moonlight.

Ramide yawned.

"Always the sleepy one," Seondzus said. "Sleep over there, Big Boy. We don't want you to roll over and crush everyone."

"As you wish," he said, his voice low and guttural. Ramide moved on, and as he did bits of sand scattered down to the platform.

"We can certainly stand guard," Adventus told Ariosto. "You don't have to. None of you have to."

"I will do so alongside you all. In fact, I think I will join you." Ariosto floated up to one of the dunes so he could be closer to the white dragon. "I would like to speak of the past."

"Much of our memories are gone," Adventus said.

"That may be true, but there has to be something." Ariosto looked down at the others. "Rest. Tomorrow, we open the ziggurat, discover its secrets, and move on to the Harvest Mountains."

Twillo awakened to find Ariosto crouched over him. "Have you ever seen sand wraiths?" he asked in a whisper.

"I have not," Twillo told him. "But I've heard of them."

"There's a group moving not far from here. Destroying them will provide all of you a chance to recharge your dragonessence before you venture into the ziggurat."

Twillo sat up to find Anneli and Princess Embla huddled around the campfire, the pair using coals to boil water. Vradon was still sleeping, the monk with his back turned to the others. This left Katashi, who was seated in meditation at the top of one of the dunes. Twillo wondered briefly if he had been inspired by Ariosto.

"We're going to recharge, and we need to figure out how to crack open this ziggurat." Twillo approached the campfire, one that Ariosto had crafted from a particular type of dried cactus and some of the debris he'd found in the area.

"Aware," Anneli told him. "We've been up for an hour."

"I can't believe I slept so hard." Twillo took a cup of the hot water from Princess Embla. There were some roots and a cactus flower in it, which gave the water an earthy taste that had a hint of mint. It was refreshing.

He looked over to the dragons.

"How challenging would you like this to be?" Ariosto asked as Twillo continued to sip the hot water.

"I think the challenge is here," he said as he motioned to the platform.

"Yes, I've been examining it. Come."

"You really didn't sleep?" Twillo asked the warrior monk as they approached the platform with ancient runes scrawled across its surface.

"No, but I'll be fine. I've seen these sorts of runes before. It isn't a very hard puzzle to solve. It was designed for water harvesters, which is why Vradon couldn't figure it out. One rune must be activated by the wind, another by water, and the final by stone. Easy enough."

"That's it? That's hardly a puzzle."

"Correct."

"Will we have to get the water harvesters again?"

"No, we will be able to do it ourselves," Ariosto said. "In fact, if you want to do it before we head out to deal with the sand wraiths, just to prove it is possible, we could certainly do so. You look like you're still waking up."

Twillo cleared his throat. "I slept better than I thought I would in the desert. I have no problem admitting that. But I'm awake."

"It's not the first time I've heard about a good desert slumber. There's something about the high desert that lulls someone to sleep. Since most people don't travel through it, they don't know about it. It is peaceful in its own way," Ariosto said, a hint of fondness in his eyes. He looked down at the three runes and rubbed his hands together. "Let's begin."

The warrior approached the rune on the left and swirled a bit of wind over it. The rune glowed with dragonessence. The spark that started in the center of the rune pressed outward and formed a complete circle around the runic script. It twisted to the left, Twillo hearing a locking mechanism on the other side.

"The first one was a success. Let's move on to the next. Grab a few of those rocks," Ariosto said as he motioned to some pebbles near the base of the platform. Twillo picked them up and returned. "Toss them at that rune there."

Twillo tossed the rocks onto the rune on the far right. Doing so produced the same glow in the center that eventually spread outward, the entire circular stone twisting counterclockwise.

"And the final one." Ariosto unscrewed a canteen he kept on his belt. Water curled out of it, forming a hook in the air. He flicked a bit of this at the rune in the center of the platform. "I would step back if I were you."

Twillo stepped off the platform just as it started to shake.

It rose several feet into the air and pressed backward, the disturbance waking Vradon. The monk turned, and was sitting up just as the platform settled.

"By Livia," Vradon said as he rubbed the sleep out of his eyes. "You did it!"

There was now a set of stone stairs leading down under the ground. A cold draft, one that smelled of wet earth, reached Twillo's nostrils. Katashi slipped down the sand dune and joined them.

"It looks deep," he said, his fox ears folding back.

"Are you sure you want us to deal with the sand wraiths first?" Twillo asked Ariosto.

"It is probably for the best. We definitely don't want them bothering us, or perhaps joining the four of you below. There are still four of you going, correct?"

Twillo exchanged glances with Anneli and Princess Embla. "That's right."

"Yes, it's for the best. Let's deal with the sand wraiths." Ariosto floated into the air, Twillo, Anneli, and Princess Embla soon joining him.

They came up over a ledge, and lowered onto it. The dunes moved beyond, yet there was something unnatural about the way they shifted. It almost looked like the wind had twisted into a point where several of the dunes rose and formed into cloaked beings, ones with long arms and sharp claws made of sand and stone.

It was faint, yet Twillo saw that they glowed with dragonessence.

"How are we supposed to fight those things?" Anneli asked as the sand wraiths swirled below their feet.

"Therein lies the problem. With some effort, you can destroy them with dragonessence. But unless you can wield water or stone, it is hard to actually kill them. Galecallers can swirl them around as much as they'd like, but they can't really make them disappear."

"I can't really use dragonessence in that way," Anneli said.

"That's fine. The two of you can," Ariosto told Twillo and the Princess. "Try your best, and if they become too overwhelming, I will see what I can do."

"We really should have brought the dragons," Princess Embla said.

Ariosto grinned at her. "That would have been too easy."

Twillo went through his cards. He put Firebreath, Ripple Tide, and Core Eruption on deck. He summoned his dragonaura using the mudra he had recently learned, drew his sword, exchanged glances with Embla, and floated down to the sand wraiths. They noticed his presence immediately.

The nearest sand wraith swelled forward like a wave intent on crushing Twillo. Even though he didn't know how this would play out, Twillo hit it with Firebreath. The sand wraith was quickly consumed in burning dragonessence. It whipped about, Twillo forced to jump backward to avoid its imminent collapse. Another wraith rushed toward him and he struck it with a bolt of power from his sword.

Princess Embla joined him and fired spheres of energy at another one of the sand wraiths.

Twillo thought that they were getting the upper hand, but then he felt a shift in the ground beneath his feet.

A sand wraith sucked him under, where it would have smothered Twillo had it not been for his Core Eruption power. Even as he was choked, the sand squeezing his neck and trying to pry itself into Twillo's eyes and mouth, Twillo was able to charge up a chunk of the grains and explode it.

This had an effect that he wasn't expecting. Twillo was fired out the back, and did a complete flip before landing on his stomach. "By Livia," he said as he got to his feet, just in time to avoid a slash from one of the larger wraiths. Twillo took off in the opposite direction, where he hoped to circle back around.

One of the wraiths struck him across the back with what felt like a lasso of sand. The pain was instant and vicious, like a thousand miniature daggers made of glass embedding themselves in his skin. For a moment, he thought that it had ripped through his clothing, when he circled back around, Twillo wincing at the pain, he didn't feel any tear. Nor did he notice any blood.

Not yet, anyway.

He performed the mudra for Scaled Lash, Twillo able to dig into the sand wraith as it tried again. His attack didn't completely kill the desert monster, but it did cut it in half. What happened next reminded Twillo of the ash warriors that he had once fought. The sand that was left reformed into a smaller wraith, one that was almost comically sized.

Any comedy from the visual was quickly squashed once the smaller sand wraith zipped forward, Twillo barely making it into the air in time. It lunged for him; he dived to avoid it. He used Dragonflight to send himself up and over the smaller opponent. Twillo landed, but did so with his sword cutting straight down the middle of a sand wraith that was giving Princess Embla trouble.

There were only a few left now.

Pulling his hand back, Twillo fired a flash of dragonessence at the smaller sand wraith as it turned toward him.

It moved so quickly that it seemed like the surface of the sand itself was bubbling. Twillo was sucked back under. Yet again, he was able to fight his way out of the sand, this time using his dragonaura to launch himself to safety. It was maddening, the way the sand made him feel claustrophobic, the way it managed to get beneath his clothing and send pinpricks up and down his spine.

He managed to fight it back and cast Ripple Tide, Twillo able to take down another one of the wraiths. He turned to Embla.

The princess lunged for the small sand wraith and stabbed it in the back, killing the final one of the group.

Out of breath, Twillo huffed for a moment as he looked back up to Ariosto and Anneli.

"This is another thing that water harvesters do," Ariosto told them as he motioned his hand over the sand.

"What you see here can become something much nastier over time."

"Much nastier?" Twillo asked.

"Creatures like this feed on stray dragonessence, of which there is more than you would expect here in the deserts of Southfall. If they grow too strong, they can become something known as a rock daemon. I pray you never encounter one of these rock daemons. They are giant rock beasts that can grow to the size of mountains and can crush entire villages. This is another thing that harvesters try to stop in their travels across the kingdom."

"I'd like not to fight one of them, if given a choice." Twillo checked himself to see if he had actually been cut. He only saw small little bits of blood, nothing too serious. Even so, Twillo was glad the fight was over.

"Agreed. That doesn't sound like a fun time at all," Anneli said.

"No, it is not. And this is why many don't reach their Rite of Fulfillment, which is reserved for those who complete seven years of service. But they know that going in. It is a sacrifice that they have made for hundreds of years." Ariosto smoothed his hands over his gray robes. "Now, the dragonessence. Absorb as much as you can and top off your reserves."

Twillo could see it now, dragonessence just hovering in the air similar to the way that it existed at vortexes outside of stave churches. He raised his hand and instantly felt the power swell into him. Once he was done, Twillo checked his stats and saw that his levels were topped off. He still hadn't ranked up yet, which was something that was starting to bother him.

He needed to get stronger.

Chapter Fourteen

Portal to Nowhere

By the time they arrived back at the campsite, Vradon was wide awake, the monk pacing in front of the entrance of the ziggurat. Before greeting him, Twillo approached Adventus and Seondzus.

"It's time," he told them, and with those words the dragons returned to the wristlets, Seondzus' voice now in his head.

"Did you have fun hunting sand wraiths?"

"I'm just glad I'm not a water harvester," Twillo said as he turned to Vradon. "Are you ready?"

"You are truly serious about me coming with you?"

"Just in case we need someone to read something, yes, I'm dead serious." He placed his arm around the monk's shoulders and turned him to the entrance of the ziggurat. "It'll be fun. Trust me."

"Fun, you say?" Vradon ground his teeth for a moment. "I don't know if we have the same definition of fun, Jhaeros."

After bidding farewell to Ariosto and Katashi, Twillo turned to the bag of supplies he normally carried with him. He checked to make sure he had certain items and soon joined Anneli, Princess Embla, and Vradon at the cellar-like opening of the ziggurat.

"Back before lunch," Twillo said as he strolled past them, right down the steps.

"Aren't you confident?" Anneli told him. This brought a chuckle from Princess Embla, and a little nervous chatter from Vradon as they started down the stairs.

"No, I'm just ready to move on to the next one. I do enjoy exploring these kinds of places, even if they are a bit dangerous. But I don't like doing so on such a tight timeline. Generally, before the Artifance, I've had nearly a year to look for relics and other rare things across the Four Kingdoms. A year."

"I know what a year is," Anneli said as she caught up to him. The two hadn't spoken as much as of late, firstly due to the separation of their groups and then Princess Embla, who was usually either hanging out with Twillo or Anneli, but not both of them together.

Twillo grinned at Anneli as they continued down the stairs, the light dimming. It became pitch black, all of them able to see just fine because of their elven bloodlines.

"How much further do you think it goes?" Vradon asked from the back.

"If I knew that, I would have told you at the top. Don't worry," Twillo told him. "We will reach the bottom at some point, and we will go from there. But do stay alert."

"You should take your own advice," Anneli told him.

"You're not wrong." Twillo slowed his pace and took in his surroundings. He noticed that the temperature had plummeted. It wasn't quite cold yet, but it would be soon. The stairs stopped just before an enormous doorway, one that was twice Twillo's height. It was open, and there seemed to be several passages on the other side.

"Wait," Vradon said as he approached the stone. "There's some text here."

"What does it say?" Princess Embla asked as she came up beside him.

"A loose translation. *Listen*, no, *harken my call. Enter not this gate... in gall.* I can't read that part. But this part says *a test of soul and mind, riddles twined. Beyond what I,* no, *eyes, perceive. Beyond what eyes perceive, the truth you shall receive. Seek the key in each domain. Fail to do so, die in vain. Leave now or take your stance, Livia and good fortune guide your chance.*"

"That was a loose translation?" Anneli asked. "That was incredible."

"I would be lying if I said I hadn't come across similar texts before," Vradon said modestly.

"What do you think, bird monger?" she asked Twillo.

"Something is deceptive beyond, and it is some sort of test. What does gall mean?"

"Impudent behavior would be one translation," Princess Embla said.

"Thanks, Emmy."

"*Beyond what eyes perceive, the truth you shall receive,*" Adventus said, repeating the phrase in Twillo's head. "And there is a key in each domain."

"Yes, a key in each domain." Twillo paused for a moment. "Makes sense. I'm going to assume that the challenge here is to be deceptive in nature. In each of them, however many there may be, we have to find a key. What is the key? I think I'd be going out on a limb here if I said I didn't think that the *key* term was literal."

"It could be literal. But it could also be the answer to a puzzle," Princess Embla said.

Beside her, Vradon wrung his hands. "I don't like this. I really don't like this."

"I can't imagine why anyone would go head first into the unknown, but that's what you do professionally, right?" Anneli flicked Twillo's arm with a finger.

"I am a relic hunter extraordinaire, as I told the water harvesters."

Embla rolled her eyes. "Please don't start calling yourself that."

"Noted. But with that spirit in mind, there's only one direction I want to go at the moment. And that is through these doors to start whatever challenge lies ahead. Don't worry," he told Vradon. "You're in good hands. Did I already say that? If so, I'm saying it again."

Twillo stepped forward, the others soon joining him. They traveled down a dark hallway, one with carvings along the walls and ceiling. Twillo recognized some of the images. They were similar to the tapestries back at their hotel in Nalig, which showed images of the legendary Tournament of the Gods. He would have stopped to admire them further, but they were on a mission now.

The group reached a circular room, one with the next logical passage blocked by a solid wall of stone. Twillo's first instinct was to approach the door. He cautiously stepped up to it and looked for any openings, perhaps an option to force their way through. He placed his hand on the door and closed his eyes. The stone was heavily powered by dragonessence.

Even if they had enough space to summon Ramide to charge the door, Twillo was certain that they wouldn't be able to topple it. And he certainly wouldn't be able to blast through with an Arcane Card.

There were two pocket openings to the left and right of the stone door. Vradon was the first to investigate, the monk bravely stepping forward and peered down at a carving on the ground. It resembled the rune that Ariosto had activated earlier.

"Should we go up and get Ariosto?" Anneli asked.

"Maybe that's a good idea," Princess Embla said. She turned to the exit of the chamber and a solid wall of stone came down, kicking up dust.

"What was that?" Vradon asked as he got to his feet. He looked from Twillo to the exit, which was now blocked. "We're trapped?" He began to panic even further. "Are we really trapped in here?" he asked as he took a step back onto the rune. "I think we're trapped. I think—"

Light poured into the circular chamber, followed by a flash of silvery green magic.

Vradon was gone.

"Vradon?" Anneli said as she brazenly rushed over to the rune. She stepped onto it and vanished as well.

"Don't, not yet," Adventus told Twillo, even though he didn't have to. Twillo wasn't about to immediately follow without figuring out what was going on.

"They disappeared," Princess Embla said as she approached the rune both Anneli and Vradon had stepped on. She stopped in front of it and looked back at Twillo, fear flashing across her eyes.

Twillo had heard something about a dungeon with runes like this, ones that were solved through a series of portals. Upon looking to the right side of the room, he saw that there was another one of these runic portals. Two portals, and a sealed passageway ahead.

Twillo understood instantly what needed to happen next.

"Come on," he told Princess Embla. "We're heading into the portal." He reached his hand out to her and she took it.

Even as both dragons protested in his head, Twillo approached the rune. He squeezed her hand, offered the Crown Ravenna a short nod, and stepped out onto the rune.

The world as he knew it flashed away.

Twillo was instantly familiar with the space. Upon glancing over to Princess Embla, he saw the look of familiarity on her face as well.

Stretching before them was a vast, oddly colored desert that resembled the Dragon Meridian that Ariosto had taken them to. Twilight had a way of adding purple hues to the sand, and elongating some of the shadows. There was none of the fluorescent fauna here, yet there was a rim of mountains in the distance, the peaks impossibly far away.

"You're here," Vradon said as he approached Twillo.

Anneli quickly joined the monk. "How do we get back?"

"We have to find another portal," Twillo said. "We activate something here, find a portal, and return. Then, we travel to the next runic portal back in the chamber, activate something there, and hopefully it will open the stone door at the front of the room."

"How can you be sure?" Vradon asked.

"A hunch. A good one."

"We both have been to a place like this before," Princess Embla told Anneli and Vradon. "Ariosto took us."

Vradon raised his eyebrows in surprise. "You've been here before?"

"This is a Dragon Meridian," the princess said. "Or, I should say they share a similar environment. Ariosto showed us one of his, a space like this. It's where we encountered Livia."

"Ah, that is what you were describing. So it's a pocket realm?" Vradon asked. "We're in a pocket realm. Whew. Heh. Wait. Who am I kidding? That's not exactly good news!"

"Yes, a pocket realm," Twillo said. "And there was a portal that took us here, and one that will take us back. I'm certain of it. We just need to find the return portal. But before we do, we need to find whatever key is here, like the riddle stated. Then we will find the portal."

"Find it here?" Vradon looked at Twillo incredulously. "You know that I rarely doubt you, Jhaeros, but look at the size of this place. We would have to travel for days to find anything."

"We could take dragons," Princess Embla said.

"No, no we can't. They aren't accessible here." Twillo glanced down at his wristlets. There was no glow to them. Same with Anneli's. The dragons were still in the circular chamber back in their world. He had a feeling that they were there as well, in some sort of transitory state while they waited to complete the task here. But he didn't tell this to the others. This was already complex enough.

Twillo produced his Pathweaver's Compass. "We need to find the key."

Upon saying these words, the compass lit up. It pointed in a westerly direction.

"Where did you get that thing?" Vradon asked as Twillo took the lead.

"We had some time to kill outside of Seondzus," Princess Embla explained. "Jhaeros spotted something peculiar on a mountain which turned out to be a sanctum. We fought a headless guardian that wielded magical chains and rode a ghostly bull. We were rewarded with this compass."

"How convenient. It sounds like Livia played her hand yet again."

"She often does," Twillo told Vradon.

They started down an incline, one that opened up into a scattering of silvery rocks. Anneli stopped to observe them. "Do you think these are worth anything?"

"I don't think we should take anything with us, if that's what you're asking," Vradon said.

"That's not what I asked."

Twillo replied for Vradon this time. "We are only here to find the key and leave. This may take some time; it is best if we leave the natural environment untouched for our own sake. We do not know what messing with these rocks will do," he said, thinking of the sand wraith. "But who am I kidding? Take a few rocks if you must."

Anneli laughed. "Maybe just a handful. A keepsake."

"Such strange places we find ourselves," Vradon said as they came down a ridge and then passed through something akin to a slot canyon.

Twillo's focus remained on the compass, the relic hunter careful of where he put his feet and very cognizant of the stone walls around them. He could imagine a scenario in which they were being crushed. He didn't want to, but he could.

The canyon opened up into a wide space. The compass stopped working. Twillo looked at it for a moment, shook it, and the piece illuminated once again.

"How can we trust this thing, Jhaeros?" Vradon asked.

"It is not as untrustworthy as it looks. Or is it? I suppose that we have no other option. That's what I meant to say."

"We're stuck in a portal without any food, a place as desolate as the moon, and our only option is an old compass." Anneli shook her head, yet there was a smile on her face. "The things I do for glory."

"Is that why you're doing this?" Vradon asked the elven orc.

"I don't really know why I'm doing it. I suppose the whole *save the Four Kingdoms* part is appealing to me because I like living here. I don't like Gods of Carnage, at least to my knowledge."

"Up ahead!" Twillo said as the ground shifted in front of them.

It was like the shadows had all pooled together. They were suddenly surrounded by spectral demons, their bodies translucent and shimmering with kaleidoscopic colors that flickered and danced. It would have been mesmerizing had it not been terrifying, their limbs long and elegant, almost graceful, yet also deformed and covered in sharp tips. The spectral beings were terrible to behold, with willowy tendrils of luminescence where their hair should be. Their bodies rippled and distorted as they moved, the demons within evident.

Twillo fired at one with his sword.

He moved into action, and struck the next spectral demon to reach him. Anneli fought them back with her sword as well, yet her strikes were much less effective. Princess Embla ended up protecting her using a blast of dragonessence, which she fired directly through the swarm of enemies.

They were soon outnumbered. Like the sand wraiths, their opponents all seemed to operate as a unit. Yet there was something more menacing about the spectral demons as they melted together and converged upon Twillo and his companions. Twillo beat some of them back with Firebreath, but he could only do so much. Ripple Tide cut through more, yet they kept coming, their numbers seemingly endless.

"Vradon, stay back!" Twillo shouted to the monk.

Vradon tried to turn and run, to listen to Twillo's advice, but he tripped on a rock and fell. The spectral demons flocked to him, the ghostly mob surrounding the monk.

Twillo rushed toward them swinging his sword, Princess Embla doing the same with her dagger. But there were too many of them. To beat them back and protect himself, Twillo amplified his dragonaura through the mudra that Ariosto had taught him. He whipped at the spectral beings with Scaled Lash and took to the air using Dragonflight. He landed and spun around with the whip of energy, cutting away as many as he could.

The spectral demons disappeared as quickly as they arrived. Twillo's eyes dropped to Vradon, who lay on his back, his hands over his chest.

"Breathe," Twillo said as he got down onto his knees.

The monk's eyes popped open, his pupils and sclerae entirely black. He sat up and grabbed Twillo by the neck, Vradon easily able to break through his dragonaura.

The two floated into the air, a possessed Vradon choking Twillo, his grip tightening.

"What do we do? What do we do?" Anneli asked, hesitant to strike the normally peaceful monk down.

"Don't do anything to him," Twillo said as he struggled to breathe.

Even as he was being choked, and Princess Embla and Anneli watched from below, Twillo focused on his dragonessence cards. He put Flash of Fata Morgana on deck and cast it, which sent the two of them straight to the ground.

A pair of spectral demons burst out of Vradon, coming out of his mouth, his eyes, and his ears. Twillo scrambled to his feet and Princess Embla went on the attack, able to destroy them with her dagger.

Anneli helped Twillo up. "Are you okay?"

"I think..." Twillo let out a deep breath. "I think I'll be alright." He massaged his neck for a moment as he looked at Vradon. "But he might not be."

While he was now breathing, Vradon was completely pale. It was clear that the possession had affected him greatly.

Twillo walked back to where he had dropped his compass and picked it up. It buzzed stronger than it had before. "We're close," he said, still catching his breath.

"Anneli, you and I can help him. Embla, you are up front. Hopefully, that is the last of the spectral demons."

"You know it's not," Anneli said.

"No, I don't. I really don't." Twillo helped Vradon to his feet. "Just try to walk with us," he said.

"Jhaeros?"

"We're going to find the key, find the portal, and then get you back to our world. I promise this will all work out, old friend. Just stay with us."

Twillo gave Embla the compass so he could help Vradon.

"I am so sorry," Vradon said, his breaths heavy and painful. "It is like everything has been sucked out of me, all of my stamina, all of my energy."

"Your life force, your dragonessence, was taken from you," Embla told him softly. "That is what happened. That's what Ariosto told us the spectral demons could do. That is why you feel so weak. It was trying to take your core."

"I would try to heal you, but my healing power only works on me," Twillo told the monk. "At least at this level."

"You're doing what you can, Jhaeros, and I appreciate it."

They came to the top of the hill.

There was a pool of energy beyond with a natural stone formation in its center, one surrounded by a growing corruption. Twillo was certain that if they approached it, the spectral demons would notice. It had to be the key.

He helped Vradon onto the ground and stepped over to Princess Embla, who was keenly observing the compass. "It's there," she said.

"Agreed."

"That has to be it," said Anneli as she joined the two of them. She pointed to the top of the stone formation, to the glowing beacon that Twillo had already noticed.

"I have an idea," Princess Embla told Twillo.

"Please, Your Highness, do tell."

"What about this?"

Embla's idea was similar to what Twillo had already worked out. The only difference was, he thought it was best if the others headed back in the other direction first. This would allow Twillo to go after the key while his companions were already in the process of escaping.

They did just that and returned to the bottom of the hill with Vradon.

"Find the portal," Princess Embla told the Pathweaver's Compass.

The compass pointed into the north.

"We will start heading in that direction," she told Twillo with a hint of uncertainty in her voice.

"I can get it using Dragonflight," he assured her. "I'll grab the key and join you. I promise there's nothing to worry about."

"Just leave me," Vradon said once the two women helped him to his feet. "It is beneath both of you to help a foolish old monk like myself."

"Old? You aren't old," Anneli said. "But you are too dramatic. We're not going to leave you. Who else is going to read all the stuff if you aren't around?"

"The dragons can."

"They can," Twillo said, "but we have to provide light for them to do so. And with you, we don't need light."

"And who has time to make light?" Princess Embla asked the monk. "Not us. We're apparently relic hunters."

Vradon gave them a playful frown.

"We will still get you there," Anneli assured him.

Twillo took a final look at the three of them. "I'll meet you soon. Just keep going. Livia is with us all."

With those words, Twillo floated to the top of the hill. He observed the shadowy corruption, the horde of spectral demons presenting an almost hypnotic sight. There was no way for him to know how many there actually were, but it seemed as if there were hundreds, their lithe bodies a ghostly nebula of malice.

If Twillo misstepped, if he lost his footing in any way, he'd fall into the cesspool, where he would be overwhelmed by the spectral demons. He saw what had happened to Vradon; it was a testament to how much Princess Embla and Anneli trusted him that they let him do this alone.

Twillo respected them for that. And he had to see this through so they could complete this realm and move on.

He looked back at the others, who were now moving further and further away from them. Princess Embla glanced at him as if she could sense his gaze, their eyes locking.

It was her choice to join him, and if it wasn't her choice, it was the choice of a goddess that had influence over their lives. Yet he couldn't help but feel responsible for what he had already put the princess and the others through, and how much their presence had changed Twillo.

Now, he had people that counted on him, true companions. People from all walks of life that had banded together to stop an evil force that many in the Four Kingdoms would never know about. But they would know about the return of dragons. Twillo was certain of this.

Rekindling a determination that had driven him for twenty years now, Twillo looked to the stone formation, and the glowing object on top. It was too shiny for him to make out, but he'd been doing this long enough to know when a relic presented itself.

Reach the platform, get whatever the key was, and join the others. That was the core of his strategy.

Twillo activated the mudra for Dragonflight and threw his arms behind his back. He took to the air, the relic hunter sailing directly over the colony of spectral demons. He landed on the stone platform, nearly fell, and was quickly up on his feet again.

What now? Twillo hesitated for a moment as he took in the brilliance that now hovered before him. It was so bright that he had to look away.

Twillo ignored the blinding golden light as he reached his hand through it. His fingers fell upon a spherical object. As soon as he touched it, Twillo felt a burning sensation that spread up his arm. The golden light disappeared, yet Twillo could feel that something had changed within him.

He had absorbed the key.

Twillo prepared to use Dragonflight again. He jumped off the platform just as the spectral demons reached the top.

They didn't shriek, which only made things stranger as he flew through the air and landed on the hill. There was no sound associated with their movement, no noise at all. It was precisely this quiet that Twillo found the most terrifying. There was no warning, and no predatory grumblings as they swarmed toward him.

They simply consumed.

And worse, the spectral demons seemed to have locked on to Twillo, the group of shadowy beings all shifting in his direction.

Twillo had to reach the others.

After a mad dash across an eerie-dark desert, Twillo landed just behind his companions. "They're coming," he said. "We have to hurry."

"Where's the key?" Anneli asked.

"It disappeared. But—"

"What?" asked Princess Embla.

"I reached out for it and it vanished. But I have it. I can feel it. We just need to find the portal now."

"What do you mean you can feel it?" Anneli asked, alarm in her voice.

"Just trust me. Come on." Twillo replaced Embla, where he was able to slip under Vradon's arm.

"Well, hello, Jhaeros—"

"How much time do we have?" Anneli asked as she picked up her pace.

"I don't know. But they definitely noticed me." Twillo tried to use his dragonessence to float forward, but this didn't work the same way while bearing someone else's weight.

"How much further do we have, Your Grace?" Anneli asked Princess Embla, who continued to hold the compass.

"It's buzzing more, but I see the demons." Princess Embla had been alternating between walking ahead of the group and turning back to check on them. She drew her dagger. "I will try to hold them off."

"It's going to take two of us," Twillo said.

"There are only a few right now. Continue." She gave Twillo the compass. He could feel it buzzing in his hand.

Twillo gave the compass to Anneli and drew his sword. It wasn't going to be easy to use it one-handed while he still assisted Vradon, but he didn't have many other options.

The first spectral demon swooped toward them, just about to crash down on them when Embla hit it with a blast of dragonessence that spiraled forward and tornadoed through her opponents.

Not a bad maneuver. It wasn't enough to fully push their pursuers back, a cluster of which was heading in their direction, but it did cut one of them down. Joining the fray, Twillo fired a bolt of dragonessence at them with his sword. He managed to destroy one of the spectral demons, but not the others.

By this point, his Ripple Tide power had reset. As they grew closer, he sent a wave of dragonessence forward, and was able to break through their ranks while still helping Vradon.

"Is that it?" Anneli asked. "Twillo, look!"

He had been so focused on the fight happening behind that he hadn't been scanning ahead. Twillo turned to find a structure in a gully beyond, one with sandstone columns erected around it. All of it had been weathered by time, yet it had maintained a majestic, almost regal aura. It seemed like it was an important structure, and as they grew nearer to it Twillo saw an anomaly of sorts in its center, one surrounded by runes.

It had to be the portal.

"Let's go!" he said, invigorated yet again. Twillo tried something he hadn't yet attempted with a group. Dragonflight exploded him up into the air with Vradon and Anneli. The pair landed right outside of the sandstone structure.

"Tell me next time," Anneli said as Twillo helped her bring Vradon to the portal.

"Don't take too long," Vradon said as Twillo turned back to help Princess Embla fight off the spectral demons.

Twillo barely nodded.

Seconds later he joined the princess using Dragonflight yet again, the pair cutting through the madness of spectral monsters, even if they would soon be overwhelmed.

"Come on!" He reached out to Embla and she took his hand. Together, they bounded into the air with Dragonflight, and landed softly right beside one of the stone pillars.

"Are you certain about this?" she asked.

"As certain as a relic hunter can be, Your Excellency."

"I'll go first."

Twillo moved aside, allowing the princess to use the portal. She vanished, and left the air charged with dragonessence just as the shadowy demons converged upon him. Twillo fired one more bolt from his sword at the spectral creatures, and stepped onto the portal as well.

The world blurred.

He felt like he had plunged into a pool of cold water as a sudden, disorienting sensation washed over him. There was a brief feeling of weightlessness, followed by this sense that Twillo was being stretched and squeezed from all directions.

And as quickly as it started, it was over.

Twillo appeared back in the circular chamber with the others, his knees a bit wobbly.

"Left-Handed One," Adventus said, his voice now at the back of Twillo's head, which was comforting in its own way.

"Thank Livia you're back," Seondzus told him.

"How long were we gone?"

"I don't know how much time has passed," Adventus told him. "This is a strange space."

"Where's the key?" Anneli asked. She was crouched next to Vradon, who sat on the ground, a disappointed look on his face. Twillo could read the shame, and he didn't want the monk to feel that way. Any of them could have been possessed.

"The key is in me." Twillo approached the blocked stone doorway ahead. Nothing moved, the wall of solid rock remaining in place.

"That's not great," Princess Embla said as she looked to the second portal, the one that they hadn't investigated yet. "Do you think we have to get both of them for it to open?"

"I don't know. I really don't know." An idea came to Twillo. He approached the exit, the doorway they had been through earlier. The wall of rock crumbled away, the exit passage open again. "At least we can leave now. But if we want to continue, we're going to have to go through the other portal."

"I can stay here," Vradon said. "In the chamber."

"Maybe, but if something happens to us, that might not be ideal." Twillo looked from Embla to the elven orc.

"What are you suggesting?" Anneli asked.

"I'm curious as well, Jhaeros," Princess Embla told him.

"You and I, Your Grace. We will handle the next portal. There will be two of us, and we will be lighter on our feet. Anneli, you can take Vradon back to the surface, where he can rest. Wait," he said as she began to protest. "There's a reason I think this is a good idea. If something happens to us, there are still several of you that are able to fulfill this task. If we all go in there, this won't be the case. If three of us go there, and we leave Vradon here, it might be some time before he's able to reach the top, or before Ariosto and Katashi come down to find him."

"How long do you want us to give you?" Anneli asked.

"I don't know. A few hours? Did it feel like a few hours passed, Adventus?"

"I do not know," the white dragon told him.

Anneli tilted her head to the side, as if Ramide was speaking to her. "Ramide says that they have been sitting in the dark for some time now, but he doesn't know how long it has been either."

"It is a risk we will have to take." Twillo approached the second portal. "Embla and I can do this."

"We can," she said, royal confidence behind her words.

Twillo could tell that Anneli didn't like his plan, yet she also saw the reasoning behind it. She finally spoke: "In that case, I will help him to the top, and we will await your return. But if it's been too long, I'm coming back. And I'll bring Ariosto and Katashi with me."

Twillo gave her a short nod. "Hopefully, it won't come to that."

Chapter Fifteen

Icenordian Summer

TWILLO AND PRINCESS EMBLA appeared on the outskirts of a city, both of them intimately familiar with their new setting.

"It can't be," Twillo said as he took a step forward, all the blood draining from his body.

He recognized the maroon roofs, the way they pressed up to the ancient surrounding walls. The buildings, which were carved from local alabaster stone, gleaned under the sun. Narrow lanes ran from the farmlands beyond to the gated entry points, which were protected by Icenor's finest. All of it. Twillo knew exactly where he was.

"What sort of cruel joke is this?" Princess Embla asked as white butterflies fluttered past. Everything was in bloom around them: moon petals known for their opaline luster; golden star-shaped elanors, which were often used in rituals; sunfire lilies, which were said to be originally imported from Southfall; snapdragons, the name for green flowers that grew into the shape of a dragon's maw.

Twillo knew that the ziggurat was toying with them. Whatever being had created this space had somehow tapped into their minds, bringing the two to a place Twillo didn't know if he would ever visit again. This was Sparrow's Rise. His childhood home. The place where he and Princess Embla had grown close over the course of what felt like long-forgotten summers, fever dreams even.

Yet here they were, standing before it all.

Twillo produced a compass, not at all surprised to see it point them to the outer walls after he asked it to find the key.

Sparrow's Rise was built long before Yanzon the Undisputable and had been gifted to various Icenordian queens. They had put quite a bit of money into the city over the years, which attracted attention, and more citizens. Hence the reason for many of the buildings now existing outside its ancient walls.

"We just need to find the key, and the portal," he told Princess Embla.

"It looks so real," she whispered, still in awe.

"I've been through something like this before, a psychological test put on by the ziggurat's keeper. It is not real. You can't think of it as real. This is a figment of our imaginations. A combined figment. And I have a feeling that it is a twisted one at that."

"Twisted? Why?"

"Just a hunch." Twillo drew his sword. "Be ready for anything."

As much as he wanted to look around and explore, to go through each home along their way and see just how detailed this hallucination actually was, Twillo knew that this was an exercise in futility. What mattered was finding the key, locating the portal, and moving on from there.

Anything else would be an obstacle in their way.

Princess Embla didn't seem to feel the same way. She stopped numerous times to do things like smell flowers, or crouch by a fence line and trace her hand over some of the names that were carved into the wood. "Exactly how I remember it," she said as she looked up at Twillo. "It's uncanny."

"The carvings?"

"I used to walk this path after you left. I was lonely here, you know. You were my only friend in Sparrow's Rise. The head of our house tried to have some of the servants befriend me, but it was never the same. There was no one to get in trouble with. No one who would sneak out with me. I took to taking long walks."

"Yeah?" Twillo imagined Princess Embla as a teenage girl walking this very lane, and the entourage that would have had to follow behind her. As she reached her teenage years and grew in beauty, her father had increased security. Thinking back now, it was a wonder that Vraizard had let Twillo hang out with her alone in the first place.

"Anyway, the carvings are the same. Sometimes I would crouch here and look at them," she said as her eyes began to water. "I'd think about you."

"Why here?"

"I don't know."

Twillo wanted to tell her that he thought about her as well during those times, but this would be a lie. Mostly, he thought about surviving. Simply staying alive and not being caught by the forces that were after him took quite a bit of concentration. There was also the lack of food, how difficult things would become in the harsher seasons, and his eventual exodus to the Kingdom of Middling.

"I bet it was hard, Emmy," he finally said.

"Whatever you went through was much harder. I know that. I'm not foolish. I can't imagine being cast out like you were, treated in such a cruel and unusual way. Even if your father was planning to do what he did, if he had tried to betray the kingdom, what does that have to do with you and your rank? You were too young to be working with him. Why strip you of your title? Of your land and your heritage? These are the kinds of things that will change when I am ruler. These unnecessary practices."

"From what I know of history, people often think they will rule in ways that are different from their current leadership, only to find later on that they ruled this way for a reason." Twillo shrugged. "It is the way of our world, Your Grace."

"I don't agree with that."

"Says a future leader."

She offered him a wry smile as she got to her feet. "From a future leader as well."

Twillo knew what she was referring to, yet he didn't say anything as he continued along the lane toward the outer walls of Sparrow's Rise. Soon, they would come in contact with the guards, which led him to pause and consider another option. "Wait. I have a better idea. The secret passage. Perhaps we should go in that way. The guards will certainly challenge us here. We can't forget that we are in a hostile environment."

"The secret passage, yes. In that case, we can go this way."

Princess Embla turned back to the fence they just passed. Twillo joined her, the two continuing along a quaint road made of huge stones that had been sunk into the ground ages ago. Twillo remembered these from his youth as well, how he always wondered where they had come from. They weren't like the alabaster or any of the other rocks that he'd seen in the area.

"I wonder if the passage is even there," she said as they came around the bend, one that twisted into the woods that surrounded the city.

"You saw your carvings."

"And?"

"This entire place"—Twillo swept his hand toward the forest they were just about to step into—"has been put together through our memories. Even the stone beneath our feet. All of it is here for a reason. It is a detail that we have either noticed or, in your case, carved into the landscape itself."

"I wonder how it would have changed had Vradon or Anneli come with us."

"That is a good question," Twillo said. "There really is no telling. I know Vradon has been here numerous times, but I do not remember any times when Anneli came to Sparrow's Rise. If they were with us, we might have been sent to a different place entirely. I don't know. I really don't know."

As they walked, Twillo took a quick glance at his status.

Name: Jhaeros Shotaro Vos
Tier: Apprentice
Rank: S
Class: Martial Arts Mastery
Rank: C
Secondary Class: None
Tertiary Class: None
Dragonessence: 246/325
[Arcane Cards]
Arms of Vikan Wood, Level 2
Codex Vault, Level 1 [Passive]
Core Eruption, Level 2
Enchanting Deception, Level 2
Eternal Cycle, Level 2
Firebreath, Level 2
Flash of Fata Morgana, Level 2
Nadakunai's Might, Level 2

Ripple Tide, Level 2
Vard's Blessing, Level 2
Warding Glyph, Level 2
[Mudras]
Level up!
Dragonaura, Level 2
Dragonflight, Level 1
Scaled Lash, Level 1

He had more dragonessence than he would have expected, but this was likely because of the nature of the place they were in. Twillo recalled from Ariosto's meridian that dragonessence wasn't used the same way here.

While he still had yet to have the time he needed to work on Voidshift, the skill that would allow him to absorb and redistribute dragonessence, at least he had leveled up his dragonaura. Twillo had a feeling Dragonflight would level soon as well. That one was something he continued to use.

Princess Embla pressed some of the branches away, allowing Twillo to pass.

"I should be the one doing that for you, Your Ladyship."

"Please."

"Your Highness? Which do you prefer?"

"Why do you think teasing me like that will get you anywhere?"

"I'm not teasing you to arrive at some destination. I'm teasing you because..." Twillo stopped walking. Why was he teasing her? "Actually, I don't know. To pass the time. And perhaps because I'm nervous. Nervous and a bit anxious about being here. I don't like when these things use my memories to make a pocket realm."

'How do you know this is your memory? I'd say there is a good chance it is mine."

"Actually, you're right, it could be yours. That would explain the carving. I don't remember there being as many guards at the front. Was that something that happened after I left?"

"It was," she said as they reached a small stream. Lithe as ever, Embla hopped across a couple of stones. Twillo used Dragonflight, which shot him above the treeline and back down to the other side. "That was dramatic."

"Heh. Just trying to level that one up."

"Anyway. The guards. Yes, there were more after you left. My father used what happened to strengthen his security. The wandering you and I used to do? That wouldn't have been possible after the incident. In fact, the carvings I made—I wasn't kidding when I said I was well-guarded. It wasn't my normal entourage. There were nine Honor Guards with me. Nine. And they were all brutes."

"Not all elven orcs are brutes, but the ones in the Honor Guard generally fit that bill. It's likely one of the reasons they're hired for the job."

"It is the main reason they are hired for the job. And there will be restructurings once I'm ravenna," she said, a hint of anger in her voice. "I understand the importance of protecting the realm and those who lead it."

Twillo raced an eyebrow at her.

"What?"

"The idea of a realm with natural-born protectors just doesn't mean the same thing to me after all of my travels. We should call the ravennaship what it is."

"Yes?" she asked.

"It's a farce to some degree, but it keeps the people happy and perhaps their happiness keeps them orderly. This makes Emperor Otonashi happy, it keeps the Four Kingdoms from warring, and we're all better off for it. Happy, happy, happy. So maybe a necessary evil."

"You consider me a necessary evil?"

"I didn't say that—"

"You consider your future role as a necessary evil, as Prince Ravenna?"

"Have we agreed to marry, My Lady? Have you provided me a copy of your yoika?" he asked, referring to the poems that traditional Icenordians had written about them that were only shared with family members or future spouses.

Princess Embla puffed her cheeks out, but ultimately didn't take the bait. Instead, she changed the subject. "A few months after you left, right before I headed to Vendir for the fall, they had the summer harvest festival."

"I always loved that time of year."

"Same. It is both joyous because it was so fun and sad knowing that winter would come again."

"And school," Twillo said.

"I quite liked school."

"I liked training with Renda, but school wasn't really my thing."

"Oh, a young Jhaeros at school. I can see it now."

"You would likely see me sleeping at my desk and being scolded by the headmistress?"

The princess laughed. "You were probably a difficult student to handle. If they did anything out of step, I'm sure your father or his representatives would get involved. Same as mine. Anyway, the Summer Harvest Festival."

"Yes?"

"Saracent Ananda Min was poison in my father's ear. She convinced him that some of the local families that she didn't like, ones that hadn't exactly agreed to her misinformation campaign against your father, needed to be dealt with publicly. It was grim. Jhaeros, it was so grim."

"I'll bet."

Twillo knew what humans and elves were capable of when they wanted to make a point. He'd seen enough heads on stakes in the Tribute Islands, a sort of victory lap for the Brethren, as well as those who had been left to die on stakes in the deserts of Southfall. The cruelty of the Four Kingdoms knew no bounds.

"They brought out the wolves."

"The wolves? You're kidding."

"They starved the wolves for several days until they were quite hungry. Kept them in cages and gathered the people that supported your father into one of the pits in the courtyard. You know the ones."

Twillo was well-aware of the walled-in pits. They were twenty feet deep, their walls etched with old Sagic writing. Thinking back, he wondered what they actually said, and how these pits had been used when they were built. Surely they hadn't been designed for something like torture.

"They released the wolves, and because I was the Crown Ravenna, my father insisted I watch. He said it was important for me to get accustomed to what seems like cruelty, but is actually good for the well-being of the public. What kind of reasoning is that?"

"Barbaric, to be sure. Yanzon the Undisputable would find that kind of action inspiring. No offense."

"None taken. It's not the first time my father has made me do something like that. And you know what?"

She turned to him. "It worked. By the hells, it worked, Jhaeros. It doesn't affect me the same way now. I don't like violence like that, but I can stomach it. And I shouldn't be able to."

"No, you shouldn't. I'm—" Twillo was about to apologize when Princess Embla collapsed into him. He hugged her back, his hand coming to her head as he held her for a moment. "I'm sorry you had to do that."

She pressed away from Twillo. "The things I've seen as the Crown Ravenna. You'd think it would bring a tear, some remorse, but it has hardened my heart. Look at me now," she said, desperation in her eyes. "I should feel remorse, but I do not. Even now, I'm not upset. I mean, I am upset, clearly, but I should be in pieces after seeing something like that." She smoothed her hands over her robes. "Thank you for that, by the way."

"Yes, Your Grace."

Princess Embla laughed. She continued on, the Crown Ravenna coming down a hill and back onto a path of stone. "You really know how to sweet talk a lady, don't you."

"I learned from the best."

"Who taught you?"

"The greatest pillowers in all of the Four Kingdoms." He cleared his throat once he read the look she was giving him. "I should clarify. Pillowers frequent relic hunter taverns, you know. It's a safe place for them to enjoy drinks without having to worry about running into clientele."

"Really? I did not know that."

"How often do you get out without having to heed to whatever your guards tell you? I'm going to assume they don't normally allow you to go to some of the seedier places in the kingdom."

"I've been to some places. But I had to sneak out."

"I'm certain you did."

"I think it is important to see how the people of the kingdom actually live. Some of my guards understood that. Rowian did not."

Twillo recalled the big elven orc, the one that Jecha had since possessed. "I can imagine that."

"He was by far the worst of all of them. Never mean, at least to me—he knew better. But to others. This goes back to my familiarity with cruelty. I saw him do things. Break people's hands, men and women, cut fingers off, things like that. Rowian didn't kill people, though. At least to my knowledge. This was why Olaf's murder was so shocking to me. It was unlike Rowian to go this far. But what do I know? Maybe I didn't see it. Maybe I didn't see any of it coming. Perhaps I had been blinded by my status."

"That's not as hard as it seems. The kind of power a ravenna wields is second only to the Emperor and a few of the higher-ups of his royal court. It is an incredible responsibility."

"Which is why I want to do it right. It's also why I'd like someone by my side that also knows of the grave consequences that come with getting it wrong." She stepped ahead of Twillo to avoid whatever reaction he may have had regarding this comment. "We're almost there, Jhaeros. I hope you are ready to take a walk down memory lane."

"I already am," he assured her.

Chapter Sixteen

Stone Guardian

THE RELIC HUNTER and the Icenordian princess reached the cave they had discovered so long ago, a place with lush flowering vines hanging over the entrance. He couldn't see the city now, yet he knew that if they followed the cave they would eventually get there.

"The compass is definitely pointing that way." Twillo glanced at the compass again, confirming this. "It's a bit of a walk, but this should do the trick. I only hope that the key is in your summer home."

"If it's not, we'll still be able to locate it."

"True. It will just take longer. Time isn't exactly of the essence; we do not know how much has passed back in our world."

"I still can't wrap my head around how strange this is," Princess Embla said. Twillo agreed. It was quite serene, summer in full bloom, a soft breeze blowing through the trees, birds chirping beyond. None of this felt like an illusion, yet it was.

Twillo stepped past her. There were markings on the cave wall that he couldn't remember. Or could he? The more he stared at then, the more memories began to take shape. He had been curious about them all that time ago. Perhaps he had always been a curious relic hunter at heart.

They walked for nearly an hour, the light gone, the cave increasingly cold. Every time they spoke, their voices echoed through the long, underground passage.

"I almost ran away right after it happened," she told him. "I wanted to come and find you. I reached the exit, and a member of the Honor Guards was there waiting for me. He was riding one of those big white horses that they use."

"The horses that wear armor?"

She nodded. "I was practically numb by the time he hopped down and made me climb up to his horse. You know that feeling of being caught. It just left me reeling, empty, hopeless. I knew from that point forward that I would never be able to use the secret passage again."

Twillo stopped walking. "You don't think it is sealed, do you?"

"If it is, we will blow through it." She laughed. "Come on, Jhaeros, you can use magic now. Doing something like that shouldn't bother you."

"Sometimes I forget that."

Twillo noticed a rustling sound ahead. He paused, his hand immediately going to the hilt of his sword.

"What do you think that was?" Embla asked.

Light swirled into the cavernous space. A trio of spectral wolves flashed into existence, the three glowing with a ghostly energy. They were large, easily as tall as Twillo at the shoulder. Their snarl produced a chilling sound that instantly had Twillo on edge, and their bare teeth were like gleaming crystals, ones that had been sharpened to strip away flesh.

It became instinctual at that point. Twillo opened fire with a blast of dragonessence, intended for the wolf on the left. The creature skittered away, and used the cave wall as a springboard to launch itself at Twillo.

He batted it down with his sword, surprised to see that it actually cut through it. This gave him hope that they would be able to defeat the monsters. But then Twillo heard a rustling sound behind him, coming from the entrance of the cave.

More wolves appeared, and as they did several began to howl, their howl haunting and loud enough that it caused both Twillo and Princess Embla to clench up.

"Begone!" she said as she used Scaled Lash to kill one of the howling spectral wolves.

Twillo's heartbeat quickened as the wolves closed in again. One leaped for him. He struck it down with an amplified fist, only to be taken off guard by another.

The wolf clamped its crystalline teeth down onto his arm, the pain excruciating. It was like being bitten and burned at the same time. Even with the sudden flash of pain, Twillo managed to torch the spectral wolf with Firebreath.

Twillo jumped away and activated his dragonaura through its mudra. He cut through another wolf, and decapitated one just about to jump for him using Scaled Lash.

Ignoring his injury, Twillo put everything he had into Ripple Tide, which created a tsunami of dragonessence that swept over the wolves, destroying most of them. This left just a few, which the princess quickly handled.

As soon as she was done, she rushed over to him. "Jhaeros—!"

"It's fine, it's fine," he said as he looked down at the injury. The wolf had bitten him just beyond the safety of his gauntlet. It was amazing that it hadn't snapped his arm.

He nursed the wound for a moment, cringing at the way his skin had already blistered, the wound cauterized by the heat.

"You can heal this, right?"

"I have a card, Vard's Blessing. It should help." Twillo cycled out his cards and put Vard's Blessing on deck.

Oblivious to his surroundings, he sat down on the ground with his back against the cave wall. He began to heal the wound. The effect was instant. It still hurt, yet Twillo felt as if the pain was slowly dissipating, filtering into the air around him. Closing his eyes, he could see it doing just that, a mist of dragonessence.

"How long do you think it will take you?" Princess Embla asked. "There may be more of them."

"In that case, I will heal as we walk." His back against the wall, Twillo managed to get to his feet. Embla brought his sword over to him and helped him put the blade in its scabbard. "Thanks."

They continued, Twillo healing himself as he walked. Soon, the pain was completely gone. His clothing was ripped, and it looked like he would always bear a scar there from the teeth, yet he was able to use his arm once again.

"I'm so glad I have this card," he told her.

"You're lucky he didn't break the bone. Mending broken bone is much harder, from what I've heard."

"Sure is. And just so we're clear."

"Yes?"

"The carvings, the cave, the wolves—this place is entirely made from your memories," he said. "Or at least, the entity that runs the ziggurat is using yours to create obstacles. Hence the wolves."

"You think the wolves are mine?"

"They aren't mine. I have wolves as well that I am afraid of, but those ones were more on the side of wolvencree. This tells me something else."

"An expert, are you?"

"I prefer relic hunter, but sure, you can call me that." Twillo grinned at her. "It shouldn't be much further now, Emmy."

Twillo and the princess came to a set of stone steps. The steps moved in a spiral pattern, each one expertly cut into the stone. There were numerous sconces on the wall, which led Twillo to imagine what it would have looked like had they all been lit. It would have been quite the sight, mysterious and ritualesque.

But ultimately, these kinds of lights weren't necessary for Icenordians. Twillo had noticed many things in the kingdom like that, installations created so that Icenor blended in better with the other kingdoms. It was completely for aesthetics. Even elves wanted to fit in.

They reached the top of the stairs. Twillo checked the compass one last time to see that it was buzzing, pointing directly to the exit.

"Well?" he asked as the princess reached out for the door. She opened it to reveal a wall of rock.

"Sealed off, just as I remember it being."

"We should be able to handle it," Twillo said.

"My only concern is that it will attract whatever is patrolling the castle."

"We don't know if something is patrolling it yet, aside from the guards out front."

"You're right. I suppose we have no other choice."

Twillo scanned the area yet again. His eyes jumped over to a sconce, which would do the trick. He worked to pry it off the wall, the iron eventually coming loose. Twillo rearranged his cards, and used Warding Glyph to charge the door.

"Please step back, Your Grace," he told the Princess.

Once she was behind him, Twillo used Core Eruption to charge the sconce. He tossed it at the door, the combined explosion bringing the wall of stone crumbling down. They had to move some of the pieces to fully fit through, but it had done the trick.

They were now in the manor. Even stranger, they were in Embla's old bedroom.

Twillo recognized everything, from the frostwool sheepskin rug to the tapestries on the wall featuring scenes of flowering fields. It was a spacious room, one filled with natural light thanks to floor-to-ceiling windows that overlooked a verdant inner garden.

At the heart of the room was a grand canopy bed, the bedframe expertly carved, Twillo instantly recognizing the honey-toned wood from the Faewoods in the west. On the far side of the room was an ornate fireplace, with cozy seating near it. There was even a vase full of snapdragon flowers, a testament to the sheer detail that ran throughout the hallucination.

"Everything is the exact same," she said as she sat down in one of the chairs. Embla looked up at Twillo. "One could get comfortable here."

"One could, and then one would be trapped forever in a pocket realm. It is best we move on." Twillo showed her the compass. "We're close."

"Where would we be without that thing?"

"That, I do not know. But I am thankful that Livia led me to that sanctum to find it."

"You act as if she stood there waving a flag at you."

"I suppose she stands in front of all the places I discover, waiting for me to test my luck."

"You met her, as did I."

"We did. And that is still something I've yet to process. Maybe in another lifetime." Twillo took a seat next to the princess and looked at the fireplace. He had a memory of sitting in this very seat drinking a tea made from icethistle petals. These petals were native to the winters, and Icenordians usually dried them out to make tea. It was subtle and sweet, perfect during the warmer days of summer.

Thinking about it now made him swallow. Twillo was thirsty.

"We shouldn't get comfortable." He pushed himself up and stepped to the door. Soon, they were heading down the hallway, Princess Embla behind him giving instructions.

"Servants' quarters, then a corridor into the guest housing. If it's not there, then I don't know where it will be."

"Wait, it's pointing up." Twillo stopped in front of the stairs and turned to it. The needle turned as well.

"Do you think the key is in my father's quarters? They are upstairs."

"It seems like a good place to check." Twillo stepped over to one of the windows. He could see one of the numerous courtyards below. He knew the pits were beyond that, the ones where they had held the gruesome public execution that had clearly affected the princess. "I have a feeling they are going to be standing in our way."

"I see what you mean," Princess Embla said once she joined Twillo by the window.

Floating above the courtyard below were Icenordian archmages, ghoul-like, their robes draped from their bodies.

"You know more about them than I do. Their powers are kept from the public."

"Only a select few in the Ravenna's court know their capabilities. We should treat them as if we were going against the Emperor's Magi. They can use Arcane Cards and dragonessence in similar ways as the Magi."

"I wonder if we will be able to get any cards from them."

"This is a hallucination. I believe those are your words."

"Right," Twillo said as he ran his hand along his chin line. "It is certainly something that we will have to be ready for. I would bet good coin that they will be the ones standing between us and the exit portal."

"Likely."

They came to a new hallway, one with statues of Honor Guard lining the walls. These were carved out of alabaster, completely white, and so detailed that Twillo was spooked upon first seeing them. He'd never been in this hallway before. The Ravenna's floor had been off limits in his youth.

They traveled down a red carpet, one with gold stitching along its borders. The pair reached a door that was twice as large as it needed to be. Twillo looked down at the compass and up to the royal crests carved into the door. "I think it's on the other side."

The room that followed was a grand space, one that radiated an understated elegance. Rather than floral prints, the tapestries all had pictures of Icenordians, mostly nude. Vraizard's bed was much larger than his daughter's. There were more sheepskins draped over it, and it was painted with gold leaf accents. Near it was an arched window that was protected from the light outside by heavy emerald green drapes. Finally there was Vraizard's ceremonial armor, which had been erected near the fireplace. All the pieces were there aside from a helmet.

"Don't touch anything," Embla said as Twillo approached the armor. It was the kind of work that he had only seen from a certain few in Icenor, the armor made of a special steel that was prized for its lightness and durability, a silvery blue sheen to it etched with intricate interwoven patterns of Sagic script. A sweeping cloak was attached to the shoulders, one with golden stitching.

"Can I have this?" Twillo asked. "Aside from the cape. Capes aren't really my thing."

"Can you what?" She gave him a curious look. "What did I say about not touching things?"

"Aside from some stuff I have in Katashi's pocket shelter, the only armor I have are the gauntlets. This would go perfectly with them."

"Would it... could it?" She looked at him with confusion. "I don't care if you take it, but would it actually come with us? Can we bring something from a place like this?"

"What's the worst that could happen? I can stash it away. There are enough blankets on your father's bed to make a sack. We can try to bring that; if it lets us take it, then so be it. If it does not, then we will still be all right."

"I suppose it is worth a shot. Let me see the compass."

Twillo gave her the compass. Princess Embla followed it to her father's armoire. She opened one of the doors, and light poured into the room.

"That would be the key. Touch it," Twillo said.

He had already started to remove the chest plate. Soon, he collected the bits of the armor that he could wear, and placed them on the ground. He used one of Vraizard's velvet blankets to make a sack to hold the armor. By the time he turned to Embla, she was ready to go.

"I have the key," she said.

"Then the only thing we need to do now is find the portal."

"Take us to the portal," she told the compass. It buzzed and the needle shifted in a new direction. Twillo followed it to the window to see that it was looking out at the courtyard, just as he expected.

It was going to be a fight.

They considered finding another way around. They consider taking to the air, where Twillo and Princess Embla would be able to fly directly over the archmages. But as they went over their options, it became increasingly clear that the only way to get through the archmages was to head them off. If they did something like go through the secret passage again, and come around to the front of Sparrow's Rise, they would be forced to fight the guards outside the city.

This was the best solution.

"All we have to do is reach the portal," Twillo reminded Princess Embla as they reached another large door, one carved intricately with famous scenes from Icenordian history. There were even stave churches in the etchings, Twillo recognizing their dragon finials.

"Then let's hit them with everything we have."

"Exactly." Twillo used Codex Vault to cycle through his cards. He put Ripple Tide, Nadakunai's Might, and Firebreath on deck. He considered going with Arms of Vikan Wood, but didn't think it would be that kind of fight, one in which he would actually sustain close combat injuries. If he could just move to the next Tier, he'd be able to use another card with the three he could already use.

"And you are seriously going to do it with a bag of armor over your shoulder?" she asked in reference to the pieces that Twillo had taken from her father's room.

He jingled them. "If it actually works, it will be incredibly helpful. If it doesn't, then at least I tried."

"Do you often live your life this way?"

"On the razor's edge or by putting my full faith in Livia and what she places before me? Because the answer to both is yes. Yes, I do."

"I suspected as much." She looked at the closed door one more time, a hint of hesitation in her eyes.

"We just need to get to the other side, Emmy. I think it is beyond the courtyard, where the pits are. I'm certain of it."

"There it is again, that relic hunter confidence and intuition."

Twillo winked at her. "It is one of my defining features."

The door creaked open and Twillo rushed out with his sword drawn. He sent a blast of dragonessence towards the first archmage. It blew the cloaked mage backward and drew the attention of the others, all of whom turned in Twillo and Princess Embla's direction.

One of them swooped down at the pair, magical sword drawn. Embla whipped the weapon out of its hand using Scaled Lash. Dragonflight took her into the air, where she grabbed the archmage by the neck and stabbed it numerous times with her dagger.

She was a whirlwind of action and he soon caught up with her, torching one of the archmages with Firebreath. Twillo stepped aside to avoid a spear of dragonessence. Had it not taken the mage a moment to form the weapon, he might have been skewered right there.

But as always, luck was on his side.

Twillo struck this mage down with his sword, and used the bag of armor to crack another one across its hooded face as it dipped in for an attack.

Spectral wolves appeared, the beasts much larger than the ones that they had encountered underground. They seemed to be coming from the pit area, which Twillo was certain was where he would reach the portal.

"The portal!" he called to Princess Embla. They could fight the enemies, or they could just get out of the area. It soon became clear that they would be overwhelmed if they stayed around.

Twillo swung his sword at some of the walls as he charged forward. Embla landed in front of him and took off as well, the two running at their full speed. He could feel his enemies on his heels, the wolves trying to bite, the mages firing bolts of dragonessence.

"That's it," Twillo said as he noticed the same structure they'd seen in the last round. It was surrounded by monolithic stone, the portal vibrant and covered in runic carvings.

They reached the portal and disappeared.

Twillo's and Princess Embla's bodies reformed back in the main chamber. They fell to the ground. Twillo rolled onto his back and let out a deep breath. "I cannot believe…"

On her back as well, Embla draped her hand over Twillo's chest and let out a deep breath. "How insane was that?"

"What has happened to the two of you?" Seondzus asked, her voice strong in Twillo's head.

"We have just taken a trip that I'll be piecing together for weeks." Twillo sat up, the armor jangling. "Do you hear this?" he asked the princess.

"I do. It seems like you've gotten lucky."

"Yet again."

"You have armor, I see," Adventus said as Twillo got to his feet. He started putting the pieces on. Princess Embla helped. Once the chest plate and epaulets were snapped into place, she stepped back, placed her hands on her hips, and took him in.

"Not bad, right?" Twillo did a complete circle.

"For a Prince Ravenna, no? For anyone else, it's a bit much."

"Where did you uncover this armor?" Seondzus asked.

"From her father's bedroom."

"That sounds salacious."

"Nothing like that," he assured the red dragon. "Why don't the two of you join us?"

Adventus and Seondzus formed into existence, both dragons in their warrior forms.

Seondzus approached Twillo and looked down at him, the red dragon a full head taller than the relic hunter. "It's not bad," she said as she knocked her fist on the armor. "Actually, you said it was from her father, right? The Ravenna?"

"That's right," Twillo said as Princess Embla turned away.

"He probably didn't have cheap armor made for himself."

"No, he did not." The princess approached the wall at the front of the chamber. Her hand glowed and the wall of stone shifted aside, revealing a new passage.

"Well?" she asked Twillo. "We've come this far."

"We certainly have."

"We could also go back up and see if Anneli wants to join us."

"We could. But we are here now. Let's see if there's another portal first. If that is the case, we will do just that. Better to have three people than two in these scenarios." He paused.

"Let me guess. Be ready for anything?"

Twillo grinned. "You took the words right out of my mouth."

"If this is a battle we must face here, you will be at an advantage," Adventus said.

"I suspected so."

The four of them pushed ahead, and traveled down a long hallway without the lighting like the last chamber.

Because of their companions' lack of night vision, Embla produced a light using dragonessence, a whispery lamp now hovering just over her shoulder.

"I did not know you could do that," Twillo said.

"I still have a few tricks up my sleeve. What about you, relic hunter?"

Seondzus laughed at Princess Embla's quip. "Never underestimate a Ravenna."

"I'm not a Ravenna yet. But soon."

Her title, her birthright, was something Embla wasn't too keen on. It was in the realm of the necessary evil, at least the way that she spoke of it. But would she actually be different? If Twillo were to join her, if that was even something he should consider, what would be expected at that point? Could he really come back from the proverbial grave and help rule the kingdom up north?

And what about the royal court? Surely they wouldn't be happy about the sudden reemergence of Jhaeros Shotaro Vos. There would be betrayals, double crossings that he normally associated with a group of people like that, all vying for attention and power.

Even the thought that he would actually entertain this idea, of marrying his childhood friend, seemed outlandish. Had he really taken things to the point that he was ready to hang up the mantle, as it were?

They came to a new space, one with a raised platform in the center. Even though there was no opening above, a spotlight shone down onto the platform, revealing a wristlet in a bowl carved out of stone.

Twillo and Seondzus drew their swords as a being stepped out of the darkness and into the light.

The male being stood over seven feet tall, its stone skin the same color alabaster as the statues back in the portal realm. A series of complex, glowing sigils ran down the length of the being's arms and pulsed with an ethereal light. While its body was stone, it still wore a cloak made of fabric, the thread platinum with a hint of sparkle to it.

You've completed the two trials, it said, the being's voice echoing through the chamber. It didn't move its lips as it spoke, yet Twillo could hear it loud and clear. *The power of the ziggurat is yours.*

As it said this, channels of light opened above Twillo and Princess Embla. He recognized this sensation instantly. It was the one he felt when his powers were recharged and amplified. Thinking about his status caused it to flash in front of him.

Name: Jhaeros Shotaro Vos
Tier: Apprentice
Rank: S
Class: Martial Arts Mastery
Rank: C
Secondary Class: None
Tertiary Class: None
Dragonessence: 400/400

It was quite a sum, four hundred points. Yet he still hadn't improved his Rank or his Tier, which was something that bothered him.

The being made of stone gestured to the wristlet on its pedestal. *One of you may take this. It will unlock the power of the dragon known as Vendir.*

Twillo had heard the name before. It was the name of the capital city of Icenor, where Princess Embla lived. Like the other dragons, all aside from Adventus, they had been memorialized across the Four Kingdoms.

"Well, I don't have any wrists left," he said once Princess Embla didn't immediately take the wristlet.

Even though this was a serious moment, Princess Embla couldn't help but grin at Twillo. "I suppose you don't. And Vendir is a city I'm quite familiar with."

You cannot remove the wristlet once you have worn it. You will be soulbound.

"Soulbound." There was no hesitation on Embla's part. She approached the pedestal, removed the wristlet, and placed it on her left wrist. The jewel glowed as she quietly confirmed something. There was a change, a flourish of dragonessence around her that took Twillo by surprise.

She wasn't going to be able to summon Vendir in such a small space, at least not in his dragon form. The princess would have to go to another ziggurat to access the vordic form and then the dragon warrior.

"Vendir," Seondzus said as she nudged her counterpart. "It has been ages. He is quite like you."

"Me?" Adventus asked her.

"You know, loyal to a fault, stoic, a bit irritable around the edges."

"You've spent too much time in the Realm of the Forgotten."

"As have you, old friend."

The man made of stone slowly tilted his chin back. He looked up at the ceiling, as if he could see something.

We are safe here.

"Safe?" Twillo asked. "Safe from what?"

They have arrived, those who would like to use the power of this ziggurat for malicious purposes.

"Are you saying Jecha is here?" Embla looked from her new wristlet up to the stone guardian, her eyes wide.

He is. And I believe your companions are doing what they can to prevent his entry into this sacred passage.

"Then we have to join them," Twillo said.

You will also be safe here. He cannot get through the walls if they are closed.

"No," Twillo told the guardian. "I think we have seen enough of this place." He turned to Princess Embla. "What do you think?"

"We do what we can, with the goal of leaving as quickly as possible and heading toward the harvest mountains."

"Right," Twillo said.

The final ziggurat? the guardian asked. *That will be challenging indeed. You should know something else.*

"Yes?" Twillo asked.

Whoever unlocks the final ziggurat will unlock all the dragons.

"All of them?" Adventus asked.

Yes. This is the way that it was set up. Many of them won't join with the God of Carnage, but as a few of you know from the past, several have been persuaded before. It is best that you hurry.

Twillo bit his lip. "We should go there tonight. No sleep."

No, you should rest, the guardian told him. *In his human form, Jecha must rest as well. You have more time than that, yet your time is slowly dwindling. Good luck. May Livia guide her robes over your journey.*

With those words, the stone guardian turned away from the pedestal and disappeared back into the shadows.

Chapter Seventeen

Frozen

TWILLO AND PRINCESS EMBLA bolted up the stone stairs, Seondzus and Adventus just a few steps ahead of them. The two dragons would have taken their vordic forms, but the hallways in the underground ziggurat were too narrow, forcing them to do it on foot.

They reached the top and the dragons burst out, Princess Embla hanging back with Twillo.

"It'll be just a moment, Emmy!"

"Hurry, Jhaeros!"

His brow furrowed in focus, Twillo used Warding Glyph to charge the side of the wall. Once they were clear, Twillo fired a bolt of dragonessence at it with his sword.

The blast that followed brought portions of the wall and later the ceiling down. This, coupled with what the guardian below had done by locking the doors, would prevent Jecha from ever reaching the inner space.

"I'm going!" Princess Embla summoned her dragon and took to the air. Vendir was similar in color to Adventus, something between white and silver, but he was much smaller, which seemed to make him faster as the two rocketed toward the main fight. Ramide and Nalig were already doing their part, the black and green dragon clashing with Senja warriors. This left Katashi, Anneli, and Ariosto to deal with Jecha and some of the elven orcs.

Twillo rushed toward them, his only focus now on Jecha, who wore sweeping black robes over thick armor.

He activated his dragonaura for additional protection and used the Dragonflight mudra to move even faster.

Twillo landed directly in front of Jecha and swung his sword. The towering God of Carnage easily shrugged off his opening attack. Perhaps Jecha would have landed his next strike too had it not been for Ariosto, who came in with an amplified punch that blew off a chunk of his armor.

Jecha stumbled forward.

Twillo hit him with Ripple Tide, which pushed him back but ultimately didn't whip him off his feet. Jecha rushed forward and grabbed Twillo by the neck. His hand was struck down by Ariosto, who flitted in with one of the fastest chops Twillo had ever witnessed.

Even with all this effort though, his rapid-fire strikes and swift kicks, the warrior monk was finally taken down by Jecha, who cracked him across the face with the hilt of his sword.

Jecha twisted his hand in the air. A group of sand wraiths came alive, the dirt-cloaked creatures lifting from the ground. "You will be consumed today," Jecha said, his voice breaking through Twillo's resolve.

His words had a way of shattering his confidence, forcing Twillo to second guess what they were doing.

Could they actually do it? Was the God of Carnage himself an opponent that a mere mortal like Twillo could even defeat?

The odds felt as if they were entirely stacked against them.

Twillo backed away, suddenly unsure of himself.

His fears were interrupted by the sand wraiths, who came whirling toward him with sharpened stone claws. He managed to beat away some of their attacks, but was quickly overwhelmed by wraiths, Twillo only barely managing to get away using his Dragonflight mudra.

He landed twenty yards away from the fight.

Upon turning back, he spotted Adventus using his enormous glaive to clear out some of the elven orcs.

Adventus turned ruthless, the armored dragon warrior swinging through them with ease and scattering their ranks. Seondzus was right there with him, her sword a blur of fury and strength. Yet a few of the orcs were also holding their own, protecting Jecha even though they should have been easily toppled by the two dragons. It was like they had been boosted by his mere presence, Jecha's sheer bloodlust.

How? How had Jecha come across such strong warriors? And how were they able to take on opponents much stronger than them with relative ease?

To amp himself back up, Twillo sent a blast of dragonessence at Jecha. The God of Carnage shifted toward him, the red bits of his sword glowing as he returned fire.

Twillo tried to block it, yet was unable, the bolt of dragonessence quickly bringing him to his knees. It kept him static, Twillo unable to move. He struggled to press himself away, only to be defended by Katashi, who jumped in his way with both his swords drawn just as Jecha approached.

The kitsune flourished his blades and went to work, spinning into action without fear, his fox tail flailing as he came in for whip-fast strikes.

Jecha blocked them with relative ease, as if Katashi was moving light-years slower than the God of Carnage. Both hands on his sword, Jecha stepped around Katashi and brought his blade to the side, hacking into the kitsune's shoulders.

"Katashi, no!" Twillo shouted. He tried to move, yet he remained frozen in place.

Twillo spotted Vradon on the outskirts, the warrior monk fretting, gathering up the courage to try to save Katashi. But Twillo knew there was no saving Katashi, not with Jecha's next attack, which saw him running his sword straight through the kitsune's midsection and pulling up, spilling his guts.

Jecha kicked Katashi's body to the ground, and used both hands to drive his sword into Katashi's back, finishing off the kitsune.

"Damn you!" Twillo shouted, the relic hunter throwing everything he had into moving. He remained frozen, held by Jecha's incredible power.

Anneli wasn't, though. The elven orc, who had been fighting off several of her brethren, turned to the God of Carnage, a madness in her eyes that Twillo hardly recognized.

Jecha seemed to appreciate it, however. He seemed to gather energy from the way that she now hated him, Anneli seething, her chest heaving up and down, muscles bulging as she sized him up.

"Do something, Adventus!" Twillo cried. "Don't let her—"

It was too late; Anneli had already charged toward Jecha.

It was as if he was witnessing a nightmare unfold, Twillo well-aware what was about to happen, how Jecha would simply shift to the side and cut her down using her own blind anger as his momentum. And he did just that, the God of Carnage causing an enormous wound that extended from her shoulders down to the small of her back.

What made it worse was how unceremonious her death was. Jecha didn't care for these people, he didn't have a relationship with them, nor did he know of their past, their failures and triumphs. They were simply obstacles in his way. And he responded like she was an obstacle. He delivered one more strike as Anneli tried to stagger to her feet, killing her.

The energy holding Twillo finally released itself, yet he could no longer move. Shock washed over his shoulders due to the deaths that he had just witnessed. Anneli and Katashi. There was a part of him that felt like he should have done something, Twillo barely able to push it away.

He could do something now. Or at least he thought he could.

His feelings on what he should do next changed when Jecha summoned both Katashi and Anneli, who got to their feet, their eyes completely black. The wounds that he had given them stitched up immediately, tethered together by a dark dragonessence as their skin paled. Yet the blood was still there, and the dead look in their eyes was something that Twillo would never be able to swallow.

"Your dragons are now mine," Jecha said. Even though Nalig and Ramide put up a fight, they were ultimately returned to their owners' wristlets, which glowed and shook, the two dragons trying to free themselves. "They will adjust," he sneered. "The rebirth of the Age of Dragons is mine. It will be a rebirth of carnage, but this is an integral part of the cycle of existence. My brother recognizes this, your Father Dawn. He might not admit it, but he knows it to be the case. And there is only one ziggurat left now. After that one is unlocked, it won't matter what you have done here. What is it like? What is it like to lose?"

"We haven't lost yet," Twillo said.

"I am a fan of beings who can change themselves, grow with time. You are not one of those beings, Jhaeros. You've only fallen. You had a chance to join me and Renda, but you turned it down. Just because you haven't seen your failure yet, doesn't mean it hasn't already happened. Dragons were once used by the rulers of your world, and this will come to pass again."

Princess Embla landed next to Twillo, her mana-powered dagger drawn. "Are you ready?" she asked Twillo.

Her words invigorated him. The doom he had just been feeling instantly dissipated. "Ready."

"Ariosto will handle the rest."

And with those words, as if Embla had conjured the wind herself, huge spirals blew through Jecha's ranks, shredding the sand wraiths and blowing his soldiers and dragons aside.

"Vendir, to me!" Embla said as she grabbed Twillo's hand.

Inspired by her sudden action, Twillo called Seondzus and Adventus back to his wristlet.

As the sand swirled in a frenzied cyclone around them, Embla led Twillo to their campsite by way of

Vradon, who had seemingly been there all along. They grabbed their things, including Katashi's pocket shelter. Holding the relic reminded Twillo of what just happened, how Jecha had killed the kitsune in cold blood. It made him want to go back to the battle and fight Jecha to the death, yet he had to trust Princess Embla. Clearly, she had a plan.

"Dragonflight," she said. "We must go. Summon your dragons once we land. Follow me." The princess bounded toward the southwest using Dragonflight.

"Hold on," Twillo told Vradon.

"Hold on?" Rather than explain, Twillo hugged the monk and the two took to the air, landing on the outskirts.

"My word, Jhaeros!"

"Wait here." Twillo quickly summoned his two dragons, which were now in their normal forms. The wall of wind had culminated in a barrier of sand, one that even Jecha couldn't break through. It left Twillo wondering about Ariosto.

Where was the warrior monk? Would he survive this?

His questions were answered a few moments later as Ariosto appeared. "It's a mudra," he said, his intensity now on the raging wind beyond, his hands trembling. A strong breeze continued to batter Jecha and his soldiers, the wind now carrying rocks with it as well.

Twillo turned to Vradon. "You know where the final one is, right? The ziggurat?" The monk had already told him this, but at that moment, Twillo was slightly delirious from all that had happened. He wanted to know that they still stood a chance.

"I do, the Harvest Mountains."

"Then that is where we will go." Ariosto dropped to a knee.

"What's happening?" Twillo asked as he came to the warrior monk, his conical hat falling to his back.

Strain appeared on the warrior monk's face, his features twitching, eyes shifting into two straight lines. "The sandstorm will buy us some time. It is my cleverest invention."

"Your what?" asked Princess Embla who had just summoned her dragon almost as an afterthought, Vendir taking his place next to Seondzus and Adventus. All of them looked like they were ready to fly.

Ariosto pursed his lips and let out a deep breath. "I created the storm so that it follows them. If they try to leave, wherever they go, the sandstorm will join them. If they try to fly, it will bring them back down. There is little that Jecha can do to thwart it. But it won't stop him. He will eventually find a way to disrupt it. And then he will get the information he needs out of Katashi and Anneli."

"He will be thoroughly disappointed. They only know that it is in the Harvest Mountains, nothing more," Vradon said. "I kept its exact location to myself."

Twillo remembered that Vradon had been on the verge of attacking Jecha. While foolhardy, he knew that the monk would have sacrificed it all to save his friends. It was an aspect about Vradon that he appreciated, but he was glad that he had thought otherwise. Vradon was the only one who knew where the final ziggurat was located.

"Good. We can discuss everything later and mourn those who lost their lives here today," Ariosto said. "We need to go."

"Relic hunter, you're with me," Seondzus said. "Adventus can carry the other two. Vendir, Her Royal Highness is yours."

"She is, indeed," the male dragon said, his voice prim and proper. "To the Harvest Mountains, yes?"

Twillo nodded. "To the Harvest Mountains. We'll regroup and go from there. And mourn. This is it. We're coming up on our last shot." Sadness filled his heart, yet there was nothing he could do now. "We have to move on."

Chapter Eighteen

Harvest Mountains

THE DESERT BELOW was stark and quiet, harsh even in the pale moonlight. At points, Twillo became mesmerized by the shadows of the three dragons. It was easier to watch the shadows float over the dunes below than it was to process the devastation he felt in his heart, the sheer disappointment in himself, the sheer rage at Jecha for what he had done yet again.

First, Olaf. And now Anneli and Katashi. But there was something else that he couldn't quite understand. Twillo wasn't the kind of person to lose his emotional touch on a battlefield. There was the adrenaline, sure, but the doom he had felt back there was something new. It was more than this feeling that they were going to lose. It was this sense of inadequacy, of abstract failure.

At some point during their flight he caught a glimpse of Ariosto, who was seated on Adventus' back alongside Vradon. The warrior monk had taken more of a cat form in his face, ears, and whiskers, yet there was a hardened look of determination in his eyes, one that Twillo knew that he should replicate.

But what if he lost the willpower? What had actually happened back there?

Maybe it was exhaustion. Fatigue from the challenges he had just faced in the portals. Yes, fatigue. It had to be something like that. It wasn't like Twillo to give up hope in that way. And who was he to give up hope? The Goddess of Luck was on his side, guiding her endless robes over his journey in profound ways that he would never fully understand.

He had to trust. Twillo had to believe that this was possible. And they still had a chance. If they could clear the final ziggurat, they would have the upper hand.

They reached the foothills of the Harvest Mountains. From the vantage of the dragon's back, the world continued unfurling over the harsh landscape below. The sand from this view was similar to the ocean in the way that it lashed against a rocky shoreline, reminding Twillo of the eastern coast of Middling and the great stone formations that separated it from the land.

Yet there was something different here, a dry coldness that worsened as the temperature dropped and the air pressure changed. Twillo started to see hints of snow scaling the peaks below. They definitely didn't have the kind of gear that would be necessary in a range of snowy mountains, but they had the pocket shelter.

Adventus found a space to land, the other two dragons following suit. As soon as Twillo was on solid footing again he set up the pocket shelter. He placed it on the ground and stood by while it grew. Soon, the relic was large enough for all of them to climb down to the platform below.

"We will speak again in the morning," Twillo told the dragons. They returned to his wristlet. Vendir did the same, Princess Embla's wristlet glowing for a moment before she joined Twillo.

"It is freezing," Vradon said as he headed down to the pocket shelter. Twillo and Princess Embla followed, leaving Ariosto to join them at the back. The platform below was exactly as Twillo had remembered it: a glowing hearth and a comfortable space where they would be able to sleep. He didn't like the fact that there were no barriers along the edge of the platform, but they had other things to worry about. Namely, how they would reach the ziggurat tomorrow.

Vradon sat, and began going through his things so he could gather his notes, Princess Embla joining him. As they sorted, Twillo removed his bags and his sword and turned to Ariosto, who stood by the edge of the platform, staring out at the void.

"One year ago."

"One year ago?" Twillo asked the warrior monk.

"Exactly one year ago, I met a young man who had a pocket shelter himself. His name was Jaden and he was an arcane cultivator. I recently saw him again, which was nice. But at the time, a year ago, he was attacked by thieves and ended up tossing several of them over the side of the platform."

Twillo looked at the great expanse of nothingness beyond. "He tossed them over the edge?"

"They tried to rob him and he acted swiftly, as any one of us would."

"What exactly would happen to someone if they went over the edge?" From the edge of the platform, Twillo looked up to the opening of the pocket shelter. It was a space he would never be fully familiar with.

"If they went over the edge? I do not know. I would assume that they would fall forever. The eternal plummet itself would be beyond any torture that one person could inflict upon another. But Jaden didn't do it out of malice. As I said, they attacked, and he responded. Anyway." Ariosto turned to Twillo. "What's on your mind?"

"How do you know something is on my mind?"

"Something should be on your mind considering what has just happened. I only wish there was more that we could have done to prevent it."

"There is certainly more I could have done. I could have used more Arcane Cards. Or perhaps I could have summoned Yasuna to help me. Or maybe I could have used my paintbrush." Twillo ran his hand along the paintbrush he had sheathed at his waist, a power he hadn't used as much lately. This was one problem with having so many tools at his disposal. Some got left to the wayside.

Ariosto didn't ask about the paintbrush or its power, and it was a moment before he spoke again. "We all have regrets. But don't let them eat at you. Is there something more that you feel?"

Twillo took a step closer to Ariosto. "I feel like Jecha did something to me. He affected my willpower. He made me feel hopeless, my sense of purpose completely drained."

"He made you feel like your only option at this point is to give in. Does that sound familiar?"

"It does. And then he was able to keep me from moving. How am I supposed to combat someone like that?" Twillo asked Ariosto. "How are we supposed to stop that?"

"Jecha has our access to Arcane Cards, same as you. Being able to control the emotions of your enemies is a powerful thing. You aren't normally one that would feel this way, no?"

"No, I'm not."

"Then you should assume that it was Jecha's influence. As for keeping you stationary, there are various dragonessence techniques that could do something like that. How did he do it?"

"Through his sword. He fired a bolt of energy at me, similar to what I'm able to do with mine."

"Yes, that power. It will be something that you have to avoid unless you are able to learn Voidshift."

"Voidshift would help me against an attack like that?"

"It is meant to absorb other attacks. Were you to wield it correctly, you would be able to simply absorb his nullifying strike."

"Then that is what I will do." Twillo felt the doom he had experienced earlier finally leave him, as if it were being sucked out of his body and fired into the nothingness beyond.

He turned to Vradon and Princess Embla, just as the monk looked up at him. "As I was telling Her Highness, I have the key to open the ziggurat. I should clarify—I mean that I can solve the puzzle. But I don't know exactly where the ziggurat itself is. It could be in one of two locations from what I have uncovered," Vradon said as he pointed at a crude map.

"Perhaps it changes based on the season," Ariosto surmised.

"You think? I was wondering why, or how I kept coming up in two locations." He launched into a detailed academic discussion of Sagic words, one that was well above Twillo's head. "Actually, that makes sense," Vradon said, answering his own query. "*Season's shift*. It is another translation of this particular phrase." He tapped on some of the script. "Season's shift."

Ariosto nodded. "We will ask the locals."

"Locals?" Vradon looked up at him. "People actually live in these mountains?"

"They do. There are small nomadic tribes and the locations they frequent. Think of them as small villages. They usually have a place that they stay most of the year, aside from the high summer. So they are less nomadic than they were, say, five hundred years ago. But they still get around and they will know. We will find some of them tomorrow. I will speak to them. They will show us the way."

"You think?" Vradon asked. "They would know of something like this?"

"A powerful structure that keeps changing locations would definitely be something they noticed." Ariosto was quiet for a moment before he spoke again. "The people that live in these mountains. They aren't like the rest of Southfall. They are a unique group, mystical in their own ways. A bit more superstitious and, well, you'll see once we encounter them."

It felt wrong eating Katashi's food, yet they needed sustenance, and it was best not to send Seondzus out even if she really wanted to go. As he drifted off to sleep, Twillo wondered if there was a way to tell Katashi's people of his death. It was rare to meet a kitsune, yet he now knew that they had a network all across the Four Kingdoms, shared homes as well.

Then there was Anneli, who had a brother that was part of the Honor Guard. But Twillo didn't know his name. He only knew how she had done her best to get away from him. So maybe that chapter was best left closed.

Twillo had a dream that night that he was back in the tavern in Padrian Sands, where he had first met Anneli. They flirted. He continued on his way to the wolvencree's lair to barely survive, only to return to the tavern and discover that the Tongue of Ravenna Megren was missing.

What followed was an adventure, the kind that he was used to going on up until this point. He used everything at his disposal, his basanic fire, Gloves of Maruth, his Enkiro Ring of Animation. Surrounded by enemies, Twillo blew the ground shell of a yandori snail into the air, creating intense visions. He escaped with trollen smoke, Twillo always one step ahead of the people he was pursuing even if he was also being chased by others.

It was a maddening dream, one that became cyclical, hard to wake up from.

He was in the Tribute Islands cliff diving, using the Gorget of Illagorn to explore sunken ruins. Then he was in Southfall, sand and wind whipping all around as he rode a camel through No Man's Crossing. He was in the deep green woods of Middling encountering enormous yokai, the likes of which most people had never seen before. And he was on Icenor's western coast, in Sorzol, planning to explore glacial crevices, where he heard rumors that there were forbidden relics discarded by a disgruntled archmage.

Twillo couldn't wake up.

The adventures came, he took them, anything to not pause and see what he had become, what he had made of his life.

When Twillo finally broke through his fever dreams the next morning he did so with a quick breath out. The inhale that followed was one that he truly savored. The nightmare was over, only for the next one to begin.

Vradon and Princess Embla were still sleeping, yet Ariosto was up, the warrior monk seated with his back to Twillo, conical hat over his head.

"Bad dreams?" he asked without turning to Twillo.

"How did you know?"

"I looked at you earlier and you were sweating."

Twillo brought his hand to his forehead and wiped some of the sweat away. "So I was."

"I'm glad you're awake," Seondzus said from somewhere at the back of his mind. "I wanted to wake you once you started twitching, but you-know-who wouldn't let me."

"Humans and elves behave in peculiar ways during rest," Adventus told her. "You know this as well as I do. How many hours have you spent watching people sleep?"

"Too many..."

Ariosto stood. The warrior monk approached the ladder that led up to the top. "Are you coming up?" he asked Twillo.

Twillo didn't respond. He merely got to his feet, grabbed his sword, and joined him.

A light snow was falling outside of the pocket shelter, something at odds with the desert they had been in the last several days. Twillo took a spot across from the warrior monk, who was in his half-human, half-cat form.

"No need for your blade, not yet. Let's work on mudras. But before you do that, let's warm up. It's cold. I'll teach you a technique that warrior monks do in environments like this, a way to cultivate inner warmth. It's necessary sometimes in the desert, especially with the light robes that we wear. Water harvesters too." Ariosto hopped from foot to foot; it was then that Twillo realized that he was barefoot.

"Do you think we will run into any more water harvesters up here?"

"They don't often come to the mountains, and they certainly wouldn't be here during the spring. If anything, they come up during the heat of the summer to search for water veins and deal with disruptive pockets of dragonessence. Remember, those can gather and create things like rock daemons, sand wraiths, and other creatures I pray you don't encounter in the near future."

Ariosto moved his hands through the air as if he were kneading something. He summoned his dragonessence core, and held it outside of his chest for a moment. It was brighter than any core Twillo had ever seen, so bright in fact that he actually looked away for a moment.

"He is incredibly powerful," Adventus said.

"Not powerful enough to defeat Jecha. Don't forget that," Seondzus told her counterpart.

"The God of Carnage versus a bakeneko who has lived a long time? He is still mortal. You're too quick to judge."

"I'm merely pointing out the obvious."

"Quiet," Twillo told the dragons. "Sorry, continue."

"Access your core, pull it out of your chest, and notice how much colder it is," Ariosto said. "This is a way to condition yourself, to realize just how much warmth you naturally possess. Once you've noted this, place it back into your chest and start fanning the flames, as it is known by taking short, staccato breaths."

Twillo did as instructed, each breath fast and tight. For a moment, he felt foolish standing out there in the cold breathing quickly. But then he noticed the warmth spread over him, as if he were sitting by a crackling fire. He exhaled, and could see his breath. How could he feel so warm yet be so cold at the same time?

"Nice, right?" Ariosto asked. "A great way to warm up. Now, place your sword down on the ground over there. Let's begin. Follow my lead. Tsuh!"

Ariosto performed a series of practice punches and knees, the warrior monk working to an internal rhythm. Twillo tried his best to match his patterns. Soon, he found himself able to fit right in with what the warrior monk was doing, Twillo even anticipating his next moves.

They both activated their dragonauras by tapping the back of their knuckles, which Twillo noticed amplified all of his strikes.

"Now, cycle," Ariosto said. "Pull back the energy just as you are about to release it."

Twillo did this as well, warm to the point now that he almost wished he could take the top of his robe off. A thought came to him as he continued following the warrior monk's lead.

There was one way Twillo knew to celebrate the lives of those he had lost. He didn't know what these villages in the mountains would be like, but if there was an option there, he would take it. He had to honor Anneli, Katashi, and Olaf in the only way he knew how.

"Focus," Ariosto said, as if he could read the look on Twillo's face, like he knew that the relic hunter's mind had drifted. "Time to learn Voidshift. Both fists back, thrusting forward, Voidshift."

Ariosto demonstrated what he meant.

Twillo saw a spherical vacuum of power flash and settle. He knew that in a real battle this would be less visible. Twillo had seen warrior monks spar before through the pilgrimages they often took in the coastal cities. They would set up, look for challengers, and grow their skill the old-fashioned way, through sheer guts and bloodshed.

He knew what it looked like when they kept striking one another, each absorbing the other's power. It was mesmerizing, yet he had never noticed a spherical vacuum of dragonessence, one that looked like a shield had formed and quickly faded. He was certain that Ariosto had shown him this to help him better understand what the power actually looked like.

And for some reason, it helped.

It took Twillo a few tries, but at some point during their session, he pulled his fists back and thrust them forward, Voidshift activating. Twillo stumbled backward, and then kept his arm up as if he were holding a shield.

"Yeah?" he asked, excited.

"Let's see how strong it is."

Ariosto came forward with a kick. Twillo went in to block it. Much to his surprise, and even though it seemed as if the kick was about to land, it didn't. It was as if Twillo had pressed the kick away, to the very threads of reality itself.

He had successfully deflected the warrior monk's attack.

"Now, release it," Ariosto said. "Release the stored power."

This made sense to Twillo. The dragonessence was stored in some void, one that he controlled. It wasn't hard for him to simply let go, which caused a wave of force to rush forward. Ariosto jumped out of its way.

Now crouched, the warrior monk looked up at him, clearly pleased. "See? It wasn't that hard. Now do it again. And after you do it that time, again."

The training became relentless, Twillo activating Voidshift a couple dozen times and releasing the power before Ariosto was finally willing to move on. By the end, he felt a new wave of confidence, which was something he desperately needed.

"Is Voidshift listed in your mudras now?"

"It is," Twillo said as he checked his status:

Name: Jhaeros Shotaro Vos

Tier: Apprentice

Rank: S

Class: Martial Arts Mastery

Rank: C

Secondary Class: None

Tertiary Class: None

Dragonessence: 316/400

[Arcane Cards]

Arms of Vikan Wood, Level 2

Codex Vault, Level 1 [Passive]

Core Eruption, Level 2

Enchanting Deception, Level 2

Eternal Cycle, Level 2

Firebreath, Level 2

Flash of Fata Morgana, Level 2

Nadakunai's Might, Level 2

Ripple Tide, Level 2

Vard's Blessing, Level 2

Warding Glyph, Level 2

[Mudras]
Dragonaura, Level 2
Dragonflight, Level 1
Scaled Lash, Level 1
Voidshift, Level 1

Twillo could see how the new mudra would be helpful, especially in the fight that was to come. Yet he still hadn't reached the next Tier.

But at this point, how much did it matter? Either they reached and completed the final ziggurat before Jecha arrived, or they didn't. That was all that mattered now.

Chapter Nineteen

Mountain Ink

THE DRAGONS TOUCHED DOWN in the shadow of a snowy peak. This was by design. They didn't want to scare the people that called the Harvest Mountains home.

"Hopefully, they haven't already seen us," Ariosto said as he floated off Adventus' back. He stopped just before reaching the ground.

Vradon jumped down, landing in a patch of snow. He stood and dusted himself off, the snow nearly up to his knees. "It won't be easy to travel that way," Ariosto told him as the wind began to pick up. Several tendrils twisted down Vradon's arms and legs and yanked him into the air.

Vradon looked down at his hands, the way that he was now hovering. "This is so strange." Twillo floated down to join them, as did Princess Embla. The dragons returned to their individual wristlets and the group forged ahead, Ariosto in the lead.

"It really has been ages since I've been in this region," Ariosto told them. "If it weren't for the signs, I wouldn't even know where to start. These people are quite hidden, you know."

"The signs?" Vradon asked. "What should we be looking for?"

Ariosto pointed to certain clumps of snow. Upon further examination, Twillo saw that these were actually stone cairns, and not small ones either. The boulders that had been moved into place were impossibly large, but it was clear that humans had done it. How long ago was another question entirely.

"How did people move those?" Vradon asked.

"Stoneshapers did. They are the water harvesters that are able to control rock and mineral veins. I don't know if I already mentioned this, but most harvesters come from these mountain communities. Not all of them. Some are from the main cities, but many grow up in semi-nomadic ways. Which makes it easier for them to become harvesters. Anyway, this is the path to one of their winter villages."

Ariosto shifted ahead. Because he was controlling the wind that was hovering Vradon, the monk trailed after him. This left Twillo behind with Princess Embla.

"How are you holding up?" she asked once the two of them were alone.

"Doing better now, I guess. At least I'm doing better than I was last night. Still trying not to dwell on what happened but I'm still angrier than I have been in years."

"Anger isn't going to help us here. Strategy is. What is our strategy?"

"Strategy? Strategy for what?" Twillo realized that this question wasn't as clear as he would have liked. He tried again: "Are you referring to the ziggurat, or Jecha himself?"

"We have no control over the ziggurat or how it will challenge us. That seems to change every time, at least according to you."

"It does. So you are referring to Jecha."

"I am. We are going to be able to beat him."

"She doesn't know that," Seondzus said, but only Twillo could hear her.

"What are you suggesting?"

"I'm suggesting that we need a strategy. I don't actually have one." Embla gave Twillo an almost bashful smile. "I'm sorry. I just want to put this thought out there. To say that I don't think that we will reach a point in strength that will allow us to stop him, even with Ariosto, isn't something I would like to tell you. But it's true. Jecha is an all-powerful being. He is the God of Carnage."

"Noted," Twillo said.

"Were you really going to play it by ear?"

"I usually do," he told the princess. "But you're right. In a situation like this, especially after what has happened, we will need a new kind of plan. One that may be a bit unorthodox."

"We still have time."

"Yet we don't know how much is left."

"Ariosto said that the windstorm he created will follow them around for another day or so," she reminded him. "Even if they know where to go, they're not going to be able to reach us in that time."

"So then we clear the ziggurat first. And bring the fight to him?"

"Bring the fight to him? You are confident, Jhaeros."

"No, I'm delusional. I'm merely throwing out options here. If you want a different one, I'll give it a try."

"By all means," she said as they came around another stone formation, one that was large enough to be a statue. It was clear that it had been placed there by humans, but Twillo couldn't quite understand the significance of the piece, if it was actually a statue, a monument, or simply a stoneshaper showing off their powers.

"How about this, Your Highness? We fly to Vendir and tell your father what is happening. He gathers all of his archmages and they, as well as the dragons, and any saracents able to soulbind, rush south to deal with Jecha by way of Middling. And yes, by doing this I'm suggesting that we would loop in Emperor Otonashi in E'Kanth, and get the entirety of the Four Kingdoms on our side. It would be the battle of the ages, one that would shepherd a new dawn for the Sagaland."

"You are beyond saving at this point."

"Beyond saving at this point? I wasn't asking to be saved," Twillo told her, a grin forming on his face. "And what's wrong with being a bit beyond. If we were anything close to normal, we would have likely died by now."

"You forget about the Goddess of Luck."

"I've yet to forget about Livia, and never will. She is my patron, after all."

Princess Embla laughed. "I think the mountain air might be getting to you now."

Twillo took a big breath into his nostrils. "It's crisp, I will say that. But you know what the winters are like up north. This might be cold, but it is nothing like that. Nothing."

Ariosto turned to them and they quickly caught up. "We've reached the outskirts of the village," the warrior monk said. "I will go ahead and lead them out to greet you. No more floating now. We are one with the people here."

"Back to the snow it is." Twillo lowered down. He stepped over to Vradon, and patted the monk on the shoulder. "How goes it?"

"I'm still trying to figure out how I feel about floating. And who would have thought it snowed this much in Southfall?" Vradon kicked at the white stuff. "It's a different kind of snow, however. Did you see the texture?"

Twillo scooped some of the snow into his hand and noticed it was powdery, not as thick as the snow they had up north.

"I do hope these people are hospitable," Vradon said as he crossed his arms over his chest. "I could go for a warm meal. Perhaps a nice stew."

"I hope they have a tattoo artist."

"Do what now?" Vradon asked, suddenly disturbed by Twillo's comment. He gave the relic hunter a baffled look. "Did you say what I think you said?"

"A tattoo artist."

"Ah, so my ears don't betray me. Are you being serious right now?"

"I'm wondering that myself." Princess Embla elbowed Twillo. "Don't you have enough tattoos? Are you sure you don't want another piercing instead? Wait, you have too many of those as well." She smiled at him. "I'm teasing you, Jhaeros. At least about the piercings. I like those. The tattoos, on the other hand, you certainly have more than any Icenordian I've ever seen before. Vradon?"

"Yes, but I have seen relic hunters with more. So maybe we are judging him against the wrong people?"

"No, this needs to happen." Twillo turned to Vradon. "And I'm going to need your help."

***

Ariosto approached with a pair of Southfallians, a man and a woman, both of them with weather-beaten faces held together by a fine crosshatch of wrinkles. Twillo took in the fearlessness in their eyes, which spoke of the conditions they had lived through, and how living through them together had made the group stronger.

"Greetings," the man said, his voice soft to the point that it was at odds with his stern demeanor. He was a commanding figure, tall and rugged like the mountains that he had lived in his entire life. The man had strong brown eyes and his long, brown hair had curls of white in it, his skin a light shade of ebony, evidence of his time in the sun.

The woman was equally captivating, slender and petite. Yet something told Twillo that she was much stronger than she looked. Her hair was auburn, braided into strands and tied off behind her ears. Her hazel eyes reminded Twillo of the way an Icenordian's eyes looked in pitch black, a gleam to them that was complex and calculating.

They both wore brown robes that bordered on maroon, thick, but not as thick as he would have expected for the people who lived so high up in the mountains. Had they visited a similar people in Icenor, mountain dwellers, as they are called, they would have found elves that were heavily bundled in furs and leathers. But the clothing worn by the two standing before them more resembled something an Icenordian would wear in early fall.

"This is Torin Spirit, and his wife, Rhea," Ariosto said. "It has come to my attention that perhaps Livia is still at play here."

"What do you mean?" Twillo asked the warrior monk.

"My student, Jaden, the one that I mentioned was competing with others in the Tournament of the Gods. These are his parents. They thought their son was dead up until about five minutes ago. But he is very much alive. And he is on his way to becoming a celestial champion," Ariosto said, which brought a warm, yet sad smile to both of their faces. The woman's almond-shaped eyes were suddenly wet. She looked away.

"You know Jaden?" Torin asked Twillo.

"No, they don't know your son," Ariosto told him. "But I'm certain they would support him in his endeavors. We are all here for another reason. But I wanted you to meet the Icenordians before we discussed this with you all."

"Another reason?" Rhea asked, after official introductions were made.

Vradon stepped forward. "We are looking for something. I have details, but I will need to retrieve them from—"

"The place we keep things," Twillo said, not certain of how much they should reveal about a relic like the pocket shelter. He knew from experience that it was a highly sought after item.

"Come, and don't be worried if the children give you strange looks," Rhea said. "None of them have ever seen Icenordians before. There are adults in our group who haven't seen Icenordians."

They passed under a long arch, one that looked to have been created by a stoneshaper, eroded over time. It was here that Twillo caught his first glimpse of their mountainside village. The people had carved into portions of the mountain itself, utilizing natural caverns and crevices to blend their homes perfectly into the range. Aside from fires, and smoke coming out of small, circular chimneys, Twillo was fairly certain if they had flown by that they wouldn't have spotted the village.

It was multitiered, and while everything clinged to the mountainside, there were flatter stretches beyond, the formations yet again human and natural. Twillo saw that they had terrace farms, where farmers and their children busied themselves cleaning snow off the crops. He didn't know what grew on the terraces, but whatever it was, it must have been hardy.

As they reached what Twillo would describe as a central plaza, the kids began to gather. They were scrawny yet strong, wild-looking things with flushed cheeks and curious faces. They instantly began speaking to one another quietly about the Icenordian ears, some of them making exaggerated gestures with their hands and laughing.

Vradon seemed to take offense at this, the monk lifting his chin up in the air and holding his head proud. His incredibly long hair, which was braided and wrapped around his neck, quickly took center stage. Some of the kids even tried to mimic this using their scarves, which they wrapped around their heads.

"They're going to remember this for the rest of their life," he said in a defeated undertone.

"Don't let it bother you," Twillo told him. "Have fun with it. Watch." He turned to the children and approached them. "Ever met an Icenordian before?"

The young girl he spoke to shook her head.

"Well, now you have." Twillo got down onto a knee and extended his hand to her. She looked to another one of the children, perhaps an older brother, for approval. He gave her a nervous shake of his head and she pushed back into the crowd.

Another child came forward, slapped Twillo's hand, and darted away.

The other children began to laugh. Twillo calmed them down by showing them his palms. "Ever seen anything like this?" He reached in his bag and found a small bottle of basanic fire. He sprinkled a little out onto the ground, producing purple flames right there on top of the snow.

It didn't melt. And soon, the children became curious.

"What kind of fire is that?" one of the younger boys asked.

"It's not a fire at all." Twillo reached in his bag again. He found his bone goggles he used up north for covering long distances of snow, which blocked some of the light that radiated off the white surface.

He placed the bone goggles over the bridge of his nose.

The younger boy who had spoken earlier crossed arms over his chest. "We have those too, you know."

"You do?"

Almost in unison, the children all produced similar goggles from various pockets on their robes. They placed the bone goggles over the bridges of their noses, and a few of them stuck their tongues out at Twillo.

"See? We share something in common."

"Not the ears," an older girl told Twillo.

"They just allow me to hear you better." He turned his ear to them, and the children laughed. One of the older ones, a teenager by the looks of it, came forward with a young girl whose cheeks were cherry red from the cold. Twillo noticed that the teen had a fresh tattoo on his hand. This also made him realize something else: most of the children weren't wearing any gloves, and none of them seemed especially cold.

"That tattoo," Twillo said as he was turning away. "Where did you get that?"

"The artist lives there." The teenager pointed at a home several tiers up.

"Good. I need to get some work done myself." To illustrate what he meant, Twillo pulled up his sleeve and showed the children all the tattoos on his arms. They came in close again, including the teenager.

"You really are something else," Seondzus said.

"It's good that he normalizes relations with Icenordians."

"How did I know that you were going to say that?" she asked Adventus.

Before the two could continue the conversation in Twillo's head, he bid farewell to the children and joined his companions, who had gathered near what he was certain was some type of signaling tower. There was a large fire here and seating. As Twillo approached, he saw Vradon getting the confirmation from Ariosto that he could reveal the pocket shelter.

"I need to show them what I'm looking for," Vradon told Twillo. "Also, I should say, Jhaeros. You certainly have a way with children."

Twillo glanced at Princess Embla, who had a softness in her eyes as she looked him over. He shrugged. "I try to be friendly when I can. It goes a long way. As for the pocket shelter, will they actually want to go down there with you?" This question was meant for Ariosto, who would know more of the hillfolks' customs.

"They have a place that they can take you," Ariosto said before he returned to his conversation with Torin and Rhea. It seemed to be about their son.

"In that case, let's do this somewhere more private. I don't want the children knowing about this," said Twillo. While some of them had scattered, others still stood on the periphery, curiously watching the Icenordians talk. He'd already seen some of the girls try to mimic the way that Princess Embla wore her hair, and he heard them discussing the color. He knew better than to pull out the pocket shelter here.

After a little discussion with Ariosto, they were led to a private space inside a spacious cabin. Vradon was able to get the documents that he needed, which he showed to Torin and Rhea. They discussed them for a moment, and then asked if Vradon would be able to visit some people with them.

"Certainly, I would. I am a representative for the group. But I would ask that we would be able to eat something soon." His stomach grumbled, almost as if it were in agreement. "I'm sorry, but I haven't had a warm meal in a while."

Seondzus laughed. "He's not cut out for this kind of life."

"No, he's not," Twillo said under his breath. But this was fine. It wasn't a life for everyone.

"My apologies, I thought we were clear," Torin told Vradon. "When visiting these homes, we will be required to eat at each place. That is our tradition. So you will be overly full by the time we return here. And the rest of you can either stay here or head to the communal fires outside. There will be food brought to you."

"One of the teenagers mentioned a local who was good at tattoos. Would that be something that is available?" Twillo asked.

Torin didn't seem at all surprised by the statement. "Yes, that is Batt. He used to live in Middling."

"Where exactly?" Princess Embla asked. "I thought most of you stayed in the mountains."

"No, some of us leave," Rhea said, the woman touching her chest. "I was gone for a while as a warrior nun."

"And I was gone for seven years as a water harvester," Torin said. "An aquaseer of the Breakers sect. Batt was like me, a water harvester. And once he reached his Rite of Fulfillment he took his payout and spent several years in E'Kanth."

"City of Dragons," Rhea chimed in. "He always likes to call it by its nickname."

"He returned, and was provided a place in our society. So there has been a growing interest in tattoos, especially among the younger men. I thought our son was going to get something that one time," he said, a comment meant mostly for his wife and Ariosto.

"But the desert mages would have prevented it. No identifying markers." Ariosto registered the confusion on the Icenordians' faces. "Once they become water harvesters—"

"I understand now," Vradon said. "Their memories are stripped. If they had tattoos, perhaps of someone's name, then it would eliminate the effectiveness of this part of the ritual."

"Precisely," Ariosto said. "And it isn't a cruel ritual, even if it seems like it is. That doesn't mean it doesn't have its faults. The problem with the ritual is when someone doesn't class. But that is a discussion for another time, and perhaps something we don't even need to touch on in the coming days. Let's visit the people you need to visit," he told Torin and Rhea. "And by the morning, we will know where we need to go."

"Vradon, before you go," Twillo said. "I need you to write a few things down for me."

"Is this about the tattoo you were wanting?"

"If I told you it wasn't, would you believe me?"

"Certainly not, Jhaeros."

"You're really going to make me go with you to get this, aren't you?" Princess Embla asked the relic hunter.

He waved her concern away. "It will be fun, trust me."

The tattooist began by selecting a handful of vibrant mineral stones from a collection that he kept on the shelf. Batt, who was hunched over and had a beard that nearly reached his navel, had already taken payment, Princess Embla's treat, even though the money was from the coins they took from Romulus.

"So in that way, Romulus' final gift," Twillo told the princess as he got comfortable.

She laughed. "The things I get into with you."

"This really is *the first beam of the solstice dawn*," Twillo said, which was a verse from an Icenordian poem often spoken before important decisions were made. He liked using these kinds of phrases with her, ones that only an Icenordian of a certain classes would be familiar with. They were playful, and he could tell that while she feigned dislike, she secretly enjoyed it.

"You plan to write poetry after we finish in the mountains here?" she asked.

"No, I plan to go to the Tribute Islands. I have information about a haunted doll there."

"A what now?" Embla asked as the tattooist began grinding some pigments together on a weathered stone slab. Batt had already explained the colors, how each of them had a meaning to their group, and how it would take him a moment to mix them all up.

Twillo continued: "I received three leads from a friend of mine, a relic hunter. I followed up on two of those leads, and have been successful. The haunted doll was the third one."

Seondzus, who had been quiet up until this point, started to laugh. "So after you save the world, your plan is to go after a haunted doll?"

"That's the plan," he said, not wanting to reveal to the tattooist that there was a dragon speaking to him in his head.

Princess Embla sighed deeply. "A haunted doll."

"A haunted doll."

"Why would anyone want something like that?"

Twillo looked at her incredulously. "Because it is haunted. Because it might do something. Because it could be helpful. There are too many reasons for me to list right now, Your—"

"No, don't call me that." Princess Embla smiled over at the tattoo artist. "If he calls me anything like Princess, or Your Grace, or Your Highness—"

"—Your Ladyship, Your Regalness—"

"—He's teasing me. I'm nobody."

"We're all nobody," the tattooist told her as he continued mixing the pigments together.

"And everyone likes a haunted doll," Twillo added.

"So that is actually your plan after all of this?"

"Thinking about it."

"How deeply have you thought about it?"

Twillo shrugged. "I kind of like to see things to their completion. I now have the other two objects that I was looking for, a paintbrush and my brooch. There is one more."

"The doll."

"The doll."

"And then you retire?"

"I think I'm ready for my tattoo now." Twillo rested back on a mat made of leather. He closed his eyes and listened as the tattooist finished his ink base.

Batt crouched over him. He had a sharp bone needle fixed to the end of a wooden handle covered in runic carvings in one hand, and a hammer with its tip wrapped in leather in the other.

"Is there anything else you need?" Embla asked, which was a strange question to ask a tattooist. Twillo didn't comment on this.

"As I told you earlier, I am familiar with the script. These three people will live on, close to your heart." With those words, Batt began hammering the needle onto Twillo's pectoral muscle. The sharp, stinging sensation quickly prickled across Twillo's chest. It was a crisp and clear pain, yet the steady drumbeat of the precision tapping had a way of reverberating through his body, which created a soothing cadence at odds with the sharp bursts of pain.

Twillo began to feel an almost electric tingle spread across the marked area. He knew to stay calm. He also knew from past experience that there was pleasure in this pain, that it was a way to hone his mind and his tolerance.

Every time the pain intensified, he thought of the three that he had lost.

His favorite memories of them, from his first encounter in the caravan with Katashi, how he had told the kitsune to be less flashy, to Olaf the monk, who had always shepherded Twillo. Anneli, her humor, her grit. He wished he had gotten to know her better. He felt the same way for Katashi, who had given up a life of leisure to join them in their fight against the God of Carnage.

The pain grew, but Twillo never gave in to it. Instead, he listened to a storm that was brewing in the mountains, the one that was preventing them from leaving that night. It grew stronger during the tattoo session, but he tried not to take this as an ominous symbol.

Livia was on his side. His friends were close to his heart. And they would soon unlock the final ziggurat.

"You will need to let this heal for several days," the tattooist said as he finished up.

"I have something for that," Twillo told the man as he slowly sat up. He leaned against the wall of his cavernous home. Even though his shirt was off, Twillo didn't feel cold. There was the warmth of a fire not far from them, and also the burn of his new tattoo.

Olaf, Anneli, and Katashi.

Twillo looked down to see his new ink. He felt a sense of elation as he continued to celebrate the lives of his friends. As his chest throbbed, he accessed his Vard's Blessing card.

It immediately began to heal.

"So that's how you have so many tattoos," Batt said as he came forward, a balm now held between his ink-stained fingers. The man himself had zero tattoos, at least not to Twillo's knowledge. This wasn't the first time he encountered a tattooist like this. There was a school of them in E'Kanth who had no visible tattoos, yet their torsos and every part of their body from the upper thigh to the shoulders were covered in ink.

"I never actually used this power on a tattoo before," Twillo said. "But it works. And thank you. What do you think, Emmy?"

Princess Embla let out a soft sigh. "I think it looks great, Jhaeros."

HARMON COOPER

Chapter Twenty

Ice Foxes

SINCE THEIR CURRENT CLOTHING wouldn't suffice, Torin and Rhea provided something more appropriate for the mountains. Twillo, Vradon, and Princess Embla now wore dark robes made of a thick wool with a detachable hood lined in fur, same as the mountain people. Ariosto kept his normal robes, but when they were in private, as they had been in the large cavernous space they slept in that night, he went for his half-human half-bakeneko form to stay warm.

It was morning now, and they were prepared to set out once they received final instruction from Torin. The group sat around a fire enjoying a morning soup, one with steam lifting off its surface. The watery soup consisted of boiled goat fat and some mountainous root that tasted like a potato, yet was much chewier. It wasn't the greatest thing Twillo had ever eaten, but it was filling, and he could tell it was meant to sustain energy over long periods of time.

"Sleep well?" Vradon asked, who had just started on his second bowl of soup.

"The robes were warm. Like being wrapped in a blanket," Embla said. "So, well enough. Jhaeros?"

"I slept fine."

"Are you a side sleeper or a back sleeper?" Vradon asked him.

"Side. But sometimes I end up on my stomach. Why?"

"That tattoo would have hurt had you fallen asleep on your stomach."

"Yes, it would have." Twillo took a sip of his morning soup and winced at the flavor. "But I'm fine. With this card, I could get as many tattoos as I'd like." He drummed his hands on his chest. "See? Completely healed. Good as new."

Ariosto, Rhea, and Torin approached before Princess Embla could say anything more about the relic hunter's tattoos.

"So, as discussed yesterday," Torin began, "the way that you would normally travel to reach this ziggurat is blocked right now because of an avalanche. But there is another way."

"I really don't like the sound of this," Vradon added, which wasn't the first time he had voiced his concerns. Twillo had already heard the plan, but it appeared that Torin wanted to hash it out again. As the man had explained previously, they were going to use a cave to bypass the avalanche. The only drawback of this route was that it channeled them through a unique feature known as an ice tunnel. This natural phenomenon formed annually, a result of sudden snow accumulation around the rocks of a specific peak.

"And the ice tunnel is bad because dragonessence pools in this place," Rhea said, "which can spawn creatures that wouldn't normally be strong enough to take a physical form."

"Sort of like sand wraiths," Ariosto said.

Rhea nodded. "Yes, very much like sand wraiths. Nasty devils, they are."

"And we can't just fly over it all because the ice tunnel will give direct access to the entrance of the ziggurat," Ariosto said, careful not to mention their dragons. "Where the puzzle is, at least according to your sources." He motioned to Vradon.

"Let's hope the scholars of the past are good sources, because otherwise, we're putting ourselves into a very risky situation for nothing. Not that visiting your people hasn't been something," Vradon told their hosts. "And at least one of us got some fine tattoos from it."

"The ziggurat is there. The key to opening it is another thing entirely," Torin said. "Anyway. If you're ready to leave for the cave, I can take you there now."

"Yes, let's get on with it," Seondzus said in Twillo's head. "You're not going to finish your soup it seems, relic hunter, and we've got dragons to free. You might give them a warning about what could happen."

Twillo nodded.

Once they started on their way, he pulled Ariosto aside to relay what Seondzus had told him. The warrior monk, who now wore his conical hat and had a scarf tied under his chin, merely grunted a response. It took them about an hour, but they eventually reached a cave at the bottom of a gorge, one with very steep walls.

Torin, who traveled with a large walking stick, dug it into the snowy ground and leaned his weight on it. "There. Head through the cave, the ice tunnel, and you will reach the ziggurat. We will keep your lodgings warm should you return tonight. I suggest you return. The mountains at night are quite dangerous. The temperature drop alone can kill you."

"Thank you," Ariosto said as he joined Torin. He walked a few paces away with him and the two spoke privately. Twillo didn't know exactly what he told him, but by the look on Torin's face, it was clear that he was heavily invested in the conversation. It was likely more about Rhea and Torin's son, Jaden, the arcane cultivator currently competing in the Tournament of the Gods.

"Well?" Twillo asked once the warrior monk returned.

"He will prepare his people, and he wishes us the best of luck." Ariosto motioned toward the cave. "Shall we?"

Twillo had once read an Icenordian poem that described the entrance of a cave as a yawning portal of icicles, a cold invite into a realm of perpetual winter. These words came to him as he pushed ahead, Twillo whispering them and trying to remember where he'd first heard the poem: *"Through a stifled vernal, in the heart of frost's embrace we tread, yawns the mouth, a door of icicled dread. An invitation to the winter internal, in the cavern's chill, mysteries yearn infernal, yawn eternal."*

The walls around Twillo were so translucent that it looked as if they were venturing through a hall of mirrors. The air was crisp and dry. It smelled of fresh snow, the thick ice instantly muffling the sounds of their footsteps.

"Oh my," Vradon said, his breath visible. He nearly slipped, yet Princess Embla caught him just in time. "Thank you, Your Grace!"

"Please, call me Embla."

"He won't," Twillo said as he moved around them.

From what he could tell, their path had just switched its trajectory, where it would gradually lead them up to its inevitable exit. While it should have been dark in the cave, and perhaps it would have been had this been a normal cave, the snow and ice reflected light throughout, illuminating the space.

It was mesmerizing in this way, ethereal.

Twillo had explored an ice cave before, years ago when going after a relic near the Icenordian city of Bravelon. But the depth of that cave had paled in comparison to this, and it had been less foreboding.

They heard a crack and Princess Embla gasped. "The places we find ourselves," she said as she lowered the hand she'd placed over her chest.

"We should be quiet here," Ariosto told her. "Treat it like another realm."

"Adventus and I could do a number on a place like this," Seondzus commented. "Vendir would surely join us. Ugh. I miss Vendir. We haven't had a chance to really catch up. He's much friendlier than you."

Adventus growled.

"See what I mean?" she asked as Twillo moved on, half-listening to the dragons in his head.

They reached a portion of the cave that had holes above that led to the surface. These had been clogged with ice, yet the sun had melted them to some degree, which created something that resembled numerous spotlights. It was a mesmerizing visual, one of many that Twillo would try to hold on to as long as he could.

Yet he knew with this order of beauty, of natural magnitude, an encounter was in order. This place was magical, and because of its magic, there was bound to be treachery.

They reached this treachery in the chamber that followed, one that opened up to what Twillo assumed was the ice tunnel.

It started with a crackling sound as several piles of ice and stone. The beings, which resembled foxes, all stood at the same time, their fur a cascade of frozen shards.

"By Livia," Vradon said as he stepped behind Twillo. "If you have a weapon I could—"

"Do not worry," Twillo told him as he drew his sword, the tip rimmed with dragonessence. Twillo fired off his first shot, which went wide and struck the side of the cave at the point that it met the ice tunnel. This caused a series of fissures to spread forward, which sounded like a malleted Icenordian instrument.

"Careful of your powers," Ariosto hissed. "We do not want to die in this ice tunnel this close to our goal."

The warrior monk whipped forward with a strike that shattered one of the ice foxes. Bits of ice spilled off to the side as the other foxes all gathered together, baring their teeth as they prepared to attack Ariosto.

One jumped for him. The warrior monk kicked it to the side, where Princess Embla finished the fox with an amplified punch.

Several of the foxes pressed forward, their tails fanning out into sharp plumes of rigid frost. The first one spun and Ariosto jumped away to avoid its attack. Twillo came in fast with his sword, which he used to cut its tail off. The sound instantly caused him to cringe, the stark, chilling note echoing through the tunnel of ice.

Twillo pressed away as another fox flitted toward them and met its demise once Ariosto smashed it with a sudden heel kick.

Whoosh!

Princess Embla fired a twist of dragonessence at the next fox, the Crown Ravenna careful not to let her strike go wide and hit the outer wall of ice.

One of the foxes brought its tail over its body and fired blades of ice at Twillo and Ariosto. The warrior monk managed to block the first round using something akin to Voidshift. Seeing him activate this inspired Twillo to do the same, yet attempting the mudra caused him to slip onto his back.

The *umph!* that followed had Twillo reeling, the pain flashing through the relic hunter as he lost his sword. A smaller fox jumped right on top of him, its icy breath and serrated teeth mere inches away from Twillo's face. The fox exploded into a mist of ice as he hit it with Core Eruption, which he'd put on deck in case they needed to blow their way through something.

Princess Embla used Dragonflight to launch herself straight through this explosion, startling Twillo as she went up and over, landing behind the foxes. She destroyed another and then another. Ariosto came through in the end with a series of strikes that finished off the rest.

"Recharge," Ariosto said as he motioned to the dragonessence now hovering in the air.

Vradon approached and offered Twillo his hand. "You alright, Jhaeros?"

"I'll be fine." Twillo found his sword and sheathed it. He shook his hands out, took a few deep breaths, and began absorbing the lingering dragonessence in the air. Once he was topped off, he joined Ariosto and Princess Embla, who were already waiting to journey through the tunnel of ice.

"How much longer do you think we have?" Twillo asked as he caught up with them.

"It can't go on for that much longer," said Vradon, the monk off to the side with his hood over his head. His heavy breaths caused puffs of white fog to appear around his head. It was clear that this was stressing him, yet Twillo was proud of Vradon for sticking it out with the group. This wasn't a life he could have ever grown accustomed to, yet he'd done well in a short amount of time.

"The ice tunnel won't go for very much longer, I don't think." Ariosto squinted at the ice. "Hopefully, there won't be any more foxes."

Chapter Twenty-One

Onward, into the Dungeon

THEY CONTINUED THROUGH the ice tunnel until they came to a grand monument, one covered in snow. Pillars had been erected around what resembled a court, perhaps a point of worship. The group cleared some of the snow away, revealing a large scatter of Sagic words carved into emerald-colored tiles.

"It is exactly as the texts say," Vradon told them, the monk excited now. He used his foot to kick away some of the snow directly in front of him and set a piece of fabric down, where he arranged some of the sketchings he had made and the notes that he had taken.

Vradon began slid the stone tiles into place, painstakingly going back and forth from his diagram to the text. "Some of the words are so old that even I can't translate them," he told Princess Embla as she joined him.

While he rearranged the tiles, Ariosto explored the area. They were completely enclosed by the ice tunnel, yet it became evident that they were on some semblance of a ledge off the side of one of the mountains. It only made the fact that the ice naturally formed this way even more wondrous.

"What a strange sight," Twillo said. "And they told you it does this every year?"

"That's right," Ariosto told him. "There are other ice tunnels like this in the mountains. They said that one of the groups that lives closer to the western shoreline actually lives within one of the tunnels and collects its water during the melting season."

"It sounds bitterly cold to me," Vradon said as he continued rearranging the tiles.

"I'm sure it is. Even with thick furs," Ariosto said. "But they must do it for a reason. The western slopes are known for the wind that they get. It is said to be the birthplace of galecallers. I would posit that this is why they take refuge in the tunnels. A cold wind would only make things worse."

"It would," Twillo said as he joined Vradon and the princess. "How is the translation coming?"

"This won't be translated. But it will be put into place correctly. And from what I can tell thus far, we are missing two tiles." Vradon, who was on his knees, looked up at Twillo. "Without the two tiles, I do not think that this will work."

"Two tiles?" Twillo approached one of the tiles Vradon had yet to place. He picked it up and examined the emerald piece, noticing the way that the words were etched into the stone. "Then they have to be around here."

"I was thinking that myself. I figured I would arrange everything first so we can see exactly what we could expect. But—"

"I may have a better solution." Twillo produced the Pathweaver's Compass. "Find me the first tile." Saying these words caused the needle to twitch. It pointed toward the left. Twillo approached the hardened wall of ice. "I think I can burn through it."

"Do what now?" Vradon started to ask.

"Let me join you," Adventus said.

"I could join as well," Seondzus added.

Twillo took a look around at the space that they had. "No, just one of you. Adventus is fine."

Seondzus groaned, but ultimately didn't say anything as the towering dragon took his warrior form. He approached the ice as well and drew his glaive, the end of which ignited with a blue fire. As carefully as ever, Adventus pressed into the solid wall of ice. He carved a door large enough for the two of them to fit through and pushed the chunk of ice forward. "That should do it."

"Yes, it should," Twillo said. "Let's find this first tile."

The snow blew past them as they headed out into the tundra. As Ariosto had surmised, they were on a great stone ledge, which forced Twillo to hover down to the next pass. Looking back at the ice tunnel, it was almost like a giant snake had died in the mountains, its body wrapped around one of the jagged peaks. An incredible formation.

While Twillo hovered over the snow, Adventus trudged through it, the dragon tall enough that his feet were actually able to reach the ground. He carried his glaive at his side, always at the ready.

Twillo kept his focus on the compass. There was more buzzing now, and he knew they were close to one of the tiles. They reached a cave, one that was barely visible in the snow.

"You think this is it, Left-Handed One?"

"I'm certain." Twillo floated inside, his eyes scanning the darkened depths. He saw his first skull and his heart jumped. He wasn't expecting it, and he especially wasn't expecting to see the way the skull had been staked to the ground, jaw hanging open and now covered in ice. "By Livia."

"What was this place?" Seondzus asked. While the ice hanging over the mouth of the cave opening made it impossible for Adventus to enter, Seondzus was privy to what Twillo was seeing.

"Some sort of graveyard," Twillo surmised after he saw more skulls. At first he thought they were staked to stones, but as he floated just a bit closer, he saw the points that were pressing out of the eye socket. These were ancient swords. "I wish we had more time."

"To do what exactly?" the red dragon asked.

"Explore. Finding something like this tells me that there are also relics in the area. There have to be. Whenever there are ancient peoples, I generally find something of value."

"You really can't shake your obsession, can you?"

"Obsessions aren't made to be shook," Twillo said as he hovered until his feet were completely horizontal. He closed his eyes and saw dragonessence lingering in the air. It was brighter in a section just a bit further back, where he caught the subtle outline of a square. Twillo reached forward and found the tile. He took it quickly, and joined Adventus outside.

"Good find."

"It is a good find," Twillo said. "And that means there's only one more left in the area. Let's return this one to Vradon and continue."

They reached the ice tunnel and came back in through the entrance Adventus had made. Just as Twillo had hoped, Vradon was completely done with the puzzle aside from the two missing pieces. The monk took the tile from Twillo and slotted it into place. "Perfect, Jhaeros. Just one more."

"Where was it?" Princess Embla asked.

"Some sort of graveyard where there were skulls staked on swords. I don't know what happened here."

"People have called these mountains home for a long time," said Ariosto, who hovered in the air with his legs crossed, his tail curled behind him. He had seemed to be in a deep meditation until Twillo had mentioned this detail. "I wouldn't be surprised if there were entire mountains made of skeletons."

"What a horror. Let's hope not," Vradon said.

"Find the next tile," Twillo told the compass. He left the ice tunnel alongside Adventus and floated to another mountain pass, following the compass yet again. This time their path took them much further than Twillo would have liked. This, coupled with the snow that brought flurries, made it nearly impossible to see where they were going.

"You will be able to use that relic to get us back, right?" Adventus asked as it grew increasingly hazy around them.

"I believe so. Worst-case scenario we have to take to the sky and find them that way."

"I don't like flying in the cold."

"Then tell him I can fly," Seondzus said. "If he's going to complain about it."

Twillo didn't relay the message.

The two started up a slope, one peppered with large stones. They came to a new place, which reminded him of the sacrificial location they had found in the Oto Mountains. There was an altar here for executions, and grooves in the stone cut for blood to flow freely.

Twillo saw more of the skulls which were frozen, all masks of horror. It was as if the snow didn't want to stay on them for long. Yet he expected this had something to do with the wind.

"We are close," he said as he began searching around the area. There was a passageway that was partially covered by a stone. It was pretty clear that he could shift to the side and head down. Had he had more time, Twillo would have done just this, especially with Adventus there to help him.

For now, he had to focus. Twillo was there for one thing, and one thing only, even if he was certain there were relics in the vicinity. As he searched around, Twillo kept coming back to the pile of skulls.

"Let's move the skulls," he said as he pried some of them away. They were frozen to one another, and he wasn't strong enough to do it without relying on dragonessence. Luckily, Adventus took over, the big dragon able to break through the ice with his glaive and easily shove it to the side. He dug for a few moments before he finally reached the tile they were looking for.

"I believe this is it," he said as he showed Twillo the piece.

"It certainly is."

Twillo took the tile from Adventus. He looked out at the horizon, at the way the sun played tricks on his eyes up here, the endless stretch of white. It reminded him of Icenor, if there was something different about it, something harsher.

He stared at it for just a moment longer and started back toward the others. The ziggurat awaited.

The ground shook once Vradon put the tile into the correct slot. They all took a step back, wary of the top of the ice tunnel overhead as the platform itself rose from the ground.

The tiles Vradon had arranged began to move in a counter-clockwise pattern. Twillo heard a grinding sound, like gears were being moved. Once the sound stopped, he examined the structure in front of them, not quite certain of where the door had opened up. The front-facing piece was still the tiles that had been rearranged, but now they were in a different position because of the way they had moved.

"It's on the side," Ariosto said.

Twillo joined him to find a doorway, one with a small set of stairs leading down. "Adventus, to me." The white dragon returned to the wristlet and Twillo moved into the stairwell followed by Princess Embla, Vradon, and Ariosto.

"You don't think we will be sealed in here, do you?" Vradon asked.

"I don't believe we have a say in the matter," Twillo told him.

"We won't be sealed," Princess Embla assured him. "We have dragons with us."

"Tell her that we're not miners," Seondzus said. The noise of sliding stone behind them caused the group to stop. Twillo turned to find that the entrance they had just traveled through was now blocked.

"I believe that answers your question," Ariosto said as he started down the set of stairs again. "We are sealed until we do what must be done here."

"By Livia," Vradon said. "And to think that someone actually designed this trap."

"Father Dawn designed it, or at least he had humans make them for him," Twillo reminded him as they came to a long hallway. There were the same kind of lanterns here that he encountered before, ones that all activated with dragonessence. Twillo handled the left side, while Ariosto handled the right.

Now lit, Twillo noticed the hallway had been completely carved out of black marble with white veining. Creating something like this in any of the cities of the Four Kingdoms would have taken several lifetimes' worth of wealth.

"The craftsmanship," Princess Embla said as she came to one of the walls. She ran her hand along the outer surface. "And it's warm."

"It's warm?" Vradon approached and confirmed that the walls were indeed warm. He crouched and placed his hand on the ground. "The ground is warm as well. How?"

"We likely won't learn the answer to that anytime soon," Ariosto said. "Let's just remain aware of our surroundings."

Twillo thought back to how the entrance looked, especially when viewed from outside of the ice tunnel. He hadn't seen the entrance fully formed, but he got an idea of the rock that it had been carved in, the sheer size. A sprawling labyrinth likely lay ahead.

The long chamber they were in came to an end. The stone door shut behind them, indicating that they weren't going to be able to go back the way that they came. Even using something like Warding Glyph would do them little good. The stone was incredibly thick.

"I hate this," Vradon said as his teeth began to chatter nervously. "I really hate this."

"It isn't ideal," Ariosto said. "But we will survive."

"I wish I had your confidence."

The warrior monk grinned at Vradon. "It has kept me going through the ages."

The room beyond had a glow on the other end. There was another passageway, but the door was sealed.

Facing the glow, Twillo noticed that there was something behind it, as if it were a semi-transparent wall of energy. He also saw something else about this particular area. There was a strange shadow in one corner, one that didn't seem natural, especially with how well lit the space was.

"Do you see it?" Ariosto asked as he approached the glowing wall of energy.

Twillo squinted yet again. Beyond the wall was a floating gemstone made of the same energy as its protective barrier. He hadn't noticed it before because all that was so bright.

"Reach your hand in and grab it," Seondzus suggested.

"He may lose a hand doing something foolish like that," Adventus told her.

"Worth a try," Twillo said as he looked around for something to throw at the protective barrier. There was nothing, the marble floor completely clean. He took a small coin out of his pocket, an electrum, and flicked it at the barrier.

As soon as the coin hit, it sizzled and melted away.

"That won't work," Vradon said as he stepped to the right of the protective barrier. "Wait. There's some writing here." He leaned in just a bit closer. "Reciting these words will remove the barrier," he read. "I think I have a solution here!"

"I knew we kept him around for a reason," Seondzus told Twillo. "Tell him to recite the words so we can get on with it."

Twillo was about to do just that when the shadows shifted off to his left.

He wasn't the first to turn to them. Always a step ahead, Ariosto had already activated his dragonaura. The shadows lunged for the warrior monk, and he beat them back with an amplified punch. The shadow tendrils hit the wall, splattering away before regrouping to try again.

"Vradon, you must recite the words!" Princess Embla said as she joined the monk. "Do it!"

"Right. Um... *shadow of the sun, light in darkness, silence in the storm. Speak this truth*. Um... *Speak this truth, and reveal the heart of courage that lies within.* That's it. Nothing is happening."

Twillo struck a bit of the shadow with his sword, his mind racing as he tried to decipher what was clearly a riddle. *Shadow of the sun, light and darkness, silence in the storm.* What could it mean? What was the...?

"It's the moon," he told Vradon.

"Shadow of the sun, light and darkness, silence in the storm. Speak this truth and reveal the heart of courage that lies within. I am the moon." As soon as Vradon said this, the magical barrier started to trickle away.

The phrase did nothing to the shadow monster, which continued to lash at Twillo and Ariosto as they protected Vradon and Princess Embla.

"Get the gemstone!" Twillo said.

"I don't know if I should touch it with my hand," Princess Embla told him.

"Handle the shadows and I will get it," Ariosto told Twillo. The warrior monk twisted away as Twillo took center stage. He wielded his father's sword with expert precision, cutting any of the shadowy tendrils aside.

The shadows were like the ash warriors in the way that they continued to converge upon them, constantly reforming. It was like fighting ink, yet there was little physical tangibility in his opponent's body. Just movement.

A blast of dragonessence struck the mass of the shadows, which forced it into the wall yet again.

"Jhaeros, we must go," Princess Embla told him.

Twillo backed away from his opponent, never taking his eyes off of the shadowy devourer. He felt Princess Embla place her hand on his shoulder and guide him as he continued to swing his sword, cutting away inky tendrils. The steel door from earlier was now open. As soon as they passed through it, the door dropped, preventing the shadows from pursuing them.

"Did we get it?" Twillo asked as he finally turned to the others.

He found Ariosto with his palm turned over, the gemstone hovering over his hand. "I think we can touch it. But until I'm certain, I'm using dragonessence to suspend it in the air for now."

"Try pressing it against the wall," Vradon said.

Ariosto sent the gemstone to the marble wall. As soon as it touched it, they heard a sizzle.

"Perhaps I was wrong," the warrior monk said. "We won't be able to touch it. But I am certain that we will need it. I will continue to hold it like this."

"Good," Twillo said. "Hopefully, there aren't many more that we have to collect."

"You think this will be a scenario in which we must collect jewels?" Vradon asked.

Twillo looked ahead toward the chamber beyond. He ran his hand over the torches on the wall, illuminating the space. "I honestly have no idea. But that's what my gut is telling me, and I sort of have a knack for these things. Onward, into the dungeon."

Seondzus laughed. "I love that phrase."

Chapter Twenty-Two

Shadows and Apprehension

A TRAP WAS IN ORDER, yet it did little to disrupt Twillo and his companions' progress as the ground beneath their feet gave way. Only Vradon fell, Ariosto able to swoop down and catch him while maintaining the hovering gemstone.

"That would have been bad," Vradon said as Ariosto held on to him with an invisible lasso of dragonessence. "Real bad. Thank you."

Twillo glanced down into the pit. He could see the gleam of sharp blades all pointing up.

They were going to have to be hyper-aware of their surroundings going forward. The place and its challenges reminded him of a dungeon that he had once conquered in the Tribute Islands. He had searched the jungle for two days to find the place, Twillo having to deal with everything from venomous leeches to poisonous plants. What made matters worse was that he had received nothing for his endeavors.

Sadly, the relic had already been taken.

Yet the dungeon in the islands and the ziggurat they were currently traversing had similarities. There was a design element that Twillo couldn't quite put his finger on, the way the chambers were likely stacked on top of one another. Occasionally they would come to a set of stairs, head down, and then continue in the direction that they had just come. It was a feat of engineering, to be sure, but it was one that he wasn't a big fan of.

The layout was designed to thwart people, discourage them in a way. Yet Twillo and his companions pushed on.

They reached a new space, and as soon as they stepped into the room, the ground shifted. It rotated so quickly that they could barely get their bearings. It rotated again. It started to do this until it was moving quickly and sporadically, Twillo now uncertain of the direction that they had just come from.

"Which way do we go?" Princess Embla asked as the ground came to a momentary stop. "We came from there, right?"

"We came from there," Ariosto said as he pointed toward one of the chambers. There were now three options available.

"Wait," Twillo said as he got out his compass. "I swear, if I had had this thing years ago... What's the direction to the nearest gemstone?" The compass vibrated as soon as he asked this question. The needle twitched and finally started to spin rapidly until it stopped at the passageway on the right.

"Works for me," Vradon said as he headed in that direction. The portly monk shrugged. "It has been right thus far. If it's wrong now, then, well, I don't know what happens then. Ha! Am I the only one starting to feel a bit delirious?"

"Delirious?" Princess Embla asked as she caught up with him.

"Being trapped down here. You all have explored more of these kinds of locations than me. Am I supposed to be feeling like this? Jhaeros?"

"You certainly aren't supposed to be feeling as if this is in any way relaxing. Because it isn't."

"No, it is not. It doesn't feel relaxing in the least bit."

"But at least we know that it is here somewhere, the point that we need to reach. I can't tell you of the countless times I've explored long-forgotten locations only to turn up empty-handed. In that regard we are lucky. This is where it is, this is the final ziggurat."

"I would be so frustrated to turn up with nothing," Vradon said.

"Yes, I have been there, but it is part of the job description," Twillo told him as they came to a room in which the marble was polished to the point that it resembled mirrors. It was uncanny to see their elongated forms caused by the murky light and the smooth stone. The most troubling part was that there was no visible exit ahead.

"Maybe your compass was wrong?" Vradon asked.

"It has been right up until now." Twillo looked down at the compass to see that it was pointing toward one of the walls. "It's saying that we should go this way."

Twillo approached his own mirrored reflection. He reached his hand out to it. As soon as his fingers grazed the wall, he was transported to another room. For a moment, Twillo was alone, but then he was joined by Princess Embla.

"Where are we?" she asked.

"Your guess is as good as mine, Your Eminence. At least it isn't Sparrow's Rise."

"You really think it is another of *those* challenges, Jhaeros?"

"No way to tell, but I suspect not."

Ariosto appeared, followed by Vradon.

"Ah, it portaled us to another chamber." Ariosto approached the mirrored surface and was just about to touch it when he stopped. "What does your compass say?"

"Let me see." Twillo followed the needle to an opposite wall. "Here."

"I wonder what happens if we portal to the wrong area," Vradon asked.

"Hopefully, we don't have to find out," Ariosto said.

"Or we could just check for the fun of it," Seondzus told Twillo.

"Let's not."

They approached the next wall. As soon as Twillo touched it, he portaled to a new chamber, one with a floor that was also highly polished. He was about to step forward when he got this feeling that he shouldn't place his feet on the ground, aside from the stone that he already stood on.

Twillo floated up. As the others appeared, he had them float as well, Ariosto taking care of Vradon. The warrior monk still had the gemstone hovering in the air near him, which gave Twillo another idea. Could it be used as a weapon?

"This way," he said as he hovered across the chamber.

"You are afraid the floor may portal us somewhere, yes?" Princess Embla asked.

"I am. Call it a hunch."

"You are the expert here."

"Yes, I agree," Ariosto said. "You have been to more of these places than any of us."

"I don't know if I will wear that as a badge of pride, but hopefully my past mistakes will come in handy." Twillo reached the wall in question and once again checked the needle of the compass. "This is the one."

He vanished, and landed on the ground of the new chamber, one with a hardened stone floor. The space wasn't illuminated like the others had been, which wouldn't be a problem for Vradon and Princess Embla.

Once Ariosto arrived, he sent the gemstone forward, which provided enough light for them to see the murals on the walls. They depicted horrific images of sacrifice and slaughter by beasts covered in flames.

"By Livia," Vradon said as he approached the stone. "What war is this depicting? I've never heard of anything like this."

"Perhaps it was something before the Age of Giants," Ariosto said. "There were conflicts then, you know, and, at least according to warrior monk tradition, there were points that war almost brought an end to civilization. We speak about these, about ways to prevent them."

"It saddens me that most will never see a room like this," Princess Embla said as she scanned the grotesque art. "A reminder to us all of what we are capable of." She reached her hand out to touch a skeletal man, one who looked like he was half starved. "I hope we don't have much further in here."

"There's only one way for us to find out."

Twillo moved ahead.

What he didn't tell the group was that he had seen similar art before, although they were more recent depictions of Icenordians and the way they handled the Four Kingdoms after the Age of Dragons. There was mass slaughter, people were moved around, deported from their homes and stripped of their land. The Tribute Islands had numerous memorials to these occurrences, ones that had only been erected in the last hundred years or so after Otonashi's reign began.

Theirs was a troubling history.

Twillo and the others reached a circular room, one with the exit blocked by a wall of stone. This room had the same magical barrier from earlier, indicating they had found the next gemstone.

The shadow guardians moved into action immediately, Twillo just able to get his sword up in time to block their advance. "Decipher it," he told Vradon as Ariosto joined him.

"On it!" Vradon rushed over to the magical barrier with Princess Embla. She stood guard in front of him as he began translating the text.

"Try to use the gemstone," Twillo told Ariosto.

Still maintaining his control over the gemstone, the warrior monk sent it twisting toward the shadows. The shadows shifted backward, yet were unable to avoid his attack as the gemstone touched a bit of the darkness. Twillo heard a sizzling sound, one followed by an acrid smoke.

"Good," he said as he batted away another tendril.

Vradon mumbled something behind him as he worked out the riddle. *"The silence that screams, the hidden in sight, the dreamer that dreams. The silence that screams, the hidden in sight, the dreamer that dreams.* What do you think?" he asked Princess Embla.

"I'm not good at stuff like this."

"Silence that screams. Perhaps it is an echo?"

"I am an echo. *The silence that screams, the hidden in sight, the dreamer that dreams. I am an echo.*" When this didn't work, Vradon continued to mumble the phrase, as if doing so would somehow unlock the words in his head.

"Let me help them," Twillo told Ariosto, who continued to thwart the shadows' advance using the gemstone.

Ariosto delivered a dragonessence-powered chop to an approaching shadow claw. "By all means."

Twillo joined Vradon and Princess Embla. "Where are we at?"

"The silence that screams, the hidden in sight, the dreamer that dreams."

"Death," Seondzus said in Twillo said. "Death. It is the silence that screams, it is hidden in sight, and it is the dreamer that dreams."

"No, not death," Adventus told her. "It is the mind. Or the vastness of the mind. Try one of those, Left-Handed One."

"The silence that screams, the hidden in sight, the dreamer that dreams. I am death," Twillo said. When this didn't work he tried Adventus' suggestion. Twillo repeated the phrase again and added, "I am the mind," at the end.

This had the intended effect he was going for.

The barrier quickly melted away, leaving the gemstone ripe for the taking.

Twillo returned to the shadows with his sword drawn again. He fought them back as Ariosto moved forward to grab the floating gemstone. Once it was secure, the door that had previously been blocked shifted open. The stone slid into the wall, allowing Vradon, Princess Embla, and Ariosto to pass through.

Twillo joined them just as the door was starting to close again. He finished his action by firing a bolt of dragonessence at the shadows.

"Two gemstones now," Vradon said as he approached the pair of jewels. He observed them for a moment, the light that they gave off reflecting onto his face. "I'm going to guess there is a third."

"Things usually come in three, yes," Twillo said. "You're getting the hang of this."

"I'm practically a relic hunter," Vradon said.

"You are, you are. But we can't be too sure of ourselves. I do not know what we should expect here, but a third gemstone is a good guess."

"I'm still wondering what we're going to do with these gemstones in the end," Princess Embla said.

"If we fight an even larger shadow monster, they will certainly come in handy," Ariosto told her. "But maybe it is something we will have to exchange. There is no way to know at this stage. But we do know one thing."

"What's that?" Vradon asked.

"The way forward lies ahead. And there are certainly going to be obstacles. Hopefully, they will be manageable."

"That would be nice," Vradon told the warrior monk. "Imagine a ziggurat without challenges."

"Ah, that sounds wonderful," Princess Embla said. "Too bad that is not in our future. I might not be as prescient as Jhaeros over here, but I can tell you without a *shadow* of a doubt—yes, I meant to say it like that— there will be more trouble in store for us ahead."

"Alas. It was wishful thinking. Maybe that will be the answer to the next riddle. Wishful thinking." Vradon laughed to himself. "Wouldn't that be nice if I'd already solved the next puzzle?"

The next chamber was large and circular, with an unusually high ceiling. The room was illuminated by the flickering light of a purple crystal near the top of the ceiling.

"That's it?" Vradon asked as he looked up at the crystal.

"It certainly looks different than the others." Ariosto stepped ahead, the two gemstones they had already retrieved tailing him.

The warrior monk was right. The crystal that floated in the air in the center of the room was vastly different from the others. Twillo got the sense that there was something off about it.

"We should probably find the exit." Yet in scanning the room, Twillo didn't see anything that looked like a way out. There was only the way that they had come, which was partially blocked by a wall preventing the shadows from reaching them.

The sound of stone on stone caught all of their attentions.

Panels opened up above, and shadowy beasts dropped down into the chamber.

They were built like demon bears, not unlike Yasuna, who Twillo could certainly summon through his brooch. Yet their bodies were completely made of a murky energy, their eyes glowing purple beads.

They jumped for Twillo and his companions, the shadows moving like predators that knew their prey was prone. Twillo slashed at one, its body instantly reforming. Ariosto tried attacking them with his gemstones, the warrior monk spinning and using them as if they were flails. This had the same effect as Twillo's sword. It beat them back, but it didn't stop them.

Twillo activated his dragonaura using the mudra that he had learned. He then went for a Scaled Lash power, which allowed him to whip at the shadows. Princess Embla did the same, while Vradon desperately scanned the room, looking for some way out, some solution.

"Summon us," Seondzus said. "It is time, relic hunter!"

Twillo nodded. He summoned Seondzus and Adventus, the two taking shape in their dragon warrior forms. The room was large enough for them to easily wield their weapons. Every time the hulking shadows tried to flank Twillo's group, or attempted to circle around, Adventus beat them back with his glaive, Seondzus doing the same with her massive sword.

This gave Twillo a moment to think. He looked up at the glowing crystal. It had something to do with that, he knew it.

"Try to shatter it," he told Ariosto.

The warrior monk sent the glowing gemstones up into the air. Yet they would never strike the protective purple crystal above. Every time he guided them, they moved away, as if repelled by its power.

Twillo tried hitting at the purple crystal with his Scaled Lash. Then he tried a blast from his father's sword. Neither landed.

"What else, what else?" he whispered to himself as he mentally scrolled through his Arcane Cards. Was there something he was missing? Something that would help them? Clearly the crystal was fueled by a dark energy, but he had nothing like that to his knowledge. Nothing aside from...

"That's it!" Twillo drew his blade across the palm of his hand. The blood appeared instantly.

"Have you gone mad?" Vradon asked. But by this point, Twillo was already sheathing his blade and going for the paintbrush, one that was fueled by blood. It was a strange relic, only useful in certain situations. Hopefully, this was the dark mana that Twillo needed to break the crystal.

While Adventus and Seondzus continued to defend them, Twillo brought his wrist back and flicked the blood-tipped paintbrush at the crystal. What followed was a kaleidoscope of strange hues, the crystal completely fizzling out in a matter of seconds.

The room went dark.

"We can't see," Adventus told Twillo, even if Ariosto's gemstone slightly illuminated the place. "Are they still here?"

Twillo had to close his eyes. Even if he could see in the dark, he wasn't going to be able to see shadows, but he would see their dragonessence imprints. He let out a deep breath as he noticed that the shadows were all gone. At least to his knowledge.

They were replaced by something else. A new being now stood in the cylindrical chamber, one that was cloaked and made of boiling dragonessence.

Twillo drew his sword again, and ignored his pulsing palm as he continued to bleed out.

The entity did the same with its weapon, its blade completely dark. The only way Twillo was going to be able to see it was through dragonessence, which meant he would have to keep his eyes shut. He moved forward just like Renda had taught him, just as he had trained, always ready to take things as far as they needed to go for him to defeat his opponent.

Their blades clashed, the echo loud and biting. He blocked another strike in and spun around his opponent, where he used his Firebreath power. This happened to be the same palm that he had recently cut, which only made it sting even more.

The fire ignited the shadow being's cloak, illuminating the cavernous space. Adventus and Seondzus moved into action while they could see it. It became too much, the being not able to defend against all three of them.

Soon Adventus landed a strike.

Then Seondzus cut off its head.

Twillo pressed on with a blow that cut into the side of its body.

As it fell, the energy was sucked to the far corners, where it made a complete circle around the chamber before fizzling out. A doorway appeared in the center of the space, one that was rimmed in dragonessence and bright enough that Seondzus and Adventus could actually see it.

"I suppose this is the way," Vradon said with a harrowed breath out.

Princess Embla stopped the monk before he could enter. "Let's wait a moment. Jhaeros, heal yourself."

"Will do," Twillo told her as he sat on the ground. He cycled through his Arcane Cards and found Vard's Blessing.

"Very curious," Ariosto said. "Very curious, indeed. This is a kind of dragonessence that I have rarely encountered in my life. This dark influence. What was that paintbrush?"

"Just a thing I picked up along the way," Twillo said.

Ariosto placed his hands on his back and examined the glowing doorway. "Amazing discovery. Let's continue."

Chapter Twenty-Three

The Chamber of Skulls

DRAGONESSENCE HUNG LIKE A HEAVY FOG in the next space, reminding Twillo of a vortex. He didn't dare use it to recharge. There was a darker aspect to it that he couldn't quite define, the dormant power giving a chill to his bones.

"Something is off in here," Vradon said, his nose held high even though there was no discernable smell here.

"Agreed," Twillo said.

"Best to move on." Princess Embla stepped down into a new chamber. Twillo noticed in the way the ground and the walls were contoured that the entire room had been fashioned of skulls.

"Horrific," Ariosto said as he moved ahead, the warrior monk light on his feet. The two gemstones hovered just above his tail and acted as lanterns as he stepped deeper into the darkened room of skulls.

"I wonder if this has something to do with the skulls you saw when you were searching for the tiles," Vradon told Twillo.

"I have no idea. But there definitely seems to be a theme."

Adventus and Seondzus began discussing the skulls, both of their voices somewhere at the back of Twillo's mind. He could feel his wristlets buzzing as they spoke, the jewels glowing blue, the metal warm. It was all speculation, yet hearing them did calm Twillo to some degree. He knew that they would come to his aid when summoned, and that they were an incredible force to be able to wield.

Their presence made things like exploring an ancient ziggurat with a room fashioned completely out of skulls less harrowing.

Once they reached the halfway point, Twillo caught a pair of bright purple eyes forming on one of the skulls. More of these eyes flashed into existence, the room soon illuminating with them. The skulls began to chatter, whispering in a language that Twillo had never heard before.

"What are they saying?" he asked Vradon or the dragons, whoever would translate.

"It is not a language I know," Adventus said.

"It isn't old Sagic?"

"No, Left-Handed One. It is something much older than that."

"Vradon?" Twillo asked as he turned to the monk. Vradon had his head tilted to the side, listening intently.

"I've heard this before," he finally said. "I know this language!"

"You do?" Princess Embla asked as the chatter grew louder.

"We use it for hymns. Don't you recognize it? They're saying the words differently, but it is an Icenordian tongue."

"I sort of see what you mean. But how do we solve this? Whatever *this* is." She motioned to the skulls. Princess Embla had since floated above them, so she wasn't standing directly on top of them. Twillo had done the same and Ariosto had taken care of Vradon.

"They are getting louder," Ariosto said. "Perhaps that is the test itself, how much of their noise we can endure."

The skulls grew louder, their whispery voices filling the chamber. They were the voices of men and women young and old, children, all of them increasing with intensity. Soon, they were yelling, Twillo forced to cover his ears.

He saw Ariosto and Princess Embla do the same, yet Vradon remained entirely focused, his brow furrowed as he concentrated on the words. His eyes flickered, but not with worldly concern, nor concern for the shrieking skulls around him. It was a dance of internal cogitation, Vradon desperate to solve the riddle.

Twillo felt Princess Embla grab his arm. She squeezed it tightly, her nails digging in. "I can't take it anymore," she said as her head started to fall forward.

Twillo caught her. "Cover your ears!"

When she didn't respond, he covered her ears for her even though this made the chants almost unbearable in his own headspace. Seondzus and Adventus were shouting for him now, but he couldn't hear them, the sound in the room overwhelming.

Twillo couldn't hear Vradon either as the monk threw his arms out and yelled something.

The skulls all stopped. Twillo gasped, their collective voices absent, the chamber now filled with silence. The skulls in one of the walls began to tumble forward, revealing an exit. Their myriad purple eyes all faded at the same time, their ramblings nonexistent, jaws still.

Princess Embla blinked her eyes open and stared at Twillo for a moment. She placed a hand on his cheek, and gave him a funny look. She slapped him. "Let me go."

Twillo did as instructed, but rather than touch her feet on the ground, Princess Embla merely floated in the air again like the rest of them.

"That is some way to thank you," Seondzus said. "Those skulls would have devoured her whole."

"They weren't going to eat them. They were going to destroy them with sound," Adventus told his counterpart. "Drive them mad."

"You don't know that."

"How did you do it?" Ariosto asked Vradon. "How did you solve it?"

Vradon let out a deep breath. *"I blur the lines between truth and deceit. Above a crown of white and phantom peaks. Day after day, I cloak the world in bleak. What am I?* Mountain fog. You are mountain fog," Vradon said. "That's what they were all saying."

Ariosto nodded his head in appreciation. "Brilliant."

"We would be dead without you," Twillo told Vradon. "You know that, right?"

"You would have figured it out, Jhaeros."

"No, no I most certainly wouldn't have. This challenge, this ziggurat, requires an extensive knowledge of language. I have the dragons, and they would be able to read some of it. But to decipher a room of shrieking skulls? Do not undersell yourself, old friend. We couldn't have done this without you. Olaf would be incredibly impressed."

These words caused Vradon's shoulders to drop. "Maybe. He always said that I over-studied."

"I'm glad you over-studied," Princess Embla told him. "You are a scholar of the highest degree. When all this is over, when I become the Ravenna of Icenor, I expect you to take a place in my court as a trusted advisor and Royal Sage, Keeper of Wisdom."

Vradon's face went pale. His mouth started to drop open and he stopped it. "Keeper of Wisdom? Icenordians haven't used that title in hundreds of years, Your Ladyship. I do not believe I am qualified."

"I will bring it back, and I'm certain that you will use your power, your access to knowledge, to help all of us. I'm counting on you to do so."

"This isn't over yet." Vradon turned to the passage that had just opened, the monk hiding how red his cheeks had become. "We still have to defeat Jecha, and I think we still need to get out of this place first. Unless I am mistaken."

Twillo laughed. "Yes, we are dreaming of the spoils of the future while stuck in the dungeon of the present. Didn't someone famous say something about that?"

"Not to my knowledge," Vradon said. "Come on. Let's see what else this ziggurat can throw at us."

They entered a new chamber, where they found one of the gold gemstones floating on a pedestal. It wasn't protected by a barrier, and the passageway beyond was wide open. Even so, Twillo scanned the shadowy corners, all but expecting something to lunge for them.

"We now have three," Ariosto said as he floated the new gemstone over to the others. He brought them in closer so he could observe them, their golden glow shining brightly on his face. "Such strange magic."

"All of this is strange," Vradon said. "No one would believe it."

"Some stories aren't meant to be told," Princess Embla said. "There is a draft coming from this next chamber. Do you feel it?"

Twillo stepped over to her and noticed a subtle breeze, one that was bitingly cold. "You think it leads outside?"

"It leads somewhere that is quite open," Princess Embla said.

Ariosto confirmed this with a grunt. "We may be reaching the end here. In that case, let's see if we can make it out with our lives intact." He grinned at the three of them. "And live to suppress another story."

"I'm definitely telling part of this story," Twillo said as they continued on. "But I will hide some of the details as to what we were doing, or who I was with. Do not worry, Your Grace. Your secrets are safe with me."

She didn't even try to hide the smirk on her face this time. "Where would you tell the stories, Jhaeros?"

"The relic hunter bar. Where else? These are the kind of stories that we swap late at night over warm glasses of kvoss on hot summer nights in Middling, the days when the sun sets late and almost pushes into morning."

While he was being playful, Twillo could see it now in his mind's eye, the strange orange of the sky as it began to shift purple only for it to become orange again. It was a summer phenomenon, one that was even greater up north in Icenor. But he preferred to experience it in Middling, where the alcohol was better and cheaper. Or maybe it was better *because* it was cheaper.

Twillo shrugged at his own inner monologue.

It was easier to focus on these kinds of memories than it was to think too deeply about what lay ahead. Not just the ziggurat itself, but Jecha and their impending clash. Twillo had an idea of how he could deal with him now. He just had to set things up, and had to make sure this time that he wasn't frozen in place.

As he looked ahead, his eyes fell upon Ariosto's shoulders. The warrior monk would help in this regard, Twillo was certain of it. But would he go for his plan? Twillo planned to reveal it to them tonight, and he would discuss it with the others.

It was one of those ideas that was so crazy, it just might work.

"We're certainly getting closer to the exit," Vradon said as more cold air whistled into the passageway. Soon, little bits of snow came twirling in. "By Livia, I've never been happier to see the snow. And I don't much like the snow myself."

Light spread into the passage as it reached an opening with ice hanging above it. They stepped out and found a small alcove, a mountain grotto carved into the side of one of the peaks, hidden by the thick clouds that shrouded the top.

"It's an altar," Twillo said as he came to the stone structure. He began wiping the snow off it, and was soon joined by Princess Embla, who was able to move more of the white powder using her sleeve. They continued to clean it up until they revealed three grooves carved into the surface of the altar.

"Is there any writing?" Vradon asked Twillo.

"None that I see. But I believe this is clear enough. We need to insert the gemstones into the grooves. Ariosto. And do be careful, we do not know what will happen once they are in place."

"Summon us," Seondzus said.

"Not a bad idea," Twillo told her as he pulsed his power, the two dragon warriors taking shape behind them.

"We will be ready for anything," Adventus assured the group. "Just focus on setting the gemstones."

Ariosto, who now stood in front of the altar, carefully floated the first gemstone into place. It set. A golden energy traced over the altar, forming an impossibly detailed image that swiftly faded away.

"We are on the right track," Vradon said with bated breath. "The next one."

Ariosto slowly lowered the gemstone into place. Yet again, as soon as it locked, the altar filled with more golden lines, these strings of mana morphing into geometric images that Twillo couldn't quite place.

"And one more," Princess Embla said.

Ariosto set it into place and then stepped around to join them on their side of the altar. The ground began to shake.

The group braced themselves for what was to come.

Chapter Twenty-Four

Stony Visage

THE SNOW ROSE INTO THE AIR and a swirling wind picked it up, pressing it together and forming into a translucent butterfly made of ice. Dragonessence fluttered around the contours of its wings, giving the icy butterfly life. Twillo was focused on the butterfly such that he didn't see the other being that had formed out of the snow, a cloaked entity in all white.

The butterfly landed on the entity's shoulder as dragonessence sprinkled down over their shoulders, recharging their reserves. Even if he had just been rewarded with dragonessence, Twillo slowly brought his sword to the ready. Instinct. The beam showed no signs of malice, yet he expected a challenge, especially with everything that they had been through up until that point.

"You will not need your sword," came a voice on the wind, one that was feminine in nature yet so much more. The sound seemed to radiate all around Twillo as if it were the voice of the realm itself.

"What are you?" Princess Embla asked.

"An emissary. Come."

The butterfly lifted off the being's shoulder and floated away from the ledge. As it did, a bridge of crackling ice formed beneath the bottom of its robes.

Ariosto was the first to step out on it. He looked back to the others, nodded, and continued. Twillo followed, then Princess Embla and Vradon. Twillo wasn't afraid of heights, but he did his best not to look down as they followed the mysterious emissary. The path soon became rigid as it merged into steps that climbed toward the summit of the mountain.

Once they reached the top, the emissary turned to the horizon.

Twillo looked out into the light gray fog that hovered over the mountain beyond. The fog began to clear, as if it were a set of drapes being parted in the middle. It revealed a set of towering peaks that sat like a crown around a summit defined by large boulders covered in a thick snow.

The butterfly left the emissary's shoulder. It trailed in the air slowly toward the mountain that had just been revealed.

"What is happening?" Vradon asked, the monk standing on the tips of his toes as he watched the unnatural phenomena play out.

Twillo looked over at his old friend and saw the monk with his eyes fixed on the emissary and its butterfly, Vradon's cheeks puffy and red from the cold. He wished in that moment that Olaf was here to see Vradon and how brave he had become. He would have said something to lighten Vradon's mood. And while it may have sounded harsh to others, it would have been funny to both of them. It would have worked.

Twillo's thoughts were interrupted as the snow on the peak beyond began to fall.

Rocks tumbled toward the ground as an avalanche picked up. Yet this didn't send puffs of snow and jagged boulders all the way down the peak. The debris magically stopped at the midpoint of the mountain, hovering in place. A swirl of wind circled around the detritus, the fallen snow and boulders forming something. Twillo had to blink twice. He had to blink three times. Twillo had to rub his eyes and stare in disbelief as the impossible took shape.

He now looked out at a face that took up the entire midpoint of the mountain. The face was that of an old man with a beard, and even though he shouldn't have, even though all the artists of the ages hadn't gotten it perfect, Twillo recognized the man immediately.

Twillo and his companions were staring at Father Dawn.

"This is impossible," Vradon said as the snow continued to settle around the chiseled mountain face. "Unheard of."

Twillo looked down at his hand to see that it was trembling. He had met Livia, he had met Jecha, but Father Dawn and Mother Dusk were said to be the king and queen of all realms. This was beyond divine, it was an experience that would sit with him for the rest of his life.

Ariosto got down onto one knee and bowed his head. Vradon did the same, Twillo and Princess Embla dropping as well.

"Please, back to your feet," the emissary near them said.

They stood. The emissary swept to the side to allow them to fully view Father Dawn.

"You have done it," Father Dawn said, his voice strong and proud. As he moved his lips, snow fell from his brow, the mountain and its crags still adjusting to the fact that his face was suddenly there. "You now have the power to free the dragons."

"How do we do it?" Twillo asked. He cleared his throat and tried again. "How?" This time, his voice was amplified, Twillo feeling that it was just as loud as Father Dawn.

"The gemstones you possess. When pressed together they will open a portal that brings the dragons back from the Realm of the Forgotten."

The gemstones hovering above Ariosto's tail were suddenly in a glowing satchel, one that lowered to the warrior monk's hand. He glanced down at it and handed the small satchel to Twillo, who was able to feel the gemstones through the outer material.

Even though Father Dawn was hundreds of feet away, it sounded like he was standing directly in front of them. Twillo still couldn't make sense of the visual, yet he accepted it and listened as Father Dawn continued: "You will meet Jecha the day after tomorrow, on a battlefield south of the Dunes of Endrus."

Twillo thought of the Harvest Mountains. If he wasn't mistaken, that was directly east from their current location.

"Jecha is a fool if he thinks he is going to be able to destroy this realm. I know that Livia has been working toward this moment for the last fifty years or so. I also know that she is watching now and that you cannot see her. I applaud her endeavors. She has made it so that I do not have to intervene; she has chosen the right people for this task."

"He can't mean us," Vradon said, his head still bowed.

"He does mean you," Ariosto told the monk. "He means all of you, and those you have lost."

Twillo thought of his father. He thought of Olaf, Anneli, and Katashi. He also thought of Renda, their final moments together. It had been such a struggle to reach the summit, to stare across the void and speak directly to the most powerful god in all of the realms.

"I want you to do it," Father Dawn told them as more snow tumbled down the mountain. "It would be easy now for me to crush the army that he has put together, to bring sandstorms and lightning bolts and earthquakes to my brother all at the same time. Jecha has taken the body of a mortal, as you know. The only way for him to possess the power that I have would be to completely control the realm, to sacrifice every living being and amplify his own strength. But that won't happen. You will defeat him."

Twillo let out a deep breath. To hear Father Dawn this confident in his abilities filled Twillo with a newfound sense of self-worth. Yet he wasn't the prideful type, and he didn't trust this feeling. He also knew what Jecha was capable of, Twillo uncertain if he actually had what it took.

"Do not let doubt guide your heart. Livia has selected all of you for this task. You will prove to not only my brother, but all the gods, that mortals are even more capable than they may think. The Age of Dragons will begin anew, and all of you will have played your part. But your story won't end there. The dragons with you will regain their fame and respect. You will guide a kingdom to a better destiny," Father Dawn said, and even though he was far away, it was clear that he was talking to Princess Embla. "You will continue to live the life of a legendary being," he told Ariosto. "You will redeem your family name, become a legend yourself, and prove to an entire kingdom the power of redemption and cunning," he told Twillo. Father Dawn shifted his focus to Vradon. "And you will bring about a new Age of Knowledge, one that will guide the future to come."

"Me?" Vradon asked.

Twillo placed a hand on Vradon's shoulder. He did this for the monk yet also for himself. It was a lot to take in, and to hear Father Dawn say these things left him feeling speechless. Who was Twillo to question such a powerful being? Why didn't he feel that he would live up to these incredible expectations?

"Tomorrow, a kitsune named Preshka will join you and act as my representative. She will lead you to an optimal position just beyond Jecha's forces. It is here that you will execute your plan."

"We have a plan," Twillo said, even if he hadn't completely run it by the others.

"We do?" Princess Embla asked.

"I'll explain later."

Father Dawn continued: "I have considered what I should do to help, if there is anything that would truly give you an advantage over Jecha. But I believe there isn't. Livia has painstakingly put these pieces together, and I champion her for that. Jecha may think he is all-powerful, but he doesn't possess the cunning of the four of you and your dragons. He doesn't possess the skills, nor the willpower. So I'm not going to intervene in that regard. I'm not going to give you a boost in any way. Because I don't believe you need it."

Twillo swallowed hesitantly. He appreciated the faith, but he'd also been head to head against Jecha and knew what the God of Carnage could do.

"I told you before, Jecha isn't the only god that needs to see firsthand what humans are capable of. It is time that the others do as well. Perhaps it will lead them to stop their meddling in human affairs, doing things like hosting tournaments, and taking lives at their own whims. There is so much that they do, my fellow gods, so very much. And I would like this to be a point that causes them to pause, to take heed."

"As you wish," Ariosto said, but something about his tone told Twillo that he had more on his mind.

"If you have something to say, speak freely," Father Dawn told him.

"If you want to stop the gods from meddling in human affairs, then do so. They will listen to you. Using us to make an example is certainly a way to go about this, but I don't see it is as the best way. I can think of a number of things you could do to help stop the gods considering they are all under your control."

Vradon's mouth dropped at the way Ariosto had just challenged Father Dawn's wisdom.

"You are suggesting I become more active in my punishments? Because if that were the case, I would have been forced to punish Livia years ago for the way she thrust herself into Shotaro Vos' life. Among other things. If you knew the result of all timelines, you would be very wary to try to mold them to your liking. Had I done so then, we wouldn't be speaking now. So there is a process. And you all are very much part of this process. When it is time, when Jecha turns his forces on you, unite the gemstones. The portal will open and the dragons will come. All will be settled shortly after. Good luck. The gods will be watching."

The face on the mountain collapsed, rocks tumbling forward, snow puffing into the air. The sound was terrifying, yet it was entirely controlled, none of the debris falling much further than the midpoint of the mountain. By the time it cleared, the emissary was gone as well, leaving the four of them on the summit.

The dragons veered toward the ground, Seondzus in the lead. Twillo was on her back, Adventus carried Ariosto and Vradon, and Princess Embla rode Vendir as the group moved up and down the slopes, a frigid wind whipping past.

They decided to camp closer to where they would eventually meet Jecha, at the foothills of the Harvest Mountains. This had been Twillo's suggestion. He didn't want to involve the villagers in any way. It was best that they moved on, especially being in possession of the pocket shelter that they would use for the night.

They flew for hours until they reached the edge of the mountains, where the start of the desert became apparent. There was the concern of water, but Ariosto was able to mitigate that once they landed, the former water harvester able to find a deep reserve and distribute the resources.

"This should do fine," he said as the water lifted from a hole in the ground and curled, not unlike Ariosto's tail.

"Water secured. I will find something for dinner," Seondzus announced with her usual flair.

"I believe I will join you," Vendir told her.

"You don't think I can find it on my own?"

"A dragon wants to stretch his wings. Is that not something I'm allowed?"

Seondzus motioned her neck toward Embla. "Ask Her Highness."

Princess Embla gave the silvery white dragon a nod. "Have at it."

The two dragons pushed away, and as they did, Adventus morphed into his dragon warrior form. He took guard, standing with one hand holding his glaive upright, silent and stoic as ever.

Princess Embla turned to Twillo. "Your plan. I'm dying to know what you've decided without consulting us."

"My plan," he said as he got the pocket shelter out. He placed it on the ground, and watched as the relic fully formed into a square large enough to pass through.

"I'm curious as well," Vradon said. "What have you come up with, Jhaeros?"

"It may sound crazy."

The monk laughed. "I expect nothing less."

"I would posit that Father Dawn already knows of your plan, especially if he is able to see the future.

Therefore, whatever it is, however strange it may be, I suppose I will support it," Ariosto said.

"You are giving him way too much confidence," Princess Embla told him. "We should at least hear it first. Perhaps there are some adjustments that need to be made."

"We can't defeat Jecha," Twillo said once the group quieted down, "but we do have something that he doesn't have."

"Our wits?" Vradon asked.

"Our combined strength?" asked Princess Embla.

"No. We have this." Twillo gestured toward the pocket shelter.

The princess gave him a skeptical look. "A relic? What are you getting at, Jhaeros?"

He pointed downward. "We have to get Jecha in there. That's what I'm trying to say. You told me about that student of yours, the one who had a pocket shelter," Twillo reminded Ariosto. "You said that he was able to throw thieves over the side. I have wondered myself what it would be like to step over the edge of the platform below. According to Katashi, one would fall for all eternity."

"You want to shove Jecha over the edge of the platform?" Vradon asked, a baffled look on his face. "I don't even know—"

"It would trap him forever. He wouldn't be able to escape because he would be stuck in a realm with no exit."

"Wouldn't the top of the pocket shelter be an exit?" Vradon gestured toward the square. "He could just fly out, Jhaeros."

Ariosto's eyes lit up. "No, it would not. Jecha would be caught up in a vacuum of reality. These shelters were crafted by insanely talented arcane artificers. They created a pocket dimension for the shelter to exist. But none of them were strong enough to create a fully contained pocket dimension. Meaning that anything beyond the edge of the platform would be touching infinity itself. What I'm saying is there would be no escape from it."

"So the God of Carnage would be no more?" Vradon asked.

"The God of Carnage would be no more," Twillo said. "We would just need to get him down there."

"We are about to go up against an army, one that has several dragons," Princess Embla said.

"We will have more dragons," Twillo assured her.

"Perhaps, but that won't make this any easier. And your plan is to lure Jecha to the pocket shelter, and then what? Or, I guess I should say, how? How would you even go about doing this? Wouldn't he know? Wouldn't there be too many distractions already?"

"He is very confident in his power. Even if he knew it, he may not fully understand what it is we are trying to do," Ariosto said. "The problem would be if and when he uses his power to shift your willpower. We still do not have a way to prevent that."

"There's no mudra?" Twillo asked the warrior monk. "You must know something."

"A mudra to prevent the spell power of an Arcane Card? You know, there is one thing that might work, but it would have to be timed just right. Let's try something. Step over there and use one of your cards to attack me," Ariosto told Twillo.

"Is there a preference you would have? Fire? A wave of dragonessence?"

"Perhaps the wave. That would be a good test for what we are about to do."

Once Ariosto was in position, he went through the motion of activating Voidshift. Twillo hit him with Ripple Tide, the warrior monk able to fully absorb his attack.

"Just as I suspected," Ariosto said as he lowered his arms. "Even something from an Arcane Card can be blocked by Voidshift. The only problem is, neither of you are at a level that you would be able to block his mind attack. I'm thinking theoretically now, but to do something that would affect your willpower like that, that would be a very strong, and very legendary card. So in that case, I guess I will be doing the blocking and luring."

"Into the pocket shelter?" Twillo asked.

Ariosto nodded in response. "Yes, where he will meet you. You will have a limited amount of time to act. I have ways that I can force him into it, I believe. The rest of you should try to stay as far away from the proceedings as possible," Ariosto told Princess Embla and Vradon.

"I assumed I would be riding my dragon," she said, "doing what I can from the sky."

"Good. That is a good place for the future Ravenna," Ariosto told her.

"I'm not so useful in a fight," Vradon admitted. "But I want to be helpful. In that case…" The monk bit his lip. "In that case, I'll go into the pocket shelter with Jhaeros."

"Absolutely not," Twillo told Vradon.

"It wasn't a request. I want to be there. I want to do my part. Even if it is simply distracting him while you throw Jecha over the edge. Notice I said throw. He doesn't need a shove."

"Actually," Ariosto said, "it would be helpful to have another distraction in the pocket shelter. But you'd be on the platform, and that itself would be incredibly dangerous."

Vradon continued to gnaw at his lip. "I'm prepared for that," he finally said.

"You don't have to."

"No, I have to," Vradon said Twillo, a rare hint of defiance in his eyes. "For Olaf and for our realm and its future. I need to be there with you."

Chapter Twenty-Five

The Void Beyond

SEONDZUS AND VENDIR returned later with a male elk with a gorgeous coat that was a mixture of earthy tones and specks of white. The elk had a massive rack of antlers, larger than Twillo had seen in some time. He hated that they were going to have to leave its carcass behind and was glad when Ariosto drew a quick plan to deal with the body. After they had stripped the elk of its meat, the warrior monk volunteered to fly with Adventus to the mountain dwellers to drop off what was left of the body, which would allow them to put the coat, the antlers, and certain organs to good use.

"I can take you," Seondzus said. "Perhaps we can pick up another elk along the way. There were several."

"That is fine. The rest of you should rest," Ariosto told Twillo, Princess Embla, and Vradon. "Tomorrow is an important day of training and preparation."

"What about you?" Vradon asked the warrior monk.

"I will survive. I hate to see something as beautiful as this creature go to waste. Besides, I would like to spend a little more time with Torin and Rhea. I want to assure them that their son will be fine. Jaden has quite the challenge ahead of him."

Having just met Father Dawn, and already having met Livia and Jecha, Twillo could only imagine what the young man must have been going through. Twillo was twice his age, and he could barely grasp the undeniable power of the gods. And to be actively challenging them. That seemed riskier than what he was doing.

Twillo shook his head. "At least eat before you leave."

"I will gladly dine," Ariosto said.

Princess Embla and Vradon prepared the meat by laying it out in strips on a large stone. The outer layer crisped under Vendir's sudden heat, small trails of fat drizzling down the rock. Vendir had quite the control over the intensity of his fire, and soon, the air filled with the scent of roasting meat.

They ate and it was good. Afterwards, Seondzus left with Ariosto on her back. The remaining dragons returned to their wristlets, and Twillo, Princess Embla, and Vradon headed down to the platform.

"I still can't believe that we have all agreed to your plan," Princess Embla said as she prepared a place for her to sleep. "Yet it is the only thing now that makes sense to me. How else would we stop him?" She gestured out to the void. "Our only chance is to vanish into a realm of endless falling."

"Do not worry about the plan, Your Grace, let me do the worrying for you." Vradon dropped down onto the ground and let out a deep sigh. "I'm good at worrying."

Twillo sat down on his knees near Princess Embla. He removed some of the bedding and placed it on the ground a few feet away from her. She gave him a strange look. Her eyes jumped from the relic hunter to the space between them as if she were trying to close the gap.

With what Father Dawn had hinted at, Twillo took this as a sign to place his blanket just a bit closer to hers. He had a destiny that was beyond his control at this point. Twillo was also starting to feel a fondness for the Crown Ravenna. It wasn't something that he was willing to admit, but the longer he was around Embla, the more he didn't want to leave her side.

It only happened briefly, but the thought crossed his mind of what things would be like once all this was over, especially if he went his own way and didn't become the Prince Ravenna. There was a very real chance that Twillo might never see her again. He didn't want that. He enjoyed the princess' presence, and he especially enjoyed their shared history, how they were able to help each other piece together memories.

"I'll see you both in the morning," he said as he relaxed onto his back. Twillo stared up at the opening above, the top of the pocket shelter.

The stars had a way of lulling him to sleep. Eventually, Twillo shifted to his side and faced Princess

Embla. He would only discover the next morning that she was facing his direction as well.

Twillo awoke to find Ariosto seated in meditation, the warrior monk's head bowed. Twillo let out a soft yawn and spoke: "How did it go?"

"It went well. They were happy to receive the items. They were happy to learn more about their son."

"That must be something," Twillo said as he quietly got to his feet. Once he had his boots on, he headed up, intent on doing all he could to improve his power over the next day. He had a limited amount of time to level up, and he planned to reach that plateau.

"Do you mind if I join you?" Ariosto asked just as Twillo was about to access his dragonessence core.

"By all means."

"Let's begin with meditation."

The warrior monk guided him through a meditation that lasted about thirty minutes. Once he had finished,

Twillo cycled all of his Arcane Cards. He tested out each of his powers, one at a time. For his Vard's Blessing card, Twillo cut himself using Kestrel's letter opener, his penknife that turned into a rapier.

"That is certainly an interesting object," Ariosto said as Twillo healed the small wound. "Where did you get it?"

"Yes, it is a good one, and that's a long story for another day. I haven't had the chance to use it as much as I would like lately, but that comes with the territory with my collection. Not everything can come in handy at all times."

"That is true. But if you have them when the time is right, you will be glad that you went to the trouble of keeping it."

"Isn't that the hoarder's maxim?"

"The what?" Ariosto asked.

"The hoarder's maxim. *At some point, it will come in handy. Better keep it.* They have a group of those hoarders in the Tribute Islands. It's harder to get things there, you know, and they collect any and everything that comes their way. You should see their homes. You'd need a map to get from the front door to the bedroom."

"I'm sure they are quite cluttered." Ariosto activated his dragonessence by tapping his knuckles together.

Twillo did the same. "They are. I'm assuming you want to work on mudras?"

"I only wish we had enough time for me to fully train you on more. But for now, we will just work with what you can already do. Voidshift, Dragonflight, and Scaled Lash. Let's do this."

Ariosto came in quickly with a series of chops. Twillo managed to activate his Voidshift power and block some of the warrior monk's rapid-fire strikes. It was amazing how quickly Ariosto flitted around, his movements reminding Twillo of a hummingbird. He got the sense that he was going light on him, that the warrior monk was operating at about half his normal speed.

Twillo released the energy that he had stored from Ariosto's chops, and forced the warrior monk to jump backward.

"Not bad," Ariosto said as he twisted into another attack, one that took Twillo off guard. Even though he struck Twillo, even though Twillo should have felt the incredible force behind his strike, he didn't. It was uncanny how swiftly Ariosto had moved and hit Twillo, yet had caused no pain.

"Are you pulling punches? How?" Twillo asked.

"It is something that elite warrior monks do when they spar. We don't need to hit each other at all yet we can use our full force. Voidshift and its sister mudra, Voidrift, allow for further options with this technique. But you can reach a level where you can hit someone fully without causing any damage. Now, Scaled Lash."

Twillo performed the mudra for Scaled Lash. He whipped a cord of dragonessence at Ariosto's feet. The warrior monk did a backflip and landed perfectly, his tail always keeping him stable.

"Use your sword, your mudras, and whatever cards you would like. I'm ready for you to push this to whatever limit suits you."

"Are you certain?" Twillo asked.

"I am."

Twillo drew his sword. His opening attack was a burst of dragonessence, one that caused Ariosto to cartwheel to the side. He used Ripple Tide because it was already on deck, and also Enchanting Deception. Twillo sent a fighting replicant himself forward so he could try to distract the warrior monk.

Ariosto didn't take the bait. But Twillo did manage to get close enough that he was almost able to land a strike. And he would have as well. Twillo was going full force now, his mind on what would come the following day as he faced off against Jecha. He had to be fast on his feet.

As soon as Jecha reached the platform, Twillo had to force the God of Carnage over the side. Not only that, he would have to hit Jecha enough that he wasn't able to simply fly back onto the platform. This gave him an idea for later, and in thinking of this idea Twillo missed his next strike.

"Focus," Ariosto said.

"We need to test the platform," Twillo told the warrior monk.

"We can later, when we take a break. You must reach the next Tier, even if it takes us all day and night."

Twillo took a look around at the desert all around them, the way that the wind scattered grains of sand. The sun was just coming up, the dunes with a golden glow to them. It was stark, it was beautiful. Beyond him were the

Harvest Mountains, where he had met Father Dawn. They were so tall that he couldn't see their peaks now, a metaphor for the secrets hidden in the mountains that had yet to be discovered.

"I'm ready," Twillo said as he settled all of his thoughts, from dreams of relic hunting to fears of tomorrow.

They could wait.

Twillo and Ariosto took a break. During that time, the two headed down the platform to find Princess Embla seated with Vradon. The Icenordians were enjoying warm cups of tea which they heated on the hearth that was always burning in the far corner of the platform.

"We wanted to test something," Twillo said as he produced a couple of small stones. He stepped back and tossed a stone over the side of the platform. The stone was sucked downward, where it dropped as if it was being pulled into a vacuum, some type of magnetic whirlwind.

Twillo took a step closer to the edge of the platform, butterflies in his stomach.

He looked over the edge, pulled his arm back, and tried to throw the next stone even further. Even with his attempt, it was immediately pulled down into the cold infinity.

"You just need to get him over the edge," Ariosto said. "I don't believe even with his power that he will be able to pull himself back on the platform."

"Perhaps." Twillo tossed another stone.

He wanted to get used to the mechanics of the void beyond. There was another thing that he considered needed to happen after Jecha went over the side. They would need to do something about the pocket shelter.

"We should bring anything of importance up to the top. We will search around for a place to put it, but I believe the rocks just a bit beyond will be fine. Anything of value," Twillo said as he took a look around. "Once we send Jecha over the side, we need to destroy the pocket shelter."

"That is a good idea," Ariosto said. "We will assure that he is trapped in a place that no longer exists."

"I like the sound of that," Princess Embla said. "It is fitting for the God of Carnage."

"Yes, it is," said Vradon.

"We will be able to help as well," Adventus said. "You have yet to discuss that with us."

"You're right. We will discuss it now. Let's head up." Twillo turned to the ladder. He was soon joined by Ariosto, Princess Embla, and Vradon.

Once they were up top, Twillo summoned the two dragons, both of whom appeared in their warrior forms. Princess Embla summoned her dragon as well, who smoothed his wings behind his back as he perched near them.

"What do you think?" Seondzus asked Twillo. "We honestly won't be able to fit down there with you and the monk."

"You will be up here with Ariosto," Twillo said, seeing it all play out in his mind's eye. "Ariosto will block his attacks with Voidshift. The two of you will be responsible for helping him get Jecha down into the pocket shelter. But you can't be there to help me push him over the edge. I don't know what would happen if one of you went over."

"We could return to your wristlet," Adventus said.

"Maybe, but we don't know if that is what will actually happen. It would be ideal," Twillo said. "But we don't know. And we can't operate with those kinds of unknowns." He wanted to tell the dragons that he couldn't lose them, but he couldn't quite get these words out. Both of them meant the world to Twillo. They were also soulbound. If they went over the edge, perhaps he would follow.

"In that case, the princess and I can move things out of the pocket shelter," Vradon said. "Or, I can do most of it."

"I will certainly help," said Embla. "The dragons could help as well. We can bring things to the top and they can carry them onward."

"We would gladly help," Adventus told the princess.

Seondzus turned to her counterpart. "Speak for yourself. I want to train with the relic hunter."

"Yes," Ariosto said. "It would be good for the two of you to train. And I will watch. You do have a goal of reaching the next Tier sooner rather than later, and time is running out." He clapped his hands together. "Let's get started."

The training began soon after, Twillo and Seondzus battling for the next hour. He did everything he could, yet she always was able to strike him down, to push him to his limits.

As she often did, the red dragon wielded her sword recklessly, which was something Twillo liked about her fighting style. It kept him on his toes, even if he was able to do things like blast her with Firebreath, or use a mudra to take her feet out from beneath her, she was always back on her feet in a matter of moments swinging her blade like the butcher she was, never tiring. In that way, Seondzus was indefatigable, which only made Twillo push himself even harder.

Twillo felt something at one point as their swords clashed. It was a surge of power, one that actually forced her to take a staggering step backward.

"I think I did it," Twillo said as he accessed his status. "I did. I made it to the next Tier!"

Name: Jhaeros Shotaro Vos
Level up!

Tier: Adept
Rank: D
Class: Martial Arts Mastery
Rank: C
Secondary Class: None
Tertiary Class: None
Dragonessence: 450/450

He added an additional card to his deck. Twillo knew he couldn't stop now. He needed to bring them all up to Level Three.

"The Adept Tier, yes?" Ariosto asked.

"Yes. Rank D, but I'll take it."

"And you weren't offered a secondary class?"

"No, I was not." Twillo looked at his details again.

"Yours is a broken, no, *modified*, system, but it will work. You will be able to still do plenty with it. Now, your cards. I am guessing that you would like to do what you can to increase their levels as well."

"That's exactly what I was planning to do," Twillo said.

Seondzus leaned her weight on her heels. "You're still going to need me, right?"

"I'll always need you," he said, which caused her to laugh awkwardly.

"Remember that you are already betrothed, relic hunter."

"To whom?" Twillo glanced over to find Princess Embla standing just outside the pocket shelter, directing Vradon and Adventus. "Oh, her."

Seondzus shook her head. "You're going to be the worst husband. But at least your children will be cute. Actually, maybe you will be a good dad. And I will be a good aunt, and Adventus will be a good uncle. You will let your children ride us, correct?"

Twillo got into position after arranging his Arcane Cards. "I really have not thought that far. And now that you bring it up, I don't know. I really don't know."

"Children love dragons. Or at least they used to." Seondzus brought her sword up. "I can't wait to be an aunt."

Chapter Twenty-Six

Father Dawn's Emissary

TWILLO DROPPED TO HIS KNEES. He let out a deep breath and brought his arms down, releasing a tension that had been building up, a combination of injury and sustained combat.

"On your feet, relic hunter." Seondzus held her sword out in front of him, pointed directly at his chin. "It would be easy, you know."

"If you kill me, you kill yourself," Twillo reminded her.

"Not necessarily. I'd just go back to the Realm of the Forgotten. Maybe another wayward Icenordian would summon me. Who knows?"

"Please," Adventus said, who stood near them balancing his weight on his glaive. "Enough games, Seondzus. Lower your blade, or I will forcibly lower it for you and make you regret the day you decided to be so bold."

She grinned, Twillo seeing the whites of her teeth. "Bold? I'm only being playful."

"You're being foolish," her counterpart told her.

She turned to him. "Should we see how foolish I can become?"

"Enough, both of you," Twillo said as he healed the wound on his arm. "All my Arcane Cards are at their peak level," he told the two dragons and Ariosto, who stood on the periphery. Twillo's eyes traced over his status, which glowed in front of him.

Name: Jhaeros Shotaro Vos
Tier: Adept

Rank: D

Class: Martial Arts Mastery

Rank: C

Secondary Class: None

Tertiary Class: None

Dragonessence: 321/450

[Arcane Cards]

Level up!

Arms of Vikan Wood, Level 3

Codex Vault, Level 1 [Passive]

Core Eruption, Level 3

Enchanting Deception, Level 3

Eternal Cycle, Level 3

Firebreath, Level 3

Flash of Fata Morgana, Level 3

Nadakunai's Might, Level 3

Ripple Tide, Level 3

Vard's Blessing, Level 3

Warding Glyph, Level 3

[Mudras]

Dragonaura, Level 2

Dragonflight, Level 2

Scaled Lash, Level 2

Voidshift, Level 1

Seondzus put her sword away and offered Twillo her hand. He took it; the red dragon warrior helped Twillo to his feet. "You're getting stronger," she said, "I'll give you that. But you'll never be stronger than me."

"This isn't a competition," Adventus told her.

She grinned again. "I suppose not. But I do like being soulbound to a strong mortal. It makes it so I, or I guess I should say, *we,* don't have to carry as much of the weight." She shrugged and her scaled armor clinked against her body. "Relic hunter. Tomorrow is the day."

"I'm aware," Twillo told her.

"Yes, tomorrow. And this fox has yet to show up. Where is the kitsune?" she asked, referring to the emissary that Father Dawn said would meet them. "Do I need to go find it myself?"

"I'm sure they will be here soon enough," Ariosto said. "Come, let's rest and break bread."

"I wish we had bread." Twillo was hungry, and for some reason, warm bread with butter sounded delicious at the moment. He licked his lips.

"Elk isn't good enough for you?" Seondzus asked as they turned back to their campsite, where they found Vradon seated by a fire. "Would you prefer a charred rabbit?"

"Where's the princess?" Twillo asked Vradon once he had reached the monk.

"Her Highness went out for a flight. She should return soon. Or at least I hope she does. I have no idea how long it has been. I've been watching the flames. Hypnotizing, you know." He grinned. "Do I look nervous?"

"Yes and no." Twillo sat next to his old friend and leaned his weight on him.

"You're sweaty," Vradon told Twillo.

"I've been training all day." Twillo pressed away. He saw a plate with some meat on it and took some. The elk was warm, meaning Vradon had already eaten his share.

"I've been mentally preparing myself," the monk told him. "And the space downstairs is clean." He motioned to the pocket shelter. "Aside from the big rock you wanted."

"To charge, part of the trap." Twillo almost got to his feet to take a look but decided he could do it later.

"It will be ready for tomorrow, Jhaeros, and I will be there with you." Vradon locked eyes with him. "For Olaf."

"For Olaf, Katashi, and Anneli," Twillo said as he returned his gaze.

The fire grew in intensity as Seondzus approached. She took a seat next to Twillo and the ground shook. After a yawn, she stretched her feet out to the point that they were practically in the campfire itself. Twillo felt his wristlet buzz as Adventus returned. "No need to waste additional power," the white dragon said.

Ariosto joined them. Rather than sit, the warrior monk hovered in the air with his legs curled beneath him. "I wish there was more we could do to prepare," he said once he'd settled, "but I believe that is a normal feeling the day before a conflict. I honestly have nothing to compare this to. I've never been at a point where my actions would be the difference between the life or death of the entirety of the Four Kingdoms."

"That's one way to think of it," Vradon said. "Or we could just think of it as something that is necessary. Something that we have been put here to do."

"Yes, perhaps that is a better perspective."

Twillo heard the wind rustle above. He glanced up to see Vendir circling, Princess Embla on the dragon's back. Vendir tilted toward the ground and came down quickly, spearing right at them. He disappeared just above Twillo and the others and the princess floated down to join them.

"Some entrance," Seondzus told her. "I'll have to add that one to my repertoire."

"You're more than welcome to." Princess Embla pushed her hood off her head. She smiled over at Twillo, the light of the fire adding just a hint of shadow to her face. "Jhaeros, Vradon. I trust that everything is well."

"It is, Your Grace," said Vradon. "We were just eating and discussing tomorrow."

"Of course you were. I needed a flight to clear my head. I can't believe I'm able to say something like that." She pressed back onto her hands. "I remember reading about saracents as a child, about how they'd say the very same thing. *A flight to clear the mind*. Something to that effect."

"What books were you reading?" Vradon asked. "I don't recall any stories of saracents on dragonback, and I certainly would recall a phrase like that."

"Ah, the Ravenna's private collection. You'll have access to that as Keeper of Wisdom. There are journals that have been kept and rescribed numerous times to keep the information alive. The written word is powerful in that way."

"It is even more powerful when it is hidden from the general population," Twillo said. "We should allow all the journals to be released. Any stories of the past would surely benefit the population now."

"For those that can read," Vradon said. "But if they can't, others will read for them. Emperor Otonashi has been very good about literacy. There are still those in the far-out places who cannot read, but that's changing. The past should be studied and accessible, Your Highness."

"I agree, and you'll be able to see to it that this happens," she told him. "As Ravenna, I'll be able to make sure no one in the court can stop you."

"You're serious?" Vradon asked, the monk going a bit pale. "I haven't even considered what it would be like to be part of something like that."

"If the Ravenna supports it, it shall be done," she said. "I guess there's always the Prince Ravenna to consider, but I'm guessing he will support it."

Twillo laughed. "I can't have this conversation right now." He got to his feet and headed down to the platform. Twillo set his bedding up and was soon asleep. He barely remembered his dreams that night, but he did wake up knowing that he had been dreaming about training. Considering he'd spent the entire previous day doing just that, this made sense to him.

He also discovered Princess Embla sleeping next to him, his arm wrapped around her body, his face close to the back of her head.

Twillo thought about moving but he stayed this way for another thirty minutes. It felt incredible to be beside her. Aside from the occasional pillower if his mood was right, it had been a very long time since Twillo had been this close to a woman.

He expected Seondzus to comment but she didn't say anything. Twillo held the princess for just a bit longer before finally removing his arm.

It was time.

He took the ladder to the top of the pocket shelter to find Ariosto and a white fox, one with numerous tails, just as Father Dawn had foretold.

"Ah, he's up," Preshka the kitsune said, her voice indicating that she was female. "We should leave soon. Prepare your things."

Something about the way she said this caused Twillo to pause. "You mean we'll travel there by our normal means, right?"

"By dragon?" she asked. "No, not by dragon. I will portal you there. It is a unique trait that I have. You should know something else about me."

"Yes?" Twillo asked.

"I am currently a vessel for Father Dawn. I will be watching everything as it happens. Now please, prepare. Your surprise attack is in order."

After Twillo made sure all his armor was in place, he sat with Princess Embla and Vradon for a short amount of time while the monk said a prayer to Livia. Twillo knew this wasn't necessary. Livia had led them up to this point, and she was likely watching him at that very moment. Yet it seemed to make the princess and the monk feel better, both of them with a hint of relief in their eyes after the prayer was over.

"What will you do after?" Vradon asked Twillo, a hint of urgency in his voice.

"I—" Twillo glanced over to Princess Embla. "If I am lucky, the Crown Ravenna of Icenor will read me her yoika poem so that we can make this official. If I'm not as lucky, I'll be in the Tribute Islands looking for a haunted doll to possibly sell at the Artifance next year. So either way, I'm lucky?" Twillo grinned at the monk.

"You'll marry?" Vradon asked, his voice filling with joy. "Really? How wondrous!"

"If she'll have me, sure."

Princess Embla blushed. "You've really put me on the spot here, Jhaeros!"

"You're the one that has been poking him about this all along," Seondzus said, even though no one could hear her aside from Twillo.

"I think this is absolutely wonderful and befitting of your status as a saracent, Left-Handed One," Adventus said.

"What a blessing," Vradon said, gushing now. "A true blessing! We are about to face something so important, so crucial to our survival, yet it is good to know that there is an outcome worth striving for. I would be honored to attend your wedding."

"I'm sure that can be arranged, but all in due time." Changing his tone, Twillo shifted to something that was equally important to say. "Now, ahem, we must keep in mind that we are not only doing this for all future generations, but we're also doing it for Olaf, Anneli, and Katashi. Sorry if that was a strange transition." He almost added Renda to this list but didn't, even if Twillo felt as if he were doing this for her as well. "But I thought it was important to say."

"It was. And the Four Kingdoms," Vradon said, his tone changing as well. "Keep the kingdoms and our companions in your hearts. Wedding talk can come later, and hopefully there will be no more haunted doll talk."

"Agreed," said Princess Embla. "For now..."

"For now?" Twillo asked the princess.

"Let's go," she said, the first of the three to stand. "We're wasting precious time."

Twillo would be the last to climb out of the pocket shelter. After the other two headed up to meet Preshka, he wanted a moment alone on the platform that would decide the fate of everything that was to come. Twillo circled the space several times. He imagined Jecha in Rowian's orcish body standing right there, all the things he might have to do to push him over the side.

Twillo was aware that one of his tactics was the ultimate sacrifice. If it came to it, he would bring Jecha over the edge with him. He hadn't mentioned this to the others, and no one had brought it up, but he was certain that it had crossed Embla's mind. Something about the way she kept looking at him, her gaze a mixture of fear and hope, told Twillo she'd already run this scenario.

She was smart like that, and she would be an incredible leader with or without him.

There was also Vradon, who had maintained that he would be on the platform with Twillo. The monk said this with such conviction that Twillo hadn't been able to talk him out of it. This would provide a distraction for Jecha, but it would also make what Twillo knew needed to happen even harder to pull off.

He glanced back up at the opening. It would take a lot to lure Jecha down, but he was confident that Ariosto and the dragons could do it. Perhaps one of them would be on the platform as well. Twillo didn't yet know.

Once he was ready, he took the ladder to the top to join the others. He picked up the pocket shelter as it morphed back to its transport size and placed it in his bag. "What about the dragons?" he asked as he approached.

"What do you mean?" Ariosto asked.

"We've yet to discuss when we will free them from the Realm of the Forgotten. I assume the gemstones will be what Jecha wants, if he even knows of their existence."

"You will free the dragons at the start," Preshka said in an eerily calm voice. "Jecha will descend into madness, as he has before. He will come for you, specifically you," the white fox told Twillo. "And whoever is luring him into the pocket shelter will stoke the fire in his heart, which will aid in your attempt to deceive and ultimately thwart him."

"And then we will take him over the edge," Vradon said.

"You don't have to—"

"I will be down there, Your Highness," Vradon told her before she could suggest otherwise. "I am not normally brave, as you know. And I've caused this group troubles in the past due to my lack of training. But I am rather large. And I am stronger than I look. And if it comes to it, I will push Jecha over the edge myself. Do not put the entirety of this burden on Jhaeros' shoulders. All good plans must have a back-up plan. I am that back-up plan," he said.

No one could deny the passion in Vradon's voice, and no one did. Instead, they gathered around the fox, whose seven tails started to glow.

"We will be on the outskirts of Jecha's troops in a few moments to set up. From there, it is up to you to prove why Livia chose the four of you in the first place."

"Seven," Seondzus said in Twillo's head. "Correct the fox."

"Seven of us," Twillo said.

The red dragon wasn't wrong.

Chapter Twenty-Seven

Battle Hardened

THE HARDTOP CONTINUED toward the east, the stretch of sheer nothingness interrupted by Jecha's troops. There were hundreds gathered, and they weren't just the Honor Guard and the Senja Warriors. Even with his brief glimpse of what was to come, seconds after they appeared courtesy of Preshka's portaling, Twillo saw the telltale signs of lower-level grunts and Brethren mercenaries. How had Jecha been able to gather such a force in such a short amount of time? How had he done it while being pursued by Ariosto's roving sandstorm?

Twillo knew the answer.

It was through the sheer power of his influence, the way the God of Carnage was able to corrupt the minds of mortals, as he had done to Renda. That was the only answer. But to see the troops in front of a group of dragons, including Ramide and Nalig, told Twillo something else—Jecha's power extended past mortals. He could control dragons.

This also meant that Anneli and Katashi would be at the fight as well.

Twillo steeled himself for this. He didn't know if there would be an encounter, but he suspected as much. Twillo knew Jecha well enough to know that he was an expert at psychological warfare, that Jecha would use their presence to turn the tide of the battle.

He wasn't going to let that happen.

Twillo's focus shifted to setting up the pocket shelter. Once it was in place, and Vradon was down on the platform, Twillo summoned Adventus and Seondzus.

A hill was the only thing between Jecha's forces and his group. It was a smart location, one chosen by Father

Dawn himself to give them advantage. As soon as they breached that threshold, as soon as they crossed that hill separating them from Jecha's forces, it would be on.

And Twillo wanted part of it.

He had to be part of it, at least initially. All that had happened since his fateful meeting with Adventus, from the attack that had ripped Twillo's body in half to later joining forces with Princess Embla and learning even more about the dragonessence system—it was all for this moment, all leading up to this epic encounter.

"I am ready," Seondzus said, her sword gleaming from the pink morning sun. Her tone, while often comical, had shifted. Adventus stood by her with his enormous glaive. Even though his face was mostly concealed, Twillo could read the grave look the dragon warrior carried. It was one shared by Ariosto, the warrior monk standing with his fists at his side, energy flaring around his knuckles, face obscured by his conical hat.

"Let me know when I should summon Vendir," Princess Embla said.

Preshka stepped forward, the white fox's seven tails all held upright. "Before you do, you must open the portal to the Realm of the Forgotten. That is the surprise attack that will destroy Jecha's focus."

"Very well." Ariosto produced the strange satchel that they had received in the Harvest Mountains. He opened it carefully and the golden gemstones floated out. Hovering them, Ariosto pushed the gemstones to a point overhead, about ten feet up, where they grew in luminosity.

The gemstones spun, faster and faster until they ultimately collided in the center. This produced a shimmering glitter of dragonessence that rushed upward, scattering toward the clouds.

"That's it?" Vradon asked, his hands trembling.

"It will be any moment now," Preshka said.

The entire world seemed to quake as purple lightning crackled, splitting the dark clouds. The sky above the battlefield churned as a turbulent vortex of silver and green took shape. Reality itself folded backward, the seam of existence undone, the skyscape untethered. A dark abyss formed at the center of the dazzling vortex, one flashing with bolts of dragonessence and prismatic light that pulsed and twitched.

"I'll go," Adventus said as he changed into his vordic form. "Someone must instruct them. They'll know who I am!" He took to the sky, his enormous serpentine body slithering higher as if he were on land. Seondzus bristled, as if she wanted to join her counterpart, but she ultimately stayed in her dragon warrior form as the portal continued to roil with power.

Twillo looked to Princess Embla, who shook, his oldest friend holding her wrist with her other hand. She bowed, as if she was making some pact with herself, and summoned Vendir. He appeared directly behind her and stretched his wings. The white dragon tilted his head up toward the vortex, one that had caused great winds to whip over the future battlefield. Once the princess was mounted, Vendir took to the sky.

"Let's go to the top," Ariosto said as he pointed up the hill.

They reached the top just as the portal's edge started to shiver. Like a cascade of falling stars, dragons poured forth from the celestial portal. Ethereal flames flickered off their bodies as they continued to press through the open skygate. They were met by Adventus, who valiantly floated in front of the arriving dragons.

It was only a few moments later that the dragons all shifted to face Jecha's forces, all of whom scrambled to address the inevitable.

More dragonessence flared around Ariosto's fists. "Are we ready?"

"I think we are," Twillo said as he activated his dragonaura through the mudra. "Livia, with us."

Ariosto nodded. "Livia is here. She is here, her robes are behind our every move. Let's go! This is our chance!"

Twillo beat back the elven orcs with Firebreath, which ignited parts of their armor. A few pushed through the mana-fire and came in swinging, only to encounter Adventus and Seondzus. The two dragon warriors cleared through some of the ranks until Jecha's own dragon warriors appeared on the scene, the epic clash imminent.

Adventus batted his glaive at an incoming assailant and managed to knock a sword away. His staggering opponent followed up with a technique similar to Firebreath. Ducking the next attempt, Adventus swung through the flames with his glaive and was met by a mana-powered shield that had appeared on his opponent's arm. A Brethren assassin tried for him and Adventus struck him down with his fist, instantly killing the man.

Flash of Fata Morgana disoriented an incoming group of grunts. Twillo cleared through them as the men and women tried to get their bearings, his sword drawing wounds and death. He needed to find Jecha, but had yet to see the God of Carnage in the pandemonium that had ensued since the release of the dragons.

Above, the collisions in the sky mirrored the clash on the hardtop.

Dragons laid down fire, the fight soon defined by intense plumes and sizzling heat interspersed with cries of agony. Yet the skies had enemy dragons as well, who swept into the ranks of the good dragons. Occasionally, one of the dragons would fall out of the air, which would smash into the forces below, killing more of Jecha's men.

Where was the God of Carnage?

Twillo ducked under a sword and came up with a spinning cross-slash that cut his opponent down. Another tried to run him down but was thwarted by Ariosto, who throat-chopped the man, flashed behind him, and struck the man so hard in the small of his back that Twillo was fairly certain he had killed him.

"Any sign of Jecha?" Twillo asked.

"Not yet, but be prepared for—"

Ariosto didn't have a chance to finish his sentence.

Zombie Katashi and Anneli stood before the two of them, their wristlets glowing.

"You've come far enough," Katashi said, only his voice wasn't his own. It was the voice of Jecha.

Katashi summoned Nalig the dragon, who tried to fight his influence but quickly came under Jecha's spell. Anneli did the same with Ramide, the towering, horned dragon instantly taking to the sky.

Ramide slammed into a smaller dragon, one that had been released from the portal, grabbed it in his huge jaw, and tore it in half. The top of the dragon's body fell right in front of Twillo and Ariosto just as Adventus and Seondzus stepped up, their blades at the ready.

"We have no other choice, relic hunter," Seondzus told him. She transformed to her vordic form and bolted upward, the red dragon twisting toward Ramide.

"Do what must be done, left-handed one," Adventus told Twillo as he too morphed into his vordic form. He raced toward Seondzus with plans to aid her in her fight against Ramide. Nalig the green dragon, who had been hovering over Katashi, took off as well.

Twillo and Ariosto exchanged glances. "Which would you prefer?" the warrior monk asked.

"Neither."

"In that case, I will take Katashi. He will prove formidable."

Princess Embla flew overhead and dropped to the ground. She was up on her feet in a matter of moments, now holding her dagger. "We have to," she told Twillo as she fired a searing shot of dragonessence, one that struck Anneli in the shoulder.

As much as it pained Twillo to attack his former companions, he knew that it was necessary. They were dead, and Jecha was merely controlling their bodies. This also meant that they fought like they were possessed, Anneli moving faster than Twillo had ever seen her move before. She was on Princess Embla in a matter of seconds, Embla narrowly missing her opening strike.

Zombie Anneli kicked the princess to the side and came for Twillo, who blocked her next attack. He could feel her intensity, which was at odds with her empty black eyes.

Anneli seemed to sneer at him as she twisted to the side and drove her sword directly into Twillo's chest. At least that was where her sword would have turned up had it not been for the armor that he had taken from the pocket realm. The chestplate protected Twillo, her forward trajectory causing her to stumble. Twillo brought his sword around, yet was unable to finish her off for good as he was hit by a stray bolt of dragonessence.

The blast sent him tumbling backward, straight into a pile of fallen soldiers.

He pushed himself out from the pile just as Nalig released a plume of fire overhead, one meant for Twillo. After rolling out of the way, Twillo used Core Eruption to charge a helmet that he just so happened to pick up. As Nalig came in again, he prepared to chuck the helmet directly at the green dragon. He waited until she was just close enough that she wouldn't be able to change her flight path and released the charged helmet.

The explosion tore through her wing and caused the dragon to sail toward the ground. Twillo looked up just as a large shadow came over him.

He started to run, and ultimately used Dragonflight to catapult himself away from Ramide, who struck the ground, a victim of Adventus and Seondzus' concentrated attacks.

Twillo had no time to see how they had done, or what had become of the two dragons. Anneli had already started engaging him again, the elven orc swinging her sword with the intensity of a berserker. "You'll never win," he told her, a message for Jecha. "You have failed."

The words caused Anneli's eyes to twitch, the woman seething by the point she came in again for another attack. She swung at who she thought was Twillo, her sword going straight through his body, and found out the hard way that the real Twillo had used Enchanting Deception to conjure a replica.

After landing behind her through the power of Dragonflight, Twillo put all of his force into his next strike, one that saw Anneli's head leaving her body.

He thought he was done, that the gruesome decapitation would have done the trick, but then Anneli's headless body turned to Twillo and brought her sword up.

"By Livia—"

Seondzus swooped down, grabbed Anneli with her claws, and careened upward before Twillo could say anything else. The red dragon spiraled back toward the ground with Anneli in her claws. Seondzus dropped her at the last second, the splatter that followed enough to make Twillo look away.

"Sorry for that," Seondzus said as she hovered before Twillo. She was huffing now, and looked injured. "I'll give the cat man a claw as well. He could use it."

The red dragon moved toward zombie Katashi. She whipped her body into him, caught the kitsune, and zipped into the air. She came down fast and slammed Katashi's body against the ground, causing another unceremonious death.

Twillo knew not to look at it this way, yet the notion did cross his heart for a moment. He quickly got his bearings, locked eyes with Ariosto, and moved deeper into the fight.

A group of elven orcs charged toward Twillo and Ariosto with their glaives pointed at them.

"Come on!" the warrior monk shouted. Ariosto used Voidshift to absorb the first strike that reached him. Twillo moved around him and knocked another of the weapons out of the way. Ariosto followed this up with a kick that produced a wave of dragonessence. It knocked the group back, revealing someone in the midst of battle.

Jecha was heading their way. The God of Carnage wore his tattered robes over thick black armor. Covering his face was a new helm, one shaped like that of a dragon's skull and lined with sharp protrusions that curved in random directions.

"Go!" Ariosto told Twillo. "I will lead him to you."

"We will help," Adventus said as he swooped over Twillo. He torpedoed to the ground, now in his dragon form. Seondzus did the same.

"Good luck, relic hunter!" Seondzus said as she brought her sword up and prepared to charge Jecha.

Dragonflight sent Twillo up and over the flight.

He hit the mudra again, moving like a grasshopper toward the pocket shelter. Confusion came to him upon his next landing. Twillo didn't know exactly where he was now in relation to the pocket shelter. The fog of war was too thick, the sky a mess of dragons as Twillo fumbled to get his Pathweaver's Compass out.

His heart jumped when a white dragon swooped overhead and grabbed Twillo by hooking its claws under his armor. Twillo nearly thrust his sword up in a desperate attempt to stop the dragon when he heard Embla's voice.

"We have you, Jhaeros!" she called down to him.

Even as he whisked through the air over the fight, shock roiling through him, Twillo managed a sigh of relief.

He just needed to get the trap ready.

Vendir reached the pocket shelter and dropped Twillo beside it. Much to his surprise, Princess Embla landed. She turned to him.

"Your Grace?" Twillo started to ask as she stepped forward and kissed his cheek. She placed her hand on his waist, their eyes locked.

"Jhaeros, you know what must be done."

Princess Embla's eyes never watered; she never showed any sign that she felt this would be the last time she would see him. There was defiance in her gaze, there always was, but there was also love, and Twillo could sense it in that moment. Whatever hesitation she'd had earlier was gone.

He felt a tremor in his chest; her genuine affection for Twillo transported him away from the battlefield. It was something he wouldn't soon forget. Not only was he doing this for the Four Kingdoms, for the three friends he had lost, he was doing this for his future.

Their future together.

"I will be back, Emmy," he said, almost as an afterthought. "And we will destroy the pocket shelter after. Have Vendir ready."

"I will be ready," the white dragon assured him.

"Go," Embla told Twillo, "and make sure Vradon lives as well. Our court will need a Keeper of Wisdom."

"Can I get another kiss before I go?" he asked, the words leaving his lips before he could fully process how bad his timing was considering they were on the outskirts of an active warzone.

"No, but you can after." Embla floated up to her dragon. "Livia is with you."

Twillo watched the dragon take to the sky. "Livia is with us all," he said before turning to the pocket shelter. Rather than take the ladder, Twillo hovered down to the bottom to find Vradon pacing near the edge of the platform.

"How is it going up there?" the monk asked, squinting upward. "All I can hear is dragons roaring and swords clashing."

"Sounds about right," Twillo said. "And as to how it's going, everything should come to a head soon. Are you ready?"

"I will do what I must."

"Are you sure? You can head up now, before Jecha comes. It will be safer. The princess needs her Keeper of Wisdom more than she needs a disgruntled former saracent turned relic hunter out of Sparrow's Rise."

"Prince Ravenna is an important role as well, Jhaeros, and Keeper of Wisdom is a title that is earned." A rare darkness formed on his face. "I will earn it today, and your name will be renewed. For the kingdoms."

"For the kingdoms." Twillo crouched in front of the large stone at the center of the platform to prepare the trap.

Chapter Twenty-Eight

Done and Dusted

THE WAIT WAS EXCRUCIATING. There were several times that Twillo thought about heading up and checking on Ariosto and the dragons, making sure the trap was in motion. Yet he remained, mostly because of Vradon, who always sensed that the relic hunter was itching to leave.

"We have to stick to the plan, Jhaeros," the monk would say. "It is the only way. Ariosto will make it happen. If anyone can do it, it's him."

"The only way, the only way," Twillo said under his breath as his eyes traced over the large stone in the center of the platform, the one he'd charged with Warding Glyph.

"The places we find ourselves," Vradon told him at some point, after what felt like days had passed on the platform, their fates postponed.

"That isn't the first time you've said that."

"If ever I was to get a tattoo, that would be a good one."

"In Old Sagic?" Twillo asked.

"Why not Modern Sagic?"

"Because the old script looks better." Twillo brought his hand to the tattoo on his neck, the one directly behind his ear. He remembered getting in E'Kanth at the start of all this, in the days before binding souls with Adventus. He lowered his hand to his chest, where the names Anneli, Olaf, and Katashi were written vertically. His newest work.

Twillo heard some commotion above. He squinted up at the opening as a dragon he didn't recognize flew overhead.

"Friend or foe?"

"It's hard to tell with the dragons," he told Vradon. "But we should be ready."

"Jecha lands, I distract him momentarily, and you push him over the side. Or the other way around," Vradon reminded Twillo.

"Or you just stay back and let's see if I can't take care of this. If I am forced to make the ultimate sacrifice, give my utmost apologies to Emmy."

"Emmy? Her Highness? Yes, wait. No. No, you absolutely are—" Vradon huffed. "Why are you saying this now? Don't say this now, Jhaeros! That is not part of the plan."

"Because—"

Twillo and Vradon heard the sounds of a struggle above. This was followed by Jecha's voice, which seemed to amplify into the space of the pocket shelter.

"Where is he!?" he screamed.

Twillo watched a shadow move over the pocket shelter, one that belonged to Ariosto. The warrior monk pointed down into the shelter.

Twillo tapped his knuckles together, activating his dragonaura. "Here it comes."

"Then I will deal with you next," Jecha said. A wave of force struck Ariosto before he could use Voidshift, freezing the warrior monk in place.

Jecha approached the pocket shelter, his torn robes beating in the wind over the opening. He peered down into it and lowered instantly. He stood before Twillo, the wolfish grin on his face mostly disguised by his grotesque helm.

Before Jecha could say anything else, Twillo struck him in the chest with a blast of dragonessence. This caused the God of Carnage to stumble backward, his heel hitting the rock that Twillo had charged. The explosion that followed pushed Jecha to the right, just a few feet away from the edge of the platform.

Twillo activated Voidshift, the power tracing through him.

Jecha twisted and brought his sword in Twillo's direction. This produced a wave of power that would have tossed Twillo over the other side of the platform had it not been for Voidshift. Twillo's heels ground into the stone surface, yet he held strong, Jecha's first strike completely absorbed.

Jecha sneered. "The cat-man has trained you well, but it will all be in vain. I didn't believe him when he'd said you were hiding in here. But I see that you are a coward as well. A true Icenordian coward."

Twillo hit him with Ripple Tide, which seemed to pass right over his assailant's shoulders. The God of Carnage rushed forward with a strike.

Klank!

Twillo was able to block it and release the stored Voidshift power at the same time.

This forced Jecha back. He brought his blackened sword up and turned to Vradon, the look in his glowing red eyes telling Twillo that he'd known the monk was there all along.

Twillo used Scaled Lash, which sent a whip of dragonessence forward that struck Jecha in the shoulder. He came upon the God of Carnage with his sword overhead, fury filling his heart as he tried to deliver a strike that would force Jecha closer to the edge of the platform.

He didn't care now. Twillo didn't care if he went over the edge with Jecha. Vradon had to survive and the Kingdoms needed to live on.

Much faster than Twillo, Jecha swiveled and knocked his sword out of his hand, his strike so strong that Twillo could feel it in his bones. Twillo watched in horror as his father's sword hit the edge of the platform, spun, and went over the side, his blade disappearing into the void.

The terror he felt at being weaponless shifted to something else, something much worse as Vradon used this opportunity to tackle Jecha. The monk's girth made this feat much easier than it should have been. The two hit the platform, just a few feet away from the edge.

Twillo watched them scramble for a moment, his mind racing as he finally summoned his Enchanting Deception card. Jecha began to beat Vradon across the back with the hilt of his demonic sword. He got to his feet, and prepared to deliver a deathstrike to Vradon when one of Twillo's replicants appeared.

Rather than kill Vradon, Jecha swung his sword at the replicant. Twillo used this opportunity to come at Jecha from a different angle. He shouldered into the larger man, who fell over Vradon, the monk on hands and knees, wheezing as he tried to get up.

"Fools!" Jecha was even closer to the edge of the platform now.

Yet he was also on his feet in a matter of seconds, where he was able to fire a bolt of dark mana from his sword. It struck Twillo, freezing him in place.

Unbeknownst to the God of Carnage, the relic hunter had anticipated this. Twillo stood there across from Jecha, almost completely frozen, his hand trembling over his demon bear brooch.

Twillo's eyes twitched as he watched Vradon get out of the way, the monk breathing heavily, clearly wounded. Jecha, who stood at the edge of the platform, removed his helm to reveal Rowian's orcish face. His skin was pale, evident of how long the body had been dead.

The God of Carnage smiled, his teeth jaundice yellow. "You have lost—"

This smile quickly shifted to surprise as Yasuna the demon bear came barreling in his direction. She struck Jecha and the two went over the side of the platform, straight into the void beyond.

Vradon looked over to Twillo in shock. "How?" he began to ask.

Fwwwip!

The demon bear brooch returned to Twillo, the piece tottering on the platform just before his feet, Yasuna safe.

Twillo, who remained partially frozen, felt a tension leave him, one that seemed as if it had been bottled up for years. "By Livia..."

But then he saw Jecha's clawed hand slap onto the side of the platform, the God of Carnage still hanging on.

"I've got it!" Summoning all the strength he had left, Vradon pushed to his feet and stomped Jecha's hand. He kept at it, fury writ large, the monk putting everything he had into each stomp.

Twillo wanted desperately to help him, yet the effects of Jecha's attacks were still preventing him from movement. Was there something else he could do? Twillo cycled through his Arcane Cards in his mind, his mudras, his relics—nothing.

All he could do was have faith that Vradon would be successful. The monk took two steps back and came at Jecha's hand with a running kick. This did the trick, the orcish fingers finally forced backward off the platform.

"Nooooo!" the God of Carnage cried, his voice echoing through the void even though it shouldn't have.

Silence followed, one peppered with the breaths of two Icenordian elves who were experiencing an adrenaline the likes of which they'd never felt before.

Reality rippled and folded around an explosion of radiant luminescence. Preshka stepped out of the heart of this spectacular display, her seven tails settling, her presence transforming the very air around her.

The white fox sat, and shifted her gaze to the void beyond, where Jecha could still be heard screaming. "You have done it," she said, Father Dawn clearly speaking through her. "Now, you must destroy the pocket shelter. I will make sure my brother stays here until you are able to get to the top. I'd like a few words with him, the last words he will ever hear."

Twillo could move again. This sensation was so sudden that he nearly tripped over his own feet. Vradon joined him, the monk limping.

"By Livia," Vradon said, tears in his eyes.

"We did," Twillo told him. "Let's get you to the top." He helped Vradon reach the ladder. Once he was up, Twillo floated out of the shelter to join him.

Vradon hugged Twillo, full on sobbing now. "I don't know why I'm crying," he said. "I've never been this... this happy and scared and relieved in my entire life."

"That would explain the tears," Twillo told him as he patted Vradon on the shoulder.

The frame of the pocket shelter started to tremble. They heard a booming voice, one that seemed to ripple across the expanse of desert as if it were in a deep cavern.

Ariosto, who stood several yards away from the pocket shelter, limped over to join them, his face yet again obscured by his conical hat. The warrior monk looked to the sky just as Adventus, Seondzus, and Vendir shifted in their direction, Princess Embla on the smaller white dragon's back.

Twillo gave her the signal, the relic hunter so overcome with joy that he couldn't speak.

It was time to burn the relic. Vendir laid down a trail of fire, one that ignited the pocket shelter. He made another pass, plumes lifting from the ground, the pocket shelter cackling in the heat.

The dragon landed with the others, and soon, Princess Embla joined Twillo, Vradon, and Ariosto to watch the pocket shelter turn to ash. She slipped her arm around Twillo's waist, her head pressed against the side of his chest. "I knew you could do it, Jhaeros," she said as the flames grew higher. "The God of Carnage is no more."

Epilogue

The Relic Hunter and the Cursed Grove

-One Year Later-

TWILLO STOOD before the Miyaji Red Gate. The monument pierced the churn of restless waves, its opposing presence a testament to how well Tributarians had mastered their ocean environment over the years. Seagulls twisted in and out of the air above the gate, the brown-faced birds diving into the water and returning with small blue-shelled crabs. As many crabs as there were in the water, there were even more on the white sand beach, enough that Twillo was certain that it was mating season for the blue-shelled crustaceans.

"Dinner will be easy tonight," said Seondzus, her voice currently in his head. "You were planning on bringing some back to Illagorn, right?"

"Crab is an excellent meal, Left-Handed One. For once, I agree with Seondzus."

"You are so agreeable," the red dragon told her counterpart. "It's your weakest trait."

"And I am certain he would like to bring some back to—"

"Give me a moment," Twillo told the dragons as he produced the Pathweaver's Compass.

According to the relic hunter named Garnax, the haunted doll was somewhere near the Miyagi Red Gate, in a box buried beneath some ruins.

He turned back to the jungle beyond, one that had nearly overtaken the white sand beach Twillo currently stood on. "I really hope it isn't underwater," he said as he looked down at the compass, the sun gleaming off its scratched surface. "Find the haunted doll."

The needle began to twitch. A blue-shelled crab crawled over Twillo's boot as he watched the needle spin and finally come to a stop. It pointed in the direction of the jungle.

"Good." He placed his hand on the hilt of the machete he had acquired from Illagorn, the capital of the Tribute Islands. The machete hadn't been a cheap weapon. According to the dwarven blacksmith, it was the same one that the Brethren used for local 'missions,' as she had called it.

"Are we going into the jungle? We're going into the jungle, aren't we?" asked Seondzus, the red dragon suddenly excited. "It's about time we do something adventurous. The last several months have been the most boring of my life."

"That is called stability," Adventus told her. "And it wasn't boring at all."

"Care to join me?" Twillo asked, stopping the dragons before they could bicker.

"I'll stay here," Adventus said. "I detest the jungle and will only join you if I must."

Seondzus took her dragon warrior form. She threw her arms back and inhaled deeply through her nostrils.

"Smell the air here! It is so fresh." She approached Twillo and placed a hand on his shoulder. "Do you want me to go ahead? I'll clear out all the vines and scare anything away that is stupid enough to try to bite you." She stepped around him and brandished her sword. "Perhaps they'll put up a fight."

He shook his head. "You can just scare things away if and when they come. But I doubt they will. I'm so lucky to have this." Twillo showed her the compass. Seondzus turned back and looked down at the relic as he continued: "I guess I could have come to the gate here and explored on my own, but it likely would have taken much longer. Weeks, even."

"Isn't that the fun in it?"

"It is, but it is also nice to know you are looking for something that actually exists. If the haunted doll didn't exist, the compass wouldn't work. But I wouldn't know that without the relic."

"I didn't think of that part. Clever."

"I prefer lucky."

"You are Livia's favorite pet." Seondzus patted him on the head. Twillo didn't like it when she did this, but she seemed beyond correcting at this point. She turned away, brought her sword back, and struck down the first vine she came to. "Try to keep up."

"Yes," Twillo said as he drew his machete. "Let's see what we can uncover."

Twillo noticed a strange heaviness in the air as the pair pushed deeper into the jungle. It was entirely at odds with the light wind that he'd felt on the beach earlier.

Twillo was certain they were close.

To think it had taken him a year to get to this point, a year that he was still processing, from defeating the God of Carnage to everything that had happened after. Yet here he was, finally able to go after the haunted doll.

There was always the question of why he would even do such a thing, but anyone that knew the relic hunter by now knew that these kinds of questions were ultimately futile.

Twillo was there because it would be a challenge. He was there because he was a completionist when it came to mapstones and any trustworthy rumors he picked up from reliable relic hunters like Garnax. He was there because relic hunting was an integral part of his life force, the very blood that pumped through him strengthened by adventure and discovery.

The jungle grew in denseness, much of Twillo's time spent cutting through the foliage. Seondzus helped, and when it became too much, Adventus begrudgingly joined her, the white dragon swinging his glaive with expert precision.

"What would you do without us?" Seondzus asked Twillo after they'd taken down a particularly tangled mess of underbrush.

"I've often wondered that myself." Twillo sliced down a flowering vine and waved away the colorful pollinators that buzzed into the air after. "But if we're being honest, I would have likely cut my way through. The only difference is it would have taken several days versus several hours."

"And you'd camp here overnight?"

"I would," Twillo told the red dragon. "It wouldn't be comfortable, especially with the mosquitos." He slapped the back of his neck to prove his point. "But I'd make it work. I always do."

"Wait, I think there is something here." Adventus used his glaive to clear away more of the brush. He revealed a tomb-shaped stone with Sagic words carved into its surface.

"Nice find, Adventus."

"Thank you, Left-Handed One."

"What does it say?" Twillo asked as the dragon warrior got down onto a knee so he could better read the text.

"In the heart where sunlight clove, death and beauty intertwine, lies the Cursed Grove, where the green seeks to dine."

Seondzus angrily hacked her sword into a tree, startling Adventus.

"What has gotten into you?" he hissed at his counterpart.

"I'm sick of these blasted riddles! Why must there always be riddles? Do I need to go get the monk?"

"No, you don't. He's no better at solving riddles than him," Adventus said as he nodded at Twillo. "What do you think?"

"The Cursed Grove, where the green seeks to dine." Twillo wiped sweat from his brow. "It's obvious to me."

"It is? How?" asked Seondzus. "I hate riddles!" She struck another tree with her sword.

"We're going to have to fight the foliage itself. It will try to eat us, meaning we will have to fight it."

The red dragon grew excited. "Do you mean to say I'll be able to burn most of this jungle down? If so, then I'll gladly accept that challenge."

As if on cue, the heavens above erupted, the orchestration followed by a sudden and intense rainshower.

Adventus laughed. "Oh, that is ripe. That truly is ripe."

"I can still produce fire in the rain," Seondzus told him.

"But its burn power will be limited."

Seondzus shouldered ahead. "Well?" she asked Adventus and Twillo. "Are we going to the cursed grove or not?"

Twillo checked his compass to confirm they were heading in the right direction. "Apparently, we are."

The rain and the heat caused an instant humidity, one that soon reached the realm of unbearable as Twillo and his two dragons hacked their way deeper into the jungle.

Occasionally, they'd spook an animal, which would always cause Seondzus to laugh and point out the fact that the creatures living in this environment should be sharp enough to see a swashbuckling Icenordian and a pair of dragons coming along.

The humor in her tone changed once the ground started moving.

It began with the roots, which slithered like serpents as they all pulled back toward a copse of enormous trees towering over the jungle. Twillo expected to fight the branches at that stage. What he didn't expect was for the trees to uproot themselves and knock any of the foliage in front of them to the side as they all came for Twillo and his dragons.

"Blasted rain!" Seondzus said, the fire from her palm having much less of an effect.

"Perhaps we should take a larger form," Adventus told her.

"You take something larger. I'm going to hack these trees into—"

The white dragon burst into the air, Adventus now in his vordic form.

Wham!

He smashed into the first tree to reach them, giving Twillo just a bit more time to figure out a mode of attack. While Seondzus protected the relic hunter from incoming branches—cursing the entire time—Twillo cycled through his cards and decided Core Eruption and Warding Glyph would be of use here.

He activated his dragonaura and charged toward the center of the enemy trees, where he used Dragonflight to narrowly avoid one of their club-like branches. Twillo landed beside one of the trees and touched it with his bare hand. While it moved, he ducked down and found himself in a groove created between the trunk and its roots, one that shifted as the tree charged toward Seondzus.

Once Twillo knew it had been charged to the point of no return, he used Dragonflight again, the explosion that followed filling the rainy sky with a mixture of dragonessence and splinters as the tree ripped in two.

"One down, good!" Adventus swooped over Twillo to protect the relic hunter from another of the killer trees. He was met by a thick branch that shot him to the side. Seondzus rushed forward next, the red dragon also in her vordic form to help her companion.

While the dragons distracted the trees, Twillo moved onto his next target. He grabbed onto a swinging branch, and used it to carry him to a tree in the middle of the mayhem.

As he flew through the air, Twillo charged the branch using Warding Glyph. He bailed, landed on the ground, and bounded into the sky again with Dragonflight just as the branch he'd charged was triggered by the movement of another branch.

The trees lurched as the explosion tore into their trunks and limbs. The ones that fell did so violently. Still combative, they twisted toward Twillo and the dragons, trying to take them out in their fall.

Using his body as a shield, Adventus whipped through them, and was able to bring a few more animated trees down in the process.

As Seondzus hacked away limbs, Twillo summoned Ripple Tide, which sent a tsunami-sized wave of dragonessence forward, one that left him feeling ecstatic as the dust settled.

The sound of the rain reached his ears, what was left of the grove peaceful yet again.

Catching his breath, Twillo watched as Seondzus speared her blade into one more tree. He scanned the area, his eyes darting across rain droplets as they plinked against puddles in the mud.

Realizing that mud would only get worse, Twillo hovered a foot into the air. He checked the compass and found the needle twitching. Twillo wiped the face of the relic with the front of his shirt and looked down at it again.

"I think it's pointing down."

Seondzus shouldered up next to Twillo. Her action would have sent him stumbling forward had he not been ready for the dragon and her constant aggressive presence. "Down? As in, the haunted doll is buried?" she asked.

"I think so. Garnax said it was buried beneath some ruins, but I don't see any ruins here. This tells me that it is underground. Maybe there's a bit more to this cursed grove than meets the eye."

"Meaning?"

He shrugged her question off. "I don't know. Let's take a look around, but be prepared to dig."

"With what?" she asked him.

"Your claws?"

"Please. I won't muddy myself in that way."

Twillo smirked at the red dragon. "We'll figure it out. We always do."

Digging in the mud during a rainstorm was no easy task, especially without the right tools. The dragons were able to help, Seondzus with her tail and Adventus wielding a wedge-shaped piece of wood with his jaw, but it still presented complications. Twillo used his machete to shape a flat spade out of one of the branches, yet he was never able to clear as much dirt as the dragons.

"And you're sure it is down here?" Seondzus asked after they had made a hole about six feet wide and four feet deep.

Twillo wiped his mud-caked hands on his pant legs and checked his magical compass. "I'm pretty sure." He took in a deep breath, the smell of fresh mud and rain invigorating even if he was starting to tire from all the digging.

"Pretty sure? I don't like the odds there. It's raining, it's muddy, and it will soon be night, yet you still want to continue?" She flicked some mud off her tail. "You're making me regret coming here."

"Do you have anything better to do?" Adventus asked her, the branch in his mouth garbling his words.

"I can think of a number of things that would be more fun. For one, we could take a swim in the sea and clean the mud from our scales. We could go do that now and be done with this. I can only imagine what they will think once we deliver the relic hunter to Illagorn covered in mud." She laughed. "You should see yourself."

"I'm aware that I am covered in mud," Twillo told Seondzus as he continued digging. "It comes with the territory."

"It's in your hair and on your face."

"It will wash. We can both take a dip in the ocean. For now, let's keep digging. I think we're getting closer."

"And what makes you think that?"

Twillo gave the dragon a wink. "Call it a relic hunter's intuition. Don't leave home without it."

They continued digging, their chatter replaced by the sounds of the jungle, from the hum of rain on the foliage to the melodious tones of tropical birds; from the buzz of mosquitoes and insects that seemed to take a liking to the relic hunter to the distant sound of falling limbs.

He swatted them away and continued digging until he hit a bit of solid stone. "I found something!" Twillo moved more of the mud as he reached a solid structure.

"Dig down the sides here along the front," he instructed the two dragons. Twillo stood atop the structure as the pair moved mud, stone, and dirt out of the way. He lowered once he was able, Twillo now standing directly in front of a door made of stone, his back to a wall of dirt.

"I think it is some sort of mausoleum," he said once he noticed the spiritual carvings and the overall shape of the building.

"All of this for a haunted doll?" The red dragon was now on top of the mausoleum and looking down at him.

Twillo ran his hand along the stone door. It was smooth to the touch aside from a few gooey hunks of mud still attached to it. "Let's blast it open, but do so carefully. We should also give ourselves a bit more room before we do so. Then we can head inside, collect the relic, and get back to Illagorn by morning."

"Do you think this will take all night, Left-Handed One?" Adventus asked.

"That seems like a real possibility. But at least we're almost there. We're almost there."

After the dragons cleared more space in front of the door, Twillo charged the stone with Warding Glyph. He flew back up to the top and found a rock about the size of a melon. He used Core Eruption to transfer dragonessence into the rock and tossed it down toward the door, which he figured would be plenty of charge.

The explosion that followed sent up a cloud of dust that was quickly cleared by the falling rain.

Twillo could now see the hole that he'd caused in the door, how it had cracked the stone and caused a large chunk of stone to fall outward. It was going to take a little bit of work to further expand the hole, but they were almost there.

"I can't believe we're doing all of this for a haunted doll," Seondzus said as Twillo lowered into the pit they had dug.

"All in a day's work," he told the red dragon. "Let's see what's inside."

The place certainly felt ancient. As Twillo stepped into the mausoleum, he was greeted by a biting cold at odds with the sticky humidity outside. The air smelt of wet stone and decay, which caused him to shift to breathing out of his mouth.

Seondzus, who was the first to step inside, moved a bit closer to the relic hunter as if she was frightened by the interior of the mausoleum.

"This place gives me the creeps," she said as Twillo peered deeper into the dark.

It was quite the building, some twenty feet in length with covered tombs on either side of a walkway made of sandstone. Even after all the years since the mausoleum had been open, the sandstone was still slick, as if it were recently polished.

A dark shadow stretched into the room, one caused by Adventus, who now stood in the doorway poised to fight anything that would try to harm Twillo.

"Move. You're blocking what little light there is," Seondzus told him.

"It's best I stay here, just in case," he called back to her.

"In case what?"

"Your guess is as good as mine."

The temperature dropped even further as Twillo reached the end of the mausoleum. He checked his compass in the dark to find it vibrating. Twillo glanced around. There was nothing here aside from a child-sized sarcophagus.

"Find the haunted doll yet?" Seondzus asked, even though she was right behind him.

"You would know if I found it." Twillo focused again on the small sarcophagus. He traced his hand along its stone top and noticed that it was warm to the touch. He also felt a groove, one just big enough to fit the blade of his machete.

"It's in there, isn't it?" she asked.

"Let's find out." Twillo placed both hands on the grip of his machete. He drove it into the opening and used his body weight to pry the lid to the side. The stone hit the ground, the sound loud enough that Twillo felt for a moment as if his eardrums had popped.

Twillo looked inside to find a doll with a porcelain-colored face, one that had been smeared with the grime of age, its painted features almost a mockery of innocence. Its tunic, which was once vibrant, had faded to a morose hue, pieces of which were tattered to a point beyond repair. The doll's tangled hair, once meticulously styled, was curled at the ends.

"Ugly, isn't it?" Seondzus asked.

"I wouldn't call it that," Twillo said as he continued to peer down at the doll. "I'm sure a dollmaker would be able to get it cleaned up."

"And what does the doll do?"

"What don't I do," said a scratchy male voice, one that sounded like that of a teenager.

The inside of the mausoleum came alive with fire as Seondzus released a plume from the palm of her hand.

"Easy!" Twillo told her. The flames rushed past, nearly singing his arm hairs.

"What in the blazes was that?" the same voice asked. *"Who let a firebeast in here?"*

"So it's you," Twillo told the doll, the face of which had started to twitch.

"It is me. To whom do I speak? I ask because your very life depends on what you tell me next."

"You would kill me?" Twillo asked carefully.

Adventus stepped into the mausoleum. "I'm coming."

"How many times do I have to tell you I'm already here?" Seondzus shoved past Twillo and aimed her palm at the doll. "Unless you want to truly understand the power of a dragon, I'd suggest you change your tone."

"Do you know what I am?"

"A haunted doll," Twillo told the voice. "At least according to what we've been told."

"Who speaks of me behind my back?"

"I am a relic hunter by trade. I learned of your existence from another relic hunter. I do not know where he heard about you, but he was right."

"Do you know what a haunted doll does?"

"I do not." Twillo felt his heart constrict as if someone had reached into his chest and squeezed the organ. He choked and took a step forward.

"That's it, I'm torching—"

"Wait!" Twillo told Seondzus. "Release me, doll!"

"The name is Kodaiye."

"Kodaiye, release me, dammit!"

Twillo felt the pang in his chest subside. "I believe we got off on the wrong foot," he told the haunted doll. "My name is Jhaeros Shotaro Vos, but you may call me Twillo."

"He should call you—"

"That doesn't matter right now," Twillo told Seondzus. He returned his focus to the doll. "You have been locked away in this tomb for some time. I am here to free you, if that is what you would like."

"Free me?" The tone of Kodaiye's voice changed, now tinged in sadness. *"So they're actually dead?"*

"Who?"

"The family. Someone put me in this stone cradle while I was sleeping."

"You sleep?"

"Is that the lady firebeast? There are two, are there not?"

"Two dragons, yes," Twillo told the doll. "I am Icenordian and I travel with two dragons. They are Seondzus, the lady firebeast, as you called her. And Adventus."

"That is rather impressive."

"You said you were placed here."

"I was," Kodaiye told Twillo. *"I assumed my family was upset with me. I can be a bit overprotective, you know. But I swear, I swear I've seen the errors in my ways and I will not curse people as quickly as I have in the past. I swear!"*

"You cursed people?"

"You are aware of what I am, are you not? I am a doll that protects a family. If anyone, and I mean anyone, even looks at my family in a strange way, and I find out about it? Heh." Kodaiye started to laugh maniacally and then stopped. *"Let's just say it will be the worst mistake of their life."*

"I see," Twillo told Kodaiye as he considered his options. "In that case, if you are interested in coming with us, you are more than welcome. I can also leave you here. But you should know that the family you looked after for so long has certainly passed, and by the age of this mausoleum, they may be closer to dust than they are skeleton."

"Ah, that's a pity. They weren't so bad in the end. Murderous Southfallians, but is there another kind of Southfallian?"

"There are now," Twillo said.

"Maybe you're right. Maybe it's best if I go. I honestly don't know how people will receive me now. My body is falling apart; I look like a doll several times my real age of what I'm guessing is a couple thousand years. Go figure."

"The doll is vain?"

"We all are when we've had this much time alone, firebeast," he told Seondzus.

"I'm fairly certain I can get you fixed up, but if I do, you can't talk to the craftspeople that repair you. Even if they are a bit curious regarding your age or where I found you."

"Do I really look that old?"

"You don't look that young, but I think with a new outfit and a few touch-ups, you'll look great," Twillo told the doll.

"I see. In that case, one more question before I make my decision."

"Yes?"

"Do you happen to have a family I can protect?"

Twillo smiled at the haunted doll. "I'm glad you asked."

The red dragon veered toward the sea. "I hope you don't mind getting wet!" was all Twillo told Kodaiye the haunted doll as Seondzus breached the tops of the waves.

The doll, which he had tucked under the front of his robes, didn't seem to mind at all as the red dragon broke through the surface of the water. She spun a few times to really get the bubbles moving.

"Again!" Kodaiye shouted as they came out of the sea.

Twillo laughed. "Fun, right? Much better than bathing."

Adventus, who was in his vordic form, dipped beneath the waves, the sight momentarily startling Twillo. He'd been soulbound to the white dragon for a year now, yet seeing him come out of the water with a shark in his mouth was unexpected.

"Looks like Adventus has a snack." Seondzus dipped back toward the surface of the sea. She tore through a school of fish. They exploded out of the water, Kodaiye laughing maniacally as Seondzus soared even higher.

"Again, again!"

"We'll need to settle a bit once we get near Illagorn. Dragons are still feared. It has only been—"

"As they should be," Seondzus said, interrupting Twillo.

"We'll need to land on a shore outside of the city. I think it's still dark enough for us to get in relatively close."

"Don't be such a Middlinger," Seondzus said, which was a phrase Icenordians used to describe someone from Middling who was too hesitant. "We'll fly high above the city, drop you, and you can fly down to your destination."

"Do what?" Kodaiye asked. *"You can fly?"*

"I can do a number of things," Twillo said, not wanting to go into detail with the doll. "And yes, Seondzus. I suppose that will work. But only because it is still dark."

"Higher it is!" The red dragon shifted upward. It wasn't long before Twillo and Kodaiye were completely dry, the powerful winds having an effect on Twillo's hair.

Adventus pulled up beside them and noticed this. The white dragon laughed. "You look like a lion, Left-Handed One."

Twillo roared in response, which had Kodaiye cracking up.

"Now that is funny! I haven't experienced humor in—"

"Thousands of years, we know." Seondzus twisted into a barrel roll.

With a powerful thrust of the dragon's mighty wings, Twillo and Kodaiye ascended rapidly. Surging skyward, her head locked in focus, her muscles rippling beneath her scales, Seondzus seemed to pulse with the wind. Higher and higher she went, the sea below becoming a murky tapestry of tropical blue, hidden by wispy clouds.

The air thinned, the stars seemingly larger, the sky an unfathomable purple tinged in wisps of twilight. In the thunderous silence that enveloped, Twillo could hear the rustling of her wings, the steady rhythm of her heart. He didn't know how fast they were traveling, or how far up they were, but he certainly could feel the effects in his lungs.

The world began to dim, but then it grew bright again, the ocean far below replaced by a glowing patchwork of homes and seaside businesses indicating they had reached Illagorn.

"We're here. Are you prepared, relic hunter?" Seondzus asked.

"Sure." Twillo made sure his bag was tucked under his clothing. "I'm going."

With Kodaiye held tightly to his chest, Twillo tilted over the side and began his plummet.

"By Livia!" Kodaiye shouted as the pair sailed toward a castle below.

The relic hunter and the haunted doll freefell for a few excruciating moments before Twillo finally took hold of the dragonessence all around him. He swooped up as if he were a dragon himself, and hovered for a moment as he located the castle.

"Almost there," he told Kodaiye. He felt his wristlets buzz, indicating both dragons had returned.

Twillo shifted toward the castle and landed on a wall walk.

He prepared for several of the guards to come running, and they did, the elven orcs all with weapons drawn.

"It's just me," he told the captain of the Honor Guard as she closed in on him, a woman named Zolsa.

"My Lordship?" The elven orc bowed her head and slowly lowered her sword. "Have you lost your bloody mind? What has happened to... your hair?"

Twillo started to laugh. He liked Zolsa for this reason. Regardless of his title, she still spoke to him as an equal.

"I haven't lost it yet. As for my hair. You don't like the new look?"

She shook her head. "No, Your Lordship, I do not."

"Zolsa, meet Kodaiye." Twillo moved his arm away from his chest to reveal the haunted doll's face.

Zolsa brought her sword up again, the men around her doing the same.

"It's fine, he's with me."

"What is this thing you possess?" she asked. "What has happened to its face, Your Lordship?"

Twillo looked down at Kodaiye's to see that the saltwater mixed with strong winds had completely removed the chipped paint on the doll's face.

"We took a bath. Let's call it that."

A wooden door slammed open and more of the Royal Guard came forward.

"At ease," Zolsa said. The elven orc bowed her head again as Vradon, the Keeper of Wisdom, approached, the monk in a maroon nightcap.

"Jhaeros, what are you doing?" Vradon couldn't help but laugh upon seeing his old friend. "Why do you look like you've been through hell and back and have the hairstyle to prove it?"

"No one seems to like my new look."

Vradon squeezed his large body through the rank of soldiers to get a better view of Twillo. "What do you...?" The monk gasped. "You found it, didn't you?"

Twillo grinned. "Yes, I did. Just as I said I would. I'm surprised you doubted me."

"I didn't doubt you for one minute. But was it worth it?" Vradon gave the doll a skeptical look. "It is quite ugly."

"You aren't so handsome yourself, fattie."

Vradon hopped backward and was nearly cut down by one of the elven orcs as the guard drew his blade, the others following suit.

"Easy, everyone," Twillo commanded them. "If you had given me a moment—"

"What was that voice?" Vradon asked. "Is Seondzus being crass?"

"Pfft!" Seondzus said in Twillo's head.

"He has a point," Adventus told his counterpart. "You are the crassest of us all."

"Relax, everyone. It's the doll," Twillo explained to Vradon and the guards. "His name is Kodaiye. Kodaiye, say hello to everyone, and don't insult my oldest friend. *He is family.*"

The Honor Guard lowered their blades yet again, this time on Zolsa's command.

"Hey everyone," Kodaiye said. While his voice was certainly strange, what made the doll even creepier was the fact that he didn't move at all. What was left of his smeared facial features remained frozen, and he wasn't able to lift his arms or twitch his legs.

Vradon turned away in disgust.

"What?" Twillo asked him.

"Her Highness isn't going to like that."

"Oh, she'll love it. But maybe I shouldn't wake her up to show her the doll."

"Or the twins," Vradon said. "She finally was able to put them to bed a few hours ago. I fear I will be attending your memorial if you try to disturb them now."

"In that case, I will find a different room to sleep in." Twillo gave the monk a playful smirk. "And I suppose I'll bring my doll with me."

A knock woke Twillo the next morning. He sat up and ran his hand through his white hair, which was still puffed out from the wind. It now had a big indent in it from his pillow.

"Your Lordship, the Ravenna has requested your presence," Zolsa said from the other side of the door. She knocked again. "Your Lordship?"

"What time is it?" he called back to her.

"It is mid-morning, Your Lordship."

"Right, give me a moment." Twillo put a gown on. He then ran his hand through the water in a basin and smoothed his hair back, making himself more presentable. He looked at Kodaiye, who was propped up on a chair. "Ready to meet the rest of your family?"

"I've been ready. You; the monk named Vradon; the Ravenna."

"Her name is Embla, my wife."

"You never said you were royalty back in the jungle. I might have spoken to you differently had I known. I might not have attempted to end your life prematurely."

"Well, I am," he told the doll as he rubbed the sleep out of his eyes. "The Prince Ravenna, Saracent of Sparrow's Rise, to be precise."

"And there was mention of twins?"

A fondness came over Twillo's face as he thought of his children. "Yes, born two months ago. A boy and a girl. The boy is Katashi Vraiz Vos Jhaeros. The girl is Olafia Anna Vraiz Vos Jhaeros."

"That's a mouthful. Icenordians take their father's first name as their last name, do they not?"

"Correct, they do."

"Where did you get the name Katashi?"

"A kitsune who was a dear friend of mine. Vraiz Vos is a combination of Vos, my father's middle name, and Vraizard, Embla's father."

"And Olafia Anna?"

"She is named after a monk who was murdered last year, a man named Olaf, Vradon's partner. She's also named after Anneli, an elven orc who sacrificed her life for the Kingdoms. But all of that is a story for another time."

Zolsa knocked again.

"I am going to have a word with that incessant orc one of these days," Seondzus said.

"She's just doing her job," Adventus said. "Although she can be annoying. Perhaps you are right, one of us should have a word with her."

"Zolsa is fine," Twillo told the voices in his head. "Anyway. We should probably make you look a little less scary."

Kodaiye laughed. *"A faceless haunted doll who can talk is scary? Since when?"*

"Let's just keep you in a blanket for now. Once we're back in Vendir, I will hire the best dollmakers in Icenor to fix you up. Then, you will be presentable, and later, after the children are older, they will be able to play with you."

"They can play with me now."

Twillo shook his head at the grotesque doll. "If they want nightmares, yes, they could. But they already have trouble falling asleep at night. Let's not complicate that. One more thing."

"Yes?"

"Keep quiet until I reveal you to my wife. This might take some convincing."

Zolsa knocked at the door again and Twillo ignored her. He put his boots on, made sure his gown was tied tightly around his waist, wrapped Kodaiye in a blanket, and finally joined the commander of the Honor Guard.

"My apologies, Zolsa. I had trouble waking up this morning."

She bowed instinctively then held her chin high with annoyance. "Right this way, Your Lordship. Her Highness is waiting."

Zolsa led Twillo down a hallway and into a room with a long table and plenty of light from a trio of enormous stained glass windows. It was here that Twillo found Embla, the Icenordian Ravenna seated at the end of the table surrounded by a pair of custom Vikan wood bassinets. Two nursemaids stood behind her, ready to help if need be.

Embla, who held Olafia in her arms, smiled at her husband. Her white hair was pulled into a topknot, Embla too busy as of late to braid it like she normally did. She'd gained a few pounds during her pregnancy, but that was already starting to change, her cheeks increasingly gaunt.

"My love." Twillo placed the haunted doll on the other side of the table. He kissed her cheek and then took Katashi into his arms. The baby, who had wisps of white hair over his forehead and cute pointy ears, made a cooing sound.

"Husband," Embla said as she glanced over to the bundle. "I was told that you returned late last night."

"That I did. Later than I would have liked. I appreciate you coming here with me. You didn't have to."

"It is spring in the Tribute Islands. This weather will be good for the children." Her smile thinned. "Jhaeros."

"Emmy?"

The Ravenna's eyes darted across the table and back to him. "What's in the blanket?"

"I'm going to give you two guesses," Twillo told her with a smile.

"What does it do?" she asked.

"How about I let him tell you."

Seondzus laughed as Embla paled to some degree. "He can talk?"

"He most certainly can." Twillo summoned the nursemaids. "Please take the children to another room. Just for a moment. I have a surprise for the Ravenna. You can leave as well," he told Zolsa, who stood guard near the opposite door.

"Right, Your Lordship," one of the nursemaids said as she took baby Katashi from his arms. The other one did the same with Olafia, and soon, Twillo and Embla were alone.

"So it looks a little strange, but that is only because he—his name is Kodaiye—is thousands of years old. We'll get him fixed up in Vendir. Anyway, I'm actually surprised he's been quiet this entire time, but here he is."

Twillo removed the blanket and sat the doll up so Embla could get a good look at Kodaiye.

The Ravenna placed a hand over her chest. "No. Absolutely not, Jhaeros! That is not going anywhere near our children."

"Nice to meet you, Your Ladyship. As your husband has told you, my name is Kodaiye, and I am now in your

possession. I may look a little worse for wear, but that is merely cosmetic. I will protect you, your family, and the monk. Although I don't believe he is actually part of your family."

Embla's eyes narrowed on the doll. "And how will you protect us?"

"Through curses and various other means. If anyone double-crosses you, if anyone tries to do anything to you or your family, I will curse them and they will die. Or I'll just kill them myself. Or, I'll tell you, and your people can handle them. Mark my word, Your Ladyship, I might seem like a harmless doll, but I am not. And you are my new family. I protect my family."

"And how would you kill anyone?" she asked. "You cannot move."

"I can do certain things."

The chandelier above the table moved as if a sudden wind had come into the room, which was impossible considering the stained glass windows didn't open.

Kodaiye continued: *"I've yet to reveal this to your husband, but I suppose now is as good of a time as any. I can hear it when someone lies. I can also hear things from very far away. Like right now, in the kitchen two floors below, a rogue chef has added a sleeping agent to the porridge that will be served to your Honor Guard. I believe he is testing how well it will work with the hopes of eventually getting to you or your husband. That part I'm not certain about. I suggest you tell the swordmaiden outside to instruct her men not to eat anything for the time being."*

Twillo exchanged glances with his wife. "Well?"

"Tell Zolsa," Embla finally said.

Twillo left the room to find Zolsa standing guard outside.

"Your Lordship?" she asked.

"We have been informed that there may be a poisoning set to take place."

Zolsa maintained the hardened look on her face. "A poisoning?"

"I do not know the full details, but we believe one of the chefs is trying to poison the Honor Guard, your men. Do not eat any of the food until we have verified this."

"I will let them know," Zolsa said. "We will bring all the chefs to the dungeon and find the traitor by any means necessary."

"No, not like that," Twillo said. "I will head down with Kodaiye in a bit. He'll know which one it is."

Both her eyebrows raised at the same time. "The doll can see through walls?"

"Something like that," Twillo said, not wanting to give all of the doll's powers away. "We will test the porridge on the chef planning to serve it to the Guard."

"Yes, Your Lordship."

Twillo returned to find Embla still examining Kodaiye. "Emmy?" he asked as he approached his wife and placed his hands around her waist. Twillo kissed her neck and Embla relaxed to some degree, melting into his arms as she often did these days. "Can he stay, my love? Please?"

"Yes, can I stay? Please, Your Grace?"

"I believe…" A wry smile formed on Embla's face. "I believe that will be fine. But let's make haste in getting him cleaned up. He looks horrendous in his current state and the children cannot see him until this changes. No offense."

"None taken. Perhaps you can have the artist add elven ears to my face as well. The children will like that."

Embla elbowed her husband playfully. "I'm sure that can be arranged."

Twillo, who still held Embla in his arms, smiled down at the haunted doll. "Welcome to the family, Kodaiye. I would like to believe that we won't be calling upon your services as frequently as we might, but I'm likely wrong in that regard. Let's head down to the kitchen to see about this rogue chef."

"Find out his reasoning first, Jhaeros," Embla said. "Perhaps there is more to this story than Kodaiye is able to detect."

Twillo kissed his wife on the cheek. "Will do, my love, will do."

HARMON COOPER

Author's Note

Thank you for reading *The World According to Dragons 3* from start to finish.

Please take a moment to <u>leave a review</u> or a rating.

I am an indie author, and your reviews go a long way in helping other readers decide if Twillo's journey is one worth taking. It is, after all, likely how you stumbled upon this book.

Also, people hesitant on the series might continue after reading your review. Thanks for taking a moment to rate and review this series!

If you're not sure what to read next, I'd recommend Arcane Cultivator, the next series set in the Four Kingdoms of the Sagaland.

It is an action-packed LitRPG fantasy cultivation series story water harvesters, a story that was hinted at in this book. It follows the life of Jaden, who is forced to compete in the Tournament of the Gods. You've also met Jaden's parents in this book, Ariosto, and you already know the dragonessence system. But there is so much more to enjoy!

Thanks again for reading and rating my books.

Yours in sanity,

Harmon Cooper

THE WORLD ACCORDING TO DRAGONS – BOOK THREE

HARMON COOPER

THE SAGALAND CHRONICLES

ARCANE CULTIVATOR

Jaden has 10 days to go from zero to hero. Epic journey. Epic odds. Will you join him?
Start Arcane Cultivator, the next series set in the Four Kingdoms of the Sagaland.

Other Books by Harmon Cooper

I have written over seventy books (!). Here are some of the highlights.

An instant bestseller. Pilgrim follows the life of Danzen Ravja, a former assassin trying to make amends with his past.

THE WORLD ACCORDING TO DRAGONS – BOOK THREE

War Priest is a progression fantasy/cultivation series about a healer forced to multiclass to survive. Expect intrigue, tournaments, combat, humor, training, and a ton of world-building based on Japanese mythology.

Cowboy Necromancer is a heavily researched post-apocalyptic LitRPG set in the Southwest that continues to thrill readers!

The World According to Dragons – Book Three

GameLit before it was a genre, The Feedback Loop was published between 2015-2018. Volume One collects books 1-4 and has a ton of extra content. If you enjoy audiobooks, it is performed by the legendary LitRPG narrator Jeff Hays.

Scan the code to sign up to my newsletter, follow me on Twitter, Instagram, Facebook, or Amazon. Soon, I'll have a Tales of a Relic Hunter story about one of Twillo's past journeys for my newsletter to read. Be sure to sign up.

Here are some Facebook pages you should join:
My Facebook Group
(Join the above group to get exclusive content, see cover reveals, get updated release schedules, connect with

other Harmon Cooper readers, check out dope memes, and so much more!)

LitRPG Books

GameLit Society

LitRPG Forum

If you so choose, here are some other ways to support my books:

1. Join my ARC group on Facebook – this is where I give away free books before they are released.
2. **Review my books**, which generates more interest from other readers, which makes me write faster because (carrot dangling from the stick!)
3. Join the Harmon Cooper mailing list or follow me on social media.
4. Join my Patreon where you can read exclusive content (from cover design to future release ideas and chapters).

To learn more about LitRPG, talk to authors including myself, and just have an awesome time, please join the LitRPG Group on Facebook.

Printed in Great Britain
by Amazon